Jim & MaryAnn

Thanks for your
friendship and
interest in my
Work. Enjoy

Ken

ALSO BY KEN STICHTER

Death on the High Route
The Water and Murder Flow South

TRAIL OF MADNESS

KEN STICHTER

TRAIL OF MADNESS

This is a work of fiction. All of the characters, names, incidents, organizations, and dialogue in this novel are either the products of the author's imagination or are used fictitiously.

iUniverse books may be ordered through booksellers or by contacting:

iUniverse
1663 Liberty Drive
Bloomington, IN 47403
www.iuniverse.com
1-800-Authors (1-800-288-4677)

ISBN: 978-1-5320-3050-5 (sc)
ISBN: 978-1-5320-3051-2 (e)

Library of Congress Control Number: 2017917743

Print information available on the last page.

iUniverse rev. date: 01/03/2018

For

Julie Ann,
Wife, best friend, and partner.
You have tolerated my musings, wanderings,
And writing.

Our family,
Mark and Nancy,
Todd and Crystal,
Jennifer and Greg.

And
The grandkids:
Karli, Andi, Daniel,
Keefer, Maddy, Eryn,
Juliann, Mason, Logan.

Acknowledgments

I love to wander, and I covet solitude. Whether on the trail, reading books, working on home projects, or writing, I am comfortable with my own thoughts.

I confess this inwardness because long ago I realized that although writing is a cloistered endeavor for me, the product depends on the input, reactions, influence, and feedback of others. I am grateful to all who have judged my writing. As such, I owe thanks to my family, teachers, professors, and colleagues for serving as critics.

Trail of Madness reflects the contributions of family and friends.

Mark read multiple drafts and provided critical input regarding the story line, criminal investigation process, and law enforcement semantics. He also kept reminding me to remain faithful to the way things are and not to the way I would like them to be.

Julie was an early and often reviewer. Her questions and suggestions kept me from making excessive assumptions. She also pointed out when my narrative fell short of common sense.

I have shared fifty years of wandering and backpacking with Jim Roberts. Together we poked around most every historical, geological, and geographical site in the Eastern Sierra. My work would not be possible without our friendship.

Todd has solo hiked the JMT, and together we have hiked many trails and explored hidden basins. These experiences have found their way into my story line.

Thanks to Karli and Andi for ideas that found a way into *Trail of Madness* and their inspiration for the cover.

Thanks also to all with whom I have shared Sierra trails and the high country. My father, a wanderer at heart, introduced me to backpacking and fly-fishing. My brother Ron and I hiked the JMT and countless other trails. With Phil, Loring, John, Steve, Boy Scout friends, teaching colleagues, and former students, I have hiked, backpacked, fished, bagged peaks, and climbed. To all of you, please know that you have influenced my thinking and writing about the Sierra.

Finally, thanks to the editors and staff at iUniverse. I cannot imagine *Trail of Madness* without the support of Kathi, Dan, Elizabeth, and others.

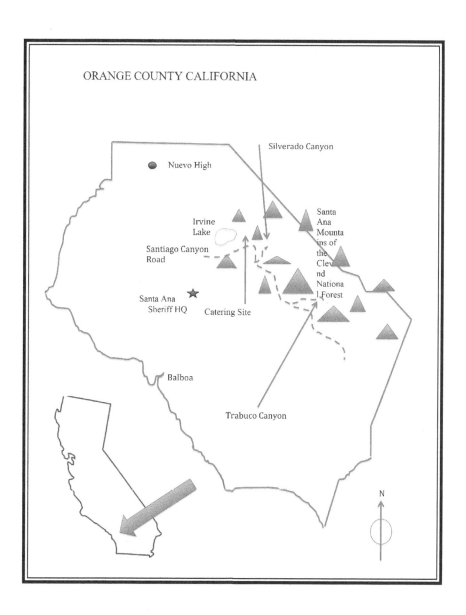

ORANGE COUNTY CALIFORNIA

Silverado Canyon

Nuevo High

Irvine
Lake

Santa
Ana
Mounta
ins of
the
Clev
nd
Nationa
l Forest

Santiago Canyon
Road

Santa Ana
Sheriff HQ

Catering Site

Balboa

Trabuco Canyon

N

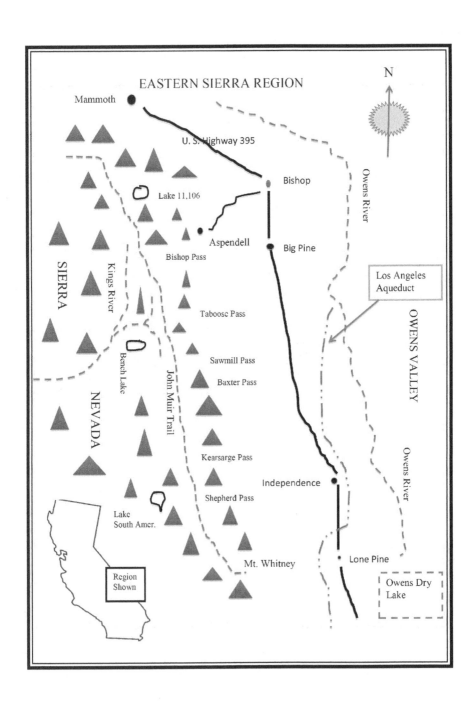

EASTERN SIERRA REGION

Introduction

The morality of an action
depends upon the motive from which we act.

—*Samuel Johnson*

Morality is relative. What one does and what others see may be worlds apart.

Most of us live in our own domain even as we bow to the norms of our times. But for some, the homage is distorted when norms are slighted in favor of redefining morality through the lens of madness.

When madness takes over, reason is reclothed, and a heinous act can look respectable.

Polonius, counselor to Shakespeare's Hamlet, after listening to Hamlet's logic, concludes that it is madness. But he also senses a certain order to Hamlet's madness and comments aside, "Though this be madness, yet there is method to it."

Writing in the eighteenth century, Irish cleric and novelist Lawrence Sterne added that "madness is consistent, which is more than can be said of poor reason." Reasoning can question morality, but the mad are not likely to waver from perceptions of what is thought to be moral.

History is replete with the biography of great minds that suffered from madness. Many "a first-rate" mind has exhibited madness, says Nassir Ghaemi, MD and author.

It should not surprise us, then, that it is often left to history to determine whether the actions of madness are acceptable or reprehensible.

And so it is that morality is sometimes defined by circumstances. Winston Churchill observed, "A man does what he must—in spite of personal consequences, in spite of obstacles and dangers and pressures—and that is the basis of all human morality." Actions are defining.

Of course we recognize that madness is a mental illness, referencing it often as insanity. But even as we classify acts of madness as a mental disorder or even criminal conduct, there are occasional public reactions of sympathy. Who among us has not been sympathetic to the madness of someone seeking what we regard as justifiable revenge? Who among us has not rendered verdicts as self-anointed judge and juror? Who among us has not thought to justify certain evils through a less-than-favored method of punishment to transgressors? There are few who can say they never submitted to the thought, *He got what was coming to him*, even as the system of justice did not agree. Does such thinking suggest we are all mad?

Or is it only the mad who think they are sane? The Cynic philosopher Antisthenes suggested that rejecting social norms was the ultimate form of pleasure. As such, madness becomes acceptable.

PART 1

MEMORIES OF YESTERDAY
LONG PAST

When to the sessions of sweet silent thought
I summon up remembrance of things past ...
—Shakespeare, "Sonnet 30"

SITTING ATOP HER bed, with legs pulled up and arms wrapped around knees and forehead leaning on thighs, Allison gave way to reflection. She was alone but not afraid as yet again the cascading memories invaded.

Allison remembered as though it was only yesterday, but it had been long ago.

The house was no longer there. Still, she saw it—the small ramshackle two-room wooden shack on the outskirts of Big Pine— her place of birth. She could not forget it. She remembered everything about it: the smell, the roof leaks, the unkempt yard, and the efforts of her mom to make it livable. Allison remembered the poverty of it all.

She also remembered the small town in the middle of the valley and beneath the towering peaks of the Sierra Nevada where it was cold in the winter and hot in the summer. It was a quaint, raw, and remote existence.

Those had not been pleasant years, but she held on to the moments alone with her mother. Closing her eyes, she let her mind wander back to the small house and to the bedroom and to her time alone with *Mom*.

She could see it all. She could see it clearly again in her mind's eye …

Reading. Reading out loud. Reading, talking, and reading some more.

Propped up on elbows and lying side by side on the sagging bed, she followed along as her mom read.

Time stood still, but it didn't. It was just that reading was a pause from it all. An escape. He wasn't home. There was no fear. They were at peace atop the bed, reading.

She stared at the pictures in the book and listened, though she already knew the story. She knew how it would end, but she wanted to hear it again from Mom.

Feeling fingers running gently through her hair, she turned to look at Mom, at the smile and friendly eyes and the glint from shiny-silver-and-turquoise earrings. There were always earrings.

They both looked back at the book. There were only a couple of pages left, and Mom began reading aloud again:

> The young Boy, his clothes torn and dirty, and with a small cut on his lip, gathered his legs beneath and once again tried to get to his feet. The other kids had run off. It was just he and Butch the Bully.
>
> Always, it came down to just the Boy and Butch.
>
> The Boy did not know how today would end. Probably no different than in the past, but he would keep getting up. Maybe, with the other kids gone, Butch would get tired and just leave. But maybe he wouldn't. Maybe he would keep hitting.
>
> Again Butch hit the Boy and knocked him down.
>
> "Are you ready to give up?" demanded Butch. The Boy said nothing. He just shook his head and started once again to get up.

This happened several more times until Butch mumbled disgust and walked away.

The Boy remained quiet. He got up and watched Butch leave. Someday it would be different. Butch would be on the ground, and the Boy would walk away. It would happen. The Boy knew it would happen. It had to happen.

For now the Boy smiled. He hadn't won, but then he hadn't lost.

Mom closed the book and laid it aside. It was quiet. Mom, leaning on elbows and with hands together and fingers interlocked, turned toward her. A soft "Hmmm" escaped Mom's smiling lips. "And how does this story speak to you?" she asked.

Looking at Mom, she thought about her response. When she responded, there was a nod. There was kindness. And always the earrings.

CHAPTER 1

———— ∞ ————

THE DEATH OF ARCHIE CONNORS

1966
Sierra Nevada Backcountry

I T WAS TIME. It was the right time. It was the right place.

A dense canopy of pine trees spread darkness on the forest floor as if it were a moonless night, although it was not. Elsewhere in the canyon, beyond the forest and in the open where the glacier polished granite and quiet meadows dominated the setting, the moon shone brightly.

It occurred to her, *The darkness here is good.*

It was also cold, colder than usual for this time of year. She suppressed the desire to shiver.

Allison sat on the boulder with her back against the large Jeffrey pine. Anticipation kept her focused, and nervous energy pushed away any sense that she might be uncomfortable. It was a matter of waiting.

She was good at waiting. She had been waiting years.

She didn't need to look at her watch. Time was not important. All that was important was his predictability. She knew her course of action once he stirred.

It was always the same. In all the years she had backpacked with him, the behavior pattern never changed. Whether it was a two-night trip or a weeklong trip, his nights were the same. She knew the beast was drunk again tonight. He would stir during the early hours after midnight and then emerge to relieve himself.

She shifted her body slightly, unconcerned about the sound it would produce. The fast-running and cascading river below would drown out any sound. She was counting on that.

The Middle Fork of the Kings River was her partner. When it was over, they would both move on.

Allison knew the beast would emerge. She had seen to it that he would. The thoughts that crossed her mind about the events earlier in the evening were disgusting, and she felt a shudder of revulsion. But it was all part of the plan. The beast would abuse her no more.

— m —

Last week he had called her about ten in the evening when he knew she would be home from work and studying. Her roommate had answered the phone and interrupted her in the walk-in closet she called a "study cave." Allison's father was on the phone.

Allison had long ago stopped calling him *Father*. It had been easy because for many years he had not acted like a husband to her mother, and his relationship with Allison was anything but fatherly. At first he was Dad. Later she just referred to him by his first name, Archie. With time, he became the *beast*, a title she used pejoratively in her personal thoughts. The beast, a title he deserved. It was a description but never a proper noun, never to be capitalized.

She knew why he called—it was the annual *you owe me* call.

She expected the call, and she was ready. Her summer session would end in a few days, and he wanted her to accompany him on a backpacking trip into the central Sierra Nevada. She had managed to suppress her usual response by planning ahead. For the first time, she was ready for his summons; it would not be the same old journey of fear. She would play along as she had in the past, but it would end much differently.

As expected, he tried to leverage guilt. She could probably manage the costs of going to college on her own, but there were just enough debts and doubts that any funding he provided was a welcome contribution to her already limited budget. So he played the usual cards, softly at first: "With the summer session over, I was hoping that you could take a few days to go into the backcountry." Her initial response had been to plead that she needed to work and really did not have time. She did so knowing how he would respond. He followed with "Well, if I knew my daughter was so ungrateful to her father for his financial support, I'm not sure why I continue to send her money." She tried to convey a strong response and said no again. They argued, he continued to try to play the guilt angle, and his agitated comments evolved into a threat. She found herself increasingly agitated, angry, and wanting to vent her worst thoughts. But she did not. She stayed in control and played her role as she had in the past. It was part of her plan.

The conversation ended with him restating his request and the threat of cutting off her funds. Then he abruptly terminated the call. It was his way of trying to control her. Afterward, she sat thinking; it had gone as expected. He would never change. Perhaps that was why she was comfortable with her decision. It was time to put an end to it all.

She let him stew and then called him back later. It was important to sound contrite and then consent to his request. It was also important to control carefully-thought-out conditions. She would take a bus to the Owens Valley and meet him at the trailhead on the first day of the trip. She did not tell him in which town in the valley she would disembark from the bus. She would not go to his residence. She was not going to be seen in the valley towns near where he lived. He would not see her until they met at the Bishop Pass trailhead, twenty-two miles southwest of the town of Bishop and at an altitude of 9,700 feet.

He resisted her request, but she knew it was not necessary to state her reasons. Both knew why Allison did not want to go on the trip. They had similar arguments before when he asked her to accompany him on a trip. Always they had argued, and always she eventually relented.

This time was different. On this trip, she would be in control. She only needed to make him feel like he was in control.

—⟋⟍⟋—

The entrance into the backcountry over Bishop Pass was familiar ground. Allison had begun many a backpacking trip at the trailhead, and she was thankful he suggested it this time.

While hiking along Palisade Creek and the Kings River, they would be on a portion of the John Muir Trail, and they were assured of good camping. Allison's goal was to find the right campsite. She would have three or four chances. The campsite needed to be near one of the rivers where the water was moving fast among large and small boulders that disrupted the flow to create an environment of treachery. There could be no other backpackers or packers camped nearby. The river had to dominate the scene.

—⟋⟍⟋—

Allison's thoughts came back to the present.

She was committed. She waited. The drunken beast didn't disappoint.

First she heard the rustling inside the tent. Then a series of grunts and groans, sounds of disoriented exasperation as he tried to get out of the tent, right himself, and make his way several steps toward the edge of the riverbank.

From her deeply shadowed spot, she watched him hurriedly stagger forward while trying at the same time to get ready to urinate. He was struggling to get it out. He had to go badly. Shuffling in a crouch, his left hand tried to open the fly while the right hand groped.

His semiconscious goal was to pee off the riverbank. It never happened.

Allison pulled the nylon cord tight just before he tried to take the last two steps. The cord stopped his feet but not his forward progress, and soon he was launched over the riverbank and headfirst down toward the rocks below.

While he was in midair, Allison was up and quickly following him down the steep screed of the bank. He hit the gravel and small boulders with his head and let out a shallow grunt. Rolling head over heels, he then encountered the water and large rocks along the edge of the swift river.

When he stopped, there was a moan. Then there was the impact *thud* of the round grapefruit-sized river rock Allison had in her gloved hand. It hit him on the side of his head with force and stunning effect. And then there was just the sound of the river. The beast did not move.

Allison felt for a pulse. He was still alive. Quickly she rolled him over and into the water facedown.

Archie Raymond Connors died without a whimper.

It had been easy.

And then she knew. Quid est nisi miserabilis insignia. "What is this but wretched madness?" It was a confession, as St. Augustine would have it.

Allison knew what she was.

CHAPTER 2

SOURCES INDICATE

Independence, California

INYO COUNTY SHERIFF's Detective Ryan Pollard couldn't believe it. Once again the *Inyo Register* had information about a case that was not yet public. He read it.

> The body of Archie Connors, longtime resident of Bishop, was brought out of the backcountry by mule Tuesday. He died along the Kings River. His death was reported by two backpackers who encountered Archie's grieving daughter Sunday morning.
>
> The backpackers, whose names are being withheld by the sheriff's office, were on their way out of the backcountry when the daughter, Allison, flagged them down. She had found her father facedown in the river early that morning. At press time, the *Register* was not able to verify cause of death, but available information suggests drowning.
>
> The backpackers hiked out to South Lake and called the sheriff Sunday afternoon. It was too late in the day to send a helicopter to retrieve the body. Two Forest Service Rescue personnel hiked all night to reach the site early Monday morning. A packer

and sheriff's investigator were sent in on Monday morning. However, strong winds and low cloud cover kept the helicopter grounded.

Tuesday the body was brought out by the packer and handed over to the coroner.

The *Inyo Register* has learned that Mr. Connors and his daughter, a college student, were backpacking a loop trip that started at the Bishop Pass trailhead.

Mr. Connors was born in Bishop and graduated from Bishop High School in 1946. Mr. Connors was forty-four years of age.

Mr. Connors married Mary Jo Harden, also of Bishop, in 1947. The two separated, and she moved to Orange County about 1953. They were subsequently divorced. Mrs. Connors took her own life in 1963.

Services are pending for Mr. Connors.

Ryan tossed the paper aside. *I best see the sergeant. He won't like this at all,* he thought.

Kennedy was on the phone and motioned for Ryan to sit. Kennedy looked agitated. He could tell the sergeant did not like the conversation with his lieutenant.

"How should I know how all of this gets in the news?" Kennedy rolled his eyes at Ryan while he listened. "Yeah, I'll look into it and get back to you. Okay, I'll do that." Kennedy was short on patience. "No, no! We'll follow up. Okay. I'll call you." He hung up.

"Shit!" Kennedy leaned back in his chair. "Tell me you did not leak this crap."

"No, Sergeant. I read the article too. Everything appears accurate but didn't come from me."

"Well, the lieutenant is pissed. He said the sheriff was in his face this morning, wanting to know how the newspaper learned all this."

"I don't know." Ryan did have his thoughts. Best to keep them close. He had learned long ago to keep quiet about any investigation. However, he knew every other person who was aware of the investigation was fair game for reporters. Off the top, he could think of several, including the coroner, packer, funeral home, and the two backpackers.

"I didn't think you had anything to do with it." Kennedy had piles of paper on his desk and seemed to be searching for something. Not finding it, he turned back to Ryan.

"Well, anything new? Anything I don't already know? Anything that could surprise me?"

"No, Sarge." Ryan could see that Kennedy was distracted. He was sorting through papers on his desk. Kennedy always seemed to be in two places at once. He had to wait until Kennedy's thoughts came back to the topic at hand.

"Okay, Pollard, you've had a night to sleep on it. Whaddaya think?"

"Daughter's probably right. Connors gets up to take a leak. He's drunk, staggers, falls, and hits his head. Lands in the river and drowns."

"Think the autopsy will support that?"

"No doubt! The investigator who went to the site found an empty bottle in the tent. Said the place reeked of booze."

"Who is this Connors anyway? Why've I never heard of him? Any record?"

"Grew up in Bishop but never caused us any trouble other than being drunk. Seems he didn't get belligerent. More'n I can say for most of the drunks in this valley."

"And the daughter, Allison?"

"She's a third-year student with a dual major in English and history. Some kind of brain, I'd say. Older brother and sister, but she doesn't know where they live. Classic dysfunctional family." Ryan stopped and looked at Sergeant Kennedy.

"Anything else?"

"Let's see here. Okay, Connors bounces around the valley. Welder at Mammoth and at the old Rovana mine. Done odd jobs in Lone Pine, Independence, and even over in Furnace Creek. Never held a job more'n a couple years. Fired a couple of times from DWP."

In his usual gruff voice and manner, Kennedy reacted. "Fired? Who the hell gets rehired after being fired?"

"Anyways, Allison said they kept in contact, and he sent her money for college. Only time they got together was once a year when they would go backpacking. Rest of the time, they only communicated by phone."

"So we can say that even though they did not get together very often, their relationship was not really so estranged since he sent her money for school and she was willing to go backpacking with him. Sounds odd to me. Damn strange. What about the other two kids?"

"Brother left home when she was about ten. Never came back. Last she heard, he's living in New York City where he's an attorney."

Kennedy's attention perked with the information about the boy. "Obviously the old man didn't get in the boy's way. Can't help but think that a kid who leaves home at sixteen must be at odds with a parent, perhaps abused, something like that."

"I asked. She said he left because the parents were always arguing. Seems he was a bright kid, and Connors did not like being shown up by his kid. Bernard, that's the boy's name, managed to save some money and cleverly disappeared. He left a note for Allison and Mary Beth, the sister, saying he couldn't take it any longer. Allison did not hear from him for a couple years."

"You located him?"

"No. Allison has no address for him. I have Millie trying to track him down. Daughter says Bernard has changed his surname but did not tell her what it was. He said it was in her best interest to not be connected with him."

"Sounds like interesting brotherly advice. And the sister?"

"Allison thinks Mary Beth lives somewhere in the valley or maybe in Inyo, Mono, or Alpine Counties but doesn't have any idea where. Sister's a drug addict and only shows up when she wants some money."

"Any luck tracking her down?"

"None. I've checked our records, Mammoth PD, and I have calls to Mono and Alpine. So far nothing. She could be under another name or long gone. Allison hasn't seen her since her mother's funeral."

"Any photos, documentation?"

"Well, this part is strange also. Allison says she does not have any photos of her brother or sister. Seems Connors wrote both of them off and destroyed any photos."

Kennedy chuckled and mumbled, "Shit, guy was really screwed up. Where did he live?"

"In my search of Connors's shack—"

"Shack?" Kennedy, who was again sorting papers, looked surprised.

"Yeah. He lived in a rented shack on the old Triple Peak Ranch. Did some work for old man Ramondson, so the old man let Connors live in an old bunkhouse. He's lived there for about a dozen years. Ranch manager says Connors paid irregularly but was no problem, except when they sometimes found him drunk and passed out on the porch."

"So, what did you find?"

"Not much. Clothes, some unimportant paperwork, and odds and ends. Place was a bit of a mess. No records, no photos, and no letters. Nothing to link him with anything. All he seemed to do was eat, sleep, work when he could, and drink. No phone. Ranch manager said he used the ranch office phone but not often."

Kennedy stopped what he was doing and looked at Pollard. "Shit! A real piece of work ... a drunk people seem to like. Go figure. Connors's vehicle?"

"Beat-up old Ford pickup. I searched it. Nothing."

Kennedy said, "Allison seems to have been forthcoming. What was your take on her?"

"It was not what one would expect. I would say it was one of shock and confusion but not one of out-of-control sadness or grief at a loss of a parent. She was not close to her father and knew him as a heavy drinker. Accepts that his death resulted from his addiction."

"She cry? Kids, even the strong ones, cry."

"Teared up a little but no sobbing if that's what you mean. Like she said, she loves backpacking, and the two of them have gone many times. Seems when they would go, he always drank heavily. She seemed resigned to a longstanding belief alcohol would kill him."

"I'm wondering. Was there any abuse here?"

Ryan was expecting the question. "Sarge, I tried probing that issue. I got nothing that supports the idea. Allison is not a small girl. She's at least as tall as Connors, maybe taller. She's strong, and I bet she could outhike most men. I'm thinking that if he tried to assault or abuse her in any way, she would have resisted, and there would have been evidence of a struggle. There was no evidence. Our investigator at the scene supports that."

"Okay, let's go over it again."

With patience, Ryan spelled it out in simple terms. "Okay, Connors gets roaring drunk. Daughter is used to it. He gets up in the night to pee. She does not hear him. If she does, she is used to it and goes back to sleep. Connors goes out to pee and loses his footing near the embankment. He is unstable. He falls down and hits his head a couple of times and drowns without a sound. Even if he made a sound, it's to be drowned out by the noise of the Middle Fork. It's a raging river. The investigator and rescue people say the camp was close to the river, and the noise from the roaring river was loud. She finds him facedown and dead in the river in the morning. Simple as that."

"Sounds reasonable to me. Unless there's other evidence to the contrary."

Kennedy raised his eyebrows. "Unless she pushed him?"

CHAPTER 3

—◊—

THE JOHN MUIR TRAIL

The JMT

O F ALL THE monuments to great Americans, none is more iconic than the John Muir Trail. Stretching 220 miles from Yosemite Valley in the north to Mount Whitney in the south, the trail offers hikers and backpackers insight into the life of a humble and visionary naturalist. It also offers them a route into the rugged interior of California's Sierra Nevada.

John Muir introduced America to the wonders of the range—its unique geological history, its flora and fauna, and its glorious opportunities for adventure. He also introduced Americans to the concept of preserving for posterity the opportunities of future generations to explore, escape to, and revel in what he called "the Range of Light."

The trail that bears his name was not Muir's idea. It was the dream of those who followed in his wake and who, like John Muir, grew to love the rugged and rewarding experience of hiking.

A professor at the newly established University of California, Berkeley, Joseph Le Conte, is credited with investigating and documenting the general route of what was to become the John Muir Trail—or, as it is often known as today, the JMT. He started his work in 1908, and eight years later, a rough route had been created.

Since the 1940s, the JMT has gained in popularity. Today, people come from all over the world to taste the wonders it has to offer.

—w—

The JMT offers many options. A continuous hike of 220 miles is complicated by the fact that barring resupply by friends, packers, or a side trip to another trailhead, one must carry the necessary supplies and food for a two- to three-week trip. Accessing the JMT from other locations along the way makes it possible for many to hike it in pieces of time lasting as little as a day or two to as long as a week or more. The more northerly sixty miles between Yosemite Valley and Mammoth Mountain allow for easy access to the trail for day hikes or overnight trips. The remaining 160 miles are much less accessible, requiring in some instances a long day or two to gain access or to exit the trail. This is especially true along the last hundred miles of the trail from Evolution Basin to Whitney Portal where the trail hugs the western side of the Sierra Nevada's eastern escarpment. This section of the trail takes one over six passes of twelve thousand feet or higher. Between the passes, one drops down into canyons at about eight thousand feet, only to begin the long ascent back up to the next pass. These final hundred-plus miles of the JMT are rugged and consistently strenuous.

Though doable for most who love to backpack, the JMT is not without its obstacles. Objectively, one must sometimes deal with challenging stream and river crossings where the water is running high and there is no formal bridge. Wading a fast-running stream can be especially hazardous. Rain can cause streams to swell quickly. Often passes, especially early in the summer, are clogged with snow, and travel is precarious. Above tree line and on exposed ridges, lightning is an extreme danger. Generally, rockslides are not a problem, but the trail takes a beating from use and exposure, so one must be cautious, especially with steep descents.

Given the quality of modern gear, backpacking along the JMT can be a pleasure in spite of the challenges. On the other hand, poor-quality gear can change the equation when one is not properly conditioned for the strain physically and mentally. Dehydration and altitude have rendered many helpless, and in some rare instances, death is the result. Blisters start small but can ruin a trip within a day or two. A severe sprain, twisted knee, or broken arm are common and made more agonizing when one must wait, sometimes days, for help. Proper nourishment in the form of protein and calories is important, as backpacking results in the burning of thousands of calories per day. The calorie intake required to offset the strenuous hiking demands is well in excess of what most hikers would normally consume when not backpacking. Those not prepared to address such demands over many days of hiking will find the going very difficult.

For many, a backpacking trip along the JMT is an outing without equal in grandeur and pleasure. However, in recent decades, the demand for time on the trail has increased to a point where the US Forest Service and National Park Service have had to institute quota systems to control the impact of too many hikers. Both federal agencies have also increased backcountry supervision. The JMT is not immune to the disruptive, if not destructive, impact of a few. It is not immune to intrusion of those who would cause harm to the environment and even to others on the trail.

Ninety-nine point nine percent of those backpacking along the JMT seek the range of natural emotions promoted by such an experience. However, our interest is in the less than 1 percent. Though they may find in nature a personal need, they are not beyond acts of violence that we deem reprehensible in nature and criminal to humankind. These are the selfish rarity found more commonly in the developed communities and urban environments where most of us gather. But to think they do not exist in the backcountry is to ignore reality.

The JMT in the mid-1960s was much different from what it is in the twenty-first century. The number of hikers was nothing like today's horde. One could hike days without meeting anyone along the trail. Today, one is likely to meet someone every hour or two. And yet the JMT continues to attract those longing for the freedom of the hills.

CHAPTER 4

ENID AND INGAR

1969

Along the Southern JMT, near Baxter Creek

A LLISON KNEW IT was time again. She knew because it made sense. It was necessary.

Allison breathed deeply. It was not a breath of anxiety. It was a breath of calmness. The short rain had been refreshing. Her mind was clear, focused. She had a job to do.

Earlier in the day, she had encountered the young couple now bedding down in their tent about two hundred yards away. She knew them for what they were, but she really did not know them, and they did not know her.

When they had met along the trail, the boy, a semiexperienced backpacker, did all the talking. The girl had never backpacked and seemed unsure and naive regarding her involvement. They were university students. She was younger than him. They professed to be here to spend a few days on the John Muir Trail. Like so many others of their generation, they were attracted to the backcountry experience. Their manners, dress, references, and take on life made it evident they were from the San Francisco Bay area. For them, everything was open and optional. Life was experimental.

To Allison, there was contradiction in their words and actions. It was an affront.

Now, later in the evening, Allison sat and waited. She knew what would happen inside their tent. It was only a matter of time now that it was getting dark and the temperature was dropping. So she waited and listened.

It was quiet, and except for the muffled tones from the tent, Allison knew the only other sounds would be wind or the distant running of the creek. There were no other hikers camped within a mile. She had verified that. It was not a moonlit night, and the late-afternoon rain would have driven backpackers to camp early. There would be no night hikers on the trail.

Like so many other areas along the trail, the setting was peaceful. Allison had been here before. She knew the area well.

She also knew that the young couple in the tent brought to this area a general disregard for their future. It was all out of balance. They did not belong here. This was her world, and they brought unwanted memories into her world. They brought an unacceptable future.

The boy knew what he was doing. The girl had no clue about future consequences.

—ɯ—

Hours later, the early-morning chill was fading. The view out across the meadow was unspoiled, and except for the sound of the small stream nearby, all was silent.

Allison gazed, seeing all and seeing nothing.

For a few moments, her thoughts and images returned to a different reality. She was here but only physically. Absentmindedly, she pushed back her golden hair and rubbed the right earring as she thought. Her mind's eye quickly brought up images of her mother.

Mom would have loved it here, she thought.

But their relationship had been a struggle to maintain. Often there was only time alone together reading and talking. The beast was never far away.

She remembered Mom's resolve: "We cannot easily control today, but in our minds we can control what we see, hear, and want. We can, in time, control tomorrow."

So it was. *Mom had been content to read and wait.*

Mom was smart. She had read. She knew where the lessons were.

Once Mom told the story of a young girl accused of stealing at school by three so-called friends. As a result, the girl was punished and later sent away to another school. The girl knew she was innocent and also knew that her three peers were the ones guilty of the theft. But no one would believe her. The three came from good families, and no one would ever think that the children of those families would do anything wrong. For the accused girl, the situation was different, as she came from a poor family with an abusive drunkard for a father. It was easy for people to believe the poor girl committed the crime.

"What happened to the girl?" Allison had asked.

Her mom's answer still resonated. "The girl never forgot. She did well in the new school but never lost sight of her need to set things straight. She had been unjustly punished, but the day of their punishment would come. She would not forget."

"How long would it take?" asked Allison.

The response surprised her. There was no set time: "The girl would know." Mom was clear about the need to take one's time and not rush into judgment or reaction. If the system of justice rectifies the situation, so be it. If not, it may be necessary for another to do so.

Later Allison would find that literature and history were replete with stories of retribution and vengeance. The story of the young girl was similar to the circumstances and subsequent response of Edmond Dantès who was falsely accused in *The Count of Monte Cristo.*

Throughout history, there is evidence of those with little means being falsely accused by others. The only resolution for these victims was revenge.

"Then there will be peace again, Allison."

—ɯ—

The meadow seemed so peaceful. Even the struggle for survival that ruled the life of every meadow creature seemed peaceful. That some animals would pay the price of death at the hands of survivors seemed to contribute to the serenity of it all. There was nothing out of place here. All was as it should be.

Allison removed her earring and studied it as she rubbed it between her thumb and index finger. The earring brought a flood of memories. She smiled.

Then she got up and walked back across the trail and well into the forest. When she came to the recently downed ponderosa pine, she stopped and tossed the earring onto the two bodies in the gaping pit that had once housed the root ball of the towering pine tree now on its side. Then she began the long process of filling in the pit with rocks. It would take all day, but she was not in a hurry.

The trail was peaceful again. It was whole. Her world was again serene and as it should be.

The future was again normal.

CHAPTER 5

MONIQUE FENWICK

1976
South along the Muir Trail, near Glen Pass
Kings Canyon National Park

HIKING FROM NORTH to south along the JMT, the backpacker looks forward to seeing the Rae Lakes, a trail highlight. At 10,600 feet and 172 miles south of the start in Yosemite Valley, the backpacker crosses the land isthmus between the two large Rae Lakes.

Ahead the backpacker sees Glen Pass two miles further on, but the lakes represent a milestone. For the through-hiker, at this point in the journey physical conditioning is such that there is no drudgery. The challenge of the pass is easily dismissed. The scenery can be taken in and enjoyed. Stopping to view the landscape and photograph is essential.

The two young backpackers leaned their packs against a rock. Rummaging through a top compartment of her pack, Rebecca took out some crackers and cheese and tossed the bundle to Monique. Already Monique was seated on the polished slab of granite and mixing powdered lemonade in her water bottle. It was lunchtime.

For a second day in a row, they had not passed any other hikers along the trail. The last backpacker they encountered was near Bench Lake on the north side of Pinchot Pass. They had been impressed. She had introduced herself as Alexi. Rebecca and Monique had considerable experience hiking, but they had never encountered a physical specimen like Alexi.

Alexi had told them she started in Tuolumne Meadows and was following a route that paralleled the Muir Trail much of the time. From time to time, she crossed the JMT and often went over the same passes as others, but she was trying to stay off the official trail as much as possible. She had been hiking about as many days as they had, but after their discussion, Rebecca and Monique concluded that Alexi must have traveled twice as far. That was no easy accomplishment because they figured they were covering about twelve miles per day.

Over lunch at Rae Lakes, Rebecca and Monique discussed the hike ahead and the possibility that they would encounter Alexi at Charlotte Lake. Both commented about how interesting, although aloof, Alexi appeared. She was certainly a first-class backpacker and very bright woman, but she was also unlike anyone either of them had encountered.

Strangely, they found themselves both drawn to and repelled by Alexi. On the one hand, she was friendly and engaging in conversation. But there was also an element of detachment as if to suggest she was not comfortable discussing personal matters or preferences. Alexi was pleasant but distant. Rebecca and Monique thought of themselves as contemporary in many ways and thus savvy to the beliefs and ways of the discontented generations that inhabited the streets and college campuses. Alexi was the opposite. She was withdrawn from the larger society. It was not just that she appeared to be a loner; it was more about a world of her own making. Alexi was intelligent and articulate and experienced in the backcountry. But she was vague about her life beyond the wilderness she loved.

Later that evening, about a half hour before dark, Rebecca and Monique were relaxing in their seasoned campsite at Charlotte Lake. They had eaten, cleaned up, and were enjoying a hot cup of cocoa while they discussed the days ahead. Tomorrow they would go over

Forrester Pass in the early afternoon and stay the night at Lake South America, about a mile off the Muir Trail. The next day, they would camp at Crabtree Meadow and then go out over Whitney a day later.

As their discussion began to wind down, they were both caught off guard as Alexi walked in. She was camped nearby but gave no specifics. Instead, she just stopped to talk.

Rebecca and Monique were pleasantly surprised at the conversation. While they both had solid credentials as graduates in history from UCLA, they were blown away by Alexi's knowledge and how well read she was. She was a high school teacher, but both thought later that she should be a university professor. Her knowledge, recall, and ability to link theory and literature exceeded anything either of them had encountered as undergraduates and now as law school students.

Very liberal in their thinking, Rebecca and Monique probed Alexi on her political and social take and were surprised to learn that Alexi tended toward a traditional bent. Given her hiking prowess and her intellectual talent, the two realized later they had misread Alexi.

Rebecca and Monique were taken aback when the discussion came around to their interpersonal relationship. Later, when they thought back on the discussion, both thought Alexi seemed uncomfortable when they shared their living arrangements and closeness. Alexi avoided comment and moved the discussion to other topics.

Later, as Alexi was leaving, both noticed she did not have a flashlight and offered to loan her one. There was no moon, and it was very dark. Alexi thanked them but declined and moved off without a sound. *Another element of strangeness,* they thought.

—∭—

The next day, the two backpackers looked for signs of Alexi as they left camp but found nothing. They hiked on toward Forrester Pass, crossing it about eleven thirty in the morning.

About two miles south of Forrester Pass, they left the Muir Trail and contoured west and around a ridge to pick up the informal trail to Lake South America. It was early afternoon when they arrived.

Named because of its shape like the southern continent, the lake sits in a basin at twelve thousand feet, well above tree line. One of several lakes in the basin, Lake South America is at the headwaters for the great Kern River, which flows south to the terminus of the Sierra Nevada. Because of the altitude, the lake offers no protection to the camper. Since it is well off the Muir Trail, the lake is isolated and the perfect spot to unwind in quiet repose.

Rebecca and Monique anticipated a restful afternoon. They could bathe in the lake without worrying about spectators, and then they could take a nap. It was just what they needed before their final two-day march to the end of the JMT.

Two days later, a despondent Rebecca packed up her belongings and prepared to leave the lake. She could not take all of Monique's gear—just the personal items she thought she should take. On the chance that Monique would return, she left Monique's backpack and remaining gear on a large boulder and weighted down by rocks. She attached a written message to Monique and any possible passerby. She did not know what else to do.

On the afternoon of their arrival, they had made camp and decided to bathe. It had been days since they were really clean, and the privacy of the lake allowed them to strip down and submerge. They felt like two little girls—naked and enjoying the water and the intimacy it encouraged.

Afterward, Rebecca opted to take a nap, but Monique said she was going to scout around the basin. She would not be long.

Rebecca slept far longer than she intended. When she awoke, it was after six in the evening, and Monique was not there. Rebecca was worried at first, but the worry quickly escalated as six o'clock gave way to seven and then eight. She yelled and scanned the basin. She walked around the lake. She went up the slope of the ridge to the east of the lake in search of a good viewing spot. But all to no avail. She found nothing. By then it was dark.

Certain that Monique would turn up, Rebecca kept her flashlight on until the batteries were depleted. Then she found Monique's flashlight and did the same. When morning arrived, there was still no sign of Monique.

Rebecca was frantic. She was scared. And she was panicked. Of all her experiences in life, nothing had prepared her for this, and she was at a loss about what to do. Should she go off searching? What if Monique was injured and returned and Rebecca was not here? Even if she searched, where should she go? She had no idea what direction Monique had gone. She must have been injured. Why else would she not return?

Rebecca hoped that someone would come along who could go for help, but no one did. She searched again the area around the lake. She found no sign of Monique.

After a second night, Rebecca knew that she had no choice but to head toward Crabtree Meadow. Along the way, she hoped to encounter someone who could help her. If not, there was a backcountry ranger station at the meadow. It was her only hope.

Glancing back repeatedly, she walked south and over the small col separating the lake from Tyndall Creek and the JMT. All she saw was the lake, the tundra, and the lone olive-green pack atop the rock where they had camped. At the col, she took one last look and then moved on.

CHAPTER 6

—∿—

TRAIL MYSTERY

January 20, 1979
Los Angeles Times *Article*

E ARLY ON A sunny morning last August, Charles Reems lifted his pack onto his shoulders. He hugged his girlfriend, Jamel Castro, and assured her he would be careful. He then set off on another backpack trip into his beloved Sierra Nevada. This was not to be a long trip, just a few days of adventure among the peaks and valleys well known to him.

Castro left Reems at the Mosquito Flats trailhead, twelve miles west of US Highway 395 near the small community known as Tom's Place. She was to pick Reems up five days later at South Lake outside the town of Bishop.

Reems never showed up at the South Lake trailhead. After he did not show up on the sixth day, Jamel Castro reported his absence to the US Forest Service personnel in Bishop, the headquarters for the Inyo National Forest. As Reems was an accomplished backpacker, the fact that he was late did not immediately raise concern. However, after a seventh day, Reems was officially listed as missing, and search efforts were put into motion.

In an interview, Castro shared that Reems was the most skilled of hikers. He was also a noted Yosemite rock climber and well aware of how to handle risks. "He is a very cautious climber; his friends will tell you that. Charles would not take any unnecessary risks. I just can't imagine what happened to him."

Now, six months later, authorities have no idea what happened to Charles Reems. Wayne Pasquali, a spokesperson for the Forest Service, told the *Los Angeles Times*, "We spent considerable time trying to gather information from hikers and packers who were known to have been on the route or parts of the route Reems was supposed to have taken. We know he was seen about noon on the first day by a couple who spoke to him along the trail near the upper end of Little Lakes Valley. He told them he was headed for Gem Lake and then planned to go over the pass north of Bear Creek Spire. We assume he did that because late the next day, a packer talked with him near Sallie Keys Lakes. Reems was on his way down from Selden Pass, and the packer indicated Reems appeared to be in excellent condition and moving along the trail with no difficulty. That is the last reported contact with Reems."

The best estimate by search and rescue personnel is that Reems disappeared somewhere along the John Muir Trail between Sallie Keys Lakes and Le Conte Canyon, about thirty miles to the south. The reasoning is that Reems was due to exit the backcountry over Bishop Pass on the last day. The twelve-mile trail is heavily traveled, and it is not likely he would have gone unnoticed on that day. There is no evidence he made it as far as the Bishop Pass Trail. A final comment from Pasquali emphasized the frustration of authorities: "We have absolutely no information about what happened to Reems."

The trail, or JMT as backpackers call it, begins in Yosemite Valley and ends at Mount Whitney. The trail is demanding and usually requires at least two to three weeks for experienced backpackers to complete it.

According to Castro, the thirty-year-old Reems had done the Muir Trail multiple times without incident. Only during the first couple of days of his trip last summer was Reems to be on trails he had not previously hiked. Given that he was last seen at Sallie Keys Lakes, he had satisfactorily navigated these unfamiliar areas.

When asked if there were others who had disappeared, the Forest

Service indicates that they have records of other disappearances along the JMT further south. In 1969, two UC–Berkeley students disappeared somewhere along the last hundred miles of the trail. The two, Enid Ackerman and Ingar Tolkenson, were last seen near Bench Lake in Kings Canyon National Park. As with Reems, there is no evidence as to what happened to them.

In the summer of 1978, Monique Fenwick and Rebecca Anderson, students in the UCLA school of law, were hiking along the JMT far to the south. About two days before their trip was scheduled to conclude, Monique disappeared. Efforts to find her turned up no evidence. The following spring, her remains were found along the Kern River, several miles from the area where she went missing. The cause of death appears to have been a blunt force accident.

Monique's hiking partner, Rebecca Anderson, says, "It hasn't been easy. Monique just disappeared. There was no warning, no sign of any problems—she was just gone. We had backpacked many times. We were very close to each other. We lived together. I would have known if there was any health problem. There was no one else in her life. I miss her dearly."

One other disappearance involves MaryAnn Travers, a student at UC–Riverside who disappeared in 1976 near where the Bishop Pass Trail connects with the JMT along the Middle Fork of the Kings River in Le Conte Canyon. Travers was a cross-country runner who used long day jogs of 20 to 30 miles in the Sierra as conditioning. She was not a backpacker. Apparently Travers left the trailhead at Lake Sabrina and jogged cross-country for about eight miles before connecting with the JMT. She was last seen at Muir Pass around noon. She planned to hike out over Bishop Pass and expected to reach the South Lake Trailhead about 9:00 p.m. She never showed up at the trailhead, and no trace of her has ever been found.

Reems, Ackerman, Tolkenson, Fenwick, and Travers were all young and, with the exception of Ackerman, apparently in excellent physical condition and very experienced at backpacking and hiking. According to Enid's mother, the backpack trip with Ingar was not something the family liked. Enid had always been shy and reclusive until she went to Berkeley. Mrs. Ackerman, a single parent, said that Enid wanted desperately to be liked and was drawn to Ingar's nomadic style. Enid went on the hike to please Ingar in spite of pleas that she not go.

The Tolkenson family lives in Sweden and did not respond to repeated phone calls.

The father of MaryAnn said his daughter was very independent and had a reputation of being a hard-core speed hiker and that she found it difficult to have a relationship with boys because they could not compete with her. Apparently MaryAnn was obsessed with maintaining her "physical and mental edge." Mr. Travers said he was very saddened by the loss of his daughter, and not knowing what happened has been hard.

When asked it if seemed strange that within the last decade five young hikers disappeared along the JMT, Pasquali indicated that perhaps to the uninitiated it appears strange. To those who know the rugged nature of the Sierra backcountry and the level of objective danger, it is not strange. The interest in hiking and backpacking has increased markedly in recent years, and young people especially are prone to take chances. Nature is not forgiving, and venturing off the trail and not following common sense can easily lead to trouble.

Whatever happened to these five young people may never be known. That is probably the most difficult aspect of any disappearance along the JMT. Did these five young people disappear because they made bad judgments, or is their disappearance the result of other circumstances? We may never know, but says Pasquali, "We never really shut the door on such cases. The people who hike the JMT and connecting trails are usually a responsible bunch, and there is always the chance that someone will come forward with information. Sometimes the most obscure piece of evidence is accidentally discovered along the trail or in a campsite. It is also quite possible, as was the case with Monique Fenwick, that someone will find a body. It is probably the not knowing that is most difficult."

Anyone who may have any insight to one of the above cases is encouraged to contact the US Forest Service or the *Los Angeles Times.*

CHAPTER 7

—∿∿—

CHARLES REEMS

1983
Offices of the National Park Service

NATIONAL PARK DEPUTY superintendent for investigations, Nils Knudson, read through the report. The case had come to light in early July. But it had been three months before the investigation by his personnel and the Fresno County Sheriff's Department concluded.

A husband and wife who had hiked cross-country to get to the little visited Lake 11,106 found the bones. The lake had no formal name and was referenced on topographic maps according to its altitude. It sat in a small basin about 1,400 feet above and north of the McClure Meadow Ranger Station along the Muir Trail. There was no formal trail to the lake, although cross-country hikers had over time created a vague one-mile path to it.

The discovery was made in the late evening when the couple hiked up a ridge on the west side of the lake, seeking a view down into Evolution Canyon. The wife found the bones and brought them to the attention of her husband, a kinesiology professor, who soon recognized several as those of a human.

It was three days after the discovery that the resident backcountry ranger was able to notify Kings Canyon National Park authorities.

Personnel responding to the scene found the bones scattered. It appeared the remains were originally at the base of the large granite outcrop that was part of a small ridge made up of large fractured rocks and boulders.

Of course, as often happens, even with experienced personnel, the initial response was not without its issues. Knudson was irritated that the findings showed the backcountry ranger and initial responders made several errors.

Because there was no identification information found at the site, the early belief was that the bones were those of a woman. This conclusion was reached when one of the responding rangers noticed an earring. However, when NPS investigators and a homicide team from the county sheriff's department were sent to study the scene and retrieve remains, they found no earring. All of this told Knudson that the scene had been compromised. The earring was never found.

Subsequent forensics revealed that the victim was male, about five foot eleven in height, and about thirty-five years of age at the time of death.

The investigation eventually revealed that the victim was probably Charles Reems who had been backpacking alone at the time of his disappearance in 1978. Reems had covered about fifty-two miles. He had been on the trail about three days. He was obviously a very good hiker.

What was perplexing was finding his remains at Lake 11,106. According to friends, Reems had not taken any fishing gear with him, as he anticipated covering sixteen to eighteen miles per day and did not figure to have much time for fishing. Also, it was surprising that he had gone to Lake 11,106 because of its distance off the JMT, and it was not a logical stop along the way.

Finally, the only indication of the cause of death was a fractured skull. It appeared Reems had fallen and hit his head. This conclusion was supported by the location and indications the body was originally probably wedged between two large boulders. If Reems had fallen and hit his head as those circumstances, it was likely he may have been unable to move. Whether he died immediately or his death was delayed could not be determined.

Because his gear was not found, it could only be surmised that he had left the gear elsewhere and took a hike during which an accident took his life. This would suggest the death took place during late afternoon or evening. To date, no gear had been found.

Having interviewed those who wrote the report, Knudson was satisfied that in the event no additional evidence was discovered, the report was complete. Accidents are not an uncommon occurrence within the many park service venues. However, most accidents are the result of poor judgment by people unfamiliar with the level of objective danger inherent in the wilds.

Nils had to admit that Reems did not fit the mold of the usual victim of an accident of this sort. Young and very experienced, Reems was not likely to do anything foolish. Yet it was also true that experience was no guarantee of safety. Anyone could make a simple mistake, fall, and end his life with a fractured skull. Accidents happened more often than people realized.

He picked up the large topographic composite map of Kings Canyon National Park. It was a shaded relief map, which made it easier to visualize areas. With his index finger, Knudson traced the route Reems took.

On reaching McClure Meadow, Reems would have covered eighteen miles and put in a long day that included a gain in altitude of about 1,700 feet during the last nine miles. It would probably have been in the late afternoon. To go up to Lake 11,106, he would gain another 1,400 feet in about a mile.

Why would he do this? Did he carry his pack up to the lake? If not, he would then have to descend back down the trail and a campsite before night. Knudson could not see the sense in going to the lake under any circumstances.

There was another peculiarity. It was the request from the county sheriff and US Army that the information be kept from the press. It appeared that Reems, at the time of his disappearance, was absent without authorization from the military. Since Reems had no immediate or extended family, the remains were to be turned over to a representative of the US Army.

Still, Reems's death was a reality. It looked to be an accident. Nothing to the contrary was evident. Was it an unusual situation? *Yes!* Was it so unusual that it warranted an ongoing investigation? *No!*

CHAPTER 8

—ᵐ—

NUEVO HIGH SCHOOL

1999
Orange County, California

I T HAD BEEN a long morning. Jay smiled at his secretary as he entered the outer office.

"Well done, Dr. Jansen."

"Thanks, Sylvia. Glad it's over. Anything important?"

"Nothing critical. Just the usual. Everything is on your desk."

"That's a good sign."

"Also, Dr. Jensen, you will find on your desk a very quick summary of the time capsule items. My list is unpolished, but I thought you would find it interesting."

"Yes, I'll look at it."

Jay looked at his desk as he walked around it and sat down. Everything was in organized stacks and awaiting his attention. Shaking his head, he thought about the work not getting done. *I guess I'll have to come in Saturday and work through this mess.*

Sylvia entered and handed Jay several phone messages.

"Sylvia, thanks. I appreciate it." Then, with a sigh of exasperation, Jay commented, "I wonder why some of the faculty and staff can't seem to master the idea of good communication."

"You are referring to some of the off-the-cuff teacher remarks?"

"Yes. This morning's ceremony brought out the media,

superintendent, board members, and community bigwigs. Some of our teachers give pause for concern about their speaking ability. It's a short leap to questions about how well they communicate in the classroom, how well they teach. Wouldn't be surprised if a couple board members raise that issue."

"I am sure it is not a reflection on you, Dr. Jensen."

"Oh well, can't win 'em all."

Picking up the handful of notes, Jay interrupted his secretary as she was leaving. "Sylvia, unless it's important, I'd like to avoid any unnecessary interruptions. Give me about an hour to work through these messages. Then we will try to get back to normal."

"Not a problem. Would you like me to shut your door?"

"No, that will not be necessary. Just screen things as best you can."

"Certainly!" Sylvia nodded and departed.

Jay retrieved the notes for his speech from his coat pocket. As he did so, he found the ceremony program as well. A note he had written on the program reminded him that he needed to thank the custodial staff. Jack and his crew had done a remarkable job of preparing for the large crowd. Most notably, they had exposed just enough of the time capsule that it was possible to open it without having to remove it completely from the ground. The whole idea had been Jack's. The assistant principals and student body adviser wanted the time capsule removed ahead of time and placed on a table for opening. Jack recognized that doing so would have taken away some of the mystery. Why not leave it in the ground with enough of the top showing so that the woodshop teacher could use his new power saw to quickly open the capsule.

Jay leaned back in his chair and thought, *Everything worked out pretty well. Superintendent and board seemed satisfied. I can only hope the media saw success. Oh well, it's over.*

He picked up the list of time capsule items Sylvia had prepared. Looking over the list and thinking about the conversations before and after the opening, Jay began to reflect on what had brought the school to this point in time.

The senior gift of the first graduating class in 1973 was the time capsule. Thinking back on those early years when he was a history teacher just out of graduate school, Jay remembered that graduating class as a special group. They, like Jay, opened the school. The time capsule was to be opened in 2023, during the fiftieth reunion of the graduating class.

Recalling the time capsule burial, Jay also remembered it was a somber time for the school, as two juniors had disappeared after the prom the year before and had never been found. They were memorialized with some items included in the capsule.

The end of the 1972 school year had been difficult with the many volunteer hours he and colleagues spent helping students work through the difficulties of losing peers. His thoughts reminded him of the small plaque in the library that listed former students who died tragically during their high school years or in the line of military or public service duty. The two missing students from the class of '73 were the first names on the plaque—Cindy and Carlos.

Jay's thoughts returned to the day's time capsule opening. In a way, it was bittersweet. Mandatory structural changes to the school building necessitated opening the time capsule. Knowing any unilateral decision on his part would create a backlash, Jay contacted the class of 1973 senior class officers. For some time, they debated how best to relocate the capsule. In the end, the officers opted to open the capsule and not wait until 2023.

So, twenty-six years later, rather than fifty, the capsule was opened. Though there was much speculation leading up to today about the possible condition of the capsule contents, in the end everything was as it should be.

All that remained was to exhibit the many capsule items in the display cases at the school entrance. Jack's crew was now removing the capsule, and it too would be put on display. Jay was pleased. *Yes, it went well.*

Jay turned his attention to his messages when Sylvia quietly entered.

"Dr. Jensen, I am very sorry, but Jack says we have a big problem he needs to share with you. I told him you were busy, but he says it is an emergency. He will not tell me the problem."

This is not like Jack, thought Jay. It was also not like Sylvia to interrupt unless she sensed a serious problem. "Okay, show him in."

Sylvia left and returned seconds later, ushering Jack Solis into the office.

In his usual polite and respectful way, Jack removed his school baseball cap and apologized before sharing. "I'm sorry to bother you, Dr. Jensen, but I think we have a problem."

"What is it, Jack?"

"I think it would be best if you came and looked."

"You can't share it with me?"

"Yes, but I'm not sure what to say. You need to see."

PART 2

———⚬———

A COLD CASE

Every normal man must be tempted, at times,
to spit on his hands, hoist the black flag,
and begin slitting throats.

—H. L. Mencken

IS NORMALCY A reality or merely a perception? Perhaps each day begins a new reality, a new normal. Perhaps normalcy is both shunned and embraced as opinion guides each of us. Maybe it is true that there is a normality that belies the world as most of us know it.

For some, normalcy is compromised by behavior that falls short of public expectations. In some cases, transgressions are heinous and extreme. In rare instances, the violator may even see such actions as acceptable. For them, a new and very personal madness emerges.

Enter those charged to *protect and serve.* What should we expect of those investigating the crimes of the mad? Must they solve crime within the parameters of normalcy, or can they, as some would suggest, *fight fire with fire?*

Television and movies are awash with examples of the dedicated, if not obsessed, crime fighter willing to exceed the limits of reason to solve a crime. In the end, they *get their man.* But such feats of detective acumen come with a cost.

A greater approximation of detective work is dogged determination that moves at a pitifully slow pace and within the conventions of case law restraints and professional practice.

An investigator of crime can be excused if he or she has feelings as those proffered by Mencken in the quote above. The frustration of solving crime can push police work to the edge; perhaps the edge of sanity in those cases where the crime is horrific and the perpetrator elusive.

But it would be inaccurate to suggest that solving crime is strictly a procedural matter where tried and tested protocols are the key. Whatever normalcy there is within the rank and file of detectives probably pays deference to popular expectations of fairness and the restrictions of legal experience. It is probably equally true that for some, the art of solving a crime has evolved at a personal level, and the methods used have their own shades of oddness.

The key for effective detective work in those hard cases, the ones that have eluded the best, would seem then to be that of finding the fine line between a normal approach and one that exists outside the box. Or, as Kurt Vonnegut has advised, get as close to the edge as you can without going over. "Out on the edge you see all the kinds of things you can't see from the center."

CHAPTER 9

—⚍—

PRESENT DAY

Orange County Sheriff Department
Santa Ana, California

INVESTIGATOR VAN VANARSDALE, approaching the small office,
noticed the nameplate still identified his predecessor as occupant.
Oh well, he thought, *it's been a whirlwind of events. No big deal.*
He long ago learned that a little anonymity was something to be
treasured.

Entering, Van saw several cardboard file boxes stacked just inside
the door. *Must be Rasmussen's things. Tough way to end your career.*

The desktop was barren, and he dropped his shoulder bag on
top. Walking around to the swivel chair, he knew this would be the
cleanest he or anyone would see the office. If past was prologue, it
would be a mess within days.

A courtesy knock caught him unexpectedly. He looked up to see
Sergeant Fenton.

Fenton was the archetype sergeant—trim, six feet tall, poised, and
all about command presence. They had known each other for years,
first as deputies and later as investigators. Occasionally they had
worked together out of the South Orange County substation when
both did a stint on the Direct Enforcement Team.

For the past seven years, they had been on different professional
tracks. But an investigator's past crossed distance and time. Reputation

was both precedent and baggage. Van knew Fenton to have been an excellent investigator, and the fact that he was now a sergeant within homicide was testimony to his talent. Van also suspected his own current assignment was probably partly attributed to the fact that he was a known quantity to Fenton.

When Van had entered the office earlier in the morning, the sergeant was there to greet him. Rapport was easily renewed.

"Van, here are some cold files. These were the cases Rasmussen was working. I took them off his desk a few days after he went to the hospital. Didn't want them sitting here when people found out he probably wasn't coming back."

"And the active cases?"

"Took those too. However, I have distributed them among the others for now. My practice for anyone new is to give 'em several days to read through their share of the colds before putting them on the rotation list. Otherwise there's a good chance they'll be up to their ass with new cases and no time to read the colds. I figure you'll be ready for your share about next weekend. That gives you four days to get settled in."

"I appreciate it, Sarge."

"Of course, if there's a crisis and the bad guys have a field day before then, hell, you may find the honeymoon cut short."

"Understood! Thanks."

"Also, I'll give you a few minutes, and then we need to meet with the lieutenant. He knows we've worked together before. He'll want to get to know you. You ever met him before?"

"No."

"Well, he's not your run-of-the-mill lieutenant. Vargas likes to know things that aren't in the file. Don't get me wrong, he's not nosy, but he believes that a good administrator knows his team well. Anyway, come to my office when you're ready."

With that, Fenton left. Vanarsdale took a seat and out of habit began to search through things, beginning with the desk drawers.

Typical investigator's office was a quick conclusion. The drawers were filled with everything from paperclips to countless pencils and pens. There were notepads of numerous sizes and origins. A cursory perusal indicated there was probably no need to request anything from the secretary. No telling what was needed. There was no order to it. The file drawer on the left side had files, but the labels looked confusing. He would need to look through them later. The file drawer on the right housed a collection of miscellaneous things, everything except files.

The computer keyboard looked little used. Van turned the computer on, and it booted quickly, and the user ID and password request popped up. That was a good sign. Although he knew he was a bit old school in the eyes of some, he had become a skilled user of the computer and internet benefits to investigations. He made a note to find out how to access the information Rasmussen would have saved.

He got up and walked over to the obligatory four-drawer metal file cabinet and checked each drawer. Again, no order. Lots of stuff but nothing that stood out. It would take time to review.

Van knew he should not be one to question someone else's idea of order, but he liked to think that he was considerably more organized than Rasmussen seemed to have been.

Returning to his chair, he took the stack of cold files and began to quickly scan them. He did not know Vargas, but he did not want to chance going into a meeting with Vargas without familiarizing himself with some of the cases.

—⟋⟍—

Twenty minutes later, he left his office and walked across the room of cubicles. Poking his head through the sergeant's open door, he said, "I'm ready when you are."

"Oh, good. Let's go." Fenton quickly exited the computer program he was working. *A good sign*, thought Van. The feds were big on never leaving your computer with files open on the screen. Too many eyes and too many chances to compromise critical information.

As they walked, Fenton said, "Listen, the lieutenant sometimes comes across a bit gruff, but he backs us to the wall. You can be open with him. Folks here like him. He's gone to bat for us."

"Good reputation?"

"Yep, but I'll give you the details later. There is one thing though. Best you not bring up one of the cold cases, the Ashae and Fuentes case. We need to talk about it some before you move forward."

"Okay by me." Further discussion would be important, but already Van sensed the case was outside the norm for cold cases. He would need to listen closely and get comfortable with the details well before doing anything.

Lieutenant Vargas met them just inside his office door. "Investigator Van Vanarsdale, it's good to have you on board. Fenton sings your praises, but I can't trust a damn thing he says, so I asked to meet with you …" The intended humor was accompanied by the lieutenant's smile.

They exchanged greetings. Then Vanarsdale spoke. "Lieutenant, with replicated first and last names, I tell people to just call me Van. No sense making it a tongue-twister."

"I take it you have a lifetime of experience with that challenge."

"Oh yeah. When I was a kid, it was a real problem, and there were times I swore that when I grew up I would change it."

"Why didn't you?"

"I guess when I got into college, I realized it was sort of cool to have a unique name. Then I learned in biology they have a term for a duplicated name for genus and species, like *Bison bison* for the American buffalo. It's called a tautonym. It just seemed to me that having something in common with the iconic buffalo was a distinction I could not reject."

Though a bit on the intellectual side, the humor of Van's comment was not lost on the two officers, and there were nods of appreciation.

"Okay, Van. Have a seat and bring me up to speed. You're coming here from a special assignment on sudden notice is a bit unconventional, but I can live with that. What I need to know is a little about you. Fenton will tell you, I always like to know my people. The better I know them, the better I can serve them."

"Fair enough, Lieutenant."

"Tell me a little about the special fed assignment you've been on the past seven years and how you got into that."

"Okay. Well, I went to the Direct Enforcement Team as a deputy for a couple of years. Had a great experience, especially working a big forgery case that involved the tri-county area. When I left DET, I was promoted to investigator and assigned to South County. Three years later, one of the DET investigators left to take a job up north."

Fenton said, "That was Brenda Robertson, Lieutenant. I think you worked with her when she came out of the academy."

"Yes, I remember Brenda. Went up north somewhere."

Fenton clarified. "She's now working for the PD in Mammoth Lakes. She says it's her dream job. Has a family, and they all ski, fish, hike—you know, the outdoor things."

The lieutenant's eyebrows went up as if to say *lucky her.*

Vanarsdale returned to his narrative. "Anyway, it was unusual, but I found myself back in DET. Things were different. Increasingly, DET was focusing on complex cases involving other agencies outside Orange County. One of the cases was a big extortion ring with connections to the Seal Beach Naval Weapons Base. The more we followed the evidence, the more it led us to an international component, but we couldn't tie everything together. So I decided to spend some time researching on my own. Probably too much time."

"You really took it that serious?"

"Yes and no. My wife was ill for several years and passed away in 2001. Our two kids were out of college and on their own by then, so I found that immersing myself in work was a great escape. It helped me cope. I became a workaholic I guess."

Vargas said, "So how did this all lead to your special assignment with the feds?"

"You've heard the rumors?" asked Van.

"You mean the idea that you got so deep into your work that soon you butted heads with the FBI and others and they had no choice but to seek your assistance?"

"Yeah, but it really didn't happen that way."

Fenton interrupted. "I never thought there was any truth to that rumor, but then I never heard a better rumor to replace it." The humor brought smiles from his colleagues. The internal secrecy that seemed to be so much a part of life in the police profession fostered an environment where rumors were ever present and the truth often never known. The department thrived on rumors.

"I can tell you, it was an interesting ride. During those years right after 9/11, the feds were looking behind every bush for evidence of terrorist involvement in all sorts of criminal activity. I just happened to stumble into the hunt."

"How so?"

"While still with the department, I started going to special conferences focused on cases involving international crime organization. I was able to use some of what I learned back here. In time, I was able to participate in discussions with counterparts across the country and then internationally. Then I was asked to give some presentations."

Vargas said, "So you became an expert in demand."

"Something like that. Anyway, my lieutenant then was Ray Masterson." Fenton and Vargas were nodding that they knew Masterson, who was now a special assistant to the sheriff. "He informed me that the feds had a task force working on connections between local crimes and international terrorism. The task force had requested that the department grant me a leave of absence to work with them for an indefinite period. The question was whether I was interested."

"Were you?"

"Yes and no again. That is ... I was interested but wanted to think about it. They said I had a week. The more I thought about it, the more I considered declining the offer. But my kids talked me out of that decision. They knew the loss of Anna Marie had left me restless and that I needed to be immersed in work. In time, they said, I would move on. So I agreed."

"Just like that, huh?"

"Pretty much. Things moved fast. Within days, I was told the department would give me a leave. I would not lose seniority or service credit."

Vargas was curious. "Any regrets, I mean working for the feds?"

"No, I think my kids were right. Looking back, it was a good learning experience."

The lieutenant leaned back in his swivel chair. He was waiting for more.

"Look, Lieutenant, I was a workaholic then. Still am to some extent. I was just relentless, and one way to get the bad guy was to outsmart him by spending so much time doing the research that I could begin to put the puzzle together when there were only a few pieces on the table."

Lieutenant Vargas looked over at Fenton. "Tell him what the word is in the department about his methods."

Vanarsdale knew that what he was about to hear he had probably heard before.

"Word is that you have developed the ability to think inside the bad-boy box. You get inside the mind of the asshole and begin to think like him and not like a detective. That allows you to anticipate when others can only react."

Van smiled. Yes, he'd heard this logic before.

Fenton went on. "Granted, you are a bit unconventional, but the word is also that you always work within regulations and are not a problem for your superiors. If anything, you're relentless and just outwork everyone."

"I'm not sure how to respond. Is it a compliment or a complaint?"

"Probably a bit of both. Depends on the colleague," said Fenton.

All three understood Fenton's comments. For those who saw their work as just a job, they looked on people like Van as making them look bad by working beyond required hours. For those who had a sense of pride in solving cases, investigators like Van were respected.

"Tell me, Van, how was it working with the feds? You always hear how they look down on those of us at the local level."

"Actually, those were my thoughts going into it. I'd heard the same things. However, I'd have to say that from my perspective now, such fears are unfounded. I was fortunate."

"How so?"

"The sheriff clued me in ahead of time. She called me into her office before I left. I think it was during her early weeks of tenure here. She gave me a couple pieces of advice." Van realized too late that he had just left a door open by suggesting she gave him advice.

"And?"

Vanarsdale paused to think about his response. "First, she said that I'd find none of the feds were any smarter. That I could match wits with the best of them."

"No doubt true. And the second?"

"Well, this was a peculiar piece of advice. She said that in the federal organizations, it was all about being first. There was a level of competition between and among the different agencies. She explained that although they work as a team on the surface, they individually take all the credit, even if someone else really did the work. Her advice was to always put things in writing and send CCs to others. That way there was a record of who did the real work."

"Was she right?"

"Sort of."

Vargas said, "That's our sheriff—always one to give those who do the work credit. Big difference between her and her predecessor."

Fenton was curious. "Was she right about you being equal to the feds intellectually?"

"For the most part, but they have some different resources."

"More money, I would guess."

"I don't know about that; I think it was more their size and reach. There was one gal … She was different. Dr. Patel was her name, Adrian Patel. Bright lady. She was part of the task force but not one of them. She was a professor type on loan from an Ivy League university. I learned some new things about investigations listening to her talk and work with some of the teams."

"A professor type? Interesting. How did she fit in?" asked Vargas.

"She had been doing research for years, using statistics to evaluate the effectiveness of investigative techniques."

With his head cocked to one side and eyebrows raised, Vargas said, "Stats?"

"Yep, but not just that. She had developed a system that used both statistics and qualitative methods. The term she used was *mixed methods studies*. Some of the people on the task force swore by her skills. She taught them to approach investigations using a *mantra*."

"Mantra? What was it?" asked the lieutenant.

"Why not?"

"Why not what? What kind of philosophy is that?"

"It was her mantra to always ask, 'Why not?' She was not confrontational. When someone explained the approach they were taking, she would follow by asking them to explain why they were using the tactic. Once they concluded their explanation, regardless of the soundness of their logic, she would ask them if they had considered another approach. If they said no, she would ask, 'Why not?' The whole idea was to get you to think on a macro level before going to the micro level. That kind of thinking helped avoid assumptions.

"Dr. Patel believes assumptions are the biggest nemeses in law enforcement investigations. She drew an analogy with research methods. Good researchers test assumptions experimentally. They know competing colleagues will challenge anything that suggests a study was done ignoring key assumptions. Law enforcement never really tests assumptions, which she likens to hypotheses. We bully our way through out of experience and habit. We don't take stock of the relationship between methods and results."

Van's comments revealed his comfort with what he had learned working with the feds. "She contended that all too often investigators get into a rut of practice; sometimes whole departments do the same thing. They seldom approach things differently. They operate from longstanding assumptions. They become very good at saying what will work and what will not work. They develop tunnel vision and really cannot see any other way to approach a problem. Dr. Patel was a master at getting people outside their investigative comfort level and trying other approaches. She was able to encourage certain more catholic approaches because she had the data to show that they worked."

Van caught himself saying *catholic* and reminded himself to be careful about use of terms that could put others off. He knew all too well that his reputation was influenced in part by the perception he was overly intellectual in word and action.

Vargas and Fenton nodded, and Van sensed they understood. "I remember Dr. Patel saying it was her experience that leaders were at their best when they empowered supporters to criticize their boss by asking *why not* questions."

Vargas was quick to understand the implications of Van's comments. "Of course, it's all a matter of circumstances. We take our direction from those who lead. If they're trusting of others, leaders can effectively empower. If they're sanctimonious, followers soon learn to keep their mouth shut."

Fenton said, "We've all experienced that, haven't we?"

There was a quiet assent among the three. Names were not necessary to confirm the point.

Later, thinking back on the conversation, Van realized the discussion had not been the usual cop talk. Instead, it had been more of an academic endeavor where colleagues listened to an open exchange of ideas without prejudice. It was refreshing.

The conversation began to move away from Van's experience with the feds and toward the department and the lieutenant's expectations. None of it was new. Every organization has its rules and boundaries—much of it explicit, and most of it cultural, a matter of history and leadership. Van was okay with that so long as expectations were clear and practice consistent.

The lieutenant's expectations and his adherence to the chain of command were consistent with law enforcement at all levels. The message was clear: do your job well and operate within regulations. Van was to keep Fenton in the loop on everything. Fenton, in turn, would keep the lieutenant advised in a timely manner.

"As for your cases, Van, you will find little interference from me unless you draw unneeded attention to our team or you do not follow proper procedures. Procedures exist to be followed, and we would be a sorry lot if we worked outside the guidelines and limits. Am I clear on that?"

"You bet, Lieutenant." Van knew that the lieutenant was saying what any good superior officer would say. The intent was to emphasize standard procedures and to not inhibit Van's work. There was a fine line, and Van was well aware that he would need to work carefully to locate that line with Vargas. For the time being, Van was satisfied. The focus was as it should be—good practice and no heroics.

"Good. Well, Fenton says you're good at what you do, and I'm counting on that. There'll be occasions when I'll ask you to come in and talk with me about a particular case, but almost always I will want Fenton, and any other pertinent investigator, present as well. We are a team. I'll leave it to Fenton to get you settled in."

The discussion ended, and Fenton and Van walked back toward their offices.

"Lieutenant is a good man, Van. He lets us do our job and always has our back. He expects results, but he doesn't micromanage. Can't ask for much more."

"Hey, Sarge, I won't be a problem for you or the lieutenant. But I do have a question."

"Shoot!"

"Well, you said earlier I shouldn't bring up the Ashae and Fuentes case. I looked at the file and know little about it. Vargas didn't bring it up. What's the deal?"

"You'll want to look through that file in greater detail. You'll have questions."

"I take it the case is sensitive."

"More than that." Fenton entered his office. "Come on. I'll fill you in."

—⟋⟋⟍—

In police work, as in many professions, there are cultural habits that play a role when transitioning between tasks. For cops, it's grabbing a cup of coffee. In Van's case, it was a cup of tea. With their respective beverages in hand, they turned to Fenton's commentary.

"You'll find a lot of history in the file. The case wasn't Rasmussen's from the beginning. He inherited it in the second phase after both Torres and Inskeep retired."

"Second phase?"

"Yes, but let me back up. The case first surfaced in 1972 when two kids at Nuevo High School went missing after the school prom. The vehicle was discovered the next morning. It was burned out and found by hikers near Irvine Lake. There were no bodies. The investigation went on for months. Very high profile, but they never found the two kids. Got a lot of attention in the news, and the department pressed hard, but there was nothing to go on. Lots of speculation. Over time, the case grew cold, damn cold.

"Then about twenty-seven years later, the case grew hot again when the remains of the girl were discovered in a Nuevo High School time capsule."

"I remember hearing about that. I was a deputy."

"Yep, got a lot of attention locally and nationally, but again the trail grew cold quickly."

"Why the sensitivity with the lieutenant?"

"Couple reasons, I think. First, his dad, Anthony Vargas Senior, was one of the investigators on the case in 1972. He took the case very seriously, perhaps too seriously. It affected him, and some say he treated every lead as if it was the answer to the case. As a result, he began to see evidence where there was none. Alienated his partner and eventually pissed off everyone else."

"I've heard that scenario. Lose your objectivity. Really need to be taken off the case."

"That's what happened. Vargas was reassigned. But he wouldn't let go. Started spending off-duty hours following up on every damned lead. Was warned but didn't stop. Eventually he was busted down to deputy and assigned patrol, but again he exceeded authority. Had enough years in by then and was gently forced to retire."

"The case doesn't seem unusual for the time. Two kids disappear from prom and are never found. Probably not the first time in this country."

"No, it wasn't unusual on the surface. That brings up the second reason. What is unusual is that Investigator Vargas had a younger sister who had been killed after a school dance in 1958 by a hit-and-run. Apparently he was very close to her and took her loss very hard. They never were able to identify the driver, and the case went unsolved. People didn't realize how hard it impacted Vargas until the 1972 case came along. He wouldn't let go. It was as if he was investigating the death of his own sister. It was a kind of transference, I suppose."

"I see. I venture there's a connection between that experience and the decision of our Lieutenant Vargas to go into law enforcement?"

"That's what some say. Not unusual."

"No, I suppose not."

"The lieutenant's father died of a stroke within a year of retirement. Seems that even in retirement he was poking around on the case and became so agitated and narrow that his health quickly declined."

"I've never been that consumed by a case, but I can understand how a case can be consuming."

CHAPTER 10

GETTING UP TO SPEED

Sheriff's Department Homicide Office

V AN SPENT THE remainder of the morning arranging his office to fit his style.

It crossed Van's mind that he should give some thought to how he might arrange his office aesthetically, but such thinking was only superficial. He would do some little things. Nothing fancy. He could bring in some photos later. Or maybe he wouldn't. He wanted it simple.

As for files, they were categorized into two formats.

Every active case was represented by one private file that was to be kept in the lower left desk file drawer. This file contained his notes, ideas, and theories as well as more speculative information pertinent to a case. However, there would be a second file located in the formal file cabinet, properly labeled and containing requisite information and records. This second file was the official source. This was not typical procedure, but it was a protocol Vanarsdale had adopted many years earlier. His college roommate went on to become a high school assistant principal who long ago told Van that he always maintained two files on a problem student—one with the required information and a second with personal notes and information, including speculative observations he would not want public. When Van inquired as to the reason, his roommate noted that school records were public documents and could be requested or subpoenaed. With the two-file system, he could always hand over the primary file, and it would appear complete and up to date. The other file would remain insulated.

Van found this approach useful because his work was a mixture of professional procedures and protocols on the one hand and his own thinking and observations on the other. Acting on a request, he could always provide a superior or others with a file of a case that was consistent with expectations without cluttering it with information and observations that could raise concerns.

During the morning, several people in the department stopped by to greet, introduce, and welcome him. A couple drop-ins were now ranking officers from other divisions; they had worked with Van years earlier. One had gone through the academy with him. All were pleasant, and most made references to the unfortunate circumstances surrounding Rasmussen's death. It was evident that Rasmussen had been a well-liked fixture in the department. Van concluded Rasmussen was well liked as a gregarious team player who was not a problem for others.

Thinking about Rasmussen, Van realized that others would soon see that he and John were very different. Van saw himself as pleasant and easy to get along with, albeit as more of an introvert. Since Anna Marie's death, he knew he was much more inward. She had always managed to bring him out of his shell, but with her gone, he slid back to the personality he had before they met—inward and focused. These two traits were both a blessing and a curse. Too much of either was problematic for someone working in a high-profile public position.

Given his introvert tendencies, Van was always conscious of his need to balance personal affinities with purposeful efforts to get outside himself. With this in mind, it did not escape Van that the homicide floor was filled with support staff, and he needed to actively spend time getting to know them. He made a mental note to get a list of birthdays so that he would not be embarrassed when those days came around. Whether one was an investigator, deputy, or any other rank, it was best to acknowledge the support of those who were not sworn officers.

—⧏⧐—

Not one to eat big lunches, Van started the afternoon drinking iced tea and nibbling on cheese and crackers while he began the task of more closely reviewing the half-dozen cold-case files.

Most were cases older than ten years and involved the deaths of individuals of little note—male and female. Two involved killings that were clearly tied to gang rivalries. The chance of either ever being solved was remote. Experience told him that for most in law enforcement, solving such cases was a low priority. Another case involved the rape and murder of a South County housewife. There had been many leads and suspects, including the husband. However, the crime scene had been so contaminated by the six people who discovered the body that the compromise of evidence hindered the case unreasonably. Forensics and DNA testing had not helped. Another case was perplexing because the body was so decayed and scattered at the time of recovery there was little or no evidence regarding the cause of death. The identified victim carried drug-dealer baggage. There was reason to believe death was the result of a drug deal gone bad, and the list of possible perps was long. Several suspects had since died, disappeared, or were in jail.

Van had purposefully avoided looking at the Ashae and Fuentes case until late afternoon when the office was relatively quiet—not that the department was ever really quiet, but at least most of the support staff had gone, and it was quieter. He wanted to look at the case with the fewest possible interruptions.

—⧏⧐—

Laid out on the desk in front of him were the contents of files regarding the Ashae-Fuentes case. There were, as Fenton called it, two phases to the case. First, there were the notes and reports from the original investigation during the months after the disappearance in 1972 and the years to follow. Second, there was the investigation paperwork that developed after the remains of Cindy Ashae were discovered in 1999.

Because of the burned-out VW van and the publicity surrounding the disappearance, the case was from the start treated as a potential homicide. There was, of course, the speculation among public figures and department personnel that Ashae and Fuentes could have run off together. It happens all the time. However, they had been dressed for the prom. There was absolutely no evidence that they had made preparations to run off. As time went on, the idea of them running off waned. Kids that age are not likely to remain detached from family and friends beyond a few days. Moreover, kids are not likely to keep such plans secret.

The assigned investigators were Vargas and Damon. The records clearly indicated that Investigator Vargas did most of the work and then some. In the early stages, all the student friends of the two kids were interviewed. As expected, the teenage friends provided the investigators with all kinds of information, most of it speculation, hearsay, and filled with bravado. Separating fact from fiction is never easy, but it is especially difficult when interviewing teenagers who seem to be compelled to say something regardless of value and provenance. Nevertheless, the files appeared to include the results of comprehensive interviews of friends, teachers, and acquaintances.

Every student at the prom had been interviewed. The gist of their comments was that Ashae and Fuentes left the dance at the end when everyone else did. According to statements, the two appeared to have a good time at the dance, did not have any visible disagreements, and did not have any problem encounters with other students. After saying goodbye to friends, Ashae and Fuentes left in his VW van. One statement even noted that Fuentes commented that he "had to get his date home before her mom came unglued." However, several others indicated that they would not be surprised if the two went somewhere to be alone for a couple of hours. On the latter point, neither investigator was able to obtain any evidence to suggest that was what happened.

Comments from the friends of Ashae suggested that her mother was not likely to let Cindy stay out all night. Also, Cindy had a very good relationship with her mother and would not want to disappoint. This suggestion was confirmed in interviews with Mrs. Ashae.

As for Carlos Fuentes, students thought his parents, especially his dad, would let him stay out all night. Carlos was well regarded by classmates and teachers, and most suggested he would not take advantage of Cindy or disregard Mrs. Ashae's expectations.

The trouble with interviewing parents, and others, so long after such an event is that recollections are often jaded by time and reflection. But even as he thought about the time factor, Van knew he would be interviewing the parents, provided they were still alive.

Damon's notes indicated teachers and administrators working the prom kept track of students who left early. Carlos and Cindy were not among those. Several teachers remembered talking with Ashae and Fuentes during the dance and as they were leaving around eleven o'clock. As he considered their departure time, it seemed to Van to be a bit early. His recollection of the experiences of his own kids attending formal dances in the 1990s was that they did not end until midnight. If Mrs. Ashae expected Cindy home by one in the morning, the two kids had two hours to travel from Balboa to North County—about forty miles. It was more than enough time to travel and to engage in *extracurricular* activities along the way.

While sorting and scanning the mounds of documentation, Van noticed a local newspaper article published several months after the disappearance.

A Sad Start to the School Year

School is back in session for many districts this week, and for high school seniors throughout the county, it is the culmination of a thirteen-year experience. But for the seniors of Nuevo High School in North Orange

County, it will be a bittersweet year. It starts without anyone knowing the whereabouts of two classmates, Cindy Ashae and Carlos Fuentes. Cindy and Carlos went to the school prom last April and have not been seen since.

The missing students represent a dark cloud over what should be a banner year for Nuevo seniors, who will be the school's first graduating class in June. Nuevo opened its doors in September 1969 with only a freshman class. This year, for the first time, there will be four grade levels, and this year's seniors have had the privilege of establishing school traditions.

Student body president, Melissa Pearson, said, "We will miss sharing this year with Cindy and Carlos, but we aim to remember them, and we plan to dedicate the year to their memory." Founding school principal, Lou Berlioz, echoed Melissa's comments by noting that he and the teachers have been amazed at how sensitive all the students have been about events surrounding the disappearance of Cindy and Carlos.

Unfortunately, it appears that the sheriff's department is no closer to solving the mystery than they were in the days after the prom. Department spokesman Lieutenant Anthony Nieto noted that investigators have talked to everyone who was at the prom. That includes students, faculty working the dance, photographers, and employees of the Balboa Pavilion where the prom was held. They have gone door-to-door in the area around the Pavilion looking for anyone who may have seen anything.

The only real clue in the case is the VW bus Carlos was driving. Friends saw the two drive away after the dance ended at 11:00 p.m. on Saturday, April 29. When Cindy did not return home by 2:00 a.m. Sunday morning, her mother, a single parent, called the homes of some of Cindy's friends. One of the parents active in the school PTA had the phone number of Principal Berlioz and called him to report Cindy was missing.

Berlioz called the sheriff's department. It is not clear what exactly transpired at the department, but missing persons was not notified until after dawn on Sunday.

About 10:00 a.m. Sunday morning, hikers in an area east of Irvine Lake discovered a freshly burned-out VW van. They called the sheriff's department from Irvine Lake about 10:30 a.m. By nightfall, the department confirmed that the van belonged to Carlos's father, Miguel Fuentes. Apparently Mr. Fuentes and his wife work nights and were not aware that Carlos did not come home from the prom until early Sunday morning.

According to Nieto, the department has followed up on countless leads but all to no avail. Nieto noted that in the beginning there were all sorts of rumors. However, once investigators began to question every lead closely, it became clear that 99 percent of the leads did not pan out. The other 1 percent, says Nieto, represent leads that have been next to impossible to follow up on. When asked about these difficult leads, the lieutenant said he was not at liberty to discuss them.

As it stands, sheriff investigators continue to work the case. However, by their own admission, the further they get away from the date of the prom, the colder the trail grows.

It remains to be seen if this year's Nuevo High School seniors finish the year knowing what happened to two of their classmates. There is a remote chance that such a resolution will add some satisfaction to the year. But it is increasingly likely that commencement day will be no different from tomorrow; the class of 1973 will be short two students.

Van set the article down. This was a peculiar case in the beginning since it provided no real leads. Cases involving young people usually provide some leads even if they do require considerable work to ferret out what is credible and what is hearsay. Kids hear things and are notorious for not being able to keep secrets. But no one seemed to have a clue about what happened to Ashae and Fuentes.

Strange, thought Van. *It doesn't compute. Teenagers don't keep secrets well.*

Van resisted reading the second-phase work. Experience had taught him to take his time with evidence. Spend the needed time to consider what the evidence from the original investigation suggested before moving on to review information from events of years later. The logic to this approach seemed apparent to Van, so he physically removed the material from the second phase and stacked it atop his file cabinet.

He returned to his desk and began to once again read over the work of Vargas and Damon.

The evening gave way to night, and Van did not go home until about ten o'clock. The minimal staff at that hour, along with the scattered deputies and officers, glanced his way as he was leaving the building, but they did not know him and only nodded.

CHAPTER 11

DAY TWO

Homicide Office

Investigator Vanarsdale leaned back in his chair, raised his arms behind his head, and stretched.

Last evening, his mind kept reviewing the information from the initial Ashae-Fuentes investigation in 1972. Twice during the night, he turned on the bed-stand light and jotted down some thoughts. This morning he arrived early. Since sleep was not going to happen, he made the decision to get up and go into the office well before sunup.

He picked up the legal pad and looked at his notes. He wondered if there was anything he should add. But no sooner had the question occurred than he tossed the pad back on the desk with a sense of frustration. *Best I go back over what I know.*

Frustration was not new to Van. Almost every case had elements of irritation that caused feelings of consternation about what to do next. But Van sensed the Ashae-Fuentes case was bothering him because he knew the obvious often hides in the mundane minutia of a case, remaining hidden in the cognitive recesses of an investigator's thoughts until stumbled upon, often by accident. It is a reality that makes a mystery mysterious.

And so he methodically retraced the sequence of events surrounding Cindy and Carlos. He tried to take notes, believing that doing so would cause him to better grasp where the details fit in the larger picture. But he had no illusions about the difficulties in solving a case that was almost four decades cold.

Cindy and Carlos had not been dating long, probably only for a couple of months. They had gone to different elementary and junior high schools. But they had known each other as classmates since ninth grade. They were in the first freshman class at a new high school, Nuevo. The school had a small population, so it was like a small town where everyone knows each other and knows each other's successes and failures. In such environments, it is hard to hide issues.

It was also true that small-town milieus foster countless rumors, and the gossip mill often clouds any hope of knowing the truth. But rumors and gossip usually have some basis in reality. Working backward through hearsay can reveal useful truths.

By the time they were in the spring of eleventh grade, students would have been together for three years. It was hard to imagine anything clandestine was going on involving Cindy and Carlos that remained unknown to others.

There was no indication their families knew each other, at least not on a personal level. Van jotted down a note to check this out more thoroughly. Had there been any contact between the families, siblings, parents, or relatives? History was critical to any in-depth investigation. On the surface, events can appear simple. But distant history often contains latent information that does not come to light unless all parties involved are vetted thoroughly.

Cindy's mom was single at the time. Father and mother divorced when Cindy was seven, and there were no siblings. According to Vargas, who interviewed the mother extensively, she had no boyfriend, and she had not dated much since the divorce. There had been no men in the house since the divorce. Mrs. Ashae's divorced husband had remarried and lived miles away in Monrovia, where he worked as a city building inspector. His new wife and her kids kept him busy, and by the time Cindy was in high school, she seldom saw her father. According to Mrs. Ashae, Cindy had no real attachment to her father and did not seem to care whether he came around. Mrs. Ashae worked part-time for a small business. She received child support. Cindy and her mom lived in a small bungalow she had received as part of the divorce settlement.

Prior to Carlos, Cindy had not dated anyone and had never *gone steady* with a boy, according to her mother. Others said Cindy was quiet and had a small circle of friends. She had no summer or after-school jobs. She was not really involved in school activities but seemed to be interested in the Ecology Club. She was a B+ student according to records. She talked about going to junior college after high school but had not really made her career intentions known.

What set Cindy apart was her attachment to her mother and her tendency, said friends, to always consult with her mom on any decision of note. Cindy was very protective of her mother. Cindy's mother returned the favor by always being worried about Cindy and doing things for her. In the eyes of friends, Cindy's mother was not controlling. She and Cindy were very close, and Cindy would never do anything that would disappoint her mom.

Cindy and Carlos were juniors, and there were no seniors at the prom. It was the school's first prom. They had another year of high school left. Neither had been in trouble, and there was every reason to believe they would successfully complete their senior year and graduate.

The circumstances for Carlos, however, were different. His parents were not divorced. Carlos and Cindy lived on opposite sides of the town. Both Mr. and Mrs. Fuentes worked, although their work hours were at night. They ran an office-cleaning business and had several people who worked for them. The business was successful, and Carlos worked for his parents during the weekends and summer and sometimes during the school year when he was needed as a substitute for an absent employee. The VW van Carlos drove to the prom was an extra vehicle that the family used for business and which Carlos was allowed to drive when given permission.

Unlike Cindy, Carlos was not shy. He was gregarious. Everyone knew him. He was well liked. He was an average student and had not indicated to anyone his post-high-school intentions. Friends said they thought he would work for his parents and eventually take over the business. Perhaps this was only hearsay since neither Carlos nor his parents had ever confirmed the idea. Carlos had played football as a freshman and sophomore but opted to focus on cross-country and track during his junior year.

According to the Fuentes family and others, Carlos had dated many girls, some for lengthy periods of time. Most of the girls had been very popular, and all were very unlike Cindy. Where Cindy was shy and unassuming, the typical girls Carlos had dated were outgoing, popular, cheerleader types and almost always blonde. Cindy was a brunette.

It occurred to Van as odd that Carlos would date Cindy because she was clearly a departure from his prior dating pattern. There had to be some attraction that caused Carlos to change this pattern. *Another issue to check out.* He jotted *Carlos preferred blondes and popular girls* on the pad and then resumed his review.

Not an especially good student, teachers described Carlos as a student who did what was needed to get by. He was not dumb. One teacher described him as "bright but lazy." Several female teachers said Carlos was handsome, but he did not behave like he was better than others. Everyone saw Carlos as honest, supportive of others, and a team player.

Carlos had a younger brother and sister, but they were not yet in high school. Investigators had spent time with each but came away with nothing of value.

It kept coming back to Van that the most intriguing information regarding Carlos was the opinion of students and faculty that they found it odd that Carlos was dating Cindy when he could have dated just about anyone. A female student who had "gone" with Carlos for several months said, "Cindy was not his type."

How did this relationship develop? wondered Van. It was odd given the comments of others and the previous dating habits of Carlos.

It also occurred to Van that there was a sort of cognitive dissonance at work. Everything about Carlos as a teen suggested a consistency when it came to his social and dating habits. Something had stressed this consistency and caused Carlos to change a highly reliable social pattern even as he was continuing to move in his traditional circle of friends. Given his interest in exploring the relationships between people involved in criminal investigations, Van knew exploring this element of Carlos would be an important part of his work.

Van was also struck by the fact that Mrs. Ashae told Vargas that Cindy had not really told her much about Carlos. She had met him once before prom night and had heard from others that Carlos was a nice boy. She had wanted to take pictures of the two when Carlos came to pick Cindy up before the prom, but the camera batteries were dead, and the flash would not work. She said Cindy was embarrassed, something she had not seen in Cindy before. For a mother with a very close relationship with her daughter, it was not evident when it came to discussing Carlos.

Vargas noted these issues. There were notes suggesting Vargas was perplexed by the relationship between Cindy and Carlos, given the statements of students and faculty who also found it surprising they had been dating and then went to the prom together. Vargas had probed this concern but found nothing that linked it to the disappearance. Van found nothing in the notes of Vargas or Damon that suggested their concerns about the odd relationship between the two teens were ever resolved. He also sensed the issue could have been probed more.

The more Van considered the oddities in the Cindy and Carlos relationship, the more he realized that he would have to develop a better understanding of the two teenagers. Before he could develop any viable theories regarding what happened, it was essential that he reach a point in his inquiry where he could say he honestly understood the two students and their circumstances. Otherwise, any theorizing was little more than guessing, and such speculation could be counterproductive.

Van was well aware that reading something into a case without digging below the surface could lead to false positives. There were many examples of cases where the push to identify a suspect and get a conviction gave credence to evidence when credibility was not warranted. In the end, such investigative processes led to embarrassment if not an unjustified conviction.

It also occurred to Van that the work done by Vargas suggested a relentless pursuit of the evidence. Such relentlessness could be a negative, but Van could not find anything to suggest that Vargas, or Damon for that matter, approached the case with anything less than a concerted effort.

Van knew of others in law enforcement who lost their objectivity because they were consumed with a case. He recalled cases where those conducting the investigation actually created evidence to support a theory that was not workable or acceptable without such evidence. In rare instances, it was not that the investigators deliberately invented evidence. Rather, they actually saw evidence where there was none. They gave credibility to the incredulous. Such actions were the pathetic outcome of an investigator who fell victim to his own desires.

But much of the work done by Vargas was good police work, and those who took over the case after Vargas was removed really did not make any substantive additions.

Vargas was convinced Cindy and Carlos did not run away. Most in the department agreed with Vargas that the burned-out VW van strongly suggested there was foul play and the two students were likely dead and had likely been murdered. However, after all the work done by Vargas and Damon, there was not a shred of evidence that pointed to what actually happened.

Van decided he needed to share his observations with Sergeant Fenton. Fenton knew the history even though he wasn't in the department then. Fenton's background might provide a foundation for questions that Van had not yet considered. Bouncing things off other professionals was often very useful and an approach he came to find very helpful while working with the feds. Federal agencies have a reputation of not sharing information with each other. However, such a reputation is not the rule.

When Van was on loan to the feds, he went into his position unhampered by the cultural protocols of communication between the various federal agencies. As a result, he did not hesitate to go outside the FBI in search of information or input. He soon learned this was frowned on, but it worked for Van, so he kept doing it. The feds were not his career, and eventually he would go back to the department. To accomplish what he needed, he did what so many others did not do: he called other federal agencies and asked for input and assistance. What he found was that people were usually most willing to help, but seldom was their assistance requested.

For now, he would keep working the evidence in an effort to draw nearer to what motivated the actions of Cindy and Carlos leading up to prom night. Somewhere along that trail were as yet unknown details about their relationship, about their world, and about those who knew them. Van was sure of this logic, but he was also sure that following this logic would require unconventional thinking.

CHAPTER 12

BUILDING A THEORY

Office of Sergeant Fenton

I T WAS ABOUT noon. Fenton was at work on his computer. He did not notice Vanarsdale step partway through the door. "Sarge, got a minute?"

"Yeah, Van. What's up?" Fenton motioned to one of the two empty seats.

Van thought, as he was taking a seat, that Fenton was much more conscientious about his office appearance. There were family photos, awards, diplomas, and pictures of the sergeant at functions with department and county dignitaries. The sergeant knew how a sergeant's office should look to visitors. "I hope I'm not interrupting, but I know you have no time this afternoon, so I thought I could bounce some ideas off you now."

"You look serious, and you have one of those electronic tablets." Fenton smiled and commented sarcastically, "Gives your visit a sense of importance. Damn, it must be official."

"Lieutenant is big on the technology. It was something Rasmussen never did, and the lieutenant was always trying to get John to go to training. He did once. Damnedest thing. Came back early. Said the instructor couldn't teach. Never went again. John just couldn't change."

Nodding toward his desktop computer, Fenton said, "I use

the computer for email but still take notes by hand. I guess I'm living in competing worlds. My kids are always reminding me I'm old-fashioned."

Fenton had the big smile that said he was not afraid to laugh at his own expense. Van knew what it meant. The sergeant was not insecure. He could have an open conversation with the sergeant without worrying whether he was stepping on any toes. Such working relationships were essential to Van's philosophy of bouncing ideas off colleagues. An office environment that was not open to a free exchange of perspectives regarding case methods and interpretations of evidence ensured a narrow focus and cut off opportunities for new ideas and objectivity.

"Well, Sarge, I wanted to talk about the Ashae-Fuentes case."

"I knew this was serious. What do you think?"

Van continued. "I've only studied the work done during the first phase of the case. I've done so to keep my mind focused on what came out of the early investigation without being influenced by the discovery of the girl's remains years later."

Van picked up his tablet and opened the notes icon. "For the past two days, I've reviewed the case. Without imposing what we know today and considering the technology in 1972, I think Vargas and Damon did a good job initially. But there were a couple of anomalies I want to review with you because neither of us was around then and I'm interested in your take and whether you think I'm going down the right track."

"Let's have it."

"On the initial investigation, it seems the right people were interviewed and meticulous notes kept. However, I don't think Cindy's mother or Carlos's parents were pushed hard enough. I also don't think the close friends of either student were pushed hard enough."

"How so?"

"I'm well aware that probing parents of a recent victim is a delicate endeavor under the best of circumstances. Parents are already disposed to emotional, if not irrational, reactions. I'm sure Vargas and Damon knew that and also knew pushing hard could backfire, especially if the media saw it as harassing or making parents out to be suspects."

Fenton acknowledged with nods.

"However, these two kids weren't meant for each other." Van went on to share the personalities and dating history of the two. He noted that on the surface, the two had nothing in common. Also, Cindy's relationship with her mother changed subtly when she started dating Carlos. Carlos could have dated any girl. Prom was the biggest dance of the year, and he chose to take a "nobody." It didn't add up.

Fenton said, "Interesting. I'm sure Vargas and Damon realized that. We all know from domestic violence cases that opposites can attract."

"I don't think I'm wrong here, Sarge. Something tells me I need a better understanding of the relationship between Cindy and Carlos. I just don't think Vargas and Damon dug deep enough into the relationship. I don't know if the oddities of the relationship had anything to do with Cindy's death, but I feel sure it holds some insight into what happened that night.

"I know the investigators saw the mismatch between the two kids. But I just feel they could have spent more time pursuing what was behind that."

Van glanced back at his notes. "Also, I'm intrigued with the photos of the burned-out VW location. A couple of hours ago, I drove out to the spot where the van was parked when it was discovered. According to Damon's notes, the location was leased by a large catering company and used for outdoor parties. It was as isolated a spot then as it is now. Good place for noisy gatherings. The road into the location takes one well away from Irvine Lake and away from Santiago Canyon Road, the main access to all of that area. The catering company no longer exists, but I found an old guy who works out at the lake launch ramp who remembers what it was like back in the seventies and eighties. He said that the catering company used to hold parties for large groups, such as churches, big businesses and company parties, very large weddings, and other events. He said the site had ample parking, and he remembers when the big parties would have a bonfire, one could see from a mile away.

"A lot has probably changed along Santiago Canyon Road since then, but I did locate the catering site. The old bonfire pit still exists, though it hasn't been used for years, maybe decades. I could see where the VW would have been at the time."

Van looked up at the sergeant. "There's something odd about the situation involving the VW. I just don't think those two kids went out there to have a good time. I grew up in this county, and I knew where guys went with a girl when they wanted some time alone. That site was too much trouble to get to, and a kid from North County wasn't likely to know about the place. And even if he did know, he couldn't know that on that warm evening there would be no event being catered at the location. Not only that—there's the question of how he was able to drive in."

"Was it locked?"

"The report by Vargas indicates the catering company said it was locked most of the time and that it must not have been locked that night because the chain and lock were unbroken and laying on the ground. According to those interviewed, people were always forgetting to lock it. But they also said it wasn't a problem because in those days no one ever vandalized or misused the site. Also, the hikers who discovered the van in the morning said it didn't surprise them that the gate wasn't locked. But those kids wouldn't have known when it was and wasn't locked. It was a long way to go, not knowing whether the gate was locked. There were lots of other options in North County where they were from."

"So what else is it that gets your attention?"

With aplomb, Van responded, "Everything! Sarge, I'm convinced those two kids weren't in the VW when it was driven to the site where it was set ablaze. I say this for the following reasons: First, I don't think those kids even knew of the place. Second, whoever drove the van there knew the site and knew how to leave without a trace. According to investigation notes, there were no other tire tracks. It couldn't easily be done with two teenagers involuntarily in tow.

Third, the VW burned; it did not explode. Whoever set it afire knew that others would just assume there was a large party there that night and what was visible was the usual bonfire. The gas had to have been drained before the fire was started to prevent a big explosion. From a distance, it had to look like a bonfire. Fourth, the location was the only place in the area where one could have burned the VW without worrying that it would start a general wildfire. Whoever burned that van was conscious of the need to avoid starting a wildfire. The usual murderer is not that picky. This person was environment conscious."

"Damn compelling, Van. Where's the evidence?"

"I know. I haven't found it yet, but I'm confident I have a potentially viable preliminary theory." Van knew the use of qualifying words plus the word *theory* suggested all manner of professional gut feelings and unverifiable speculation. The sergeant would not be doing his job if he did not call Van on such guesswork. "I think those kids were murdered elsewhere and the VW was later located to that site and set afire to destroy any evidence. Whoever did it then left on foot and made sure there were no tracks or other traceable evidence."

Van did not wait for a response before going on. "Suburban, middle-class kids in the early 1970s were not likely to carry on clandestine activities unknown to any friend. They were products of an environment where rumors and gossip had some basis in reality. The slightest knowledge of plans to carry on a late-night romp in some remote setting would become gossip fodder. Furthermore, any place where Nuevo students were likely to go for such activity would be local to North County and not twenty miles away. Even cursory gossip on this matter would have come out in the interviews of Vargas and Damon."

Leaning back, Fenton said, "Of course, finding the remains of Ashae on campus in 1999 refocused the investigation to a murder by someone who had access to the school and knew the kids. You're also suggesting the killer knew the burn site but the kids did not."

"Yes. I don't know if there was long-range planning, but the perp knew what he was doing."

"You think you can solve this one?"

"Possibly. What I do know is that with my current perspective, I think my review of the investigation following the discovery of Cindy's body will be different than it otherwise would be."

"You think Vargas and Damon screwed up the early investigation? You know why I ask."

"What I think is that they took the investigation very seriously and followed protocols. However, two things interfered. One, Damon was young, and it appears he was stretched thin, having to work on the Ashae-Fuentes case while he was deeply involved in another murder case that was demanding considerable time from the DA and was about to go to trial. Second, Vargas, as you know, became consumed. He wanted to solve the case at any cost, and his relentless and dogged approach to the case began to irritate his relationship with Damon. As a result, the two ended up not working well as a team, and that got in the way of good police work. That's pretty much all I have at this point."

Fenton appeared to be thinking and did not respond.

Van added, "But I do think this case is solvable. I say that because there's enough, at this point, to suggest the person or persons responsible for the death of Cindy Ashae, and probably that of Carlos, was someone who knew them, who knew the VW burn area, and who may still be out there, alive after all these years."

"And Carlos was also killed."

"Yes, buried or disposed of elsewhere for reasons unknown. We may never find his body."

"You gonna now look at the work done since the discovery of Cindy's remains?"

"Yeah. I'll let you know what comes from that. No guarantees here, boss. There's a long ways to go."

"Not to mention the fact that starting next week you go on the rotation for new cases, and who knows how that'll play into your available time."

Van started to leave. "Thanks, Sergeant. It's good to know I have someone to bounce my quirky approach to things off of." The comment was purposeful. Van knew all too well that down the line he might need some flexibility from Fenton. If the sergeant was confident Van was keeping him informed, the need for extended flexibility would likely be forthcoming.

CHAPTER 13

REVIEWING PHASE TWO

Homicide Office

L EAVING FENTON'S OFFICE, Van went down to the break room and purchased a bottled iced tea and some chips. Returning to his office, he checked his phone and email for any messages, but he knew there would be little of importance since he was not yet on everyone's radar. Once he was handed breaking investigations, the phone would become both tool and nemesis. It used to be that investigations were all footwork and office phones. Now it was cell phones and computers and, when needed, footwork.

Opening the iced tea, he took a long drink. The cold tea was refreshing. He was reminded that most law enforcement officers accumulated cups, as coffee was the drink of choice. He, on the other hand, preferred hot and iced tea and tended to accumulate cups along with plastic and glass bottles. In the early morning, he drank hot tea he made in his office. As the day wore on, he switched to iced tea. It occurred to him that he should look into a small refrigerator for his iced tea. But that would isolate him even more from others in the building. *Probably not a good idea.*

There was another oddity about him. He made his hot tea with distilled water. A friend once told him that distilled water was best for tea because there were no minerals to mix with the tea and alter its taste. Since then, probably twenty years or more, he had used distilled water when he had a choice. This practice was not without its drawbacks. He constantly had to purchase plastic containers of distilled water and lug them up to his office.

And yet Van knew his connection with drinking tea was more than just a preference of taste. Many years earlier, he had encountered the art of brewing a cup of tea. It was a practice rooted in history and carried with it timeless artifacts that had long intrigued him.

His interest began when as an eighth grader he became enamored with the Boston Tea Party. It did not make sense to him that the event would generate such historical interest—until he learned that tea at the time was very expensive, and thus throwing crates of tea into the harbor was a significant destruction of personal property. It was not lost on Van that his career involved investigating crimes, and the tea party was, in fact, a crime.

But it was more than that. Van had learned that in colonial America it was the wealthy who could afford to drink tea. In most homes of the wealthy, there was a tea caddy—a lockable wooden case about the size of a small shoebox. In it would be two containers for tea—one for tea from China and another for tea from India. A person could scoop a teaspoon of tea from either source, or mix them together, in a cup. Hot water would be added for brewing. The caddy often had a small container for sugar to mix with the brewed tea. A lock on the caddy ensured others could not access the expensive tea without permission.

Van loved these peculiar elements of the tea story. Somehow it provided a special connection with history, the subject he had always loved. But he was also well aware that there was sophistication to these thoughts, and he knew others probably judged him accordingly. This tendency toward complexity and refinement was also at the root of his approach to problem solving. Properly brewed tea, like well-written history and problem solving, could not be rushed. All required patience and attention to details.

He took another quaff. "Back to work," he mumbled quietly.

Collecting the various files scattered across his desk, Van stacked those from the 1972 investigation, took them to his file cabinet, and neatly arranged them into several hanging file folders. He wrote "Ashae-Fuentes" on a yellow Post-it and stuck it on the outside of the file drawer. Content that in setting up the file he was now officially pursuing the case, Van picked up the second-phase case files from the top of the cabinet and moved them to his desk. For the rest of the day, he would study the case events as they had unfolded in 1999.

Seated, Van opened the desk file drawer and removed his personal file for the case. It consisted of many pages of notes he had taken on the initial phase. Before the day was through, he would add several more pages.

Flipping through the legal pad to where he found a blank page, Van wrote *"Phase II investigation"* in the upper right corner. Beneath, he wrote the date and *"Page 1."* Each page would get the same heading with title/purpose, date, and appropriate page number in sequence. It was how Van organized his notes. Identification in the upper right so that it could not be confused with actual notes justified left. It was another quirky method.

—⁂—

When Cindy's remains were discovered in a separate container beneath the original time capsule at Nuevo High School, the principal did his level best to keep the situation quiet until deputies arrived. It was afternoon on a weekday. School was over for the day, and there were few people around, but as usual, the media picked up the scent quickly, and though it missed the primetime evening news, it did make the eleven o'clock news and was nationwide by morning. Even the *Today Show* contained a segment regarding the discovery of a body in a high school time capsule. In fact, it was not in the actual time capsule, but the media altered that reality.

Luckily it was an indoor school, so investigators, forensic techs, and coroner were able to keep things manageable for a couple of days as they laboriously removed evidence. Given when the remains had to have been placed below the actual time capsule, it did not take long for rumors to point toward the two students who disappeared after the prom in 1972. Of course, it was some time before a DNA match with the mother confirmed the bones were Cindy's, but by then everyone had pretty much concluded that the remains were those of one or both of the students.

The discovery put the case back on the front pages, and there were numerous copies of newspaper articles in the files. The pressure was back on to solve the case. But the situation in 1999 was much different. It was a clear case of murder, and finding the remains on campus shifted the focus to a suspect or suspects who worked at the school, or at least had access to the school. There was optimism that the narrowness of the focus along with newer investigative techniques and technology would make solving the case more likely.

From the perspective of 1999, Van calculated that at the time the remains had been deposited in the spring of 1973, there were perhaps 150 adults who could have been interviewed. The number would have included about sixty-three teachers, five administrators, four counselors, many coaches, fifteen clerical staff, custodians, district maintenance crews, a couple dozen part-time staff, and numerous parents. In addition, there were also all the students. But twenty-seven years is a long time, and tracking down and interviewing all of these people, plus the endless list of possible students, was impossible.

With the discovery in '99, then sheriff Stan Rains wanted two experienced investigators on the case, and the department singled out Marshal Inskeep and Ted Torres. Both were not only experienced but also good at solving cases. Orange County did not have a large number of homicide cases, so the department did not have a lot of investigators focused just on homicide. However, both Inskeep and Torres had been around a long time and were probably the best the department had at the time.

The two wasted no time. They surmised, based on the coroner's initial observations, that the body was probably that of Cindy Ashae. While they awaited confirmation, they began the task of interviewing anyone who was around in 1972. Since the victim was female, they tended to believe the perp was male. They spent countless hours talking to custodial staff, coaches, and male teachers. They were especially interested in the shop teachers since the bones were found in a prototype of the primary time capsule. Both capsules were built by students in the shop classes. The prototype was experimental and not intended to be used. The actual time capsule was better built and more secure than the prototype.

However, the woodshop and metal shop teachers had died. The only living shop teacher from 1972 was the auto shop teacher. He had been a young teacher at the time the school opened. He was not involved in building the time capsule.

The big question was why the prototype model had not been found missing. Did anyone ever ask where it was? Inskeep and Torres could not imagine how the fact that it was missing did not raise any red flags. When they were shown the storage rooms for all the woodshop and metal shop projects over the thirty-plus years of the school's existence, they knew the answer. Schools and teachers are collectors. Things just pile up, and nothing is thrown away. As Torres noted sarcastically in his summary of their tour of the facilities, "There could have been a body or two in those storage rooms, and we would not have found them." Teachers are packrats.

Inskeep and Torres interviewed a couple of long since retired custodial staff. Both had worked at Nuevo in the early years. The information proved useful, as the investigators were able to ascertain what transpired with the burying of the time capsule.

When the school was built, there were numerous planters incorporated into the design of the school interior. There were no bottoms to the planters, just the soil beneath the building that was very compact as a result of the grading requirements before construction. The hole for the capsule was dug by the custodial staff in the large planter in the center of the indoor school.

Originally the hole was dug about six feet deep, but then the plan changed to put the capsule closer to the surface and encase the top foot of the capsule with cement, which would have a plaque mounted on it. That way, when it was opened fifty years later, the concrete could be broken and the capsule opened without having to dig it completely out of the ground.

The capsule box measured eighteen inches in width on the four sides and was thirty-six inches tall. Van mentally calculated that the interior of the time capsule was about six and a half square feet. It was made of three-quarter-inch plywood, and both the inside and outside were covered with fiberglass to make the capsule impervious to water. The metal shop students made a sheet metal liner to fit into the box. When the time capsule ceremony took place in 1973, all that showed above ground was about the top ten inches of the time capsule. The wood and metal-lined top was off. Preselected items were placed in it during a school assembly. The ceremony ended with the lid being placed on the capsule, and a rubber gasket and fiberglass were used to seal it shut. Later that day, a concrete slab was poured over it. The plaque was secured atop the cement two weeks later.

The student assembly to load the time capsule took place on a Monday morning. Inskeep and Torres figured that the prototype had to be placed in the hole and below the actual time capsule sometime during the weekend. To bring the hole from its original depth of six feet up to a depth of two feet, the custodial staff had backfilled the hole and compacted the dirt. On Friday evening, they placed the time capsule in the hole and packed dirt around it, with only the top foot showing. They covered the entire planter with a tarp. It was ready for the Monday-morning ceremony. Since the school was indoors, they did not think anyone would tamper with it over the weekend.

Inskeep and Torres soon realized that no high school, indoors or otherwise, was unused on a weekend. There were always events, clubs, and athletics. Coaches, students, teachers, and administrators, not to mention parents and some outsiders, traipsed through the campus on Saturday and Sunday. Whoever buried the prototype had three nights to do so—Friday, Saturday, and Sunday. The person or persons who did so needed to gain access to the prototype, deposit the remains, and find a time to place the prototype capsule and then backfill and replace the original capsule.

The big challenge facing the person who buried the prototype involved the soil displaced. It had to be removed and was probably deposited on the school's agriculture farm. The task of placing Cindy's remains in the prototype and then burying it was deemed enormous and suggested something about the perp or perps.

The task of burying the remains in the prototype reinforced the belief of Inskeep and Torres that the suspect was male and was probably a custodian, coach, or teacher whose physical capabilities were substantial. They were inclined to think there was more than one suspect. In this sense, they narrowed their focus to about half the male population of school employees plus several district maintenance workers. Unfortunately, they were able to contact only about one-third of those who fit their profile. Twenty-seven years had taken its toll on available suspects. Also, since they did not have any knowledge of any other crimes that could also be attached to the disappearance of Cindy and Carlos, there was no additional evidence to help narrow the list.

The unsettling piece of evidence in 1999 was an earring accompanying Cindy's remains. This was a fly in the ointment of the Inskeep and Torres theory that the perps were male.

In Van's mind, Inskeep and Torres, and later Rasmussen, by default, had committed the assumption sin. They were good candidates for Dr. Patel's question, *why not?* Why exclude all the other males on campus? Why exclude the females? Van had to admit that the case suggested a male, but that did not exclude a female as a participant.

An effort was made in 1999 to interview anyone who was still alive and who may have been on campus over that weekend. Clearly the two investigators were not able to interview all who fit that profile, but they did interview thirty-seven people. In return, they got nothing. Many people could not be located, some were deceased, and some were in no condition to recall what happened. It had been too long, and of those interviewed, time and rumors had clouded accuracy.

Those they did interview were often unclear or unsure about their experience and, at best, hesitant to suggest they remembered the pertinent weekend. Time had taken its toll on memories.

None of this surprised Van. He too had occasion in past cases to interview people long after an event. He had found that many who had claimed to be at the scene of a crime were in fact nowhere near. Van often thought of these people as evidence of the Woodstock syndrome—the desire to be a part of something they were never a part of. Also, those who had actually been at the scene often really did not witness anything. Sometimes they did not know they had been in the midst of a crime until it was over. Other times, those who had been in a position to witness had forgotten much and often were confused regarding what they did see. It was not uncommon for statements given many months or years after witnessing an event to contradict what the witness had said when interviewed soon after the event.

Of course there was the three-monkey group of witnesses—those who professed to see no evil, speak no evil, and hear no evil. Perhaps this group was most frustrating because, for reasons unique to each, there was no desire to get involved. While everyone knew these individuals saw or heard something, there appeared to be a fear of involvement.

As for the Ashae-Fuentes case, Van was of the opinion that the 1999 interviews were focused on the wrong issues. Thus, the interviews yielded little. He could understand the uncertainty of former employee recollections about prom weekend. Based on the interviews of 1972, he was inclined to think that in 1999 more questions should have focused on observations by others regarding the evolving relationship between Carlos and Cindy rather than the specifics about laying the time capsule or events of prom night. It was Van's opinion that many homicide cases often have a long prelude. Investigations need to thoroughly probe the history.

In reality, witnesses were both valuable and notoriously unreliable. Initially they may be firm in their recounting what they saw or heard. Under cross-examination later, they were just as likely to back away from the strength of their earlier statement. It was a rare witness whose testimony remained solid and unchallengeable under questioning. And, of course, the value of witness testimony was often only as good as the questions the witness was asked.

As Van reviewed the materials in front of him, the day moved into the evening, and he finally turned to the coroner's report and the findings from forensics and the accompanying case summary report from Inskeep and Torres regarding what they surmised had happened.

Ashae and Fuentes had disappeared a full year before the time capsule was buried. The coroner and forensic documentation indicated that most likely the body of Cindy had been kept at a location where it decomposed over a period of about twelve months before the remaining bones were placed in the prototype capsule. The remains contained no soil, so it could be concluded that the body had not been buried directly in the ground during the twelve months. If it had been buried, it was insolated from soil in some sort of container. There was nothing to suggest the whereabouts of the remains during the decomposition period.

However, decomposition was aided by the use of lye. Though apparently cleaned before placed in the capsule, the bones carried trace amounts of sodium hydroxide, which would explain why the bones in the capsule were devoid of any soft tissue.

Most likely the cause of death was a single blow to the left side of the head with a hard and blunt object about the size of a softball or small melon. The blow did considerable damage, enough to cause death, although how long the body functioned before death could not be known. There were no other broken or damaged bones to indicate additional contributing factors.

The report indicated the blow was likely delivered from behind, given the orientation of the impact. Most people are right-handed and would deliver the blow to the right side of the head when doing so from behind. Thus, a left-handed person probably delivered the blow to the head from behind. Were they looking for a left-handed person? If so, it narrowed the field of possible suspects considerably. However, heeding Dr. Patel's caution, to make such an assumption was not wise. Consider it as part of the investigation but do not adopt it as reality.

All of this was evident to Inskeep, Torres, and Rasmussen. They knew the coroner was only giving the best estimate. They knew there was no guarantee. There were always exceptions to what looked to be the truth.

—⚏—

It had taken several hours to review the files and reports from 1999 and subsequently the work of Investigator Rasmussen.

Van reached for his iced tea. The earlier coldness of the beverage had long ago vanished. It tasted tepid, and there was nothing refreshing about it. He set it back down.

Then he picked up the photograph of an earring. The earring was found with the bones. Looking at the ruler that was alongside the earring in the photo, it appeared to be about two inches from top to bottom and about an inch wide. The earring was intended for a pierced ear and would hang down from the lobe. The design was simple. The end of a fine one-inch diameter wire loop went through the ear lobe and hooked to its counterpart end on the back side of the lobe. At the bottom of the loop, a small oblong piece of turquoise threaded on the wire hung free.

The report suggested the earring was cheap and probably handmade. According to Torres, it fell into the category of "cheap jewelry like that sold by Native Americans along tourist routes in the Southwest or sold by hippie types at low-end art festivals."

Van's thoughts were the same as earlier detectives. *Was it a signature or was it accidentally dropped by whoever put the bones in the capsule?* The distinction was not easy, as the earring ends were not latched, which suggested it could have fallen off or been deliberately placed.

Efforts in 1999 to locate the source of the earring turned up no leads. None of those interviewed could say they recognized it. Inskeep had spoken to some arts and crafts types who made jewelry. They said the earring was nondescript and could likely have been made by an amateur, even by the person who wore it.

Photographs from the yearbook and from Cindy's mother gave

no indication the earring belonged to Cindy. Mrs. Ashae said her daughter would not have worn it. Mrs. Fuentes said she had never seen it before and it looked like something a hippie would wear.

Van agreed with the observations of Inskeep and Torres. The earring was not an accident. It had meaning. It had been placed there. Evidence did not confirm this conclusion, but past experience did. Whoever murdered Cindy left a signature. But this signature suggested the killer could have been a female. That was the piece that troubled Van and previous investigators. It went against their instincts. Everything about the disappearance of Carlos and Cindy said it was the work of a male suspect. But again, the caution of Dr. Patel reminded him to keep an open mind.

What concerned Van even more was another conclusion based on experience. The signature earring suggested a serial killer. Were there other bodies with earrings? If they ever found the body of Carlos, he had no doubt there would be an earring. A homicide committed in haste was not accompanied by a signature. The victims of a serial killer often did.

Van wondered if the earring was still around.

—◊◊◊—

As Vanarsdale concluded his study of the most recent work on the case done by his predecessor, John Rasmussen, he did so with the conviction that there were certain determinants.

The death of Cindy, and probably Carlos as well, was not an accident. How much premeditation went into the killings was uncertain, but the killer did so with a degree of planning, and the victims were selected. Moreover, they were not killed at the site of the VW fire. They were killed elsewhere, and the VW was moved to the location to be destroyed. The location was selected for several reasons, not the least of which was a desire to avoid setting off a general wildfire. This said something about the killer. The killer had a respect for the environment. *Leaders of the Nuevo Ecology Club?* Van was inclined to see a possible connection.

The killer was likely someone who knew the two students, and the field of suspects could probably be narrowed down. It was likely someone who worked at Nuevo High School. It could also be a friend of one of the families or a community member who knew one or both of the students. But it seemed to Van that access to the indoor school during the night on a weekend would be problematic for a parent or community member because they were not likely to have keys. It also seemed much too sophisticated for a teenage student. Van did not see this as a crime committed against two students who were in the wrong place at the wrong time.

The time capsule burial pretty much supported the school employee conclusion. The killer may have worked at the prom, but a good argument could be made that he or she was more likely to have been waiting until Carlos and Cindy left, or waiting at a location where it was known the two kids would visit following the prom.

Although it was hard to imagine, Van was beginning to feel that there were probably two killers and at least one of them was female. The earring suggested a female. It would not be easy for one female to subdue a seventeen-year-old male who was by no means meek or short on strength along with his seventeen-year-old date at the same time. Add to that the torching of the VW and leaving the scene unnoticed. Someone drove a second vehicle.

All this suggested two killers. Unfortunately, Vargas, Damon, Inskeep, Torres, and Rasmussen did not make the connection between the burning of the VW and its location and the environmental concern element.

But as interesting as this conjecture was, Van also kept coming back to earlier observations about how the investigations of both phases were conducted. The emphasis tended to be focused on the evidence from interviews about events leading up to and during the prom night. Though such focus was logical and the corresponding interviews important, the reports of both phases of the case suggested little information was uncovered regarding the mind-set of the two victims. The inquiries of Vargas and Damon were focused on identifying possible perps. This was a reasonable approach. In 1999, the focus was again on the question of who could have committed the crime. Again, the focus was on looking for someone who had motive.

From Van's perspective, all five previous investigators had not really developed a deep understanding of the two students. Van was certain he needed to gain such understanding if he was to have any success with this case. Of course, the expanse of time since their deaths would make doing so difficult.

Similarly, if his instincts were correct, it would be necessary to push the buttons of several people who had known Cindy and Carlos. This would include parents, friends, and school employees, perhaps other adults. He could not afford the time to track down all the employees at the school. He would have to be selective. He would leave that to his instincts.

For Van, it was equally important to gain the perspective of those with problem-solving skills but not necessarily in the homicide investigation line of work. His list of confidants on such matters included his gang of six—a statistician, a qualitative researcher, a history professor, his brother-in-law, a self-employed computer-based researcher, and a retired FBI contact. Their only common thread was an ability to think outside the box. Each was bright but also a bit eccentric.

He needed input from others.

Van knew involving nonpolice types was a delicate issue that must be carefully managed. He needed the support of his superiors.

CHAPTER 14

LAY OF THE LAND

Santa Ana Mountains
Cleveland National Forest

THE CATERING SITE was in the foothills of the Santa Ana Mountains. The range is part of the Trabuco Ranger District of the Cleveland National Forest. It sits along the eastern border of Orange County. To the east is Riverside County. The southern tip of the Trabuco District extends into San Diego County.

The Trabuco District ranges in altitude from about 500 feet in the Orange County foothills to 5,687 feet at Santiago Peak, often referred to as Saddleback because of its shape.

The Santa Ana range is home to rugged terrain and dense foliage. Trees include incense cedar, Jeffrey and Coulter pine, Douglas fir, and the indomitable live oak whose bulk and spreading canopies thrive in many canyons. Shade from these hardy trees provides welcome relief to both human and animal in an environment that is often hot and dry. In addition, there is the abundant sage, yucca, mountain mahogany, and manzanita, all of which combine to make up the chaparral, a dense thicket that in many places is almost impenetrable to humans.

Within the Orange County portion of the range, there are several areas where housing first took root over a hundred years ago. These are usually narrow strips of unchecked development that follow canyons intruding into the national forest. Most are accessible from State Route 18, also known as Santiago Canyon Road, which parallels the western edge of the national forest between Irvine Lake in the north and Cook's Corner, about ten miles southeast.

Driving along Santiago Canyon Road, sometimes called SCR, from the north, one enters the low-lying hills of the district from the west and then passes man-made Irvine Lake. Numerous dirt roads and remnants of old dwellings hint at the earlier days of ranching in the area. After passing the cutoff to the old catering site, which is not identified as such, the road continues in a southeasterly direction until arriving at the turnoff to Silverado Canyon.

Silverado Canyon is perhaps the most developed area in the district, but it is initially hidden from view. It is only after turning off the main road and driving about a mile toward Silverado Canyon that one begins to realize they are entering a community. Silverado Center, the unofficial commercial focus of the canyon, is about two miles after the turnoff. The center has a store, post office, and several other very small endeavors. It is another three and a half miles along a very winding and at times one-lane road to the eastern end of the canyon at the Maple Springs Trailhead. California Historical Landmark #202 at road's end notes that the canyon gets its name from the 1878–1881 silver mining frenzy in the area. The original name for the canyon was Canada De La Madera, or Timber Canyon. Today the canyon is thick with trees, but many are not native. Evidence of the silver mining past is scarce.

The residents of the canyon live in a wide range of dwellings. Sitting side by side are very rundown homes and expensive million-dollar-plus homes with equally expensive sports cars and SUVs in the driveways. The canyon is a mixture of wealth and poverty. This peculiar quality is also reflected in the variety of personality types among its inhabitants.

South of Silverado Canyon, and on the east side of Santiago Canyon Road, is the old Silverado Elementary School. The large ranch-like estates in the area are horse property, and the only cattle in sight are probably little more than a hobby. The original ranches are long gone. The modern manors with their guest dwellings and riding facilities suggest a lifestyle of misplaced cowboys and land baron wannabes.

Further south, in Modjeska Canyon, is another enclave of homes. The canyon is much smaller than Silverado but nonetheless sprinkled with evidence of the disparity in wealth among its residents. The canyon is named after the nineteenth-century Shakespearian actress Helena Modjeska, whose name can also be found on a local peak, roads, and several parks in the county of Orange.

Scattered among the hills and canyons elsewhere in the national forest are other groups of homes. Notable for their rustic and makeshift quality are some ramshackle dwellings located at the eastern end of Trabuco Canyon where it intersects with Holy Jim Canyon. These homes are on leased federal land and generally used on a seasonal or weekend basis only, though a few hardy inhabitants have lived on a semipermanent basis. The area is accessible by a four-and-a-half-mile drive over an unimproved dirt and gravel road that is often washed out during storms.

For those who enjoy four-wheeling, the Trabuco District is crisscrossed with dirt roads that make it possible to access some very remote and scenic areas. It is possible to drive to the tops of several peaks, such as Santiago, Trabuco, Bedford, and Modjeska. It is also possible, using these roads and the trails, to travel from one developed canyon to another.

Santiago Canyon Road exits the Trabuco Ranger District south of Trabuco Canyon and enters densely populated neighborhoods in south Orange County.

In 1972, much of the western front region of the Trabuco District was open space, and housing developments in cities like Orange, Tustin, Irvine, and Mission Viejo were just beginning to push to the edge of the public lands. One could drive Santiago Canyon Road on a weekend and not encounter large numbers of cars. During the week, a drive into the national forest was a drive into a quiet, remote, and wild area. Silverado and Modjeska Canyons were sparsely populated, and places like Trabuco Canyon were miles from nowhere and seldom visited.

Today the region is much different. In many places on the outskirts of the national forest land, there is little evidence of the remote and wild, open space that not long ago dominated the area. Today, housing developments from surrounding cities crowd the flanks of the national forest. It is hard sometimes to know where the national forest begins and the cities end.

—⚊⚊—

It was early morning.

Investigator Vanarsdale drove east on Santiago Canyon Road. He passed Irvine Lake and then the entrance to the old catering site. A quarter mile further, he turned north on a rough dirt road. After a short distance, he realized his car was not equipped to meet the unimproved conditions. Pulling off into a rutted turnout, Van parked the Crown Vic and retrieved his notepad and binoculars. He recorded the mileage. The notepad was an improvised spreadsheet with a compellation of recorded distances between different points along Santiago Canyon Road.

The dirt road continued on to the northeast and up a hill. There was a chain across the road further on, and Van walked toward it. A small post with white letters on a brown background indicated its national forest status as NF3977.

Van continued up the hill until he had gained enough elevation to see out over the immediate area. About half a mile away and well below was the former catering party site. Several days previously, he had walked around the site looking for trails or old dirt roads that may have radiated out and away from the site.

There had been no roads, but there were paths. He did not think them to be trails. They were more like informal paths that may have been made by animals or hikers. The paths did not go back toward Santiago Canyon Road. There was only one road in and out of the

gatherings there in the 1960s. When I read about the van being burned there, I could picture it because the place had a big bonfire pit, and the land around it was cleared off." This independent observation supported Van's sense as to why the VW was torched in that location. It also confirmed Van's suspicions about the mentality of the killer reflecting a sense of concern for the environment.

Van asked, "If some kid had driven the van there and set it afire, how easy would it have been to hike out of the area to a car hidden somewhere well off Santiago Canyon Road or a nearby house? What was the surrounding area like then?"

"Oh, boy, very different. Chapman road over Orange Hill was one narrow lane each way and was used mostly by people headed for Irvine Park. If you were headed on past the park, Chapman turned into SCR. You were probably going to Silverado or Modjeska. People lived there then. One big difference then is that there were still a couple of ranches along the road before you got to Silverado and another between Silverado and Modjeska. Ranchers were running small herds of cattle then, but that practice died out by the end of the 1970s."

"For what other reasons would someone travel SCR?"

"Well, Irvine Lake. It's been popular ever since Santiago Dam was built around 1931. Some years, the lake is way down, but when it's full, it's always been the only good fishing in town."

Barry's engaging and matter of fact way of talking made Van comfortable and provided credibility to what was being said. Van knew all too well that sometimes an old-timer was more BS than a viable source of information. Thankfully that was not the case with Barry.

"There was also the old Silverado Elementary School, which was closed several years ago. It was always small, and the kids came from many directions.

"Of course, people took the road if they were headed to O'Neil Park and Trabuco Canyon. Both were a long ways on SCR, which was not as well built or maintained then as it is now. Back in the fifties, fishing was pretty good in Holy Jim Canyon and along Trabuco

Creek. People turned out in droves for the annual opening day each spring."

"Driving at night?"

"Dangerous! In the fifties and sixties, the road was not a place to drive at night. Very dark! If traveling too fast, you were in trouble. It's dangerous today but was much more so then. Absolutely no light on a moonless night. Very dark out there now at night. You can imagine what it must have been like back then."

"What about hiking away from the catering site back then?"

"If there was good moonlight, it could be done, but there are no formal trails. If you've been there, you know most of the paths are the result of animals. However, a couple of those animal paths later became good trails for hikers. There's one trail out of the catering area that is now an acknowledged hiking route. In 1972, it would have taken someone who was a skilled hiker and who knew the area. Not many people fit the bill then."

"I notice there's an old firebreak road that runs sort of in a northwest and southeast direction about a quarter of a mile above the catering site. Was it there then?"

"Yes, and to answer your next question, it would not have been easy to access it from the catering site. Very steep climb to do at night. However, if one could get to it, they could travel a good distance in either direction. Could've made it over to Black Star Canyon with good light. Of course, they would've had to be good at hiking and know where they were going."

"I'm wondering, could a person travel about most of the Orange County portion of the Cleveland National Forest without using major roads or paved roads in the early 1970s?"

"Sure. If you knew where you were going. They would've had to be good though."

"How good?"

"Expert hiker who knew the area like the back of his hand is how I'd describe 'em. Remember, you didn't have the improved trails and signs then."

"Do you know anyone who could have done that at night in 1972?"

"If you're asking if I know anyone who could be a suspect in your case, I would have to say no. Anyone who could have accomplished that had to have been an exceptional hiker. No one comes to mind."

"So I'm back where I started. It is possible that the VW was dropped off and the person hiked away without being seen. But, from your recollection, the population of people who could have covered any significant distance at night was very small and unknown to you."

"Yes, except for one other thing. The people who lived in some of the canyons like Black Star, Silverado, Modjeska, and Harding were not very public. They didn't rub elbows with most others. The canyons then were much more isolated. You didn't have all the four-wheel drive vehicles and million-dollar homes then. The people in the canyons were solitary types who didn't like visitors. Some were strange. Those of us who hiked the canyons didn't trespass."

"They were unfriendly?"

"Sometimes, but mostly they just wanted to be left alone."

"You think anyone who lived in the canyons could have killed two kids, disposed of the bodies, driven the VW to a remote site and burned it, and then left without leaving a trace?"

"Maybe. I suppose someone could've done that, but it assumes they planned it very well, and that wasn't the nature of most of the people in the canyons. They were likely to be impulsive and not meticulous in planning."

"How do you know that?"

"Just take a drive up there. Look at their homes and the land around it. If you look at the older dwellings, those people are and were collectors, and they just got by. They weren't organized. Yeah, there're some million-dollar homes now, but those are pretty new. None of those in the old days. Most of the places in those days were the adding-on style of home. They were a conglomeration of constant projects. Whoever you're looking for doesn't fit the mold of the typical canyon resident in Orange County even today. It was even more so in 1972."

"You know any of the people?"

"Sure, but I also know that none of them would have done what you're thinking happened. These people were reactive. They may take action, but they weren't likely to give it a lot of advanced thinking. You gotta remember that people up there didn't want attention. Killing, even unnecessary harassment, would bring the cops, something they wanted nothing to do with."

"What about a female?"

"Listen, Van, people in the canyons are of one mind. However, I will say this, I would probably be more afraid of a smart female in the canyons than a smart male."

"Why is that?"

"If there were any real smart people in the canyon then, they were probably female. Men were not known for their patience or their willingness to do a lot of planning or even work."

Barry's opinion seemed strange to Van. Were the women who lived in these canyons that strong and independent? If what Barry said had a bit of truth, then Van sensed he needed to be careful and not underestimate any possible female suspect.

Van took out a folder and removed several new topographic maps of the area. All were the newer seven-and-a-half-minute series. He also had a Cleveland National Forest map.

Barry was a wealth of information as he pointed out the various inaccuracies in the maps and noted where major changes had occurred along Santiago Canyon Road over the years. Then he described the quality of the dirt roads and firebreaks in the area.

Van made notes on his iPad and on the maps. Barry gave him much to consider, not the least of which was his comment that the smart people in the canyons were female. It was interesting insight that would not have occurred to Van. But it did support the idea that a female could have been the killer, or at least one of the killers.

"Why do you say that in 1972 you would be more concerned about a female than a male?"

"Hippie era. The men were more likely to be opinionated but lacking in guts. They took the whole *make love not war* thing too serious. The women were the thinkers, made the money, what little there was, and were the ones who usually had to think ahead about living needs."

Sitting at his desk with the maps, Van reminded himself that the contour lines were more important to any interpretation of distance than the straight-line ruler of the map scale. He remembered Barry's emphatic comment, "You don't move in a straight line in these mountains. Try it and the chaparral will shred you like a well-honed knife skinning a rabbit."

The old maps McMurry gave him suggested an Orange County much simpler in 1942 when the maps were produced. There were no freeways or toll roads. The towns were smaller, and open space separated them. By 1972, it was all changing, but McMurry said that the areas along Santiago Canyon Road and the communities of Modjeska, Silverado Canyon, Trabuco Oaks, and many of the other side canyons were better represented on the 1942 series maps.

Staring at the maps, Van could see many "truck trails," as they were labeled. In addition there were numerous unpaved roads following the major canyons. In a few places, McMurry had noted hiking trails that he said were popular. Some of the trails followed the dirt roads and firebreaks. Others connected various roads and canyons.

It seemed to Van that a savvy hiker could move about much of the Cleveland National Forest by staying on the trails and dirt roads and firebreaks. They could remain out of sight. But moving about off-trail would require both skill and familiarity with the area on a scale not understood by an outsider. A mile as the crow flies could easily be two or three miles by trail. The implications were dramatic.

Van jotted a note. *Need to understand how one could move about at night. I need to hike it.*

CHAPTER 15

SHARING INSIGHTS

Homicide Offices

I T WAS LATE in the day when Van walked to the lieutenant's office. The outer office was smartly decorated with the dutiful department paraphernalia that included citations of merit, photos with dignitaries, law enforcement artifacts of the past, and a nice collection of sheriff department badges from counties across California.

The decorations were common in offices of the higher-ups. He wondered about the effect.

For Van, there had never been a need for trophies. As a kid, he had not been interested in posting or displaying the products of performance. His parents were accomplished people, but they were humble and never felt the need to display diplomas, awards, or even photos of any significance. Somewhere at home he had a couple of certificates he had received from the department, but he could not recall what he did with them. Of course he had his college degrees, but neither he nor Anna Marie had ever displayed their diplomas.

For many years, Anna Marie displayed photos of the kids when they were young, but the practice tapered off as the kids got older. He thought photos never really told much about a person. The Nuevo yearbook photos of Cindy and Carlos were poses and provided no insight into their personalities. He made a mental note to try to locate family photos of the two.

Van's reflection ended when Charlene spoke. "You can go in now, Investigator."

When Van entered, the lieutenant and Fenton stood to greet him. Van was not surprised that the two met before his arrival. *The sergeant was probably giving Vargas a heads-up on my ideas.*

Vargas took control. "Van, thanks for coming. Among other things, Fenton was just filling me in on your work in the Ashae case." Vargas motioned the two toward the small round table.

Van recognized the tactic. The small table around which they sat afforded a more casual setting in lieu of the lieutenant's desk, which would suggest a more formal meeting where title and rank were operative. The lieutenant wanted this to be an open conversation among peers.

"Fenton tells me you've quickly drawn some conclusions about the Ashae case."

Van noted that for the second time in a matter of seconds, the lieutenant referenced the case as Ashae and not Ashae-Fuentes. The truncated title was not a unique practice. In an age of acronyms, the preference for brevity trumped the need for formality. But the reference to the "Ashae case" was more than that. It was acknowledgment that they had confirmation of only one murder. In the absence of the other body, the focus was on the murder of Cindy Ashae. But then again, thought Van, given the penchant for brevity and abbreviation, A preceded F, and in the in-house parlance of homicide, it would simply be the "Ashae" case.

"Well, I don't know about the credibility of any conclusions. They're tentative at best and based only on my limited observations of the work done by others and my recent visits to the site where the VW van was found. I suspect I have more questions than anything else."

Vargas got to the point. "Why don't you give me an overview of what you've found."

Van reviewed everything he had shared with Fenton two days before. He noted the findings of Vargas and Damon and their general feeling that the two students were probably murdered and disposed of by more than one person. Though they could not rule out a crime of opportunity, the two investigators felt that there was more than one perp and that they were persons known to the students.

"Of course, with the events of 1999, it became more likely that one or more school employees who knew the two committed a well-planned murder. On the other hand, the lack of evidence provides equal value to the idea of a crime of opportunity committed with some degree of skill and cunning. With the earring from the time capsule, I agree with Inskeep and Torres that at least one of the perps was a female."

"Serial?"

"I don't think the earring was lost into the time capsule in haste. I'm confident it was a signature. Of course, this conjecture is not new."

Fenton said, "Do you know of any other murders with a similar signature?"

"No, and that's puzzling. A signature is usually acknowledgment by the killer that he expects the body to be found and the signature noticed. Cindy's killer knew when the remains were placed in the time capsule that it would probably be fifty years before they were discovered. That is not typical behavior for a serial killer."

Vargas interjected. "I'm wondering if we'll find an earring if we ever find Carlos."

"That has occurred to me as well, Lieutenant. But I'm inclined to see the murder of Cindy, and probably Carlos, with some different questions." Van knew he was now on his own. He was presenting his ideas independent of any previous investigation. "I can't help thinking that two seventeen-year-old students, one who was a strong athlete and likely to put up a fight, would have resisted the efforts of one killer and in doing so left some trace of their resistance. It appears Cindy was killed with a blunt object. What are the chances one killer could effectively, and without fostering vicious resistance, kill both students with a blunt object?

"But the idea of more than one perp keeps nagging at me. So I drove out to the catering cite for a third time. In an effort to ascertain if one or two persons were involved, I looked closely at distances from the site to other areas where a second vehicle could have been left that would have been undetected. I wanted to determine how far one would have had to walk to a parked getaway vehicle if there was one.

"There are two ways to look at the VW situation. One, the kids were murdered there and then removed and taken somewhere before the van was torched. Second, they were murdered somewhere before the fire. I'm inclined to think the murders took place before the VW was moved to be burned. In either case, the person who moved the van needed assistance to flee.

"Keeping in mind things were very different out there in 1972, I looked for old dwellings and roads, trying to avoid the impact of the new toll road and other changes. I have work yet to do on all of this because I need to study the area more. I really caution against too much in the way of conclusions. I need to follow up by talking with people from the Nuevo, the catering company, forest service, and old-timers from the area, and members of both families."

The lieutenant was nodding. "So you think there's a chance this case can be resolved."

"There's one more element. I wouldn't be surprised if the murders were a personal matter. At this point, I have no ideas about what made it personal, but I think it's related to the relationship between the victims and the murderer. To solve the case, I think considerable time has to be spent focused on that relationship as well as on the logistics of burning the VW and leaving the scene.

"So, to answer your question, I think there's enough to go on and the case merits further investigation of an active rather than passive nature. Don't get me wrong—it won't be easy. Too many unknowns to start with." Van stressed his final point. "But I do believe the work done by all five investigators to this point has provided sufficient cause to continue the investigation."

Vargas frowned. "If their work was so valuable, why were they not able to find the perps?"

"It wasn't because of what they did. Their work was very good, very thorough. However, on one point I think they came up short. In my estimation, they didn't focus enough on the dynamics of burning the VW, and they didn't get inside the heads of the two victims by pushing hard their questioning of the parents and close friends of the students. That's the only way to probe the personal nature of the murder."

Fenton said, "We know that's not easy to do in the immediate aftermath of a murder without making the interviewee defensive and wondering whether he's being considered a suspect."

The lieutenant made it more personal. "You think they went too easy in 1972?"

Van was aware that under the circumstances, this was a loaded question. "Not at all. I just think that the emotions were so strong with the parents that it was difficult to get them to admit there were signs in the behavior of Cindy and Carlos that telegraphed all was not well with some part of the bigger picture. Also, interviewing teenage friends would be hard because they get emotional and really don't reflect when they think about what happened. The desire to say something upstages the veracity of what is said. I think teenagers want to be seen as important in such situations, and thus they exhibit a bit of bravado. It colors their comments rather than promoting reality."

The nods told Van that Fenton and Vargas were following the logic.

"Talking with people today may actually get us closer to what really happened, even though so many years have passed. Those '72 teenagers are now well past middle age and many years removed from the events. They may have forgotten some details, but older people tend to be a bit more reflective than they were when young. They are more likely to share thoughts and tidbits they thought unimportant forty years ago. When asked questions, they're more likely today to actually think about the event rather than being anxious to say something, anything."

"How so?"

"No one to impress. No peer pressure. They can think unfettered by what others will think."

"That's interesting thinking."

"I know, Lieutenant, it's not conventional wisdom. But research by some psychologists suggests that emotions at the time of an event, especially an incident that's high profile and subject to extensive attention and conjecture, often clouds objectivity because there's no time for the person being interviewed to sit back and think about what he or she actually saw or heard. Interviewees in those situations often say what they think others want to hear, or what others have already said, or what the world around them and circumstances suggest. Sometimes interviewees actually do not think. They react. Sometimes they actually invent because they want to be able to say they played a part in the investigation. For teenagers, anticipation of peer perceptions is very influential and anxiety fostering."

Fenton clarified. "So the truth actually never has a chance."

"I think that's a good way to put it."

Fenton added, "Then, if what you say is true, I wonder about the possibility of finding the truth in any emotional situation."

Van seized Fenton's point. "Yes, my goal with the parents of Cindy and Carlos will be to engage them in a conversation and not a question-and-answer exercise. They have done the Q&A multiple times already. I want to know what they think and why. I want to avoid responses that have them trying to be consistent with how they answered in the past."

"And you think that after all these years, you can extract some evidence of use?" The doubt was evident in Fenton.

"I do."

Vargas wrinkled his brow and commented, "That's potentially a lot of interviews. If I'm not mistaken, that was a big problem for Inskeep, Torres, and Rasmussen."

"Not really. I would have to be selective. The parents and siblings of course. Maybe some neighbors. Close friends of Cindy and Carlos. School administrators and counselors. And some very carefully screened teachers."

Van let his comments sit for a few seconds before going on. "Lieutenant, if nothing else, discovery of Cindy's remains suggests the suspect or suspects have a strong connection to the school. The murder was likely a personal matter. I'm inclined to think a teacher, coach, custodian, or other school employee is responsible. Someone Carlos and Cindy knew. I want to believe it was an adult. I don't think another student is involved, at least not alone. But I have to start with the parents and students. Otherwise I'll never find out what was going on in the relationship that prompted a motive."

Vargas turned to Fenton. "What do you think?"

"I think it's worth a try."

"What's the case load like now? Can we give Van some more time?"

"Barring any major cases breaking in the near future, I can give him a few days. We would have to play it by ear. Can't promise anything."

"Okay, Van. Work this out with Fenton. Keep me informed. Do it right so the local media don't get wind. At some point, if they hear we're making progress, it'll get a lot of attention. We need to keep it quiet for now. I'll give the boss and Public Information Office a heads-up, but I do not want any surprises. PIO will be all over us if we don't keep them in the loop."

"No problem, Lieutenant. I prefer it well off the radar. My style is to avoid attention."

CHAPTER 16

Preparing to Move Forward

Homicide Office

IT HAD BEEN a couple weeks since Van came on board with Homicide. When he pulled into the underground parking area now and made his way up to the third floor, there were still a few people who took note, maybe even nodded, their expressions suggesting they had not seen him before. That was expected. For many, his sudden appearance at department headquarters disrupted the norm. Van knew that his seven-year absence meant there were deputies and specialized personnel who had entered the department during those years and climbed through the ranks without ever knowing who he was.

At the same time, there were many in the department who remembered him and expressed genuine surprise when they suddenly encountered him in the halls or cafeteria. Others heard he was back and sought him out. Renewing old friendships with colleagues was a welcome though of necessity, time-consuming task. Handshakes, smiles, and greetings were one thing. Renewing old relationships with those he had worked major cases with, sat in stakeouts for days with, or faced violence with was quite another. During the years of service before the hiatus with the feds, Van had established some strong bonds. In most cases, he had not interacted with these colleagues for seven years. But even in the large department, the whereabouts and status of colleagues is monitored informally, and renewing old ties is an opportune event.

Having worked with the feds meant Van's career had followed a much different path from those of his colleagues. The process of renewal carried with it a host of inquiries and the need to confirm or reject rumors about Van's experience. With a tendency toward shying away from the limelight, such interactions could sometimes be awkward for Van. It was not that he wanted to avoid social interactions; he just always felt uncomfortable when a lot of attention was focused on him. To this end, Van had for many years worked hard to improve his social skills. He found himself imposing a self-discipline focused on engaging friendship encounters with a sense of appreciation and allowing time to take its course.

One lesson learned as a teenage grocery store box-boy was that friendship and respect were coupled. The successful checkers tended to take their time with customers who were regulars. The simple act of greeting them by name and showing interest in their families and their endeavors seemed to influence the loyalty of the customer. It always struck Van that the more sociable checkers would have people waiting in their line even though the lines for other checkers were much shorter.

Those in law enforcement, he thought, were much like a checker who has to work to earn respect. It did not come without effort, especially since many in the public were averse to interaction with law enforcement.

It had occurred to Van many times that effective law enforcement personnel used their social personality more than their uniform or badge. The badge represented their authority personality. An early mentor told him that when people encounter you, they already know you have the authority. The uniform and badge are enough. If you're working plain clothes, then the way you carry yourself and the ID do the same. He still remembered the advice: "Consider the uniform, badge, ID, and command presence as icebreakers. People know you're in charge; you don't need to tell them. If you want to be effective while on duty, use your social skills, not your power skills." It had proved to be good advice.

Van's parents had also helped him to develop his social skills. His father, a man everyone liked, was quiet and unassuming. He was also one to never pass up an opportunity to greet someone with a smile and kind word. It occurred to Van as a young boy that his dad treated everyone equally. Station in life was not the important quality to his dad. It was the simple fact that they were humans, and that required they be treated with kindness.

At his father's funeral, the reality of this philosophy came to the forefront. It seemed that every person who spoke with Van expressed the opinion that his dad was a friend to all. That had been years ago, and Van had worked ever since to emulate some of his father's skills. In Van's line of work, it had not always been an easy task.

Since returning to the department, Van had made it a priority to memorize the first and last name of everyone in Homicide as well as anyone else who worked the third floor. He also prioritized the task of remembering at least the first names of any support staff he was likely to encounter elsewhere in the department. That included civilians working the front gates, parking garage, grounds, building maintenance, secretarial and clerical staff, cafeteria workers, and many others. When he thought it important, Van also tucked away bits of information regarding each person's interests or character qualities. Such information allowed Van to engage others in discussions about hobbies, music interests, ages and disposition of children, and spouses. It was also a tactic he carried over into his case-related interviews. Conversation as prelude to investigative questions often put interviewees at ease and made them more willing to cooperate.

—⁓—

As he entered the third-floor offices of Homicide, the room was only sparsely populated. It was early morning, and the workday for most on the floor would not start for another hour. Those in view were finishing their night shift. On his way to his office, Van nodded and greeted several people. Responses told Van he was progressing in his effort to know everyone by name.

He dropped the shoulder attaché case on his desk, turned on his computer, and glanced at his phone to see if it signaled any recorded calls or messages. Seeing none, he poured some distilled water into his electric teapot and turned it on. He then turned to the task of preparing his tea.

Coffee drinkers had their ritual; Van had his. He took out the spring-loaded tea infuser spoon. He scooped up a spoonful of special-order loose-leaf Earl Grey tea from the quart-sized tin. Van set the infuser in his large ceramic cup. When the water was boiling, he would fill the cup. After two minutes of seeping, the tea would be ready.

While waiting, Van noted that the computer was up. He immediately logged in and located his emails. Only a handful. *This is a good sign,* he thought.

There was an email from Fenton's secretary. It was a reminder. Now that he was back full-time, Van needed to make sure he got on the weapon-qualifying schedule. He wrote a Post-it note reminder and pasted it on his computer screen. He would schedule that today.

A quick scan of the remaining items showed there was nothing requiring an immediate response. He knew all good things come to an end and now that he was on the rotation, his emails would begin to pile up. Thankfully Fenton had eased him into the rotation and he had yet to be thrown a case that would force him to set everything aside.

The tea ready, Van retrieved his cup and sat down to address his big task for the day, preparing for the Ashae interviews.

The reality of interviewing the parents of Cindy and Carlos was not lost on Van's sense of the task ahead. Parents or loved ones of victims are never easy to question. Regardless of the lapse of time, loved ones of a victim are never dispassionate. Parents and spouses never get over their loss. Even years after such tragedy, experience had taught Van that parents, spouses, siblings, and others may put up a good front and act as though they're under control, but in fact they seldom went a day without a sad reminder creeping into their thoughts. Interviews could exacerbate difficult memories.

But good investigation interviewing was an art form. A decent interviewer had to be equal to the position of the interviewee. He had conducted his share of interviews under difficult circumstances. He had also observed many colleagues conducting interviews and knew there was no one-size-fits-all method. Each investigator had to develop a personal style. Van was certain that effective interviewing for him was a combination of personality, voice, respect, listening, and strategy. All elements were almost of equal value, but being prepared was critical in any circumstance. He did not just go off and interview. His style required strategy going in.

—⁓—

Van had worked hard to develop good interviewing skills. He saw it as one of his strengths. He could not say that about some of his past investigative partners.

It was a college professor who most influenced Van's approach to preparing for the task of interviewing witnesses or persons of interest in a case. The history course focused on the role of the frontier in American history. The professor started the semester by distributing a list of twelve questions reflecting competing hypotheses about the significance of the frontier.

During the course of the semester, the professor required students to read six different books that argued a range of issues regarding the influence of the frontier on American history. After reading each book, students had to write a paper that used the author's interpretative paradigm to answer the questions. The paper was to be no more than five hundred words. It was an absolute limit.

The professor dictated the type font, the margins, and the line spacing. Failure to abide by all the format requirements resulted in an automatic failure.

Van soon learned that the quality of his work left much to be desired. After having his first paper butchered by the professor, Van began to approach the reading differently. Rather than read the book and then try to answer all twelve questions, he learned to prepare for reading the book by studying the questions beforehand. Ultimately, he realized that a book might not address all the questions. It may shed light on only one or two questions.

The key was to be able to use the historian's frame of reference and interpretation to suggest possible approaches to responding to only the pertinent questions. Van learned to approach his reading as if he was listening to a story. It was not just a matter of the verbatim text; equally important were the implications of what the historian said. He learned that there was reading, and then there was reading for meaning. There was listening—and listening for the meaning.

At the end of the semester, there was an essay exam. It had one question. *Now that you have read the interpretation of six different historians regarding the significance of the frontier experience in American history, which author do you find most credible?*

To answer the final exam question, he had to place his argument in the hands of supporting evidence. Although insight into each historian's take on the twelve questions was important, they were not of equal value. In the end, it was not which author provided the most comprehensive answers to the questions but rather how well he, the student, could argue a point of view supported by one or more of the six historians. Van, as student, was the author, and the six historians were supporting characters with varying degrees of credibility.

There was, of course, no correct answer. It all came down to how well he could play the role of historian and use the evidence of other historical interpretations to support a viable point of view. Only when Van was comfortable that he understood the value of each historian within the context of the twelve questions did he feel comfortable developing an argument in support of the credibility of one historian or interpretation. The experience taught Van the value of historiography—the methodology of studying, interpreting, and writing history.

The same challenge confronted an investigator. Is the witness credible? Why and why not? In order to interpret the implications of a witness, one had to weigh what was said. The metrics of making such a determination were not simple. As with the credibility of the six historians, one had to develop an understanding of each interviewee's logic. Sometimes it came down to the question: which witness is most credible and why?

All interviews are different because all interviewees are different. A good interviewer must learn to question, listen discreetly, and read the interviewee. Body language, eyes, expressions, idiosyncrasies, and nervous actions are all part of the interview and must be taken into consideration. It was not a simple matter of comparing the logic of a witness's statement with the evidence from other sources. Like the six historians of his class, what an interviewee did not say was sometimes as important as what was said and how it was said.

As an investigator, the key was in developing an approach to interviews that would enhance an ability to draw supportable conclusions. That meant knowing what it is one wants to know. Going in, the interviewer must have purpose and know what is being searched for. Once in, like the historian, the interviewer must work within the context of the evidence and what the interviewee is or is not saying. It becomes important to adapt and allow the comments of the interviewee to guide the process. Equally important, the interview must be kept on track. Only when one feels comfortable with the results of an interview is one positioned to draw inferences. Only when one is comfortable that they understand what has emerged from multiple interviews can one begin to answer the questions that prompted the need to interview.

Van could still recite his professor's philosophy about writing history. "The historian who develops an interpretation of events, ignorant of what he does not know, commits a sin. The historian who interprets, knowing what he does not know, commits a crime."

—⟨⟨⟩⟩—

Later in the day, Van scanned his outline of interview items. They were categories of need-to-know information that he would use as springboards to his questions. In that sense, Van saw the list as more of a graphic organizer that he could reference without appearing to look at a list of questions. Having to look at a list or spend time taking his eyes off the interviewee was a distraction he could not afford. It was Van's experience that referencing a list could intimidate the interviewee and thereby influence their response.

In developing his list, Van started with his own needs and then reviewed the interview records from Vargas, Damon, Inskeep, Torres, and Rasmussen. Eventually he had several categories.

1. Cindy and Carlos as individuals before they met
2. Relationship of Cindy and Carlos after they met
3. Relationship of Cindy and Carlos leading to the prom
4. Perceptions of parents about Cindy and Carlos's relationship
5. Perceptions of friends about Cindy and Carlos's relationship
6. Peculiar or concerning issues/events in Cindy and Carlos's relationship observed by others
7. Conflicts between Cindy and Carlos and others
8. Perceptions of parents, siblings, friends, and others now versus 1972
9. Interviewee suggestions about other possible sources/interviewees

The categories were conceptual. They did not dictate a sequence. Van would let each interview evolve, and he knew from experience that there would be a blending of the categories as he proceeded. Foremost in his mind during the interview would be the need to make sure all nine categories ended up on the table and that the interviewees responded on all fronts. Only then would he have the opportunity to probe the "why" of any responses. It was often in the explanatory part of a response that the real value of a question was revealed.

Of course, Van was aware that, like his reading of the six historians, it was not as simple as asking questions. Each person interviewed might provide a limited insight into some of the questions. More likely, Van could expect that in the course of questioning and subsequent discussion, bits and pieces of his questions would be addressed. In the end, he would have to make sense of it all. It would come down to his interpretation of meaning.

Van would start with the parents. There were three of them, and they reportedly lived locally.

As for friends, it appeared that while Carlos had many, Cindy only had a handful.

He had no illusions. The interview process would take considerable time, and it would be taxing and frustrating. And he would have to fit it into his increasingly busy schedule.

—᙭—

Late in the day, after taking time to go to the gun range for qualifying, Van turned his attention to the reports of past interviews with Mrs. Ashae. She would be his first interview.

According to Vargas, Francine Ashae was interviewed three times during the two weeks immediately following the disappearance. Though the atmosphere was very emotional each time, Vargas found her amenable to questions, regardless of the sensitivity. Van reviewed her testimony with attention to the questions asked and the responses given. Van hoped to avoid a lot of redundancy.

The questions asked by Vargas were what Van expected. They focused on the relationship between Carlos and Cindy, their friends, possible problems, and any signs that things were not going well between the two. Vargas wanted to know, "Was Cindy having any problems?" There were also questions probing the possibility that the two kids ran away. Vargas was especially interested in whether Mrs. Ashae could find anything in Cindy's room that would suggest preparations for "running off."

However, given the tactic taken by Vargas, Van felt that not enough was done to look deep into the evolution of the Cindy and Carlos's relationship and how others viewed it. Van wondered why Vargas did not probe deeper into the alleged change in Cindy's relationship with her mom after Carlos came along.

Torres had found Mrs. Ashae restless when he interviewed her in 1999, though he also found her very cooperative. Many of the questions asked were repeats of earlier questions. The new questions focused on the earring and the expected "Who could have done this?" questions.

As he thought about tomorrow's interview, Van wondered what life must be like for Mrs. Ashae. As a single parent with one child, it was likely that everything she lived for was wrapped up in Cindy. Cindy had never been a problem, and then one day she was gone—disappeared. Mrs. Ashae likely hoped beyond hope that someday Cindy would come back. But as time passed, that hope faded.

Then one day twenty-seven years later, Cindy's remains are discovered under the most bizarre circumstances. The fading hope turns into a nightmare of unknowns and media attention. Some would say the discovery of remains provides some closure, but there is really no closure for a grieving parent. In Mrs. Ashae's case, the time capsule probably opened new questions of hurt.

Now, decades after the disappearance, what is there to talk about? She has lived with every parent's nightmare. She can answer questions, but for what purpose? The department would dearly love to solve the crime, but does Mrs. Ashae really care? At this stage, how does justice that returns the four-decade-old nightmare to the front pages bring any satisfaction?

CHAPTER 17

INTERVIEWING FRANCINE ASHAE

The Ashae Residence

ALTHOUGH HIS LINE of work relied heavily on the telephone, Van preferred that initial contact with a key person in an investigation be face-to-face. He needed to see people and size them up based on first impressions, manners, language, dress, and many other tangible and intangible qualities. If he could meet with someone before they were aware their input was important, then there was a greater likelihood that the interviewee would not spend too much time thinking and anticipating before talking with him.

Van guessed the two families were not in contact. Instincts told him Mrs. Ashae would not make it known that a new investigator on the case had contacted her. She had been down the road before, and he reasoned she was not likely to give others a heads-up after he interviewed her.

Francine Ashae lived in the same home, about a half mile from Nuevo High School. It was a small three-bedroom house with a rundown look from the outside. A bungalow, it was probably built in the early 1950s. The neighborhood generally lacked character.

Van noticed nothing special in her response at the door when he identified himself and his purpose. Van apologized for not calling in advance and then asked if she had time to answer a few questions. Her response was pleasant and unemotional. She invited Van in.

Out of habit, Van compared his initial take with what he already knew about her. She was in her seventies but looked older. Records indicated she was thirty-six years old in 1972, so Van estimated she was probably married around nineteen years of age. Vargas had noted in his early interviews that she had dropped out of Santa Ana Junior College, got married, and was probably pregnant with Cindy at the time.

Overweight, Cindy's mom was dressed in nondescript clothing that hung on her. Her silver-streaked dark hair was unkempt, and she wore no makeup. Though she spoke with a pleasant voice, it was only about ten in the morning, and already she sounded tired, and her movements and behavior suggested someone who was doing little more than going through the motions of life. Van could not escape the feeling that the travails of life had pretty much defeated Mrs. Ashae.

Van kept the initial conversation informal. It was only after the usual meet-and-greet questions that he moved the discussion to his intended purpose.

"I was wondering if you could give me some idea of your thoughts during the years following Cindy's disappearance and the discovery of her remains at Nuevo."

"It wasn't easy. The not knowing was the most difficult. I kept hoping for something, but as the months and years went by, I knew I'd probably never see her again."

"Records indicate you changed jobs years later."

"Yes. I had to. My colleagues were just uncomfortable. They wanted to help, but there was nothing they could do. It was awkward. When the city maintenance dispatcher job opened, I knew it was time to change. I worked for the city until I retired several years ago."

Van had the feeling that Mrs. Ashae was not uncomfortable in answering his questions. He also sensed from her comments that she had little contact with others, and perhaps today's interview was a welcome break from a solitary, if not lonely, life.

"How did you react to the discovery of Cindy's remains in 1999?"

"It turned my world upside down again. After '72, there was

always a slim hope in the back of my mind. In '99, I had to face the reality of her passing. I struggled with it. There had to be a funeral. Hope was over. People said it brought closure. But I assure you, Officer, a mother never forgets a loss of a child. I may no longer cry, but I will never forget."

The crying and sadness associated with Cindy's disappearance and later confirmed death had long ago taken its toll. Van suspected it had beaten Francine Ashae down for so long that she no longer openly cried and showed little emotion. Life had not been kind to her, and she appeared reconciled to it. Van found himself thinking that it was a wonder she was still alive after all she had been through. *What does one do in her situation?* He could only imagine.

"I volunteer at the library. But that's about it. Everyone is sympathetic, but most of the library help and all of my neighbors are younger, and they don't understand. So I keep to myself."

Van moved the conversation to events prior to the disappearance.

Later, thinking back on the forty-five-minute conversation, it was clear that Mrs. Ashae had been interviewed so many times on related matters that her answers required little reflection. Numerous times, she prefaced a response with "As I told the other officers …"

It was also apparent that she held out little hope that anything would come from another round of investigation. She was accommodating, but Van sensed no conviction on her part that the system would someday bring justice. Nor did he sense a temperament in search of revenge. The discourse was guided by Van's questions, and Mrs. Ashae did not raise any questions or offer any theories of her own. Van had to give her credit; she gave clear responses to his questions and was never evasive or reticent about responding.

He also had to admit that she provided him with some curious information. He was as yet unsure of the value, but time would tell.

"Can you tell me about Cindy's friends?"

"Well, she only had a couple of good friends who came over once in a while. Emily Calderon was probably her closest friend. I don't know where she lives now. There was another girl, but I can't remember her name. Came over only a couple of times. But I don't know. Cindy didn't have a best friend, if that's what you mean. Maybe Emily. I know she had other friends, but they were at school and didn't come over."

Van thought Cindy seemed to be like her mother—quiet, ordinary, and solitary.

When asked why she thought Cindy did not have many friends, the response provided interesting insight into an atypical teenager. "I don't really know, Investigator. Cindy was nice to people. But she wasn't real social. Kinda quiet and shy, I guess." It left Van wondering. Was Mrs. Ashae really knowledgeable regarding Cindy's friends, or did the responses suggest Cindy really never made strong friendships? He was inclined to think that, as a parent, Mrs. Ashae didn't think Cindy had close friends. Van knew he needed to track down Cindy's two close girlfriends.

Van inquired about whether Cindy had ever mentioned any boys, other than Carlos, who were friends or who she liked. Mrs. Ashae said Cindy never talked about boys other than to describe one or two as "nice" or as "funny" or as a boy who sat next to her in class. Cindy had gone to a couple of dances but never as a date. She usually went with a couple of other girls who, like Cindy, were not real popular and not likely to be asked to a dance.

Did Cindy go to any parties? Cindy had gone to a couple of girl birthday parties where there were probably one or two boys, but she did not recall anything special happening there.

Nor was Cindy a nerd. She got decent grades but nothing of note. What about performances? Did Cindy enjoy being involved in school or community or church activities where she would perform or speak in front of others? "Not really."

Van sensed Cindy's type. She was an introvert. She avoided opportunities to join. This was an important finding since it told Van that whenever Cindy did involve herself voluntarily in something, it was likely to be a cerebral decision and not one influenced by others.

"Mrs. Ashae, my next questions are probably different than ones asked in the past, but they are important. I try to get to know my subjects on another level, so in asking these questions, I assure you I'm not trying to violate any privacy or upset you. I hope you'll understand."

"Go ahead, Investigator. It's not a problem."

Among other things, Van inquired about the kinds of books Cindy read, special interests, music and movie preferences, what she did with her free time, and whether she liked to go shopping.

The responses from Mrs. Ashae provided little information. Cindy liked to read, especially books about animals and nature. She was not musical and never had music lessons. She listened to sixties rock music but usually only in the evening. She liked television but did not watch excessively. Cindy did not go to the movies and never expressed any special interest in an entertainment hero. She did not really have any hobbies. And, "Cindy really never paid much attention to clothes until she needed a prom dress."

Mrs. Ashae's response to a question about what Cindy did with her free time was most intriguing. "Cindy liked to go for walks in the park. The elderly couple next door had a blond Labrador, and Cindy would take it for long walks. If she wasn't going for walks, she would go to the library, which is just down the street, and look at *National Geographic* magazines and books about places like the South Pole, the Grand Canyon, Yosemite, and other wilderness areas. She didn't check them out. She just read and looked at the pictures. She got to know the people at the library well. I guess that's why I volunteer there today."

Van found it interesting that Cindy liked the outdoors, even though her contact with it was limited to walks in the park. The Cleveland National Forest was the closest wilderness to Cindy. Could there be a connection between Cindy's outdoor interests and what happened that night?

Her interests aside, Cindy seemed to have lived a cloistered life. Still, Van knew he needed to look closely at Cindy's outdoor interests as he sought to understand Cindy as an individual and as a victim. But for now he needed to turn the interview toward Mrs. Ashae's thoughts regarding Carlos and the prom.

"What can you tell me about Carlos Fuentes?"

There was an extended pause. Van knew Mrs. Ashae would be expecting such a question, and yet the pause suggested an emotional change. Van could see the change in her eyes and in her effort to collect herself before responding.

The response was a repeat of earlier testimony, but it was crowded with emotion.

"Look ... I knew who Carlos was. Everyone did. He was handsome, social, and well known. But I didn't know Cindy and Carlos were seeing each other right away. I know I should've been aware, but it never occurred to me that he would take an interest in Cindy." Mrs. Ashae breathed deeply. "It sounds crazy, but I actually heard about the budding relationship from the mother of another girl. My own daughter didn't tell me."

There was no crying, but Van saw the accumulated moisture in her eyes. He also knew he was hearing a self-assessment that emanated from deep within Mrs. Ashae. He knew she was admitting that the relationship everyone thought she and Cindy had was flawed.

Van wondered, *Why would Mrs. Ashae hear about Carlos belatedly? Was Cindy hiding something by not sharing?*

Mrs. Ashae admitted the relationship with Carlos caused some "friction." Asked to clarify friction, she said that unlike the past when Cindy would usually tell her most anything, Cindy did not want to talk much about Carlos.

"Why do you think she didn't want to talk about Carlos?"

"I've asked myself that many times, Investigator. I think she was embarrassed. Not embarrassed about Carlos but embarrassed that she didn't understand her own feelings. She had never really known a boy before and wasn't sure how to talk about him, I guess. I don't think she understood what was happening to her. I suppose not having a father when she needed one was part of it. What I mean is that a father could have helped her understand boys better."

"Is that what you thought at the time?"

"No, that's the conclusion I've drawn over the years since."

The comment rang true for Van. Time and honest introspection provide insights to elusive past events.

"Knowing this now, did it seem to you at the time that Cindy was a bit naive about how to interact with a boy?"

"I guess, but I just thought that was normal."

"Normal for Cindy or normal for all girls?"

"I guess both. It was the way I was at her age. Let's face it, Investigator—I'm sure, if you've done the math, you know I was pregnant with Cindy when I married her father. I too wasn't wise to the world of boys when I was in high school. So, when the first one who showed an interest in me came along … Well, let's just say I overreacted."

He was hearing a sort of confession, but it explained a little about Cindy. Mrs. Ashae understood her daughter, but she was not sure how to counsel Cindy regarding boys. *Was it avoidance or a form of denial?* For her part, Cindy, at seventeen, may also have put two and two together to realize her mom had become pregnant before getting married. If you're a teenage girl who's having a first experience with a boy who shows some interest in you, do you know how to respond if you know only your mother's experience? Perhaps Cindy's avoidance in talking about Carlos with her mom was a response along the lines of, *What do you know, Mom? You made mistakes and look what happened to you.*

Van moved the questioning back to focus on Carlos.

Mrs. Ashae shared her recollections. Carlos did come over one time. It was an evening, and Carlos and Cindy sat outside and talked. When Mrs. Ashae went out to offer them something to drink, the two stopped talking and waited until she went back in the house before resuming their conversation. A half hour later, the two came into the house. He said a polite goodbye before he left. Cindy remained quiet and would not talk about the evening. A week later, Cindy informed her mother that she was going to the prom with Carlos and needed to get a dress and shoes.

"I really didn't know Carlos, but I was pleased Cindy was asked to the prom. But it bothered me that Cindy didn't want to talk about Carlos. And Emily and other friends stopped coming around."

The comment caught Van's attention. What was it about the Cindy and Carlos's relationship that led to friends not coming around? Mrs. Ashae had noted earlier that friends did not come around much as it was. Perhaps there was more to it. Clearly, Mrs. Ashae was admitting that her relationship with Cindy at home changed with the entrance of Carlos into Cindy's life.

Did she think it strange that such a popular boy would ask her daughter out?

"I did, but then I wanted Cindy to go to the prom. You can't imagine how much you want your only child to have an experience you never had, to be asked to the prom. I had concerns that Cindy was taking Carlos too seriously and that it was getting in the way of our mother-daughter relationship, but I was also happy for her. I guess that's the bittersweet part of parenting."

Van sensed Cindy's mom was not hiding anything. If anything, she was opening up and sharing what was on both heart and mind.

"I've thought about this many times, and I really don't think I would have done anything different. You want the best for your child, and when they have opportunities you never had, well, you tend to overlook some things you might question at other times. I guess I just rationalized it all."

"Do you think you overlooked anything?"

It appeared Mrs. Ashae was struggling to control her feelings. "I'm sure I did. I mean, I avoided being confrontational. I was willing to let the fact that I didn't know Carlos be unimportant so long as Cindy could go to the prom. That Cindy wouldn't talk about Carlos, I could overlook. I should have been pushier, but I was afraid that if I intervened, I might scare Carlos off, and then Cindy would be really unhappy. I guess you could say it was a catch-22 situation."

"Did you ever have any contact with the Fuentes family?"

"I sat next to them at a special assembly at the high school at the beginning of the next school year. It was like a remembrance, but of course no one knew what had happened to them. I think everyone just assumed they were dead. I guess I really thought that too, but inside I still held out hope. It's the last time I saw them. I've heard they moved. They didn't come to the funeral for Cindy, but I don't blame them. Carlos's body has never been found."

Van made a mental note that the Fuentes had moved. Then he asked, "Had you ever met them before the prom?"

"No, I had no idea who they were. I just knew from friends that they owned their own business, and most people said they were hard workers. I guess that was good enough for me."

"Going back to the night of the prom, did you give any directions to Cindy about when she was due home or if she should check in with you by phone?"

"I told her she needed to be home by 1:00 a.m. I figured the dance was over at eleven, and it was about an hour drive away. One in the morning would allow them to take their time and … well, I don't know what I thought. It just seemed a reasonable time then. I guess I knew if I said midnight, Cindy would argue with me, and I wanted to avoid any conflicts."

"And you never heard from Cindy after they left for the prom?"

"I didn't."

"Did you say anything to Carlos about the 1:00 a.m. timeline?"

"No, Cindy didn't want me to. She said she had already told him."

Van thought for a moment. Was it another effort on Cindy's part to insulate her relationship with Carlos from her mom? Why would Cindy not want her mom to communicate directly with Carlos? This was something he needed to consider. The seemingly close mom and daughter relationship began to change when Carlos came into the picture. Perhaps it was understandable from Mrs. Ashae's perspective, but maybe it suggested something else.

Van made a mental note and moved on to a different line of interest. "After that night and in the days and weeks to follow, did you ever have occasion to talk with any student or teachers or administrators about the prom?"

"No. But I really don't think I wanted to talk with anyone. It was hard enough to talk with the detectives and avoid reporters. Also, her father was second-guessing me."

"Has anyone who was at the prom ever shared their views with you?"

"No."

At that point in the interview, Van had not learned anything new about the night of the prom, though he had learned a considerable amount about Cindy. He turned to other items on his list.

"Did Cindy ever share with you any of her interests at school or any clubs or groups she belonged to?" Given what he knew about Cindy, Van did not expect much.

"No, Cindy wasn't very outgoing. She wasn't very talkative. She wasn't the club type. I know some of her friends tried to get her to try out for the drill team, but she didn't want to. When I asked her why, she said she couldn't dance and would be laughed at. I think Cindy was always very self-conscious about what she saw in herself."

"So Cindy, as far as you know, wasn't involved in any extracurricular activities in school?"

"Well, I remember her saying that she went to an Ecology Club meeting, and it surprised me. I think it was her junior year. I asked her what the club did, and she said they talked about the environment and things that were polluting the world. One time she said the club was going on a hike, and I thought she was going to go, but she didn't, and I assumed she had lost interest."

"You assumed?"

"Yes, well, I later found out that she kept going to the meetings and didn't go on the hike because she was afraid to ask me for money to buy a pair of boots. I think it was a requirement if you wanted to go on the long hikes."

Van remembered a note from one of the earlier investigators that Cindy was in the Ecology Club. It made sense to Van. She was already predisposed to like the outdoors. Her library reading probably fostered the interest. Of all the things that go on in high school, the Ecology Club made sense to Cindy. It fit well with her limited experience.

"Did she ever go anywhere with the Ecology Club? What I mean is, the club must have done more than hiking."

"Yes, they went to a rally with some clubs from other high schools one Saturday."

"Where did they go and how did she get there?"

"They went to Irvine Park. I volunteered to drive, but Cindy didn't want me to drive. I had a small car. She went with some other parent who had a station wagon and took a bunch of kids."

He did not let on, but Van's thoughts were immediately impacted by the mention of Irvine Park. Was that a connection? Van was not one to easily admit to coincidence, so he made a quick note on paper to not lose track of the Irvine Park connection.

"Do you know whether Carlos went?"

"I don't think so. I don't think she was seeing him yet. But I don't know for sure."

It seemed to Van that Mrs. Ashae was confirming what he already suspected. When a boy comes into the life of a teenage girl, there is an awkwardness that impacts a previously close relationship between the girl and her parents. This was not unusual; it was a norm. At that point, personal matters were more likely to be shared with peers than with parents.

"Did Cindy ever talk about the field trip to Irvine Park?"

"I remember she liked it and said that they didn't need boots to hike that day, and the leader, or one of the leaders, a teacher I think, took them on a long nature walk outside of the park. Cindy said she loved it and wanted to get some boots."

"Did she?"

"She started saving money to buy the boots, but then Carlos came along, and she spent the money on the prom."

"So you don't know if Carlos was involved in the Ecology Club at the time Cindy developed an interest." Van was seeking to clarify whether Mrs. Ashae's earlier comment was correct.

"He may have been later, but I don't know. I just don't remember what I knew then."

Her responses were interesting. Cindy had not talked with her mom about Carlos much at all. Even where the Ecology Club was involved, the two did not talk about it.

Vargas and Damon noted that Cindy and Carlos were both involved in the Ecology Club. However, it was simply noted and not probed. Kids belong to clubs, and since there did not seem to be any connection between the disappearance and the club, the matter was not pursued.

"Just a few more questions, Mrs. Ashae. How involved was your ex-husband in Cindy's life during high school?"

"He wasn't involved. He was never around. He spent nothing on her and, as I recall, begged off helping purchase a prom dress for her. Cindy and her father had no relationship."

This was odd to Van. The father didn't live that far away. But Van also knew that the parameters of divorce were not easily understood. Earlier investigations substantiated the father's whereabouts on prom night and concluded he had nothing to do with Cindy and Carlos.

"Did Cindy ever talk about any teachers?"

"She got along with her teachers. She always did. I never got a negative note from a teacher. Her report cards always had comments about how they liked having her in class."

"But did Cindy ever single any teacher out positively or negatively?"

"As I recall, she loved her science teachers. The science department seemed to be a favorite for all the students, and Cindy always talked about them. She also liked her history teachers. I don't remember the names, but she did say, after the Irvine Park outing, that they were 'cool.' I remember because it was the first time I ever heard Cindy use the term."

Van wanted to probe the death of Cindy, but he did not want to focus on generalities about what may have happened, so he focused on three specific issues.

"I know this is a sensitive question. Did you look inside the VW van that Carlos drove?"

"Only when Cindy got in. Carlos held the door open. I remember that because I thought it was a gentlemanly gesture. I was impressed. I also remember it was awkward because she had to step up, and the dress she was wearing made it difficult for her to step up into the VW."

"So the dress made it difficult for Cindy to take big steps up. Is it safe to say Cindy probably could not have easily walked over uneven ground or uphill easily?"

"Probably so."

"Did you notice anything out of the ordinary in the van?"

"No. I really didn't look at anything other than Cindy and Carlos. They were both so handsome and happy. I was mad because my camera didn't work, so I told them to make sure they got prom pictures. They said they would."

Van remembered the prom photos. They were typical.

"I know you've been asked this before, but I want you to think back to the weeks and months before the prom. Was there anything or anyone that you can recall who may have had a disagreement with Cindy or Carlos or who showed any signs of dislike or jealousy?"

"No, it's a question I've wondered about over the years. It was one of the first questions Lieutenant Vargas asked me, and it comes back to me as a question from time to time. Always, the answer is *no*."

"Just to make sure I understand your response. You can't think of anyone or any group of people—students, teachers, administrators, neighbors, or anyone else—who showed any signs of displeasure or anger or anything out of the ordinary toward Cindy."

"None."

Van indicated that he had one last question.

"Again, on a question I know you've been asked before. Had you ever seen the earring that was discovered with Cindy's remains?"

"I suppose that has been the most mysterious and troubling part of all the events surrounding Cindy's discovery. I can see that earring in my mind today. It's unlike any I ever had and certainly not like any earring Cindy ever had. I went through her possessions I had kept after she went missing, and there was no jewelry like that earring. I've looked at the prom photos and yearbook photos, and that earring isn't there. That earring came from someone else."

For the first time, Van sensed Mrs. Ashae was very choked up. She swallowed hard and worked to compose herself. A pause hung in the air. "Investigator Van, I now know that the earring is known as a kind of calling card. When I mentioned that to Investigator Rasmussen, he was not verbal in responding, but he nodded his head."

She looked down at her folded hands and then looked Van in the eyes. "Whoever killed Cindy put that earring there. I know that. I know it."

In wrapping up the interview, Van asked Mrs. Ashae if she had any of Cindy's belongs. Her response was that she saved most everything until after the discovery. She said it was sort of a way of hoping Cindy would someday come home. After 1999, there seemed no reason to hold on to the items. They just served to revive unwanted memories. She kept old photos and yearbooks but nothing else. Cindy did not keep a diary and was not one to hold on to letters and notes, so those never really existed.

Mrs. Ashae gave Van the collection of photos she had saved, and he promised to have them back to her in a couple of days. With that, he headed back to his office.

—◆◆◆—

On the drive back to his office, Van thought about what he had learned. There were a few small pieces of information that intrigued him, but he had to admit that what appeared most valuable was the insight into the changing demeanor of Cindy in the months prior to the prom. While Cindy was close to her mother, something about her relationship with Carlos disrupted the mother-and-daughter continuity. He could not help but think Cindy was very taken by Carlos. So taken that years of loyalty and sensitivity toward her mother were relegated to second place in priority. He wondered whether other students or teachers noticed this change. Certainly friends must have noticed.

CHAPTER 18

INTERVIEWING ANGELA FUENTES

Riverside, California

THE PLAN TO interview Mr. and Mrs. Fuentes hit an unexpected snag. Mr. Fuentes had died a couple of years earlier, a fact not noted by Rasmussen. Van learned this only after following up on Francine Ashae's comment that the Fuentes had moved. A neighbor provided information regarding the whereabouts of the two Fuentes children, Muriel and Donnie. They were several years younger than Carlos. Muriel lived at a Moreno Valley address provided by the former neighbor. Donnie worked for the US Border Patrol and was stationed in Texas.

In a phone call to Muriel, Van learned that Angela Fuentes, several years older than her husband, was in a nursing home and suffering from a myriad of problems, not the least of which was mild dementia. Muriel seemed bright and forthcoming when Van inquired about interviewing her mother. She suggested that it might help if she was present since her mother tended to slide into states of anxiety and as a result became unresponsive.

Mrs. Fuentes was in an assisted living residence in Riverside, a fifteen-minute drive from Muriel's home. Van drove out to Riverside Gardens on a Saturday morning.

Van found Mrs. Fuentes neatly dressed, at first subdued, but responsive to his greetings. His initial assessment was superficial. He soon realized that she seemed distant. At times Van felt she was not listening to, or at least did not understand, his questions. As a result, it turned out to be a challenging interview. Mrs. Fuentes was responsive, but she tended to easily lose focus on a question Van asked. Often she digressed. The process was slow.

Muriel was her mother's guardian and provided valuable assistance. Given the time since the events of 1972 and the age of Mrs. Fuentes, Van knew Muriel had every reason to be dismissive of Van's interview request. Van soon realized that Muriel was facilitating the interview because she had a compelling desire that the case involving the disappearance and probable death of her brother be solved.

Muriel was articulate, patient, and resolved to help Van. Though she was the daughter, Muriel came across almost as a well-dressed and trained professional investigation partner.

Later, Van was surprised that the interview proved beneficial. Muriel was most helpful, and Van had no doubt that Muriel was the reason the interview proved valuable.

Muriel, though seven years younger than Carlos, said she remembered the prom because it was the first time she had ever seen her brother so dressed up. She remembered thinking he was lucky. When Carlos never came home, Muriel was confused and could not understand how a party could make someone go missing.

Mrs. Fuentes remembered the prom and that Carlos said he would be home an hour after midnight. Cindy had communicated her mother's timeline to Carlos. Did Carlos say anything about going somewhere after the dance? "No, he said they would be home one hour after midnight." Mrs. Fuentes articulated very clearly her recollection. Van thought it curious that she did not say one in the morning.

Van asked when Angela and her husband became aware that Carlos was not home soon after one o'clock.

Mrs. Fuentes said, "We worked at night. So Muriel and Donnie stayed with my parents like they always did."

"So you would not know if Carlos got home that night?"

Muriel stepped into the conversation to help her mother. "Mom, the investigator wants to know how you found out Carlos did not come home."

"Oh, well, we found out when your uncle came to where we were working and told us."

Again, Muriel helped her mother. "Mom, do you remember what time that was?"

"Oh, it was very early in the morning, I think. I was worried, but your father was not. He just said Carlos was being not responsible and would be punished."

Van asked when Mrs. Fuentes and her husband learned Carlos never came home. He did not get a coherent response from Mrs. Fuentes, and Muriel helped her mother to restate previous testimony that it was not until a sheriff's deputy showed up after they had returned home from work.

Van was most appreciative of Muriel's assistance. But he sensed Muriel sought to make sure her mother's testimony was consistent with past comments. This was especially evident when Van inquired about friends of Carlos. Only with Muriel's guidance was he able to learn the names of some friends. With one exception, neither Angela nor Muriel knew the whereabouts of the friends. The exception was a neighbor girl who used to babysit Muriel and her brother—Annabel Rodriquez.

Van recognized several names, as they had been interviewed by earlier investigators. But it had been many years since anyone had talked with the friends, and Van was concerned that it would be difficult to locate some of them.

Asked about any clubs or school activities, Mrs. Fuentes remembered only the sports. "Carlos was a good athlete," she said many times. She could not remember any clubs, but "He was an active boy and always going somewhere."

Did he get along with his teachers? Mrs. Fuentes said Carlos could have done better. Her husband was always after him to do better in school. Carlos did not get into real trouble; he just sometimes "got into mischief with the other boys." But she assured Van that Carlos liked everyone and he never disliked a teacher. "He was a good boy" was something she said several times.

Were they ever contacted by Carlos's teachers? Mrs. Fuentes said she did not remember because if someone called, only her husband would do the talking.

Van showed Mrs. Fuentes a photo of the earring found with Cindy's remains. It triggered a response Van had seen in the report of Inskeep and Torres. "Hippie earring. I wouldn't wear it, and Carlos would never buy such things." She was emphatic.

Perhaps the most interesting outcome of his interview came from the question, "Did Carlos ever talk about Cindy?"

Van thought it peculiar that Mrs. Fuentes took her time before speaking. It was as though she had to think out her response. Muriel tried to interject, but Mrs. Fuentes waved her off. "Carlos was liked by all the girls. Sometimes the girls would come to our house. But they were just friends, and they would visit. But he didn't talk about them."

She did not answer the question. Van clarified, "So he never talked about Cindy Ashae?"

"I asked him why he was taking a girl to the prom that nobody knew. He said because she never went to a dance and wasn't like the others. I asked why she wasn't like others, and he told me she liked animals and nature things. I asked if she liked camping, and Carlos said she never went on a vacation and didn't know anything about camping. I said it was strange because how would she know she liked those things if she didn't go there. He said she liked the hiking with a school club. That's all he said."

Van did not respond, but both Mrs. Ashae and Mrs. Fuentes had indicated something about Cindy that was hidden. Somehow Cindy had developed a real interest in the outdoor environment and in hiking. Carlos was somehow connected with that. Van wanted to stay focused on the interview, but his mind kept linking Cindy's interest with Irvine Park and its closeness to the catering site.

"Did Carlos ever talk about the high school Ecology Club?"

"I don't know. Maybe, but I don't know."

"Did you ever meet Cindy's mom before the prom?"

"No, we didn't know her. None of our friends knew her. But I knew she was divorced, and Cindy was her one child."

All through the discussion regarding Cindy, Van sensed there was a cautious edge to Angela's voice. At first he just thought her responses reflected her diminished mental skills or that she was being careful about what she said, but in time he realized she was not pleased that Carlos was dating Cindy. Mrs. Fuentes believed her son could have done much better than Cindy, and her responses implied indirectly that she blamed Cindy for taking Carlos away from her.

Angela was saying the same thing her husband had told investigators when he insinuated his son was a good boy and would not have disappeared if he had taken a different girl to the prom.

The interview went slowly, and after about thirty minutes, Mrs. Fuentes began to show signs that she was growing tired. Van knew that he needed to bring things to a close. Perhaps, if need be, he could come back another day. But that was something he wished to avoid.

When asked if any of Carlos's personal effects were still in existence, Muriel answered for her mother by indicating that there was a box with photos, mementos, trophies, certificates, and other things that Carlos had collected. All of Carlos's clothes had been distributed to his younger brother and cousins. For years her mother and dad kept Carlos's personal items in a box that Muriel now had. Muriel agreed to make the box available.

Soon afterward, Mrs. Fuentes started digressing on the fact that everyone knew what happened to Cindy, but Carlos had never been found. She became increasingly anxious, and it was clear the interview could go on no longer.

After the interview, Van asked Muriel if he could somehow see the personal effects of Carlos that she said were in a box. She offered to turn the box over to him if he wanted to follow her home. He could mail it back to her after he inspected the contents.

In turning the box of items over to Van, Muriel made her thoughts known.

"Investigator, I can only hope you have more success than your predecessors. I've spent a lifetime wondering what happened to Carlos. I won't interfere in your work, but I hope you'll take the time to call me if you do solve this case. It won't bring my brother back, but I'll feel some closure."

—m—

Forensics and Support Services was in the basement of the department. The officer manning the front desk had his back turned as Van walked in. Both were taken aback when he turned around. Hofstadter was quick to respond; it was his outgoing and fun-loving nature to turn everything into a social event.

"Well I'll be, if it isn't the long-lost Investigator Vanarsdale, back from the *fed*. I heard you're working homicide."

Van smiled. "Hello, Matt. Last I remember, you were working the gang detail."

"Hell, Van, you know the department. They need someone to set things straight in a floundering area, and here I am." He tossed files to the side. "What brings you down here?"

"Well, the contents of this envelope were given to me by the family member of a victim. It has to do with a very old case. Not sure of its value yet."

"So what do you need?"

Van opened the envelope and slid out the contents. "I need these letters and envelopes, along with the photos, and a couple of old color thirty-five-millimeter slides scanned so I can bring them up on my computer."

"Shouldn't be much of a problem. This all?"

"Yeah. I need the photos high resolution, by the way."

"High resolution? You're dreaming. This isn't the FBI like you're accustomed to ..."

"Spare me. I know you can do it. I need high resolution if I'm to blow them up on the screen."

"All right, Van my boy. I'll see what we can do. I suppose you need them yesterday."

Turning as he walked out, he said, "You got it. See you around, Matt." Van knew if he stayed any longer, it would be hard to get out. Matt Hofstadter was one who liked to talk ad nauseam.

—⟨⟨⟨—

Back in his office, Van began to type his thoughts into his computer files. The actual interview was only the first part of a two-phase endeavor. He always felt that as soon as possible he must type up observations. It was while typing that he gained insights into what the interviewee had said. Equally important was the need to record his personal impressions and perspectives.

Perspective is a function of timing and diligence. Early in his career, Van had learned the lesson the hard way. He responded to a domestic disturbance incident in a very upper-class neighborhood. He was the first deputy on the scene. The husband and wife were in a heated argument with two neighbors. Van realized that before he could do anything, he needed backup, so he approached the situation cautiously to buy time.

Several other neighbors got involved, and the whole incident was escalating very quickly. There were a couple of scuffles and some minor damage to property. Finally other deputies arrived, and together they managed to diffuse things.

The whole thing took place just as Van was due to go off duty. As it was, he had to work overtime, and part of that overtime involved completing a report. Unfortunately, Van did not do diligence in writing the report. He and Ann Marie were headed out of town, and he was running late. He did a poor job of writing up the report. Two days later when he returned to work, his sergeant called him on the carpet for a poor report and told Van to write it again.

Two plus days removed from the events in question resulted in Van relying on his unreliable memory to rewrite the report. In fact, Van discovered problems in his original report but was at a loss to remember all the details that were needed to correct his errors.

After that incident, Van never again gave second shift to the responsibility of writing up incident reports. In fact, he was very embarrassed by his error and became obsessed with writing thorough and compelling reports. The first rule was now to ensure accuracy by writing up reports as soon as possible. It was a practice that had served him well over many years.

CHAPTER 19

ANNABEL, KEITH, PHIL, FELIX, AND ALLEN

Various Locations

O VER THE YEARS, Van had occasion to interview all manner of people regarding cases he was working. During the years as a deputy, he had often talked with young adults and teenagers. Sometimes they were witnesses. Most often they were just of interest because of their proximity to a specific crime or incident under investigation. However, most kids he talked with under investigation circumstances were little more than potential sources of information.

Early on, Van struggled with questioning kids because he found that they, unlike most adults, were not reticent about talking. In fact, he had found that teenagers, despite the reputation that they clam up and will not rat out what they know, often want to talk and find it hard not to talk. Later he found research literature suggesting the desire to be perceived as important and as someone in the know often prompted young people to represent hearsay, half truths, and opinions as if they were hard and indisputable facts. Separating fact from fiction was often not something easily ascertained from the comments of teenagers.

Thinking back on the days and weeks of investigation following the disappearance of Carlos and Cindy, Van suspected Vargas and

Damon were probably interviewing high school students who were dupes of the rumor, gossip, and fabricated stories mill. It was the nature of the high school setting; you are somebody if you know something or if you were there. It was the desire to be part of the group, reasoned Van. It wasn't a matter of thinking and reflecting when asked a question. It was a matter of how you wanted to be known by your peers.

For Torres, Inskeep, and Rasmussen, it would have been different. Time would have tempered views. The diaspora of Nuevo graduates, now grown and unconcerned about how old friends might view them, would be more under the influence of maturity and a tendency to reflect before responding to questions about what happened in 1972. Yet Van sensed that the interviews conducted after 1999 fell short of the thoroughness needed. This was not unusual for a cold case.

Investigators are often under great pressure to resolve active cases and have little time to do more than a perfunctory job with old cases, especially those decades old. It is difficult to track down witnesses or persons of interest. Add the time span since the original crime and how memories fade, and it is difficult to get new information. Witnesses who were sure of their observations years earlier begin to retreat from their assuredness.

Investigating very old crimes is often labored and frustrating. Law enforcement management is always aware of a case's profile in the public eye. Recent cases, especially heinous ones like murder, are often high profile and demanded attention. The media are quick to react but lose interest equally fast when nothing happens to bring perpetrators to justice. Whether a cold case later becomes active again usually depends on the emergence of new and credible evidence.

But the issue of credibility of evidence is not simple. Time compromises evidence. Sometimes it is difficult to convince others the evidence merits action. Add to that the fact that district attorneys are often cautious about pursuing a very cold case unless any new information is clearly consequential. The diligence of an investigator handed an old case is challenged more than might be expected.

Van was certain that what he needed to do was avoid asking the same old questions and focus more on questions that might provide some insight into the personalities of Carlos and Cindy during the period of their budding relationship. He was also conscious that his own interest in the case would, over time, depend on how well he pursued the potential for new insights, perhaps new evidence. Van was acutely aware that eventually his ability to stay focused on the case would be challenged by more recent and active cases.

—⟋⟍—

The conversation with Annabel Rodriquez took place just down the street from the sheriff's headquarters. Annabel worked for Orange County Child Protective Services. She was a striking professional— tall, slender, dark hair, and immaculately dressed. The introductions led Van to quickly conclude that Annabel was both articulate and poised.

Annabel had lived next-door to Carlos from the time she was five and he was six. They had become friends even though they did not go to school together. She went to Catholic schools through eighth grade and on to an all-girls Catholic high school.

In her capacity with OCCPS, Annabel had been interviewed many times by law enforcement, attorneys, and court authorities. She knew the purpose and value of interviews. She also knew the importance of speaking to the questions when responding. Van enjoyed the interview because Annabel was given to logical and reflective responses.

"You never dated Carlos?"

"Oh, no. We were friends, and we both sensed that our friendship revealed enough about each other that anything other than a friendly relationship would not be good. We did see each other occasionally at a party or some event, but everyone knew we were just neighbors, just friends."

"What was your take on the girls Carlos dated?"

"They were always popular, tended to be the all-American-girl types, and were usually blonde. I used to tease Carlos about loving the

Barbie-doll types. There was some neighborhood humor to it because none of the girls Carlos dated looked like those in our neighborhood. As you can see, I did not meet his standards."

Van smiled. He appreciated Annabel's candid responses.

Van did not want to reference statements made to investigators in 1972 or 1999 unless a contradiction occurred or unless he needed clarification.

"You told Investigator Vargas that you were surprised Carlos asked Cindy to prom. Why?"

"I believe I told the investigator that she was not his type."

"Meaning?"

"I didn't really know Cindy, but what I heard suggested she was the very opposite of the types of girls he usually dated. Most would think the girls Carlos usually dated were loose and a bit on the snooty side. However, those girls were not naive. They were worldly and more likely to be much *tighter,* if you will, than their talk or the talk of others would suggest. Cindy, on the other hand was naive. What she didn't know about boys who were turning into men made her an easy target …"

"And this occurred to you back then?"

"Investigator, an all-girls Catholic school is something much different than people's perception. You grow up fast because the primary discussions are always about boys."

"And to you, all of this suggested what?"

"Let's face it, Investigator. There was probably a motive to Carlos's decision to ask Cindy, and it went beyond just being nice. Oh, I have no doubt that she was intriguing, and he was for some reason drawn to her. But he was a teenager and not always logical. No doubt emotions and hormones played a role."

"And you know that?"

"I asked Carlos why he was taking such a shy and quiet girl when he could have asked anyone. His response was that she had never gone with a boy to a dance, and he felt that she deserved that experience. I just didn't buy that argument … I'm not saying he intended to take advantage of her, but he was a young man with the same drives of any young man his age. He was also experienced and well aware of her vulnerability."

Vulnerable. Van tagged the word in his memory. "Did you ever meet Cindy?"

"I didn't have to. I knew Carlos. I knew his friends. Since I was a good friend of Carlos, I had some status among his group, and they often shared with me as if I were one of the bunch."

Van moved on to probe Annabel's perceptions about who may have wanted to do harm. "During those days and weeks following the disappearance of Carlos and Cindy, did you ever hear any credible comments from neighbors or friends of Carlos regarding anyone who had a strong dislike or grudge?"

"No. If you're asking did I ever pick up on any names of people who could have murdered them, the answer is definitely no. Also, as for my own inclinations, I've given thought to that question over the years, and the answer to myself is always no."

Annabel was a straight shooter. She was also experienced in dealing with difficult and troubled kids. She was sensitive to their needs, but she was also a realist. Her take on Carlos was simple, and Van had no doubt it reflected her long professional experience serving as a filter to her thoughts of events forty years ago.

Keith Jefferson lived in the house where he grew up. He inherited it from his parents. He lived alone. He had been married and divorced twice, had children by his first wife, and she had full custody. His kids were now grown, and he had little contact with them. By his own admission, Keith was not much of a family man. He said he liked women, but he did not seem to like marriage. "The institution of marriage is something I've not been able to master." Keith seemed reflective; perhaps the interview would be interesting, if not valuable.

The conversation verified Van's perspective on the benefits of time and maturity in interviews. The boisterousness and bravado evident when Damon interviewed Keith was no longer present.

Inskeep's notes said Keith was guarded in 1999. Now seasoned but as yet not retired, he seemed resolved to his lot in life. Keith no longer had anyone to impress, and Van reasoned Keith was probably honest with himself.

Van approached Keith in a relaxed manner. There was no need to make him feel defensive. Initial civilian perceptions of an investigator often triggered reaction rather than cooperation.

Thinking back on it later, Van felt his approach worked. Keith was responsive. He was reflective and transparent. Now, decades removed from high school, Keith Jefferson wanted to talk, and Van's role was to guide him.

"Yeah, there was a group of us who hung around together, and Carlos was part of it."

"What made you a group?"

"Well, I guess we were all athletes. We played football together."

"I thought Carlos didn't play football his junior year."

"No, he didn't, but we'd all played Pop Warner, and when we got to high school, we played there—except for Carlos, who only played two years. But he was a good athlete. By eleventh grade, we had all been friends so long that the group just stayed together."

"So you did everything together?"

"No, not always. We all knew some of us weren't going to college. Some got good grades, and some of us didn't. Me, I just squeaked by." There was a self-deprecating smile, and then he continued. "And some of us really didn't date. It wasn't a problem for Carlos; he always had girls. We all envied him."

"So, even though you all began to go in different directions by your junior year, you still regarded yourselves as a group."

"Pretty much."

"Did you let others into the group?"

"Yeah, sort of. I mean, people hung around with us. Some weren't athletes. You know, people come and go. We were informal anyway. By junior year, the group was kind of dissolving."

"Can you explain that?"

"You know, we were all kind of doing different things. We all drove, but some of us didn't have cars to drive around. Several guys had jobs, and though we hung around at school, we had different things going on outside. You know what I mean?"

"I think so."

So the group was increasingly not a group and certainly not really influential over its members was how Van interpreted what Keith was saying.

"What did you think when you heard Carlos was taking Cindy to the prom?"

"Yeah, you know, I think we were all surprised. He could have taken one of those good-looking cheerleaders."

"So why do you think he took Cindy?"

"Well, most of us didn't think it was because he felt sorry for her, if that's what you mean."

"I don't know. You tell me."

"I mean, most of us thought it was because, well, you know, she might feel grateful to him for asking her and be willing put out a little, if you know what I mean."

"Take advantage of her. Is that what you're saying?"

"Yeah, most of us thought that, you know."

"So all of you knew this but said nothing to Carlos?"

"Well, Phil did."

This was a name unfamiliar to Van. "Who was Phil?"

"Phil Runcle. He went to Alta Vista High, but he was a part of the group 'cause he had played Pop Warner. Oh, yeah, and he was a year older than us, and his dad was the manager of the local supermarket, and Phil could score a six-pack or two when we needed it."

Keith was honest; he wasn't bragging. "What did Phil say to Carlos?"

"Well, I don't actually know, but I heard he did."

"So, Phil was a good enough friend that Carlos would listen to Phil?"

"Gee, Investigator, I can't remember everything that far back. I just remember that Phil talked to Carlos about dating Cindy. Phil thought it was a bad idea."

"Why was it a bad idea?"

"She was a loner. Carlos was outgoing. Didn't add up, you know."

"Do you know how I can reach Phil?"

"You can't. He was killed in Nam."

He would verify that, but Van was interested. Phil was someone from outside the school who was apparently influential with members of the group. Nowhere in the Vargas or Damon interviews did Runcle's name come up. "Well, what can you tell me about Phil?"

"All he ever wanted to do after graduation was join the army. Like I said, he was a year ahead of us. He graduated halfway through his senior year, January I think, and immediately joined the army. Went off to boot camp and came home for several days before he was due to ship out to Nam."

"Do you know when that was?"

"Yeah, a few weeks before the prom, he came home."

"Is that when he talked to Carlos about Cindy?"

"I think so. At least that's what I heard."

"From who?"

"Allen."

"Allen Mapleton?"

"Yeah, he was part of the group and was close to Phil because they had gone to church camp together or something. Allen said Phil was upset that Carlos asked Cindy to the prom. I guess Phil somehow knew Cindy. I don't remember how he knew her."

"So, did you go to the prom?"

"No. The girl I asked was put on restriction a few days before, so I stayed home. You know, a real bummer. Allen and I got drunk at his house because he didn't go and his parents were gone."

"What about others in your group? Did they go to the prom?"

"Felix did, but he went with a group of other couples. All the girls knew each other. Felix's parents had money, and they hired a limo. Didn't see many limos in those days. If you want to talk to Felix, he lives in Miami now. Big attorney there."

"How about Robert Segstrom? Did he go?"

"Yeah, I think so, but he died years ago. He probably went because he didn't go to Allen's house that night."

There was a break because Keith needed to use the restroom. While waiting, Van recorded Phil Runcle's name. Van was certain he had not encountered the name in any previous records.

When Keith returned, Van restarted. "Do you know of anyone—another student, parent, coach, or teacher, or anyone else—who would have wanted to harm Cindy or Carlos?"

"Definitely not. Carlos was liked. I mean, there were people jealous of his ability to attract girls, his likable personality, but that wouldn't be reason to kill, I don't think. Naw, Carlos got along with people. Some of us could piss people off and get into it because we would shoot our mouth off but not Carlos. I don't think he ever fought. He wouldn't want to risk his good looks."

"You have any ideas on what happened the night of prom?"

There was a long pause before Keith replied. Van had the sense that Keith was tentative about what he wanted to say. And then a different Keith came to the surface.

"Look, I don't have a lot of friends. Shit, the only real friends I had were in high school, and Carlos was one of them. I was pissed when he disappeared. Other guys like Robert and Allen, I knew they were going places after graduation, but Carlos would be around. When I eventually realized he was probably murdered, I was angry."

"Angry how?"

"I get depressed. Blame others. My exes will tell you. I get angry at the world. I take it out on those around me. I have medication and have had anger management. All the people I grew up with and were part of my world are gone or not around. I understood them, and they understood me. Hell, if Carlos hadn't gone to the prom, we would still be friends."

"But you don't have any idea what happened to Carlos."

"Wrong place, wrong time?"

"How so?"

"You know. Carlos and Cindy get in the van after the dance, go off to do some physical work in a remote place, and stumble into the wrong people, I guess. Wrong place at the wrong time is how I figure it. Know what I mean?"

Van was thinking, *Here's a man who just barely graduated from high school, didn't go to college, has been a truck deliveryman all these years since, and vicariously continues to live his high school years. And yet his assessment of what happened is not much different than that of professional investigators.* Keith's take on events was as credible as Van's.

But Van knew Keith's idea was not the answer. It was just the convenient conclusion in the absence of other, more substantive evidence. Van also suspected Keith, and probably others in the group, did not believe in the wrong place, wrong time theory either. It was just that they had nothing else to suggest another reason.

—ɯɯ—

Van tracked Felix to a big law firm in Miami, Florida. He thought it strange that a Southern California boy whose family was well off would garner a law degree from USC and then move to Florida to practice.

Damon had interviewed Felix. His notes suggested Felix had a chip on his shoulder. In response to questions about Carlos as a friend, Felix tended toward sarcasm that did not really speak to a close friendship. In fact, it seemed to Damon that Felix was a bit envious of Carlos.

According to Damon's notes, Felix had invited Carlos to go along with two other couples in the big limo his parents rented for the prom. Carlos had declined and said that he and Cindy wanted to "go it alone." When asked what that suggested to him, Felix said, "Maybe he thought he was too good to ride with us. I don't know. Maybe he wanted to have a different kind of fun with his date. How should I know?"

Damon found the response interesting and followed with questions about whether Felix and Carlos had some issues. "Not that I know. We were friends, but that didn't mean we always agreed on everything. Anyway, Carlos was everybody's friend, and the girls loved him. You know, sometimes people like that get on your nerves."

Damon asked if the two ever had any conflicts, a fight, or anything like that. "No, we just gave each other the space. The other guys kept us apart."

Besides football and other sports, Damon asked if the two of them ever had the same classes. "No, Carlos wasn't much of a student. I don't think he even planned to go to college. I think he wanted to take over the family business, you know, cleaning. I had honors classes."

Damon concluded that Felix was not in any way involved in the disappearance of Carlos and Cindy. He was with two other couples at the dance, and the limo did not get back to the Najarian residence until two in the morning. Felix's dad met and paid the limo driver a tip when they got home. In Damon's words, Felix was "a chip off the old man's block—arrogant and loud."

When Van finally got through to Felix, it was only because Van made it clear to the receptionist that he was investigating a homicide case and that Felix was a friend of the victim.

From the start, the interview went downhill for a while.

"Officer Vanarsdale, is it?" There was no intent to wait for an answer. "Listen, I have clients waiting for me, and your case has been cold a long time. I don't think talking to me is going to help you make any progress. What I told the detective in '72 hasn't changed."

Van knew where it was going, but he was not one to be easily discouraged by the likes of Felix Najarian. "Yes, I've looked over Investigator Damon's notes. But I also see in the files that you refused to talk with Investigators Inskeep and Torres in 1999 after Cindy's remains were found. They called you several times, and you wouldn't talk with them."

"That's right. Time is money in my business, and I had nothing new to provide. Don't have anything new now either."

Two can play this game, thought Van. The ego on the other end of the line provided an image of a type of attorney Van had encountered many times in his career. Felix Najarian bullied people with his ego, demands, and blustery comments. "But still, you agreed to talk with me."

"Listen, Investigator, there's really nothing I can tell you that you don't already know."

"I understand. But I would like to ask you just two questions, if that wouldn't be too much."

"Okay, two questions, but only so long as they're new questions and not repeats."

Van couldn't pass up the opportunity. Playing the meek, please-answer-my-questions role would only empower Felix to act more like the idiot Van knew him to be. "Counselor, you must have a good memory to recall all the questions asked decades ago."

"Listen, Investigator Vanarsdale, I'm in the business. I represent the bums you try to put away. I know how the game is played. So ask your questions or hang up the phone."

"Okay, first, several people have told me that they were surprised that Carlos asked Cindy to the prom because he could have taken any popular girl. What's your take on that statement?"

"Yeah, yeah, that was what people said after the fact, but they knew why."

Van waited, but Felix did not go on. "What do you mean they knew why?"

"Let's face it, Vanarsdale, he wanted into her pants. Simple as that. Why else would he not want a ride in the limo and choose to drive his dad's old VW van. I guess you could say that in hindsight he passed on an offer that would have saved his life."

The crude comment spoke volumes about Felix. "You don't think he may have actually found Cindy to be more attractive, perhaps even more interesting, than the girls he usually dated?"

"Come on, Investigator, who are you kidding? We were in high school, and Carlos wasn't the brightest of the bunch. But he knew what he was doing that night. It just didn't go the way he thought it would."

"I see." Van let his response stand for a couple of seconds and then decided to ask his second question. "Counselor, you have been in the business for a long time. When you look back to 1972, from your perspective as a defense attorney, do you recall if there was anyone—teacher, student, friend, anyone—who may have wanted to do harm to either Carlos or Cindy? Anyone?"

"That's a repeat question, but it's the key question, so I'll answer it again. Like Carlos, I knew most people in that school, students and teachers. Most of my teachers were different, but we all knew the same students. What happened to Carlos and Cindy, and I'm making the same assumption you are that Carlos was killed, might not have surprised people in some high school communities, but it was completely out of the norm for Nuevo. I believed then that there was no one who would want to harm either of them."

There was a pause, and Van waited. He knew there was a second part to this statement.

"Now, of course, after years as a defense attorney, I'm well aware that our world is filled with very abnormal behavior. There are people who commit crimes for reasons far removed from the reality of normal people. I know, as you do, the person or persons responsible for the deaths of those two kids could have been someone either or both of them knew, perhaps even knew well. I suppose that happens more than most people realize. Then again, I also know it could have just been their unlucky night to encounter the wrong persons in the wrong place."

Van recognized that despite his egotistical attitude, Felix understood that the world made for some strange and unpredictable people and that murder can invade the most peaceful of communities. Madness in society is all too common and sometimes leads to violence. Felix knew this firsthand.

Felix had, no doubt, defended some of those strange types. "And you've never thought that a particular person may have been involved?"

"I'd be lying if I said no. But I would be equally dishonest if I gave any credence to any of my thoughts. I say that because my experience tells me that the slightest of suggestions would not be based on any sort of evidence. So my answer is an absolute *no*. I know of no one who would have even given the remotest of thought to harming either of those kids."

Later, thinking back on the interview, Van found the transformation that took place in Felix during the course of the discussion to be the most valuable finding. The more he thought about it, the more Van concluded that Miami was probably the best place for someone like Felix to practice law as a defense attorney. He also had no doubt that Felix was successful in the courtroom and in the interview room. Felix was a performer, not just an attorney.

Van knew that in saying that Cindy and Carlos could have been killed by someone both or one of them knew, Felix was acknowledging that he had, as an experienced attorney, given thought to who could have killed them. Van also knew that Felix had never been able to come up with a viable suspect, something Felix obviously had given considerable thought to. Perhaps that was the most valuable part of what Felix had to say.

The person or persons responsible for the disappearance knew Cindy and Carlos. They were also enraged. They were so outside the norm that even someone good at screening people in a crowd would miss them. With expertise as his guide, Felix had scanned the crowd of 1972 and never found a suspect. Felix was a professional, but he admitted defeat after years of reflection.

Keith and Annabel knew where Allen Mapleton lived. Allen was a class of '73 success story, even though he derailed his own success and settled into a life most viewed as lacking glamour.

Allen, the onetime straight-A student and good athlete, was now an honors and advanced placement English teacher and head football coach at a Los Angeles inner-city high school. He had kept his youthful appearance and all these years later looked very much like his senior class photo. Van could not help but think coaching and working with teenagers helped to keep Allen looking young.

Allen was a long way from Orange County. Although it would

have been more convenient to meet with Allen at his school, they met at Allen's Woodland Hills home in the San Fernando Valley. The home was in upper-middle class suburbia. Allen said that the presence of the law on his campus, regardless of the circumstances, sent up red flags in the gang-infested community around the school. Better to avoid the curiosity it would bring and meet at his home.

Allen had gone to UCLA and graduated with a degree in English. He then went to law school in the Bay Area and practiced law for many years before going back to school to get a high school teaching credential. With a very religious and supportive wife, they and their three kids moved down to LA, and Allen secured a position at his current school.

"You have a great home, Counselor—"

Allen cut Van short. "I'm a teacher. Call me Allen. I get enough of Mr. Mapleton at school, and I'm not a practicing attorney."

There was an edge to Allen's comments. His response was curt, and he clearly sought to distance himself from his earlier career.

"Yes, but your reputation precedes you. I did some work with the FBI, and a colleague in San Jose tells me you were a good prosecutor before going into private practice for several years."

"That was long ago. I appreciate the compliment. But you're here to discuss Carlos."

Allen's desire to avoid his earlier success was clear. But Van's FBI source had mentioned there was great speculation about why Allen left a successful and lucrative career. Van was well aware that sometimes people take stock of their situation and make decisions to move on along another track. It was something Van respected; it was a kind of courage Van admired. But Allen seemed to be hiding something, and the move to a different career for Allen was more complicated. Van did not want to probe the issue now, but the intrigue was such that he would look for the opportunity at a later time.

"That's right, and you're familiar enough with cold cases to know that I wouldn't be interviewing you if I didn't have a compelling reason."

"And do you have new evidence?" There was a hint of amusement on Allen's face.

Van also smiled. "Well, of sorts. When the case was given to me, I began to ask questions about the assumptions of earlier investigators. I didn't find new evidence, but I did find that there was sufficient reason to conclude that Cindy, and probably Carlos, were murdered on purpose and not because they were in the wrong place at the wrong time, as the original investigations tended to suggest. Of course, the finding of Cindy's remains confirmed this.

"Now that we know the perpetrator was probably someone the two students knew, the focus must be on the possible suspects. That has been the focus since 1999. However, there has been no progress beyond the time capsule discovery."

"And you would like my take on Carlos, Cindy, and events surrounding their disappearance."

"Yes."

"For starters, I applaud your department for not giving up on the case. When I heard about the discovery of Cindy's remains, I thought the case would break, but obviously it hit a dead end again. So, all these years later, what can I provide, Investigator?"

Van appreciated Allen's direct and amenable attitude. "Were you surprised Carlos asked Cindy to the prom?"

"I was then but not now."

"Reasoning?"

"Carlos was a complex kid. On the surface, he was the popular, fun-loving, athletic, and good-looking high school junior, even though he wasn't much of a student. In reality, he was a seventeen-year-old young man who was beginning to realize that he was predictable; he was what others wanted him to be."

Van did not know exactly where the interview was headed, but he did know it was going to be the kind he enjoyed. Allen was articulate, reflective, and sincere. There would be substance.

"I think we all have times in our life when we turn inward and assess our status. When we do this, we kind of look at ourselves and compare it with what's going on around us. I suppose some do this, see what they see, shrug it off, and move on. Some of us see something that raises concerns, and we consider the implications and other options. I see this happening with my high school students all the time."

Allen held up the palms of both hands as if to accentuate his qualifying comment. "Don't get me wrong. I don't think it was all a cognitive endeavor on the part of Carlos. I just think maturity was leading him to question his situation when he looked at others around him. I think he actually began to think about the future." Allen smiled as he concluded, "He wasn't someone friends or teachers took seriously. Cindy may have changed that."

"Remarkable change in a short time. How do you think it happened?"

"Quite by accident, but the timing was right. The whole Earth Day thing was in vogue then, and the two got to know each other in the Ecology Club. Cindy was a very shy and inexperienced young girl, but she was developing a conscience about environmental issues. The club had meaning for her. Perhaps for the first time in her life, Cindy connected with a cause."

Van sensed Allen had given considerable thought to the circumstance of the relationship between Carlos and Cindy.

"Carlos, on the other hand, went because a bunch of us went. The two ended up in a discussion group where the topic was something about the future of a polluted planet. As I remember it, some girls made comments about the future being the fault of their parents' generation and a problem for others. They had lives to live and should not have to clean up after their parents. Cindy, who was not known to be one to speak up, suddenly became assertive and suggested the girls were selfish and cared only about themselves."

"How did Carlos respond?"

"I think he was as surprised as we all were. Cindy was an unknown. More importantly, I think Carlos was even more surprised because he had a couple of years earlier made derogatory comments about Cindy becoming an old maid, because who would ever want to hook up with her. She had never heard him say it, but he had said it to the guys in our group."

"The group with you, Keith, Phil, Felix, and some others?"

"Yes. You've talked with some of them?"

"I have, but they didn't provide any input on how Cindy and Carlos hooked up and why he asked her to the prom. Why did he ask her to the prom?"

"As a result of the encounter in the Ecology Club, Carlos became intrigued by Cindy. I guess he had never talked with a girl who was intellectually concerned about the future of the planet. He was only accustomed to conversation that was concerned with the here and now and not the future. He started going to the club meetings regularly, and the two of them talked several times. Nothing spectacular, mind you, just small talk. I remember him being kidded about Cindy by Keith, and Carlos laughed it off and then told Keith to mind his own business. Carlos said something like 'Cindy may be smarter than all of us.'"

"When did all of this happen?"

"During the winter, maybe early spring, of our junior year."

"But why would he ask her to the prom when he could have gotten a date with just about any available girl on campus?"

"Because Cindy intrigued him and grew on him. I'm not sure even he knew why, but he grew to like her. Again, I think Carlos found his past in conflict with questions about his future.

"I know, Investigator, this all sounds overly philosophical, but I assure you my years as a high school teacher have tempered my legal perspective, and I find myself looking at my own past through the lens of my experiences with teenagers."

Van moved on with his inquiry. "I've heard it said that some thought Cindy was not his type and that he only took her because he could get his way with her. How do you react to that?"

"To some degree, I would agree. I think Carlos was intrigued and wondered what it would be like to have more than just a casual relationship with a girl like Cindy. Remember, most of the girls he had dated were like the ones who thought they had no responsibility for the actions of their parents."

Ever the analytic, thought Van. No doubt this accounted for Allen's success as an attorney and now as a teacher and coach. Perhaps Allen was right in saying Carlos had an interest in Cindy for reasons of teenage ambivalence. But Van wondered about Allen's take on Phil's influence with Carlos.

"Keith told me you and Phil Runcle were close. True?"

"We knew each other from our church youth group."

"Were you aware that Phil allegedly advised Carlos not to take Cindy to the prom?"

"Yes, it happened when Phil came home from boot camp and became concerned. He also knew Cindy."

"From church?"

"Maybe. I remember seeing her there once in a while. She wasn't a regular. Phil may have gotten to know her there, but I just don't know."

"What did you think of Cindy?"

The response was not quick. There was the kind of pause that grew from years of consideration. "You know, Investigator, I think men, and boys as well, sometimes in life encounter a girl who's a little mysterious. They don't know why, but they're attracted to that girl. She's different, and they feel a need to get close to the girl. They want to understand the mystery. They're ambivalent, but some drive deep within moves them to action. Sometimes they get obsessed."

The comments spoke volumes about what made Allen successful. It also opened doors into Cindy's changing personality. Van wondered, "Do you think Carlos was obsessed with Cindy?"

"In his own way, perhaps. Intrigued might be a better word. But to answer your question, I will admit that on reflection, Cindy was an increasingly attractive girl as a junior. But her history was a personality that put most guys off. As she got older and matured, she became a little mysterious, a little attractive in a way that a guy becomes intrigued and soon finds himself falling for her. Cindy was becoming a woman, and we boys found that interesting, even if we might not admit it or understand it."

"Did she take an interest in Carlos?"

"I don't know. Probably not at first. Maybe later when he started hanging around with her. I just don't know."

"Is it safe to say that you can see how Cindy would be viewed by others as not Carlos's type, but you can also see why he was increasingly attracted to her?"

"I suppose so."

"Do you think Carlos had any intentions with Cindy that night? Intentions beyond just going to the dance and then taking her home?"

"We all had those kinds of intentions when we dated girls, but most of the time we chickened out. It was usually big talk and little performance. The difference was that I think Cindy may have been much more aware of his interests than people gave her credit for."

This was an interesting line of thinking. Allen was suggesting Cindy might not have been the naive girl they all assumed she was. "What makes you say that?"

"It was the way she could look at you. She may have been quiet and shy, but there was a sensual side to her when she was one-on-one with a boy. She actually looked you in the eyes. It was disarming. I'm not saying she had plans for sexual contact that night, but I don't think she would have resisted some of it either. I stress the *some of it*."

"You're the first person to suggest any of these characteristics about Cindy. Why you and not the others?"

"Because Phil once said that he knew Cindy and that she was not what everyone thought she was. Of course, Phil was killed soon after Carlos and Cindy disappeared, and he never knew the outcome. But I know Phil never dated her; he just had some insight the rest of us didn't have."

Van was wondering about Phil Runcle. Did he know something about the Cindy and Carlos relationship others did not know? "Did Phil say anything else about Cindy? He seemed to know more about her than anyone else. Did that ever strike you as odd?"

There was a smile on Allen's face. "I think Phil was more mature than the rest of us. After boot camp, I'm sure he saw his role more as big brother and adviser. He was one of us, but he was worldlier, and he seemed to know we all looked up to him. Perhaps he saw it as his responsibility to give advice."

Allen had been a prosecutor, and he had been a defense attorney. No doubt the question of who could have murdered Cindy, and probably Carlos, had been mentally wrestled with. "I wonder, have you ever given thought about who could have killed Cindy and Carlos?"

"I was wondering when you would get to that question. The answer to your question is, yes, I have wondered. The answer to my own thoughts has been a complete blank. I assure you, Investigator, I have absolutely no idea who could have committed the crimes. And I have to plead a logic that I believe is true but for which I have no clues—they were murdered by one or more persons who knew them. And to answer your follow-up in advance, I could not possibly venture the name of a possible suspect or suspects."

"A thorough response."

"I assure you, it's something I've thought about many times, and it has continually frustrated me. I wrestled with the question as a prosecuting and defense attorney. When I began to work with high school students, I continued to wrestle from a different perspective. Always the answer has been I don't know."

Van moved on. "How did you personally take the disappearance of a close friend?"

"The disappearance of Carlos and Cindy affected me deeply. I guess you could say it provided an epiphany because I suddenly took school much more seriously in my senior year. I feared the idea of disappearing. Actually, I was terrified of the idea that someone could just disappear. I somehow equated not growing up and not knowing what was important in life to tragedy. I needed to be somebody to prevent that from happening to me."

Van understood what Allen was telling him. Tragedy in the life of a friend sometimes serves a friendship well beyond the grave. The death of Anna Marie had affected him in many ways he could not have imagined before her death.

"You know that I've gone over the interviews conducted by the investigators in 1972 and later in 1999 and after. Two things appear odd to me."

"What's that?"

"Well, first, much of what you've shared with me regarding Cindy's growing relationship with Carlos is more substantive than what you shared in 1972, and certainly unlike the views of your group of friends in 1972 and 1999."

"Substantive?"

"Yes. You told Investigator Vargas that Cindy and Carlos, and I quote, "hooked up" midway through their junior year. But you did not expand on the insights about maturity you have shared with me. Why?"

"I suspect it's because time and experience have provided a clearer window for my perspective. I sense you're a well-read person, Investigator, so let me lend a bit of philosophy to my response by suggesting that my observations today may be a bit existential. That is, Camus may be right when he said, 'It is normal to give away a little of one's life in order not to lose it all.' In 1972, I think I was a little more sensitive to what was going on around me than were my friends, but I wasn't one to share my feelings on matters. In those days, that was sort of a no-no for a male, one of those foolish norms of teenage society. Today, I'm not threatened by what I share. By being open and not lying or boasting, I can easily hold on to the truth. I guess I'm older, more seasoned, and more concerned with my own integrity than with the views of friends."

There was again a small smile on Allen's face. "What do you think, Investigator?"

There was a certain satisfaction in responding to Allen. They were not playing the interviewer versus interviewee game. They were having a conversation that went much deeper than an interview. "Perhaps you're right. The truth never really goes away. The question is always how to deal with it. Some would say it could be a love/hate relationship …"

"Odi et amo."

"Exactly. *I love, I hate.*" Van relished the exchange. He sensed Allen Mapleton did as well. The interaction was excessively intellectual, but it was also conversation that confirmed what each suspected about the other. No kudos needed.

"What was the other oddity, Investigator?"

"There's no record of you being interviewed in 1999 or anytime since."

"I was never contacted. I was a bit surprised. However, the fact that I wasn't interviewed was an indication to me that the case was once again growing cold. Remember, as a prosecutor, you occasionally have cold cases that suddenly grow hot again. But we both know it's a rare cold case that generates enough heat to overcome a cold trail that has iced over."

"So no one contacted you, and you didn't think it important to contact anyone after 1999."

"That is correct, Investigator. I assure you that if I had felt my contributions would have been useful, I would have done so. I knew that if the case was really back on track and headed toward a conclusion, I would be contacted. However, I also want to make it clear that my assessment today is that your cold case is being warmed up again by your approach."

"Meaning?"

"We both know your approach isn't conventional. You're not only interested in the facts that everyone else is already familiar with. You're interested in the milieu of emotions and behaviors behind the story—the *why* and not just the *what.*"

"And because of that, you would not hesitate to talk with me again should the need arise."

"Absolutely. I would even go so far as to say I look forward to it."

Van was confident Allen now trusted him as both an investigator and as someone with whom he could share openly. It was an opportunity Van could not pass up. "Perhaps then you will explain why you changed professions so abruptly."

Once again there was a contemplative look on Allen's face as he responded. "Investigator, earlier in our conversation, I noted you were caught off guard by my desire to not talk about why I left private practice and became a high school teacher and coach. I also know you were intrigued enough to have contacted a source who might explain why. But now I have gotten to know you as someone to keep personal what I'm about to tell you.

"When I worked in the DA's office I found it increasingly focused on political matters and not on the need to aggressively prosecute on behalf of the people. That's why I went into private practice. By most standards, it was a good move, and I did well. But life takes its toll if one has qualms and finds they're debating within the ethical issues. Does that make sense?"

Van said, "Such as the kind of case that finds you defending someone who runs counter to everything you stand for?"

"Yes, and more. Let me explain. I know enough about you that it's best if you hear it from me and not someone else.

"As you probably sensed in my earlier comments, I found Cindy intriguing. Had it not been for Carlos, it's conceivable that I would have asked her out. But that didn't happen, and life moved on, and I put it behind me until I was retained to defend someone who turned out to be repugnant. I won't violate attorney-client privilege, but let's just say that through several months of work and a long and emotional trial, I was haunted by thoughts of Carlos and Cindy. More than that, I kept seeing my own children in harm's way. I found it difficult to rationalize my position on the defense, and I knew that the kind of people I was defending would not think twice about revenge on my family if I should fail to get them acquitted."

"And you were successful?"

"Yes, but I knew I could never do it again. I was drained. I was scared. I knew I was good, but to what end? Fortunately, my wife came to the rescue. She knew that my heart was with helping people.

Not by defending illegal actions but by helping people improve so they would not need to be defended."

Departing Allen's house, Van anticipated the drive back across Los Angeles to Orange County would not be pleasant. The afternoon rush hour was already building.

No matter, he would use the time to think back over the interview. But first he needed to find some iced tea before getting back on the freeway.

———⟨⟨⟨———

Later, as Van thought back to his interview with Allen, he was reminded how critical interviews and follow-ups are. Time, experience, and reflection often provide insights not available to a witness at the time or soon after an event. Keith called it like he saw it, because in reality Keith had never really grown up much beyond high school. Annabel and Allen, on the other hand, had the benefit of college, graduate school, careers, and parenthood experiences that contributed a perspective based on a sense of reflection and efficacy.

He was on the right track. He had to continue to focus on the Cindy and Carlos relationship.

He also had to follow the line of thinking suggested by Felix. Somewhere in the lives of Cindy and Carlos was someone who knew them and wanted them dead.

He needed to take a closer look at the Ecology Club and the faculty and staff of Nuevo High School. The interviews suggested NHS was like a small town where few things remained hidden in 1972. And yet something was going on that involved Carlos and Cindy, and it went unnoticed by others.

Van was counting on the idea that what went unnoticed at the time did so because other students and teachers did not sense its importance.

It was time to turn his attention to the staff at Nuevo.

CHAPTER 20

INTERVIEWING PRINCIPAL JAY JENSEN

Palm Desert, California

A S EXPECTED, THE honeymoon in Homicide ended abruptly. The day following his interview of Allen Mapleton, the relative normalcy of the third floor changed dramatically. A multiple-homicide case dominated the department and the media for the next couple of weeks. At the time, Investigator Maris was out because of an emergency gallbladder operation, and Melinda Ochoa was on vacation. That meant that Van and the others had to double up to make things work.

Van had made an appointment to interview the retired principal of the Nuevo High School but had to cancel at the last minute. The Ashae case was on hold.

When he did get around to meeting with the retired principal, it was a month later.

—-m—

Jay Jensen had retired six years after Cindy's remains were found. He and his wife, also a retiring school principal, moved to Palm Desert, part of a number of retirement enclaves outside Palm Springs, California. The retirement to a gated community on a golf course had long been their goal; they could bike in the morning and golf in the afternoon.

Golden Sunset Hills included a PGA-sanctioned course, and security at the entrance gate was surprisingly tight. Though Van was expected, he had to show identification before being given a map with the route to Jay's home highlighted.

The house proved to be large and comfortable. The living area was spacious, and the view from the family room and kitchen looked directly past the pool and out to the golf course. In the distance were mountains that defined the parameters of the Coachella Valley. Van wondered if they had a golden hue at sunset as the community's name suggested.

Van and Jay sat down with iced tea in the shaded porch. Jay was tan, dressed casually, and seemingly relaxed beyond what Van normally encountered during interviews. No doubt Jay had many years of experience as both the interviewer and interviewee. He also appeared to be an extrovert but not an insecure one since Jay's pleasant nature was genuine and Jay did not feel the need to dominate a conversation.

Van reviewed his purpose and added, "At some point, I need to talk with teachers. As of now, I'm not sure which teachers I'll approach. Your input could be most helpful in that regard."

Jay set his iced tea aside. "Not a problem. Anything I can do to help. The case has always been a cloud over the school. Though solving the case will not change reality, I think closure could do much to remove that cloud."

"I suppose that's true. But first I want to just make sure I have the details correct regarding your tenure at the school. You started your career as a history teacher at Nuevo when it first opened in the fall of 1969." Van looked at Jay for confirmation.

"Correct. I taught all world history classes my first year. We had only freshmen. By 1971–72, I taught two honors US history classes and three world history classes. I also coached wrestling my first six years at the school."

"And you eventually became an assistant principal and then

principal of Nuevo in 1989. So that means you spent your whole career at Nuevo?"

"Yes. It's uncommon."

"Did you ever have Cindy and Carlos in class?"

"I didn't have Cindy. In fact, I didn't know her until the events of their disappearance. I had seen her but really didn't know her. I remember looking at a yearbook photo to see if she was who I thought. She was shy and quiet. If she wasn't in a teacher's class, she went unnoticed."

"And Carlos?"

"I had Carlos his freshman year. Everyone knew Carlos—popular, gregarious, and handsome."

"How was he as a student?"

"Average. Didn't take academics seriously, but he got by. Got a C grade each of the quarter grading periods for me."

"You remember that?"

"Under normal circumstances, probably not. But the repeated inquiries regarding Carlos have caused me to remember quite a lot of things I probably would otherwise have forgotten."

"You say everyone knew him. Did you have an opportunity to observe any changes in Carlos over the two years after he was in your class?"

"That's an interesting question because as a coach you tend to see and hear about students on multiple fronts. I think teachers are very aware of a student intellectually and perhaps to a limited extent socially. As a coach, you see other sides and hear things from other coaches and from athletes. Carlos wasn't a wrestler. He played football a couple of years, but his real skill was running. He was a distance runner. To some degree, Carlos was a coach's dream because the kid could run and had a competitive side to him. In ninth and tenth grade, he did well in track, and the coaches saw him as a future league champion in the mile and two-mile."

Van watched Jay closely and noticed the ease with which the former principal responded to the questions. Jay was a conversationalist.

"But something happened in the winter of 1972. Carlos had run cross-country in the fall and did well. But when track season rolled around, I remember the coach saying that Carlos seemed to lose his competitive edge and wasn't taking his potential seriously."

"His potential?"

"Yeah, Carlos had talent, but he seemed to lose interest. Someone said, I don't remember whether it was a coach or student, that Carlos was distracted. Later I heard he had a new girlfriend. I didn't know it was Cindy and really didn't pay attention. High school is filled with rumors and gossip, so you get used to it and often ignore it all. I had enough things to do and little time to worry about a student who wasn't in my classes and an athlete not on my team."

"Who was the track coach you mentioned?"

"Dan Alpers, a gruff, old-school coach. Came to NHS from another high school."

"He still around?"

"Retired in the eighties and moved back to Arkansas. He grew up there. I think I heard he passed away in the midnineties. He was much older than the rest of the coaches, and I think he had smoked for years. But I can check it out if you need me to."

"No. State Teachers Retirement System will know if he's deceased. I'll check. Let me come back to Carlos. So you never talked with Carlos about what you were hearing from others?"

"I'm sure I greeted him in passing and maybe even engaged in small talk, but no, I didn't discuss anything of substance with him. If he had been in my class, I probably would have taken the time to probe what was distracting him. But I didn't. As I said, I wasn't aware he was dating Cindy until they went missing."

"After the prom, did you hear any more about Carlos and his distractions or loss of interest in running, or loss of interest in any other endeavors?"

Jensen was quick to respond. "Officer, that school, community, and media were overflowing with gossip, rumors, hearsay, and half truths. It was a madhouse. Most of us teachers just wanted to close out the year and get away from it all. We were all interviewed by investigators, parents, media, and administrators. Summer was a welcome break. We had summer school, but I'm glad I didn't teach. I spent the summer camping with my family."

"So you didn't work the prom?"

"No, I did not. In a way, I'm thankful that I passed on the opportunity to work the prom. I don't mean to sound glib. Not working the dance saved me a lot of time in interviews and from the probing efforts of the media."

"Do you remember the time capsule being placed in 1973?"

"Very much so. I wasn't involved in the actual time capsule project. That was handled by the senior class officers, ASB adviser, and administration. But it was talked about a lot during the spring of that year. The actual assembly and placing the items in the capsule was a big deal."

"Did you notice anything peculiar in the days leading up to the burial of the capsule?"

"I've been asked that multiple times, and I've racked my brain for any recollections. The answer is *no*, nothing unusual."

"The ceremony took place on a Monday. Were you on campus that weekend before?"

"No."

"You weren't coaching or anything that would have had you on campus on the weekend?"

"Wrestling is a winter sport. There are times when I might have gone in on a Saturday morning to do some work. However, I didn't go in on the weekend in question."

Van moved on to 1999. "I know you've done this before, but could you share with me just how the remains of Cindy Ashae were discovered?"

Jay discussed the opening of the time capsule, but before he finished, Van interrupted.

"Excuse me, Jay. Before I forget, do you remember the prototype time capsule?"

"We all do. It was put on display for several weeks in the winter. Then it was removed, and the actual time capsule was built. I never saw it after that."

"Do you remember any discussion about the prototype or any questions about its whereabouts after the actual time capsule was laid?"

"No. I think all of us just assumed it had served its purpose and was discarded."

"Okay, thanks. Go on."

Jay described the reason for opening the time capsule early and the events of the day it was opened. He concluded by discussing how the lead custodian brought to Jay's attention the existence of the prototype and its contents.

"What was your reaction to the earring?"

"I'll never forget it. It was strange. When you have an experience like I did that day, certain images never leave your mind. To this day, when I notice a woman wearing a similar earring, I'm reminded of that earring, especially if there's a turquoise rock in the design."

"It's safe to say you never saw that earring before or after Cindy's remains were found?"

"Correct."

Van pulled out an envelope from his file.

"Jay, did you ever know a student named Phil Runcle?"

There was a pause of several seconds before Jay responded. He furrowed his forehead. Jay's demeanor changed a bit when Van handed him an enlarged copy of a senior class photo of Phil.

"Yes, but not at Nuevo. He was a big-time athlete at Alta Vista. Why?"

"He apparently knew Cindy and hung around with Carlos and some other Nuevo athletes."

"Not surprising. Many of the Nuevo and Alta Vista kids went to elementary and junior high school together. But most were not in Phil's league athletically. As I recall, Phil graduated a year earlier and went to Viet Nam where he was killed. It was a big deal in the community, and there were lots of articles about him and the return of his body to the States. Several years ago, I found his name on the wall in DC. It was sobering."

"Do you recall ever seeing Phil on the Nuevo campus?"

"Can't say that I do. My only recollections are that he almost singlehandedly demolished our football team and that he was killed in Nam."

"Thanks." Van put the photo away. "What can you tell me about the Ecology Club?"

"Oh yes, the E-Club. Big deal in the early seventies with Earth Day and the whole environmental awareness movement. I remember the first Earth Day, April 1970, I think. Big day on campus as I recall. All the young teachers and idealistic students got into the celebration. They buried an old combustion engine in one of the planters. When I retired, it was still there with a small plaque above. That old steel engine is probably nothing but a hunk of rust now. Why do you ask?"

There was a pause in Van's response. Something was odd, and he could not let go. Then it came to him. At Nuevo there seemed to be something ritualistic about burying things in the planters. Within a few short years, they buried a combustion engine and then a time capsule. What other things had been buried in planters?

"Well, the Ecology Club seems to have been Cindy's only activity. There are photos in the yearbooks with members of the club and their advisers. Cindy is in the '71 and '72 books. Carlos is not. However, I'm led to understand that in the spring of '72 Carlos got involved, and it was there that he first developed an interest in Cindy."

"That's interesting. I hadn't heard that. The club was popular and had lots of kids showing up for meetings as I recall. I'm not sure many kids really stuck with it."

"They apparently took a couple of field trips to Irvine Park. The last one Cindy participated in was in April, and Carlos was there as well."

"That does surprise me. It doesn't sound like his kind of thing."

"When you say it doesn't sound like his kind of thing, what does that mean?"

"Well, I guess my perception of Carlos was that he was more into sports, having fun, and living more in the moment. That he would be involved in something that was more cerebral, if you will, is not what I would have expected. Going to an E-Club meeting was probably not his idea. He was probably along for the ride. Then again, perhaps that was part of the distraction."

"So, the E-Club seems out of his sphere of interest, but you think it possible since there was the sense among others that Carlos was being distracted."

"It's possible, I guess. If the distractions facing Carlos speak to anything, they may suggest he was changing the way he saw the world around him. It's not uncommon for a seventeen-year-old who's about to become a senior to begin to sense the future as a bit daunting. It's sort of a crisis time for some kids who do not have a clue what the future holds and what they want to do. Maybe he was becoming conscious of the world around him and not just his own self-interests."

"An interesting comment. Similar comment was made by Allen Mapleton."

Smiling, Jay nodded. "Now there was a sharp kid. I think most of us always knew he would go on to bigger and better things. But I heard he's now an English teacher and football coach. Interesting how time changes things …" Jay's voice tapered off.

Van wanted to return to Cindy and Carlos, but before he did, he had to address a nagging thought. "Just out of curiosity, while you were at Nuevo in those early years, did they bury any other items in the planters besides the engine and time capsule?"

"No. In fact, I think those were the only things ever buried. Is that important?"

Van shook his head. "No, I was just wondering. Let's go back to Carlos and Cindy. I wonder if you can tell me a little about the E-Club advisers in these yearbook photos."

"Yes, the fellow on the far left in the back row is Duncan Erickson. He taught biology for about five years at Nuevo. Very smart, left in the midseventies and went back to get his PhD. Then went on to teach at the college level. Don't know how that all worked out."

"I see." Van made a mental note. He needed to check Duncan out.

"The other person is Andrea Simms. She was also a science teacher. She was young and I think, if I'm not mistaken, had a baby in the fall of 1971. Came back to the classroom late in the fall. I think these two teachers were most responsible for the club—the leaders if you will."

"As leaders, did they arrange for field trips like the ones to Irvine Park?"

"Oh yes. They would have had to get permission from administration, arrange for transportation, and take care of paperwork to make sure the trip was legitimate and supervised."

"Would there have been other teachers supervising on those trips?"

"Sure. The leaders of the club would have to make sure the ratio of supervisors to students was met. They probably got some other teachers to help out."

Van again reached into an envelope and removed a couple of photos. "Well, I have a couple of photographs here of an April 1972 Irvine Park outing, and I wonder if you can help me identify the people in the photo. I had them enlarged, so the quality isn't great." Van did not explain that the photos were part of the collection of items given to him by Muriel Fuentes.

The first photo was an informal shot of several students and Duncan. Students were gathered casually, and Cindy and Carlos were standing side by side with his arm on Cindy's shoulder. Jay pointed to the kids he remembered but said nothing distinctive about them.

The second photo was taken from a distance. There were several kids eating at a picnic table and waving at the camera. Cindy was in the picture but not Carlos. There was an adult walking some distance behind the picnic table. Beyond, there were several other people, but they were not distinguishable.

"Do you see anything of interest in this photo?"

"Well, many of the kids are the same ones in the previous photo, but most of the boys aren't in this photo. This is mostly girls." Jay started to hand the photo back and then took another look at the photo. "That's interesting. This side view of a person walking behind the table is a little out of focus, but if I had to guess, I'd say it looks like Allison Connors."

"Who was she?"

"Allison was an English teacher and a first-rate one at that. She taught at Nuevo for several years, until the mid or late seventies I think. I didn't know she was involved in the E-Club." There was a slight pause before Jay commented, "Different!"

Different, thought Van. It was a term that piqued his interest. People labeled *different* did the unusual. They were often not normal in the eyes of others. "Different in what way?"

"Well, she was very bright, probably the smartest and best-read teacher on the faculty. When I say bright, I mean none of us could hold a candle to her intellectually. She tended to be quiet and reserved, but beneath her outward appearance was an incredible intelligence and a remarkable athlete. She was not married when I knew her, but guys were interested in her."

"Did she date any other teachers?"

"Yes, but nothing serious developed. I think Allison scared men off because they couldn't compete with her intellectually or athletically."

"Was she involved with the Ecology Club?"

"Not that I recall, but the club was popular, and some teachers who were not actual club advisers would go to the meetings and, as this photo suggests, to the outings as well."

"Can you tell me anything more about Allison?" Van was intrigued. Allison was not normal.

"Mind you, it's sometimes not easy to separate the gossip from the facts when teachers talk among themselves about each other, but Allison was in a league of her own. I remember that it was a bit of a game among the staff to try and test her knowledge by casually raising a question about an obscure piece of literature."

"Can you give me an example?"

"Well, at the lunch table, someone might say something like, 'I was reading an article about Dante, and the author described Dante using a Latin phrase I can't translate. Does anyone know what it means?' Everyone would shrug their shoulders and look at Allison. Quietly, and matter of fact, Allison would translate."

"So she was good at languages."

"As I recall, she spoke French, Spanish, Italian, and Latin. But it was more than that; she was so well read. There was just no end to the breadth and depth of her knowledge and skills. If you made a list of the great books, she had probably read them all. I remember in the 1980s when Allen Bloom's book, *Closing of the American Mind,* came out and was critical of the modern university education. I was an assistant principal at the time, and there was a heated discussion in the lounge about the relevance of higher education. At one point, a member of the English Department, one of our brighter teachers who had been at NHS since the early seventies, spoke up with something like, 'Bloom obviously didn't interview Allison Connors because a state college had done well by her. She was so well read and smart she would have made Bloom look dumb.' People did not forget Allison; she was so smart, flat-out brilliant."

Allison Connors garnered Van's interest, and he sensed Jay knew it. He could appreciate how a super-smart person would gain the respect of colleagues in a high school. He also wondered what such a person was doing teaching in a high school.

"You said she was a good athlete as well."

"First-class runner if I'm not mistaken. Word was, and it may have just been a rumor, but some cross-country team members saw her running once, and they were so startled by her performance that they couldn't wait to tell everyone how good she was. It was strange; Allison refused to talk about it. Would not even consider coaching track or cross-country ..."

It looked to Van like Jay was remembering something else. "Anything else about Allison?"

"Yes. As I recall, she was also a backpacker. Some kids wanted her to sponsor a backpacking club, but she wouldn't. The word was she spent her vacations hiking in the Sierra."

"Did she go with other teachers?"

"No, Allison was a loner. She did all of her running and hiking alone."

"I see." Van did not let on, but the red flag went up on Allison.

The term *loner* piqued his interest. She was *different*, and she was a *loner*. She *backpacked* alone at a time when Van did not think that was common practice. *Different, loner, backpacker*, Allison was unique. Individually, the three terms were harmless. In Van's line of work, the terms together suggested people of interest, if not suspects.

Van was also wondering why he could not remember any notes from interviews of Allison by Vargas and Damon. Had he missed the notes? No, he was certain she had not been interviewed. He paused and made a note to that effect. It was something he had to check out.

"Do you recall any other special qualities about Allison besides her intellect, athletic talent, and her skill as a teacher? Let me clarify. Is there anything else that you think would help me understand what made her different?"

"Not really."

"Did this Allison have any teacher friends she was especially close to?"

"No, but she was friendly. When I say she was a loner, it doesn't mean she didn't have friends and stayed by herself all the time. She ate in the lunchroom often, went to faculty activities, and contributed as needed. But she didn't have close friends among her colleagues. But it was a long time ago, so I can't really say whether she had friends outside NHS."

Van was about to end the interview when a final question occurred to him. "Jay, would you say Allison was strong?"

"Strong as in overall body strength?" Van nodded. "Not sure. I would say she was fit, not an ounce of fat on her, and that her legs were powerful ..."

"Her arms, her torso?"

"Not especially. She was tall, and her arms, like her legs, long. But my recollection is that she was very agile, her arms and shoulders trim but not muscular."

"If you think back to those early years at the school, was there anything else you remember regarding Allison Connors? Did she have any problems? Where there any issues? Was there anything that stands out about her that you haven't mentioned?"

"No, everyone liked Allison because she was just incredibly smart and never really lorded that over anyone. She was kind of humble with her smarts."

"One last question. Again, going back to 1972, was there any teacher on campus who you could say did not like kids or who had conflicts with kids?"

"No, Investigator, that's one of the questions I was asked in 1972, and my answer then and now is no. I have thought many times about that question, but always the answer is no."

—m—

Van stayed for a short lunch. He had what he came for. He was eager to get back to the office and check out Allison Connors. He had records on all the teachers at the school in 1972. He also had yearbooks, and certainly her photo must be in the yearbook.

Van long ago learned not to get one's hopes up when uncovering things of interest in an investigation. But something inside said Allison's characteristics were outside the norm, and people like her often had a closet of experience that was also outside the realm of the normal person. They behave differently.

More importantly, why had she never been interviewed? Van was increasingly certain that her name was not among those interviewed in 1972.

CHAPTER 21

EMILY CALDERÓN

Homicide Office and Temecula, California

VAN WAS SPENDING another Saturday in his office trying to catch up.

Returning to his office after retrieving a cup of ice, Van emptied a pint of brewed tea into the cup. He took a long drink and then set the cup down on the coaster—an unconscious habit instilled by his wife many years ago and never forgotten. There was evidence of a hard-learned lesson on an expensive coffee table in his living room.

He retrieved the stack of Ashae-Fuentes materials from the file cabinet and moved it to his desk. Sitting down, Van picked up the yellow legal pad on the top of the stack and began to read through his notes. He flipped through many pages and realized it was time to consolidate.

A visual learner, Van had developed a technique in college that allowed him to move from written notes to a capsulated representation of the contents. He called it *funneling*. Whether he started with notes or the highlights and underlining in his texts, he would first create a succinct narrative outline of the information. Then he would shrink that down to bulleted points under major headings. Finally he would condense the headings and bulleted items into an even more focused list of key impressions. In the end, he would have what amounted to a flow chart of information. It was a graphically organized set of concepts.

The information could be studied by focusing on the key concepts and links between them. A scaffold of facts, ideas, data, and other items in the narrative backed each concept. Van had also discovered, quite by accident, that when he engaged this process, he found himself vocalizing his thinking. Anna Marie used tell him to talk more softly to himself. As a result, when Van engaged this process, he usually tried to make sure the door was closed.

After a few minutes of scanning the pages, he scooted his chair up to the desk and began the funneling process by typing out updated information. He started with Emily Calderón.

The 1972 interviews of students included one of Cindy's friends, Emily Calderón. Emily's family moved in 1975, and Van was not able to easily locate her. Eventually county records helped him track down Emily's older brother, who had been the executor of his parents' estate. Through him, Van finally located Emily.

Emily had gone to Fullerton Junior College, but she had not completed her AA degree. Instead, she took a job working for the Parks and Recreation Department of a local city. Eventually she went back to school and earned a bachelor's degree in recreation. That led to her current director of parks position for one of the newer cities along the Interstate 215 corridor in southern Riverside County.

Contrary to the meek and diminutive person portrayed by Mrs. Ashae, Emily was a successful woman working in the public sector. She was a mother, her husband managed a retail electronics store, and the family, by most standards, was middle class. They lived in what was called the Inland Empire. The latter referenced the San Bernardino and Riverside County cities that bordered on the Los Angeles Basin.

Van had fought the afternoon rush-hour traffic leaving Orange County and headed out toward the sea of homes in the Inland Empire.

It was late afternoon, and Emily was staying at work because there was a city council meeting that evening and she was required to attend. The interview was in her office.

Emily was really Cindy's only close friend in the year or two before Cindy hooked up with Carlos. She had told Damon that when Carlos came into Cindy's life, she had tried to maintain her friendship with Cindy, but it became increasingly difficult. Now, years later, she shared with Van that before Carlos, she and Cindy studied together, ate lunch together, watched television, and talked about boys. In those ways, it was a typical teenage girl friendship.

"I noticed your photo along with Cindy's in the 1971 and 1972 yearbook section devoted to the Ecology Club. Did you go to the meetings together?"

"Yes. Cindy and I got interested in the club as sophomores because we loved our science teacher. The teacher treated us like sisters. We liked that. But I would also say our teacher introduced us to the concept of environmental problems. It was a classic example of the liberal influence of teachers." Van sensed the use of *liberal* was not pejorative. Emily was just clarifying the influential power of progressive teachers. *Passion breeds passion.*

"I've seen photos of the Irvine Park outings. You're in those photos with Cindy. What did you think of those outings?"

"Best thing to happen to me. Changed my life."

"Changed your life?" Van raised his eyebrows; it was a definitive and unusual statement.

Emily noticed his reaction. "Investigator, I'm doing what I do today because Irvine Park impressed me. I knew I wanted to work in parks. I was young and naive, so my goals at the time were really pie-in-the-sky ideals, but they shaped my future nonetheless, as you can see."

"How did Cindy respond to all of this?"

"She was way ahead of me."

"Meaning?" Van knew he was showing surprise. It was purposeful. He long ago realized that the stoic-police-detective approach, although it had value in many interviews, was not as valuable in the unconventional conversational interview. If the interviewee senses the interviewer is exhibiting human reactions, then the willingness to converse is enhanced.

"Well, when we met as freshmen, Cindy and I were very much alike. I'm sure you know we were shy, withdrawn, awkward in social settings, quiet, and easily intimidated. But by the middle of our sophomore year, Cindy began talking about how society didn't respect the environment and that our generation needed to do something about it. I agreed, but I wasn't one to go out on point. Cindy, on the other hand, began to speak up."

"At the Ecology Club meetings, you mean?"

"Yes, and in our junior year, I felt like I was just following her lead. She was still shy, quiet, and reserved, but to me and a couple of others, she would surprise us by saying we needed to get more active in the ecology movement."

"Did things change when Carlos entered the picture?"

"Almost overnight. I couldn't figure it out then. Think I have a better handle on it now. Carlos began to attend the meetings. He would sit near Cindy and want to be in her discussion groups. None of us could figure that out. He could have dated any girl on campus, and he was interested in one of our kind. He started hanging around her during the school day and even went on some of the club outings."

Van sought some clarification.

"When he asked her to the prom, I was flabbergasted. I know others were too. She wasn't his type. At least that's what I thought at the time. It was only years later that it occurred to me that we were all growing up, and the innocence of earlier years was giving way to the realities of a future that was clouded in controversy. You know, environmental issues, Viet Nam, civil rights, and the eighteen-year-old right to vote. I think some, like Cindy, were growing up faster and leaving people like me in the dust. Her level of consciousness was ahead of mine."

Van asked if she thought Cindy's consciousness regarding boys was also changing.

"I've wondered about that as well. We always talked about boys.

All girls did. You know, who was good-looking, who we liked, and all those conversations young and inexperienced girls have about the mysteries of boys. But in our wildest dreams, neither Cindy nor I nor any of our friends could ever imagine someone like Carlos would take an interest in us. When he began to show an interest in Cindy, we couldn't believe it. Then the not believing gave way to suspicions. What was Carlos really interested in?"

Emily did not answer her own question, so Van asked it again. "What did you think was happening? What do you think Carlos was interested in?"

"What all of us were interested in. The bittersweet relationships between male and female."

"Bittersweet, meaning?"

"Relationships for teenagers are seldom always smooth. We wanted to be liked by boys, but being liked had its challenges. Kind of like marriage. You gotta work at it, I guess … You know what I mean, Officer?"

"So you think Cindy was also interested in Carlos?"

"I think Cindy was further along on the maturity curve than the rest of our friends. She was on the receiving end of someone's interest in her, something none of us had experienced. Carlos was the reason, and Cindy seemed to be interested."

"I've heard conjecture that Cindy was naive and Carlos was only interested in what he might get from a girl not wise to the ways of experienced boys. What would you say to that thinking?"

"You know, Investigator, you certainly have an ability to lead one to the heart of a conversation quickly and cleverly."

Van felt a little embarrassed by the retort. "I assure you I have been accused of not being direct enough and dancing around a subject too long before asking the hard questions."

Emily smiled. "Anyway, I don't know if Cindy realized she may have been the object of desire. Certainly, one would think she must have felt something was going on."

"Did she ever say anything about Carlos's interest in her to you?"

"Not to me. No, I've always thought that strange because girls often will share with a close friend things they won't share with others. But I think she did talk with someone else."

Van was immediately aware he was hearing something for the first time. Emily had not said this to Vargas or any of the other detectives. Perhaps they had not asked the question the way he had. "Can you tell me who that might have been?"

"Well, I know she knew this guy who went to her church but didn't go to our high school. Can't remember his name. But she sometimes talked with him about things, but I honestly don't know if he was the one she talked with. Probably not since he was a boy. I just don't know."

Normally Van would not suggest a name, but Emily suggested the person did not go to Nuevo, so he asked, "Was his name Phil Runcle, a student at Alta Vista?"

"Phil, yeah that sounds familiar, but I don't know the last name. I never met him. But really, I don't know. The name Phil is familiar, but I just don't know. I can't picture him."

"So, how is it you remember Phil?"

"I'm not sure. I just remember his first name being mentioned. At the time, I thought it strange that Cindy knew someone who went to another school."

"Did Cindy share with you her conversations with Phil?"

"Oh, no. But I do remember she said Phil knew Carlos. But I can't be sure of what she said. I think it was all a mystery to me then and now."

Van tried a different approach. "Who else could Cindy have talked with? Other friends?"

"One of the English teachers, probably Miss Connors." When Van leaned in, Emily asked, "You know her?"

Van caught himself. *Go slow*, he told himself. "I remember the name as I do many of the teachers. What can you tell me about her? Go on."

"I don't know for sure if she talked to Connors, but I know Cindy liked her because she wasn't like other teachers. Connors liked the outdoors, hiking, and things. Also had a reputation of treating every student equally. There was no favoritism in her classes. Cindy once told me that if she ever needed advice, she was going to go to Miss Connors. I don't know if she talked to Connors about Carlos, but I've always had a strong feeling that she did have that conversation."

"I would remember if you had said something to the investigators in 1972 or 1999. My recollection is you did not."

"I guess I didn't then."

"Could anyone confirm a conversation took place between Cindy and this Miss Connors?"

"Probably not. None of the other girls were as close to Cindy as I was. We grew apart a little when Carlos came into her life, but even then I was the only friend she continued to talk with. Over the years, we had confided in each other, and I never betrayed that confidence, so we remained good friends. I didn't even talk behind her back about Carlos, and she knew that. Our relationship wasn't strained by Carlos; it just took a second place to Carlos."

"What makes you say that?"

"Well, Cindy always said she was careful to not hurt her mother. She was the only one of my friends whose parents were divorced, and I knew her mother was very protective. Cindy said several times that she wished she had a father who was close to her because it was difficult to have only a mother to share with. So Cindy shared things with me, and maybe Connors."

There it is, thought Van. *A chink in the armor.* Kids can be very close to parents and talk freely with them about most anything. But there are some issues that test such a relationship.

"And you think Cindy might have had a close communication with Miss Connors?"

"Yes, and on a few occasions, Cindy stayed after class to talk alone with Miss Connors."

"Why didn't you share this with earlier investigators?"

"They didn't ask. Miss Connors was a positive and not a negative."

What he was hearing was testimony to the art of good interviewing. Often the questions not asked were as important, if not more important, than those on which the interviewer was focused.

The art was to have a conversation and not just a question-and-answer session.

—〰—

The interview with Emily was another contribution to Van's theory that student insights, all these years aside, were a crucial component in any effort to understand what happened prom night. It did not mean that Carlos and Cindy could have avoided what happened or that anyone could have anticipated what would happen. It did suggest that somewhere in the context of all of this was a piece of the puzzle that would point the finger at a suspect. One just had to keep people's thoughts on the table with the hopes that at some point some insights were in the mix.

Jay Jensen had first mentioned Allison Connors. Now Emily had done so. Soon after his conversation with Emily, Van had talked again with Mrs. Ashae, but she was unfamiliar with Connors and said she would have remembered if Cindy had mentioned any attachment to a teacher. Van had also called Keith and Allen to inquire whether Carlos had ever mentioned Allison Connors. Keith remembered Connors but never had her for a class and had no opinion.

Allen remembered her as intelligent. He had her for sophomore English for a semester before a schedule change moved him to another teacher second semester. Allen's summary was to the point. "She was disarmingly intelligent. I never had a fairer, more demanding, or more intellectual high school teacher. In one semester in her class, I learned more about how to read and discuss a book than in all other classes combined. It has served me well ever since."

Could Allen ever remember if Connors advised or counseled students on problems? Allen could not, but he said that he was confident that if a student sought out Connors for advice, the student would be lucky because it was likely Connors would have provided guidance of the "… most cogent quality. I cannot imagine Connors pussyfooting around an issue."

"She was a straight shooter?"

"Always."

"So, if you did not have a thick skin or could not handle hearing what you may not want to hear, she was someone you probably would not take your troubles to."

"That would be my take on her."

—⚭—

Background info on Connors was limited. What he gathered provided a profile of someone indeed outside the norm, but there was nothing to suggest someone who would commit murder. There was a big leap from being different and an introvert and being capable of committing two murders. No doubt there were other teachers with qualities suggesting they be regarded as suspects. He had to keep an open mind, but it was not easy.

As yet, any conclusion about Allison Connors was just conjecture.

One puzzling fact was that Allison's name was Allison A. Connors, and Van had not yet been able to determine what the middle initial stood for. In the school district records, county, college, and State Teacher Retirement System records, and any other records his staff were able to locate listed only a middle initial.

On the other hand, Connors seemed to have disappeared, and Van thought it strange that someone so intelligent would simply drop off the radar. The Unabomber was a loner, an extreme introvert, very intelligent, and he went missing. It happens. But not everyone who drops out of society is capable of criminal activity. Some just want to change their life, seek solitude. He would continue to try to track down Connors.

—⚭—

Later in the afternoon. Van read over his completed outline.

Somewhere in all of this, he thought, *is the motive.* Cindy and Carlos were killed by someone or some people who knew them. Something in the strange relationship between these two seventeen-year-old high school juniors is at the root of a reason to kill them. *The term strange is appropriate,* he thought, *because everywhere I turn, someone is remembering that theirs was an unexpected relationship,* and the two changed even as the world around them remained the same.

It had occurred more than once to Van that the Ashae-Fuentes case could be likened to an operatic or Shakespearian tragedy. It was rooted in emotions, personalities, and intrigue. Was there someone who found their relationship unacceptable and would kill to prevent it from going farther? Was their demise a result of envy?

Was this oddity of a relationship sufficient enough that a friend or friends could have sought to put an end to it? But why kill both? Was someone jealous enough to kill both?

No, there was a purpose to their deaths, and that purpose was wrapped up in the relationship of the two. The time capsule was the proof. There was a calculated emotion behind the killing and the placement of Cindy's remains, along with the earring, in the capsule. It confirmed the provincial nature of the murder and the familiarity of the murderer with the school environment. The murderer or murderers were somehow connected to the school. Was it a student, classified staff, teacher, administrator, parent, or community member connection? Van's gut said staff or teacher or administrator or a combination of the three.

He faced two tasks. He had to go to Nuevo and familiarize himself with the school. And he must keep looking for the whereabouts of Allison A. Connors.

CHAPTER 22

INTERVIEWING TEACHERS

California and Massachusetts

INTERVIEWING MEMBERS OF the Nuevo staff of 1972 proved far more challenging than Van had anticipated. Of necessity he focused on a handful of teachers he felt could provide some insight because they were at the time members of the English, history, and science departments or worked at the prom. Science teachers, with the assistance of some history department members, seemed to be leaders of the Ecology Club. Interviewing them made sense. He would start with these groups and go beyond if needed.

Van reasoned that since students had an English class every year, it was possible those teachers best knew the two students. Also, because of his interest in Allison, an English teacher, Van hoped for some insight into her personality.

There was no hope of interviewing Carlos's coaches because they were all deceased. Van also realized that although many in the staff were young when the school opened, about half of the teachers had previously taught at other schools in the district before coming to Nuevo. They were older by many years than the new teachers. He could only hope a sufficient number of former teachers were still around. Those older in 1972 may have a different perspective than those who were young and new to the profession at the time.

Based on input from Jay Jensen, Van had identified four English teachers as good candidates because they had worked with Allison and, according to Jay, seemed to have a good relationship with her. As for the E-Club, only one of the two science teachers involved was still around, Andrea Simms. Van had not yet located Duncan Erickson, the coleader of the club. Andrea taught at Nuevo for thirty-seven years, retiring in 2006 as the chair of the Science Department. After retiring, she moved to Oregon.

Most of the history teachers in 1972 had been older at the time. Besides Jay Jensen, Van was able to locate only one other teacher who had been young at the time, Brandon Naysmith. Jay said Brandon was single in the early years of the school and thought Brandon and Allison had dated. Brandon was very bright in his own right and was thought to be the only teacher close to Allison's intellectual level. The relationship between Brandon and Allison did not work out, but Jay thought the two harbored no animosity toward each other. Brandon left Nuevo in the mid-1970s and was now working at an exclusive prep school in New England.

—⟋⟍⟍—

Of the four English teachers recommended by Jay, Joanne Enright lived in Orange County.

Joanne and her husband, Earl, were childhood sweethearts and grew up on farms in Iowa. They were married in 1965 and moved to California. Joanne joined the staff of Nuevo High School in 1969. The teacher in the adjacent classroom was Allison Connors.

Allison and Joanne were the youngest teachers in the department, though Joanne had three more years of teaching experience than Allison.

Van met with Joanne at the home she and Earl had built in the hills on the northern border of Orange County. Introductory remarks and a cup of tea dispensed with, Van turned to the purpose of his visit. "As I noted in our phone conversation, I'm working on the case of Cindy Ashae and Carlos Fuentes. I know you were interviewed in 1972 and again in 1999. I've had an opportunity to look over the results of those interviews and noted that you taught both Cindy and Carlos. I know you told Investigator Vargas that you knew the two students were, in your words, *going together*, and you knew they were going to the prom."

Joanne nodded.

"I was wondering, how it was that you knew they were going together?"

"You know, Investigator, that was a long time ago, so I'm not certain my memory today is as good as it was then, but I'll tell you what I think was on my mind at the time." Joann paused as if collecting her thoughts before going on. "I never had the two in class at the same time, but I had Cindy in ninth and eleventh grades. I had Carlos in tenth grade. Cindy I knew as a quiet, respectful, competent, hardworking student. Carlos I knew as the kind of kid that made you want to just hug him. He was not a great student, but he had a personality that was friendly to all."

"When you say Cindy was competent, does that imply she got good grades?"

"I would say she was a solid B student."

"And Carlos?"

"A C student when he worked."

"When did you notice they were a couple?"

"Probably in the spring of 1972, two or three months before the prom maybe."

"I want to come back to your recollection of when they first became a couple to you. But before doing so, what do you remember about Cindy in your class that semester?"

"Cindy was changing. When I first met her as a student in the fall of ninth grade, she was still a little girl. She was a shy, cautious, and unassuming girl, behind the developmental curve physically. By the fall of her junior year, she was maturing quickly. In the scope of several months, I saw the signs that she was transforming into a woman. Don't misunderstand me. She was still shy and was still dressing like a little girl, but her body and her looks and her features were changing."

"Did you sense the boys noticed the change?"

"No, I don't think they did. Maybe later. You see, I knew she was changing, but most of the boys, and other girls for that matter, were operating on earlier perceptions. Cindy had been viewed for so long as being a bit unsophisticated and withdrawn and, if I can use an old-fashioned word, a bit *frumpish,* and most kids didn't notice the changes."

"Did it surprise you that Carlos took an interest in her?"

"Oh, yes. Carlos was liked by all the girls and had a reputation of being sort of a lady's man if you will. I think most people were surprised."

"But looking back, you say Cindy was changing. Was it the kind of change that would eventually attract boys?"

"Yes. You know, there are many girls out there who are late in developing. They go into high school well behind the curve, and they come out way ahead of the curve. In four years, they go from being backward and homely to exhibiting some style and grace. I'm not saying that's what was happening to Cindy, but I'm saying she was changing significantly and would be a woman well beyond what someone could have imagined on seeing her as a freshman."

"I want to go back to the relationship between Carlos and Cindy in the spring of 1972. How did you learn they were a couple?"

"Well, I don't recall all the details, but my recollection is that I first learned of their relationship from an offhand comment by another student who expressed surprise that Carlos Fuentes had taken an interest in Cindy. I think this remark was made somewhat derogatorily in a comment to another student by a girl in the English class where Cindy was a student at the time. My recollection is that I overheard what was said and suggested to the girl that she ought to keep her views to herself."

"That was a long time ago. Why do you think you remember that incident?"

"I probably remember it because once the prom night disappearance took place, I, like many others, went back over the previous months of memories, and that in-class incident came to the surface. I'm sure that's why today I remember those two and have forgotten a lot of other students and things that happened then."

"So, after that, did you notice this relationship any other times?"

Joanne smiled. "Oh yes. One day when I arrived to class just before the tardy bell rang, I found Cindy just outside the door talking to Carlos. It was a first. I had not previously seen them together. My initial response was to tell Carlos he needed to get moving or he was going to be late to his class. Carlos left immediately. After class, Cindy came up and apologized and said something like, 'It won't happen again, Mrs. Enright.' I thanked her and then noticed a smile and radiance in Cindy's presence that I hadn't seen before. I knew at that moment Cindy's world was really changing."

"But you were still surprised that Carlos asked her to the prom."

"Yes, I was surprised since he could have probably asked just about any girl. However, I was not surprised that he would be attracted to Cindy. She was far from developing into the young lady I think would have been her destiny, but she was no longer a little girl. The transformation was underway, and any young male student worth his salt would have sensed what was happening. Many of the popular girls on campus were already there. Cindy was just now moving toward her peak, and I dare say she would have exceeded them."

Van knew Joanne Enright was an ideal interviewee. She went beyond the yes and no answers and provided insights to her observations. It was not a simple matter of memory. She had thought enough about Cindy and Carlos over the years that Joanne's insights were the result of reflection.

"Were there any other occasions where you observed the two?"

"One other time, a few weeks later in the library. It was lunch, and I was in there looking for a book in the stacks when I noticed Cindy sitting alone at one of the tables in a back corner. I thought about going over to her once I found the book I was looking for. But a few minutes later, Carlos arrived and took a seat next to her. It seemed they were having a private conversation, so I decided to not interrupt and went to check out the book."

"And they were sitting alone?"

"Oh yes. There were lots of students studying during lunch, but Cindy and Carlos were alone at one small table. But it was my observation of Carlos that has stuck with me."

There was a hint of a smile on Joanne's face. "You see, Investigator, I may have been a young teacher from the Iowa farms, but I could spot a boy on the prowl just as easy as spotting a dog in heat. They may have been talking, but Carlos couldn't keep his eyes off her cleavage. The top button was undone, and he was ogling for all it was worth."

"Did they see you?"

"No, thank goodness. I think I found it humorous and have often wondered whether Cindy acted purposefully and was teasing Carlos. I really don't know, but my instincts told me she had not yet acquired that level of sophistication. On the other hand, she may have been well aware of what she was doing and was trying out a new technique, if you will."

Joanne paused. Van was content to wait. "Listen, I don't know where Cindy was in that equation, but I have no doubt Carlos was turned on. His hormones had to be surging."

Van enjoyed Joanne's frankness. She said it as she saw it. "I appreciate your insight and candor. It tells me a lot about the two. Let me change the focus away from Carlos and Cindy and toward your colleagues. I'm sure you know that now, decades later, the case is very cold. However, I'm trying to approach it from a different direction by exploring the long-term insights of students and faculty."

He was well aware that as soon as he mentioned Allison's name, the tenor of the conversation would change because the focus would not be on just a colleague. Joanne would immediately conclude that Allison must be under consideration as a suspect. He decided to be as discreet as possible. He could not prevent Joanne from drawing conclusions.

"I'm trying to get some background information on teachers who had Cindy and Carlos as students. That has proved to be a difficult task, as the whereabouts of many is unknown. Some have passed away. So I have to ask colleagues for input regarding teachers I haven't been able to interview.

"One person I haven't been able to locate is Allison Connors, who occupied the room next to you. What do you remember about her?"

"Oh, boy, I haven't thought about Allison for many years. But I think Cindy had been in Allison's English class as a sophomore."

"Yes, she was. But I assure you I wouldn't be asking except that I would like to talk with her and haven't been able to find her. Anything you can tell me about your memory of Allison would be appreciated."

"Allison Connors was the brightest person I have ever met. I'm not exaggerating. The brightest ever! She defined what it would mean to be a card-carrying Mensa. She was the brilliant intellectual. I suppose, though, unlike most brilliant people, she could teach."

"Meaning?"

"Allison belonged in teaching but at the university level where serious students could benefit from her brilliance. She was way overqualified for our school."

"Did you know her well?" Van already knew that Jay had suggested as much.

"Probably better than most, though that's not saying much. I don't think any of us really ever got close to Allison. I probably knew her better than others, but you know how it is when you know someone because you work with them, but you really don't know them on any other level."

"Did she ever talk about herself?"

"I suppose a little but not much. Actually, probably a better answer is *no*. Allison had a mysterious side to her. She didn't talk about herself, so you had to kind of put the pieces of the puzzle together from different conversations."

Van asked, "And your colleagues would agree with your assessment?"

"Yes. Allison was intelligent beyond any of us, and she tried to be one of us, but we were all just tolerant because we really couldn't hold a candle to her intellect. Brandon, in the History Department, came close to her level, but even he wasn't in her league."

"Brandon Naysmith?"

"Yes, I remember that for a couple of years he was interested in Allison. They both spoke French and Italian. They were both voracious readers. But Brandon got frustrated."

"Frustrated? Why?"

"I don't know the whole story. I once asked Allison what she thought of Brandon. I knew they had gone out but couldn't really figure out whether anything came of it."

"How did she respond to your inquiry?"

"It was peculiar. Let me think … I don't want to misrepresent what she said even though I have often thought it peculiar." Van waited the seconds Joanne needed.

"Mind you, I'm not quoting, but her response was something like, 'He's okay but sees himself to be more important than he is.' I'm sure it was something like that. But she followed up by saying, 'He talks only about his father, like his father was some kind of adventuresome Hemingway. He despises his mother, who never went to college.' Yes, it was something like that. I figured it was more than I wanted to know."

Joanne hesitated, then went on. "We all knew Brandon as a bit egotistical anyway. Bright but all about himself. Very narcissistic I'd say."

"And Allison, was she egotistical?"

"No, never. She couldn't avoid exhibiting her brilliance. We all marveled at it and wanted to see it in action, but she never talked about herself. Her intelligence was what it was, and Allison never exhibited a sense of superiority. Sort of ironic, don't you think?"

Van nodded. He appreciated that Joanne didn't try to suggest she could quote Allison. Joanne was only suggesting the tenor of Allison's comments. "Did you know Brandon well?"

"We all did. He couldn't keep his mouth shut. Always trying to let people know how smart he was. Turned us all off, I suppose."

"Did Allison ever talk about her family or about growing up?"

"Investigator, Allison never focused on herself. As I said, she was much different than most people in that regard."

"Did she talk about students?"

"You know, I don't ever remember her overly praising a student or being overly critical of one. She was an excellent teacher, and that was her focus."

"What about her backpacking? Did she talk about it?"

"Not really. Like I said, she didn't talk about herself. We knew she backpacked, and we knew that she ran, but I don't think anyone ever saw her do either or talk about either."

"Sounds a bit boring. What did she talk about?"

"Believe it or not, Allison liked to discuss issues such as how to teach higher cognitive thinking skills within the subject content. She was all about teaching kids to read, think, write, and question. Allison wanted students to think critically."

"That's it? Sounds a bit pedantic for ongoing conversation."

"I don't think so. We could also have discussions about the literature, politics, the environment, even movies, I suppose, and any number of issues, but she was not judgmental. There was very little she was not well versed on, but she was not opinionated. She knew the content, the questions, the issues, the problems, but she was not given to passing judgment. If you asked her to express a viewpoint or tried to get her to take a position, she would turn the request around and pose it as more of a general conundrum or another question."

"You said she was well versed on the environment. What does that mean to you?"

"Long before it was popular, I think Allison was already aware that the world was altering its environment at an alarming rate and the consequences would be disastrous if nothing was done."

The reference to Allison's environmental consciousness weighed on Van's perceptions of Allison and the spacious area around the burned VW van.

"But you said she didn't share opinions."

"She didn't have to. When the discussion would come up, she would merely cite some statistical information or express the findings of some lofty research study. If asked to support her statements, she would cite the sources as the experts, never her own opinion."

"Allison Connors sounds almost too good to be true. Everything you say about her suggests someone a bit eccentric, someone people would regard as arcane."

"I told you at the start she was brilliant and like nobody I have ever known. I suspect most of the staff had nothing but respect for her."

"Did it surprise you that she left the school in 1978?"

"No, it didn't. Allison was different. When I say she was an enigma, I guess I'm saying that her intellectual complexity was such that the normal world wasn't easy for her. I remember asking her where she was going after she left Nuevo, and she said something like, 'It's time to move on.' I have often thought she was a little like the classic stoic. She separated logic and emotions. She was a bit transcendental. It was simply time to move on."

—⁕—

As he drove down the winding road from Joanne's home, her parting words came back to him. "You know, Investigator, memories are a double-edged sword. Ninety-nine percent of them are fond memories of my teaching days; only 1 percent are negative experiences such as the loss of Cindy and Carlos. Unfortunately, that 1 percent often overshadow the other memories. And here you are chasing the 1 percent and asking us all to dredge up unwanted memories. Quite a profession you have."

Looking back on the interview with Joanne Enright, Van was struck by the fact that Joanne could work every day beside Allison for several years and be the one person in the school who knew Allison the best and, even so, really not know Allison. It seemed beyond reasonable.

Van could only conclude that Allison worked hard to be an unknown, to be a teacher and colleague in name only. Could it be Allison knew all along that she was destined to a future of anonymity? Was it essential that she be aloof in order to get to that destiny?

But why be a teacher? Why even work? Van figured that for some reason Allison needed to work for a given period of years. Was it to earn a sufficient amount of money so that she would not have to work again? Or did she need the years to pass while she prepared to disappear for good? Or was she one of those people who was always searching, never satisfied?

—⟶⟶—

The interview with Brandon Naysmith was conducted by phone.

Brandon was the headmaster at a private prep school in Massachusetts. He left Nuevo to teach at a local community college in 1976. While there, he went back to school and earned his PhD in history. In 1982, he moved to Illinois to take a position as a history professor at a small liberal arts college where he rose to the position of dean. In 1997, Brandon became the headmaster at Great Northern Prep, an old institution well known for preparing students of New England bluebloods for life in the Ivy League schools.

Brandon's provenance and Joanne's warnings gave Van reason to suspect that the interview would not be easy. It was not. Brandon was arrogant and played the intellectual role. He was distant and noncommittal.

Van was curious about Brandon's relationship with Allison. Any effort, however, to get Brandon to talk about his experiences with Allison met with evasive and dismissive responses.

"Look, Investigator, that was a long time ago. I dated a lot of women and, as you already know, never married. So I'm sure you can understand that Allison Connors was just one of them. In fact, we only went out a few times, and it was never anything serious, I assure you."

"I've heard that other teachers thought the two of you had something going since you were both the resident intellectuals." Van played the complimentary card to suggest that Brandon was not alone with the title.

"Actually, Allison was really very limited in her knowledge and understanding of the world. Sure, she was very well read, but she didn't have the background or experience needed to see the wider implications and extrapolate on their potential."

For Van, the response was classic ego talking. There was no way Brandon was going to admit what everyone else at the school knew— that Allison was head and shoulders above him intellectually. Of course, Brandon had forty years to convince himself that he was her superior.

"Did Allison ever share anything about her family, her past, her goals in life?"

The self-centered edge was clear as Brandon spoke. "Listen, we went out a couple of times. We didn't share our lives. We hardly knew each other. She really didn't have much to talk about, so I initiated our discussions. I assure you, our conversations were very one-sided."

What Allison had told Joanne was confirmed. Brandon did not have much good to say about Allison because Brandon did not have much good to say about any female. Brandon was bright, but he was all about himself. Little wonder he never married.

It seemed to Van that a different approach might work, so he prefaced his question with a compliment. "I wonder, Dr. Naysmith, if you could help me understand some comments made by others about Allison. You probably knew her as well as anyone at Nuevo, so your observations could help me clarify some things." Van did not wait for a response. "I've heard Allison Connors described as different. Would you say that's an accurate description, that she was different?"

"Yeah, that's what people said. But people like her tend to be different anyway."

"I don't know that I understand your meaning. Can you help me?"

"Sure, Allison was a classic introvert. Never could understand how she chose teaching as a profession. Sure, there are introverted teachers, but Allison was more than the average introvert."

"What would make her more than average?"

"I don't think she had any intention of letting anyone know about her past or her thoughts or future ambitions. She worked hard to stay within herself."

"You said earlier she didn't talk about herself."

"Never. That's why it was hard to have a conversation with her."

"Was she defensive?"

"No, just wasn't interested in talking about anything related to her life."

Brandon was probably right in suggesting he had to carry the conversation. Perhaps Allison's comments to Joanne about Brandon were a bit tainted by the fact that Allison did not see the need for two sides to a conversation.

Van could not help but think that although Brandon Naysmith had a big ego, he was far more normal perhaps than Allison. The difference was that he made no effort to hide his ego. Allison apparently never had an ego to hide.

Van interviewed several other teachers but learned nothing additional. One characteristic of someone like Allison is that they remain so personally incognito that years later people really can't remember them.

Allison wanted to be anonymous, invisible to others. It was something she worked hard to accomplish. Perhaps that allowed her to disappear into anonymity. As far as Van could tell, Allison had succeeded.

And yet Van felt that his interviews with Jay, some of the students, and the teachers, especially Joanne and even Brandon, confirmed the complexities of Allison. Allison was not borderline different. She was so unlike anyone else that she was unknowable. He would need to run what he knew about Allison by his gang of six resources to get their take on her.

He may not understand Allison, but Van knew he had a credible suspect.

CHAPTER 23

———〜〜———

BRIEFING VARGAS AND FENTON

Homicide Offices

RAUCOUS LAUGHTER WAS coming from the lieutenant's office. Charlene smiled and told him that they were telling old stories while they waited for him. He was to go on in.

"Ah, Van …"

"Hope you're not laughing about me," said Van with a smile.

"No. No. Just teasing Fenton about his early years as a deputy."

Fenton smiled. "Believe me, Van, Vargas never lets me forget my early mistakes."

Vargas cut off the candor. "Have a seat. What have you got for us on the Ashae case?"

"Well, I would like to think there's progress, but experience tells me to be cautious."

"That's what I hear." Van's wrinkled forehead telegraphed his confusion. "Fenton tells me you have a philosophy about working difficult or complex cases."

Van glanced at Fenton, who was silently mouthing the statement "Go slow …"

"Oh, that. Well, a friend of mine whose profession is solving problems told me his philosophy was to *go slow so you can go fast*. The work one does up front should be done thoroughly and compellingly so that once it's time for decisions and action, you can move quickly.

He says that too many people shoot first and then aim. Others aim quickly and then shoot. Those with accuracy in their shots take their time aiming and need only shoot once."

"So you always go slow?"

"Not always, but I do try to control the urge to act when I'm not yet fully ready."

Vargas smiled. "You ever read Louis L'Amour?"

"The western writer? No, I guess not." Van was certain he had not, but L'Amour was enough of an icon among western fiction that his name was known.

"Well, your philosophy would sit well with L'Amour. If you read his books, the heroes, the ones who seem to survive the shootouts, may not have been the fastest draw, but they were the most accurate. They knew enough to make a shot count."

The lieutenant's comments were an interesting transition. Van had never thought of reading any of L'Amour's work, but he made a mental note to look into it. "Well, I try to be accurate. If that means slowing down, then I try to keep reminding myself of the fact."

"You don't have to convince me. Too many people around here shoot from the hip, and we all end up cleaning up the mess." Vargas rolled his eyes at Fenton. Obviously the two were on the same wavelength. Both knew someone in the department with an unflattering reputation, and the lieutenant did not need to reference a name. "But you didn't come here for a lecture."

Van summed up the results of his interviews with family members, high school friends, teachers, and the principal. He concluded by suggesting the principal and teachers provided valuable information about a colleague who was of interest.

Vargas said, "Someone of *interest*? Sounds promising. But before we go there, can you summarize for us what you've concluded regarding the disappearance?"

"Yes." Van picked up his notes. "The disappearance, and I believe the murder of both students, was purposeful. I don't know the motive, but I'm confident the killer or killers knew both of them. I also believe the killers, or at least one of probably two killers, was female. I also believe at least one of the killers worked at the school.

"I say killers because it seems to me that it would have taken more than one person to kill both students, move the VW and burn it, and dispose of both bodies."

Fenton interjected, "Do you say that with the same conviction you did several weeks ago?"

"No. I believe they were murdered elsewhere, and the VW moved to be burned. However, though my instincts tell me it was two people, increasingly I'm leaning toward one person, a female. However, I'm struggling with the idea that one person could kill both."

"Why?"

"Because I think it would take an exceptionally talented individual, intellectually and especially physically, to accomplish it all and leave no trace."

"And you think you know who that person is?"

"I do, but let me back up. Let me talk about Carlos and Cindy first."

Van was well aware that the lieutenant needed to feel there was a reasonable rational behind any theory. A gut feeling would not do.

"It appears that an odd relationship between Carlos and Cindy developed rather quickly. Comments from friends indicate they were all surprised by it at the time, but now, many years later, some of them feel it made sense because Cindy, the previously quiet and shy introvert, was growing up, and her maturity caught the attention of Carlos. At seventeen, Carlos appears to have been suffering a bit of anxiety about his immaturity and lack of any purposeful direction in his life. Cindy, who everyone thought was the lost soul, was growing up and finding purpose and direction. She was also developing into a young woman. I have heard her described that way by females and some of the males I interviewed. Thus, the two opposites find a certain attraction."

He paused. No questions. Van went on. "If I didn't know better, I'd say there was a certain Oedipus complex at work here." The comment brought smiles to his colleagues' faces. "Carlos was attracted to someone who had the mothering qualities that provided security. He was unsure of where he was headed after high school. Cindy was gaining maturity and making decisions. She was not the rah-rah cheerleader type he was accustomed to dating. Cindy had substance to her growing interests and views. That assuredness, I think, was comforting to Carlos. Though I cannot deny that I think he was also drawn to her physically for reasons many who are immature are drawn to the more mature.

"Carlos probably harbored an interest in Cindy that ran beyond her being a prom date. For her part, Cindy, no longer just a shy introvert, was becoming liberalized, curious, and outspoken."

Fenton expressed a concern. "That provides some explanation why the two may have wandered off toward the canyon area after the dance. They wanted some physical time alone. But it doesn't explain why they were targeted by a killer or killers."

"You're right, Sarge, it doesn't, and that's the big unknown. There has to be a reason for the two to be targeted, and I haven't yet found it."

"Do you expect to find it?"

"Yes, when I find out who had issues with the Cindy-Carlos relationship. I think our inside-the-school suspect has some connection with the two and those issues."

Van was well aware he was on shaky ground at this point because all he had was the input of the principal, two students, a couple of teachers, his research, and his own instincts. There were a lot of unanswered questions, and his thinking represented a leap of faith.

"When I began to realize the Ecology Club was probably the starting point for the relationship between Carlos and Cindy, I wondered how the club could have impacted the two. Everyone said that Cindy emerged from her shell at club meetings, and Carlos was taken by what he saw in her. So much was he attracted to her that he went on a club field trip that she also attended. The April 1972 outing was the second club trip Cindy had gone on. It was the first club trip for Carlos, who had never really had any interest in the club before.

"A photo taken by some student, and given to Carlos, had a picture of Cindy in it. I can think of no other reason he would want the photo. In the background of the photo, there is a teacher who was not a club leader and was not in the yearbook photos of the club. The photo is not especially good, so the image of the teacher is very grainy and not really in focus. I inquired about her and learned from the principal that she, though peculiar, was an excellent teacher—a fact born out by independent testimony from teachers and students."

Vargas raised the question. "*Peculiar*? Peculiar enough that she's a reasonable suspect?"

"The photo was taken at Irvine Park, less than two miles from the burned VW."

Both Vargas and Fenton had incredulous looks. Fenton said, "And coincidence is not a viable term in our business."

"Let me put it this way. Allison A. Connors was an English teacher of exceptional talents ... not the least of which was her interest in the outdoors. Cindy had been a student in her class in the tenth grade. Cindy apparently liked and looked up to Allison."

"What does the A initial stand for?"

"Don't know. Employment files and her college records all show only an initial. In fact, every piece of documentation I have located shows only a middle initial. Anyway, Allison, according to everyone I have talked with, was probably the most intelligent member of the faculty. Comments describe her as the resident super brain."

Van paused to switch his focus. "Also, Allison was viewed by students as brilliant, extremely fair, and demanding of a student's best performance. One very credible student described her as being very candid and a straight shooter."

"Hardly characteristic of a killer."

"But Allison was also a loner. She was friendly, ate lunch with others, and attended faculty parties, but she balanced that with considerable time alone. She was a definitive introvert. Principal said she was a classic INTJ—"

"A what?" The lieutenant's question cut Van's comments off.

"On the Myers-Briggs Personality Inventory, an INTJ is the classification for someone who's a very resilient introvert, highly self-motivated, very organized, and inclined to be very self-sufficient.

We are talking about less than 1 percent of the population who fit this description."

Van handed each a photocopy of a description of an INTJ. It was taken from the popular Myers-Briggs text, *Please Understand Me: Character and Temperament Types* by David Keirsey and Marilyn Bates. "This probably provides a better description than I can provide." He gave his colleagues some time to read the short description.

"As you can see, it's my estimation our suspect is a classic introvert. However, it's the two middle letters, the NT, that I think are critical. Our suspect is an intuitive thinker. The authors, Keirsey and Bates, liken the NT temperament to Prometheus, a Titan in Greek mythology who defies the other gods and passes on the power of fire to humans.

"I think, in this sense, our suspect sees herself like Prometheus. She believes she knows what is right for others despite what ethics, laws, or moralities suggest."

Van stopped and let his thesis sink in. He knew he was going where others in his line of work rarely went. He was blending the philosophical with the accusatorial. Not necessarily a bad practice but certainly a risky one.

Vargas was fascinated. "Shit, Van, you really do look at things differently. This is good stuff. Go on. What about the J after the NT?"

"She is judging. She likes closure. She is decisive. Once she makes a decision, she takes calculated action. There is no leaving the door open to other options. She lives in her own world and believes it is reality. She is so bright that if you provide any argument to the contrary, she is well equipped to prove you wrong."

"So ..." Fenton took his time responding. "Our suspect is a female loner who sees herself empowered to decide what is best and to do what she deems necessary to address her motives, whatever they are. Am I off base here, Van?"

"I'd say you're pretty much on target."

Beguiled, Fenton shook his head. "Christ" was his outward expression.

Vargas and Fenton seemed satisfied with his definition of INTJ.

They gave no signs of not understanding. Van could tell both were moving ahead with his line of thinking on this matter. He knew each would ponder the implications; in the meantime, he knew they wanted to know where all of this was going.

Vargas raised the logical question about motive. "So, while we look for your suspect, we need to also look at motive to understand our little Miss Greek throwback. Any ideas there?" The levity reflected the derogatory sarcasm prevalent in police work.

"Not yet. There's something inside our suspect that's related to her perception of our two teen lovers. She may have been a loner, but she was bright well beyond normal, and if her INTJ qualities are any indication, understanding will not be easy."

"But in our profession, we know all too well the strong correlation between loners and strange criminal behavior."

"That's right, Lieutenant, and it's why I've been trying to learn as much about Allison Connors as I can. It hasn't been easy. She left Nuevo in 1978 and dropped off the radar." Van caught himself. "But I'm getting ahead again. Let me fill you in on what we know about her."

Notes in hand, Van went on. "The school district records show Allison graduated with a degree in English from California State University, Long Beach. It was Long Beach State then. She also got her teaching credential there. The state confirms she was credentialed to teach English and had a minor in history. With that information, I talked with the folks at Long Beach.

"To say she was a good student is an understatement—straight As. She was brilliant. But the available information at the university is limited. Old records were put on microfiche, but by the time that was done, they had been culled to eliminate unneeded information. There is the bare minimum of data—birth date, courses, grades, units, degree, address, social security number, and some additional contact information of no value.

"The social security number checks out, but there have been no contributions since 1978. As far as Social Security is concerned, Allison A. Connors is still alive and has never filed for social security or Medicare. I can't even find California or IRS tax records after 1980."

Fenton expressed amazement. "Damn, how do these people do it?"

Van went on. "The records indicate a post office box in Bishop, California, that was given as her permanent address while in college. The phone number was that of her father, Archie Connors. He died in a backpacking accident in 1966. The only other address was located in Long Beach. The location has a new building that wasn't there in the 1960s. It was apparently the site of a home with a granny apartment in the rear yard at the time. She apparently lived at the location while a college student. Haven't been able to locate the owner or the name of any possible roommate.

"Long Beach State records show no reference to where she might have gone to high school. Bishop schools have no record of her. It's like Allison didn't exist before she showed up at Long Beach and ceased to exist after she left Nuevo."

"How the hell did she get into college?" asked Vargas.

"Perfect ACT score."

Vargas shook his head.

"Allison A. Connors is very much an enigma, but slowly information is developing, and I'll put the pieces together. If she's alive, we'll find her."

There was an expression of disbelief in Fenton's voice. "Interesting! In this social media age, it's hard to believe that anyone can just appear and then disappear. I guess we forget that just a few decades ago that was more possible. What else do we know about her?"

"She was an accomplished distance runner, but she didn't seem to want anyone to know just how good she was. At Long Beach State, it was pre–Title IX, and women's athletics was limited to informal status. As far as I know, she never competed. That's unusual for someone of her talent.

"Also, apparently some Nuevo students saw her run and couldn't believe her stamina."

Vargas said, "She must have attracted men. Did she date? Hell,

I can answer my own question. She was some kind of mental and physical freak who scared away men."

"That's the way others saw it as well. She dated, but she seldom dated anyone more than a couple of times. I did talk with one former Nuevo teacher who dated her several times. He has a PhD and big ego, and I think he found Allison a bit intimidating because she was clearly much more intelligent than he. However, toward the end of our conversation, he confirmed what others suggested. She wasn't one to talk about herself. He all but said it was very frustrating and the real reason why their relationship terminated. That goes along with the INTJ typology."

"And you don't have any idea of her whereabouts since she left the school?"

"No, Sergeant. I've called in a couple of favors with former fed colleagues in my effort to track her down. No luck yet, but I'm confident we'll find her, though it may take some time."

"Where did she live when she was a teacher at Nuevo?" Fenton asked.

"Apartment unit in Orange. It was older then but rundown and falling apart now. I was unable to find anyone or any records from 1972. All I have is the address."

"You think she left the state?"

"No, and this is more of a gut feeling at this time. She was apparently born and spent several years living in the Eastern Sierra near the town of Bishop, California. Also, according to several teachers and the principal, she loved backpacking in the Sierra. If that were the case, she would never leave the proximity of the Sierra Nevada. Of course, I have nothing to confirm that."

Vargas said, "You said the father died while backpacking. That a coincidence?"

"Don't know yet. I just found out about it and only have an old newspaper article to go on. He died in an accident while backpacking with Allison. Article says he was married to Mary Jo Harden, who committed suicide in 1963.

"Lots of work to do to find out more about the father and the mother. I do know there were two other kids in the family but have come up empty on any effort to locate them."

Fenton shared what they all were thinking. "Weird breeds weird. The family sounds very dysfunctional. Not hard to understand the difficulty in finding any trace."

"What about school records in Bishop? You check with them?" asked Vargas.

"They have no records going that far back. Old yearbooks from the high school in the 1960s turned up nothing." Van anticipated the next question. "We're working with the Orange County Department of Education to see if we can locate any information that suggests Allison was a student in the 1950s and early 1960s."

"So …" Vargas was slow to ask his question. "The father and daughter backpacked together even though the parents had divorced. Anything in that relationship look odd to you?"

"Everything about it is odd, but as yet, all I have is the newspaper article to go on. I'm trying to locate someone who worked that case."

Fenton proffered an opinion. "I share your question about one person, especially a woman, being able to carry out these murders, but stranger things have happened."

"Where do you go from here?" asked the lieutenant.

"Well, I would like to be a bit unorthodox, boss. There are three people I would like to talk with and ask their take …"

"You mean non–department personnel?"

"Yes. One of the people I worked with in the FBI was not a federal employee but an outside consultant. Her role was studying the statistical relationships in criminal investigations. She was good at identifying the questions that needed to be asked but were not being asked. You could bounce theories off of her, and she had this uncanny ability to come back at you with questions that forced you to think differently, thus providing alternative insights into the evidence."

Fenton said, "You told us about her earlier. Indian wasn't she?"

"Yes, Dr. Patel. First-rate mind and skilled at analysis."

"Yeah, I remember. Who else?"

"A political science prof with a specialty in political motives analysis. In the past, she has been helpful in identifying motives behind actions. She's a qualitative researcher. She looks deep into problem and human behavior in search of motives in political action. She is Dr. Karli Ryan. Patel and Ryan would give me feedback and not violate any confidentiality. They understand confidentiality and the need to keep things under wraps in their line of work."

"Interesting. And the third?"

"My brother-in-law." Van saw the eyebrows go up. "I know it sounds weak, but I assure you, he would be an excellent person to bounce my ideas off. He has a PhD in psychology and recently retired as a twenty-three-year veteran as a high school principal. He heads-up a consulting firm that works with troubled schools to develop plans for improvement. He lives in North Carolina. During his career, he turned four troubled high schools into model institutions."

"And you think these three people can help you?"

"As critics and analysts of my thinking. They wouldn't be active in the case."

"Lieutenant, I'll vouch for Van. If he says these three sources will prove valuable, I think it's worth the try to let him have a go with them."

"You're probably right, Fenton. But I want to be kept in the know at every step along the way. Remember, no surprises. I'll be damned if I'm gonna be happy explaining all of this to the sheriff if it gets into the news."

CHAPTER 24

———∿∿∿———

TURNING TO OUTSIDE RESOURCES

Vanarsdale Home

WHEN GIVEN THE go-ahead by Vargas to consult with friends, Van anticipated a week or two would be needed to accomplish the task. Looking at his calendar, he realized it had taken several weeks.

Glancing at his computer screen notes, Van noted he had engaged both Dr. Patel and Dr. Ryan in several time-consuming phone calls. As for his brother-in-law, there was only the three-hour lunch meeting near LAX. The timing was a matter of luck since Ray was in town doing some work for one of the West LA beach city school districts.

Dr. Patel cautioned Van about focusing too much on Allison Connors. It was not that she doubted Van's suspicions. Law enforcement, she said, is easily influenced by long-standing assumptions regarding perceptions of loners and people with observably out-of-the-norm behavior. If Van found that the evidence was not clear regarding the issue of whether there was one or more killers, then he was obliged to keep in mind that statistically there were pronounced differences between group committed crimes and those of an individual.

Loners tend to commit crimes without wanting assistance. The thought of pairing up with another person is not usually appealing. Her question kept coming back to him. What is the motive for a loner to seek out a partner to commit a crime? Also, what is the motive for a nonloner to seek out a loner to share in a crime? "If you think more than one person committed the murders and that one was female, you must wrestle with the why of such an arrangement."

A discussion with Dr. Patel was always challenging. She was not one to tell you what to do. It was more like her to ask questions and fall back to her mantra, *Why not*? Many of Van's colleagues in the FBI got frustrated with her because they were not patient and wanted answers. They were always looking for her to guide them, make their life easier. They reasoned that since she was working for them, she should be more direct and not, as one agent noted, "play the Socratic methods game."

Van, on the other hand, found her approach agreeable. She was not telling him how to do his job. She was helping him become better at doing his job.

For years, Dr. Patel had interviewed criminal investigators about their methods. Her findings revealed that typically investigators and detectives, regardless of the type of crime, tended to follow methods based on four frames of reference.

First, experience and gut feelings were the most common guides. It was not necessarily a "this is the way I have always done it" approach. It was more the result of cumulative experience and a sense of things happening around the crime. This perspective, reasoned Dr. Patel, was the classic learning approach. Experience is the primary mentor. She was not opposed to the value of experience. She only cautioned that experience is best used when one learns from mistakes and does not become overly enamored by personal successes.

Second, and perhaps an extension of experience and gut reactions, most detectives were not students of criminal psychology. Nor were they likely to stay abreast of research regarding investigation methods. In this sense, they were like most professionals who just do not have the time to keep up with changes. Compounding the problem was the reality that resources for training were increasingly limited. Unfortunately, the lack of sufficient training contributed to an incestuous attitude. In the absence of ongoing professional development, the gunslinger mentality takes over as investigators increasingly rely on their own take on things.

Third, employer environment, directives, and preferences were very significant determinants of the methods used. Despite experience and knowledge about what should be done, it was not uncommon that investigative methods deferred to the norms of the institution. Most officers came up through a system, and that system and its in-house regulations and mentors generally guided how investigations were done. The culture of a department, and especially the expectations of superiors, provided the norms.

Finally, she had found that politics—the desires of management, prosecutors, politicians, the media, and citizens—were often at the root of poor decision making in the investigative process. Even the best investigations were no competition for errant outside pressures pushing to find a cause and a suspect and to point blame. In such environments, the system of justice was sometimes abridged in favor of fast-tracking investigations. Dr. Patel often said, "A rush to case judgment is a great way to expedite your retirement."

There was other research, of course. Some of it paralleled that of Dr. Patel; some of it was in disagreement. Van, however, had found reading the research to be of benefit. Over the years, he had concluded that the single most inhibiting factor in an investigator's actions was the failure to keep an open mind and look for atypical connections. This was the biggest influence of Dr. Patel on his methods. Assumptions and experience often hindered objective thinking; it was better to take one's time, become introspective about a case, and avoid quick judgments.

Van knew he needed to continue trying to understand the relationship between the two victims and those of importance in their world. Somewhere in the milieu of emotions and human connections between and among students and staff was the foundation for the violence in 1972.

There was little doubt that at least one employee inside Nuevo was involved in the disappearance and deaths of Cindy and Carlos.

Certainly, Allison Connors was a good candidate. However, to single her out and ignore other possibilities could be counterproductive.

—m—

He had always enjoyed a good relationship with his brother-in-law, Raymond Fancher. Bright, witty, and a great reader of history, Ray had welcomed Van into the family long before he and Anna Marie got married. Somehow Ray had concluded, even before his sister committed to marrying Van, that the two were destined to be together. When Anna Marie began to slip toward death late in her illness, Ray dropped everything to come out and be with Van through the difficult final weeks. Since then, the two had kept in contact.

Ray was a wealth of information about student behavior. He stressed that students can change significantly over four years. Experience in and outside high school can be complex.

Van needed to keep in mind that the Carlos and Cindy many of their friends saw and described in 1972 came from the opinions of people who themselves were changing. It was conceivable that Cindy was ahead of Carlos in maturation even though she appeared to be a shy introvert. By the same token, the extrovert Carlos may have been harboring a sense of anxiety and uncertainty about himself as he watched the world begin to pass him by. Ray used the analogy of the middle-school kid who is the superior athlete, and all the high school coaches salivate at the prospects of him on their team in a year or two. However, it often happens that the middle-school super athlete who is the big fish in the pond at thirteen years of age has peaked and at sixteen years of age, only three years later, is sitting on the bench because the other kids who were his onetime inferiors have passed him by. That such situations create trepidation in the mind of the seventeen-year-old athlete goes without saying.

When asked about student and teacher relationships, Ray noted that in all his years as a teacher and administrator, he never ceased to be amazed that the taboo against physical, mental, and social relationships between teacher and student in high school was constantly being breached. Despite public outrage over student and teacher trysts, they continued to take place, and the media continued to make sure the public knew. The reprehensible nature of such relationships and the potential consequences did not seem to be a deterrent.

Van wanted to know if a teacher could find a cause to harm a student, even murder. Ray responded without hesitation, "Yes." In Ray's thinking, "The intricacies of human behavior know no bounds when it comes to teacher and student relationships. Whenever you think you have seen it all, you will be shocked to learn of something new. All the foibles of human vanity and jealousy can play out in such relationships. And if we think it strange that parents can live their lives vicariously through their kids, it's also true that teachers can do the same."

Ray's point challenged Van's instincts. He had just assumed the profession promoted dispassion as a necessity to set boundaries between teacher and student. The idea that a teacher could see himself or herself in a student was alarming. By extrapolation, Van wondered, *If a teacher lives their life vicariously through a student, and in doing so finds the student's actions reprehensible, was the teacher also inclined to punish herself through the student?* The thought had interesting implications.

Ray's reaction was not reassuring. "Look, Van, anything is possible psychologically. Teachers, like students, are complex and far from predictable.

"It may be that it wasn't because of Cindy or Carlos individually but rather because of the two together that they were targeted. If their deaths were at the hands of a teacher, it's likely that it was one teacher and that the teacher saw something in their relationship that he or she found intolerable. Perhaps there was jealousy. Perhaps a love triangle. Stranger things have happened."

The idea of two teachers agreeing to do harm to students seemed a stretch to Ray, though he did think it possible. More likely, if a teacher was involved, he or she would have the help of someone outside school.

Van noted that Cindy had not been in any classes with Carlos since their freshman year. Could a female teacher be jealous of Carlos's interest in Cindy? Could the same thing happen with a male teacher? Van was trying to gauge what it would take for a jealous teacher to react with such vengeance as murder. What kinds of things would make a teacher jealous? The discussion went on, and Van came away dismayed by Ray's continued reference to the vulnerability of young students under the influence of teacher psychology. Ray seemed to endorse the idea that anything was possible, and putting remains in a time capsule was confirmation.

A comment from Ray was especially disturbing. "Perhaps by putting the remains of Cindy in the time capsule, your suspect was simply returning the student to the school, the nexus between the teacher and the student. The killing took place elsewhere, and there was a need for closure."

Van also remembered Ray's final statement as they were leaving the restaurant, "If I were you, I would be looking at the question of whether the growing relationship between the two kids could have been a threat to anyone like a teacher, administrator, student, or parent. Don't underestimate the high school environment. It's a microcosm of the larger society and with minds capable of being just as twisted as we find in society at large. If anything, Columbine, the Letourneau case, and other recent evils make that clear. Take a good look at those two kids and anyone connected with them."

Van came away from his conversation wondering where all of this was when he was in high school. His own memory was that high school was fun times when he didn't work as hard as he should have. He was an obscure athlete and not an especially hardworking scholar. He liked small social gatherings, and he was not a big partier. But he did have to admit that he had, in recollection, learned much more in school than he realized at the time. Perhaps he was just naive and did not see what was going on around him. Was that what happened to Cindy?

—∽—

In retrospect, the most startling conversations were those with Dr. Ryan. Van had met Karli in Washington, DC, when he attended a conference on terrorism and human behavior. She was part of a panel presentation on political motivation and terrorist rationalities. Subsequently, while working on several FBI cases, Van had the opportunity to get Dr. Ryan's input. He discovered that often she would bring questions and assumptions into the discussion that seemed extraneous. If ever there was a model for thinking outside the box, she was it. Often, during the initial phases of a conversation, Van found her input odd, even off base, but what seemed unwarranted in the beginning soon became a reasonable line of thinking.

Though Karli had a reputation for being a straight shooter, if not a bit sarcastic, she was an academic at heart, and sometimes her conversations were so infused with unfamiliar terms and higher-order concepts that Van had to seek clarification. It was not just a matter of listening carefully; it was more a matter of follow-up study when on the receiving end of her commentary.

Van shared everything he had on the Ashae case. He knew from past experience that she liked to know three things about a situation—what was known, what was unknown, and what theories one was considering. Over the phone, she took notes and then ended the conversation. He knew that was her style. If she had questions, she would call back or email. She needed time to think and reflect before she would respond. When ready, she would set up a call to share insights.

A couple of weeks went by. When Karli finally called, Van was little prepared for the litany of questions, hypotheses, and suggestions. She had found the case especially interesting and had spent considerable time pondering it. Van apologized for taking so much of her time. She dismissed the apology as not needed since the case was unique enough that it demanded consideration of some issues she had not previously encountered.

"Listen, Van, you're not the only one learning here." Karli went on to explain conversations she had with two colleagues, Andi and Juju, whose expertise and research focused on sociopath behaviors among isolated individuals. "Don't worry, Van, I didn't share the details of your case with them. I used them much as you use me. I bounced my ideas off of them. They concur with what I'm about to share with you."

The discourse with Karli over phone and email was long and intense. Van soon discovered that he had to spend time condensing what she said before he felt comfortable understanding the implications. It started with her being convinced Carlos was also murdered.

Van looked at the bulleted notes he had developed from Karli's input.

- While the scarcity of evidence and disparate sequence of known information suggested more than one person committed the crimes, the events of 1972 were well choreographed and those of 1973 equally well planned. It is more likely one person was responsible.
- In all likelihood, a teacher or counselor carried out the murders. It was likely someone who is always in control, certain of their purpose, and meticulous—even to the point of an eventual signature a full year later.
- The perpetrator is not about attention. The time capsule suggests that even if he or she murdered for a reason, he or she was comfortable knowing that the world may never know.
- The earring, given 1972 standards, was likely worn by a female. It was accompanied by an element of compassion evident in concern for avoiding a general wildfire in burning the VW and waiting until the dance was over and the two students were alone. Together these suggest the murder was most likely the work of a woman.

- The motive(s) for the murder were rooted in the perceptions of the female killer who saw something loathsome in the relationship between Carlos and Cindy. Chances are the motive reflects the roles of both Cindy and Carlos.
- No doubt, when the body of Carlos is found, there will be an earring.
- The killer probably killed before Cindy and Carlos and has likely killed since.
- To that end, the killings are serial, and the other killings will also reveal an earring.
- The earring is a symbol of the killer's past. The more you look into the past and psyche of your female suspects, the more likely you will find the connection.
- The killer is likely not a threat except wherein she sees things in others similar to what she saw in Cindy and Carlos. It is likely that others killed are victims of relationship complexity.
- The killer kills on her own terms, on her own territory.
- The killer is bright, strong, and impeccable in her thinking.
- The killer is psychotic.
- It is not likely that the killer spends a long time planning. She is good at controlling the circumstances and thinking through plans on very short notice. That appears to have been the case following the prom.
- Given the circumstances involving what appear to be two innocent teenagers, one cannot but help wondering if the killer was engaged in some sort of punishment or vengeance killings. Again, the reasoning will be found in the suspect's history and psyche.
- Find the killer's turf, and you will find other victims. You will probably find the suspect there as well.

The use of the word *vengeance* by Dr. Ryan struck Van as especially telling. *What could Allison be seeking revenge for?* Vengeance was not an uncommon motive in crime. Perhaps it was too common. He could not help but think that beyond the mask of anonymity that

Allison wore was an experience that fostered a life of revenge. *Did it start with her family?* If vengeance extended to Carlos and Cindy, then it was only reasonable to conclude there were other victims.

Van just stared at the list. It was hard to believe all of Dr. Ryan's assessment, and yet Van knew there was substance to what she said. Dr. Ryan did not say the killer was Allison Connors, but she did not have to. Everything pointed to Allison. He must keep an open mind; he had not yet vetted the other female or male teachers. He had yet to interview any counselors.

But Connors was of special interest. There was a certain mystery to her. The unknowns were disconcerting. There were four problems. First, he had yet to locate her. Second, he had absolutely no evidence against her. Third, she had all of the qualities of a sociopath; she had withdrawn from the world of her birth and moved into another dimension. Fourth, she was a psychopath and had become psychotic in that her actions reflected a very personal and narrowly defined set of acceptable behavior standards on the part of others.

As he leaned back and took a sip of the now tepid iced tea, one of Ray's comments kept echoing in his mind. "Teachers are a judgmental lot. Using grades, humiliation, comments, and any number of other methods, they can punish. It's not such a big leap to also conclude there are rare circumstances when they can kill to punish."

The hunt was on. He had to find Allison A. Connors. But there was no scent.

CHAPTER 25

FOCUSING ON A SUSPECT

Homicide Office

THE MEETING WITH Fenton was not for another ten minutes, so Van headed downstairs. Exiting his office, he took a circuitous route through the room of cubicles so he could greet some people.

Turning toward the exit a couple of minutes later, he noticed two deputies in a discussion outside the double glass door. As he got closer, he realized they were probably on their way to see Stenzgard, the only other investigator on the floor today. Van knew the younger deputy, working night shift patrol last week, had stopped to check out a parked car he had noticed along Ortega Highway several hours earlier. What he thought was a sleeping occupant turned out to be a gunshot victim. The other deputy responded to the scene a couple of minutes later. Both deputies had been on the job for about a year, and this was their first murder victim.

Today they had to deal with the investigator in charge, Anthony "Tony" Stenzgard, a skilled and demanding mentor.

The deputies turned as Van opened the glass doors. He had caught them unawares, and they ceased talking. Officers in homicide did not wear nametags on a uniform like the deputies, but the two smiled and nodded at Van. One addressed him, "Investigator Van." Van had to smile. *Funny how in a department you can be known by people you've never worked with.* He knew investigators developed reputations. He also knew reputation was important because investigators depend on the deputies. Good deputies made an investigator's job easier. If a deputy knew what an investigator's expectations and reputation were, the deputy was more likely to respond accordingly without being told what to do.

Alienate an investigator as a result of shoddy work, and life in the department could be hell.

As he moved on, Van sensed the deputies had arrived separately and were discussing their upcoming meeting with Stenzgard. It was the old *get your ducks in a row* premeeting. Van smiled; he remembered those early years on the force.

—ɯ—

A few minutes later, tea in hand, Van walked in as Fenton was on the phone. He was speaking to Charlene and asked some questions regarding the need to cover a pending social event. Van was reminded that the lieutenant was out of town and Fenton was standing in.

The conversation at an end, Fenton expressed exasperation. "Jeez, sometimes I realize why it's not always wise to move up the damned promotion ladder. The lieutenant has to go to all these functions with the top brass, most of whom couldn't give a rat's ass if I take his place."

"He's out of town this week and next, right?"

"Actually he's at a conference for four days in Chicago and is extending it for a week of vacation. His wife's parents have a place on Mackinac Island. Lots of bucks there. I've seen pictures of the place."

"Nice work if you can get it." The Broadway melody was lost on Fenton.

"Yeah, but Vargas wasn't real excited. But we all know how family obligations are. Anyway, I've a luncheon to cover in an hour, so let's get on with it."

Just then, Van and Fenton noticed the two deputies walking toward Stenzgard's office.

Fenton chuckled. "On the carpet time. They've a lesson to learn from Stenzgard."

Van shared the humor. "We've all been there."

Turning back to Van, Fenton picked up several pages from his desktop. "I read the stuff you sent several days ago. Your friends are impressive. Any new information?"

"Yes, that's why I'm here." Van sat back and relaxed as he moved into a more conversational mode. "I'm convinced we're looking for Allison Connors. However, as you know, we haven't been able to track her down. We will, but it's not looking real good now."

"Pisses me off. Your report says Connors was never interviewed. How did she avoid it? God damn Vargas and Damon let her slip through the cracks."

"Not sure it would have made any difference. She hadn't worked prom and was probably too smart for them."

"Yeah, I'm not saying anything to the lieutenant, but his father and partner dropped the ball."

Van went on. "So, I've been focusing on as much information about her as I can find. I learned from the former Nuevo principal that Allison was an avid hiker and backpacker. That's been confirmed by teachers I've talked with.

"Allegedly, her father, Archie Connors, died accidentally while backpacking in the Sierra in the midsixties. I called the Inyo sheriff's office. They have no one working who was around then. More importantly, they couldn't put their hands on the reports of that incident.

"Not wanting to ruffle any feathers, I took a chance that Brenda Robertson could help me since she's now working in Mammoth. I figured she probably works closely with the Inyo department and could run some interference—"

Fenton interrupted. "She always had a sort of no-nonsense approach to things. Got things done but sometimes at the expense of friendly relations. A bit bitchy as I remember."

Van ignored the sarcasm. "She said Inyo County owed her a favor and she'd get back to me. She called less than a week later." Van consulted his notes. "The only person alive is Ryan Pollard, who was the Inyo detective on the Archie Connors case in 1966. The problem is that he's eighty-five years old and is in an assisted living facility in Bishop. Brenda had to go to some meetings in Bishop and stopped to see Pollard.

"Pollard remembered the case because he eventually concluded it had been an accident. When Brenda asked why, he indicated that everything pointed to it being an accident except the response of Connors's daughter. Pollard said he remembered the case because the daughter didn't live with Connors, and most people who knew Connors said the two were estranged and found it odd that they backpacked together. The real reason he questioned the accident, though, was because of what the daughter did not do. She admitted her father drank and was drunk the night of the accident, but unlike most daughters, she didn't question her own actions. She came across as very unhappy about his death, but she didn't do what most in her position would do. She didn't say things like, 'I could have prevented it,' or, 'If only I had done such and such.' There was no second-guessing."

"And the records?"

"Brenda said she was still working on that. Apparently after the Charlie Manson arrest in 1969, the Inyo sheriff's office in the little town of Independence was besieged by attention, and many of the shortcomings of the office became very public. So the county built a new office and jail, and everything was moved. Don't have to tell you that things get lost in such moves."

"So, what now?"

"Hopefully Brenda can come up with some more to go on. But in the meantime I've been looking into state records regarding missing people and deaths in the local Santa Ana Mountains and other backpacking areas."

"This is a big state, Van, with a lot of hiking areas and mountains and countryside like we have in OC, not to mention the Sierra Nevada and desert areas."

"I got back to Dr. Ryan with information about Allison as a hiker and backpacker and the circumstances of her father's death. I wanted to know if it changed Dr. Ryan's earlier conclusions. She said no. Her observations suggest additionally that the killer is probably not a loner who holds up isolated like the Unabomber guy but is someone who's active. The best bet is that she would live near the Sierra."

"That covers a lot of cities and remote locations. Good luck!"

"Sarge, I don't know much about hiking and backpacking. Do we have anyone in the department who does?"

It was several seconds before Fenton responded. "Yeah, Sergeant Ken Pierce. He's in Investigations at the South County facility. You know him?"

"Well, I know the name. We've never worked together. Don't think we've met."

"He grew up backpacking. His father and brother are the real backpackers. I know his younger brother did that John Muir Trail a couple years back. Something like two hundred miles, I think. Old man's a professor at Cal State, Fullerton, and has been backpacking all his life, and I think he authored a book or two ..." There was a pause. "If I'm not mistaken, his dad did some work with the Inyo sheriff on a case a few years ago. I'm sure Ken can help you."

—∿—

Later, Van saw the two young deputies emerge from Stenzgard's office. The earlier nervous look on their faces was long gone. They looked sober and somber. They nodded slightly to Van and moved toward the exit without looking at anyone else.

Van was aware that Fenton's observation was right on. Young deputies, in their eagerness to pursue their job, often forget their position and become more of a hindrance than an asset when things move to the investigation stage.

Obviously the two had made some mistakes, and Stenzgard, the investigator and teacher, had to bring them back down to earth. Young deputies often forget what they are told repeatedly in the academy about crime scenes–*observe, keep your movements limited, your hands on your belt, and secure the scene for the investigators.* No doubt the two exceeded their responsibilities, and Stenzgard had the task of making sure the message sent was loud and clear.

Stenzgard was a good investigator. He had been on the third floor for some twenty years and had a reputation of doing great work. One could learn a lot from him. He was old school, but his work got results.

Interestingly, Stenzgard loved being an investigator and had no desire to move up. He was good at what he did and believed it was his calling. He could easily have been promoted but chose not to be. There was an understanding within the department that many of the top brass owed much of their success to the influence of Stenzgard the mentor.

Van thought it ironic that being a good teacher did not necessarily mean one was good in other ways. Students and colleagues described Allison as an excellent teacher. She was not the nurturing, touchy-feely type, but she got results. She had high expectations and demands, and she taught students well. She taught them how to meet the expectations and fulfill the demands. She was hard, and she was fair.

Allison too could have built on her teaching skill by earning a PhD and moving on to teaching at the university level. Those who knew her held that belief. She chose not to. She taught for nine years and then just disappeared.

—⟋⟍⟍—

A follow-up on a missing person case took Van out of the office all afternoon. When he returned in early evening, the floor was almost empty. The day shift had gone home. None of the other investigators were around.

He made hot tea and sat down at his computer to make some notes on the missing person case. But as he did so, the whole idea of someone going missing kept nagging on his thoughts. His thoughts came back to Allison.

While the remains of Cindy Ashae provided some closure as to what happened to her, the absence of any evidence regarding Carlos was like a blank sheet of paper. There was absolutely nothing to go on other than the VW van, Cindy's remains, an earring, and the implication that what happened to Cindy probably happened to Carlos.

Now, not only was Carlos missing, but also the primary suspect, Allison, was missing. Every effort to find her had turned up a dead end. The difference was that Carlos, Van was certain, was dead. As for Allison, who knew? Given that she left Nuevo in 1978, she had a long head start on his efforts to locate her. She had three-plus decades to become someone else. Feeling that somewhere she was known under a different persona, Van could not get over the fact that missing people are usually only missing to those who are hunting them. To others, they are not missing.

What he knew about Allison suggested she was smart enough to make her whereabouts very difficult to locate.

The information he had about Allison also suggested a person probably more comfortable living in a rural, perhaps even a wilderness, environment. Logic said she should have gone to Alaska or Canada. Karli Ryan took a different view and supported the idea that the connection with the Sierra was strong enough to keep Allison where she was most comfortable and thus most likely to blend in.

She would be aging considerably by now, but Van did not think her frail if she was alive. She had been a fitness-focused person, and that could be benefitting her now. She could be deceased. If that had happened and if she had been living under another name, her real identity was likely to remain an eternal secret.

If Allison was a serial killer, as the earring suggested, Van's search was hampered by the fact that he was not able to link any other deaths with her, except the possibility that she had killed her father. He was certain Carlos had been killed but had nothing to prove it. Serial killers leave a trail of death. As yet, Allison had left only one signature. Unless some latent evidence was uncovered, the death of her father was an accident, and the evidence, except for the perception of one old Inyo County investigator, supported that conclusion.

But even if Allison had taken on another identity and had not committed another murder, there were qualities about her that likely had not changed. She was very smart, probably in the ninety-ninth percentile of intelligence, and such people do not just stop being smart. For them, it is truly a lifelong process of learning. They get smarter. That is, they get smarter unless they start believing their own press and begin to get careless. Then they make mistakes. As yet, he did not know if Allison had been careless and made mistakes.

Allison did not appear to be a psychotic in need of recognition. If she had killed others, she seemed content to simply move on without concern. If that were so, finding her trail would be very difficult.

—m—

Walking across the parking garage to his Crown Vic, Van noticed the cars of the top brass parked in their assigned spaces. *Must be some special event tonight*, he thought.

Fenton would be covering for Vargas. *Maybe Vargas was smart in taking this week off.*

He had to give Vargas credit. At their last meeting, the lieutenant had cautioned him not to get his hopes about finding Allison Connors easily. He could still hear the lieutenant's voice: "Remember, history is filled with the famous and not so famous who have gone missing and have never been found. Remember also, the ones who were difficult to find often were old and gray when discovered, usually quite by accident and not because of great detective work."

A few days later, Van had entered his office to find two paperback books by Louis L'Amour and a note from Vargas. "*A couple of his best novellas. You can read them in an evening. They may give you some insight into how difficult it is to hide.*"

He had taken them home, and they sat on his kitchen counter until one Sunday afternoon when he picked one up. He read it that afternoon and the sequel a couple of days later. The hero of both was a gunfighter named Lance Kilkenny. He was not a gunfighter who sought notoriety or wanted to be noticed. In fact, he did not like having to use his guns, but when he did have to, he was always faster.

He gained a reputation, but most people did not really know him since, following any gun battle, Kilkenny disappeared, and people never got a good look at him.

Finally Kilkenny went farther west in search of a high-range setting where he changed his name to Trent and tried to live unnoticed as a rancher. For a while he was successful, but when a range war started, he came to the aid of those being bullied by the large rancher who controlled the local town. It was then that Kilkenny was rediscovered. He had tried to hide, but the past had caught up with him.

Van wondered if Allison realized the law was searching for her. She wasn't famous, but Allison was smart, and Van sensed that little escaped her attention.

CHAPTER 26

———ᴡᴡ———

VISITING NUEVO HIGH SCHOOL

North Orange County

T HE PRINCIPAL'S SECRETARY had told him that it would be a
furlough day and there would be no teachers or students on
campus. *Probably one of the cost-cutting approaches to balancing
school district budgets*, thought Van. She also thought it a good day
for a visit because the principal, Cynthia Finn, would be at an all-day
management meeting. This would allow former principal Jay Jansen
to show Van around. The parking lots were empty save for a handful
of vehicles immediately in front of the administration offices.

Jay was talking to Sylvia, the principal's secretary, when Van
entered the offices. Jay had hired Sylvia during his second year as
principal. Jay had since retired, but Sylvia was still at her post. It
occurred to Van that Sylvia was the consummate executive secretary.
She was pleasant, formal, and well dressed on a day when a glance
around the office suggested everyone else had dressed down since
school was not in session.

Van had long put great stock in first appearances. The contrast
between the dress of others in the office and Sylvia's appearance,
presence, and communication skills suggested Sylvia was a loyal
employee who protected her boss and was not caught up in the usual
train of gossip that tended to infect office environments. It reminded
Van of his college days and one of the required books in a speech class

he had taken. The professor was probably right in having students read John Molloy's *Dress for Success*. At the time, it did not seem important. But Van had found in the book insights that aided him as an investigator. It helped him read people.

After the introductions and usual pleasantries, Sylvia handed Jay a set of keys. "Don't lose these, Jay, or you'll regret you ever hired me." The two laughed. Jay, in turn, responded to the intended humor. "Investigator, Sylvia was always helping me locate things I misplaced. She used to tell me that the interviews when she was hired didn't include any questions about her searching skills. She bailed me out many times."

As they walked through the office, Jay greeted the resident staff. It was clear several had worked on campus when he was principal. The friendly banter reminded Van that the presence of law enforcement, whether in uniform or not, seldom went unnoticed. Word always got around.

"They arresting you today, Dr. Jensen?" There was laughter from several at this comment.

"Not today, Trisha." Jensen smiled as they walked. He was liked, and he knew it.

Van had no doubts that everyone on campus today knew what he was doing here. But time had mellowed reality; the misfortunes of the past no longer prevented humor. Even tragedy eventually turns a corner.

The first order of business was a visit to the location of the planter where the time capsule had been buried. They exited the office area and went into what was the center of the enclosed campus.

"You can see that we're in what's called the upper commons because we're about four feet higher than the lower commons. Each is a large quadrangle, so many call these *quads* rather than commons. I use both terms. The two quads together are at the center of the campus."

Jay walked over to the steps leading down to the lower commons. Motioning to the 365-degree view, he explained, "Up here you can see large double doors that lead from the two common areas into various wings of the campus. The two blue doors on the other side of this upper area"—Jay pointed across the quad to doors about thirty yards away—"lead to the wing that in the early years of the school housed the vocational arts classrooms. Except for the band room, woodshop, and the auto shop, all those old vocational classrooms have been converted to academic classrooms. There are no more metal, graphic arts, drafting, or electronics classes."

"What happened to those classes? I remember the shop classes were pretty popular."

"Actually, two things. As the focus on academics increased, students were given fewer opportunities to take elective classes for graduation. In fact, graduation requirements have increased significantly. Years ago, kids who didn't do well and weren't going to college would take the shop classes as electives. Today that doesn't happen because academic standards are so demanding that students who struggle are channeled into additional academic classes where they get support. There's little room for the old traditional electives.

"Also, the Regional Occupation Program, we call it ROP, began to take over the vocational classes. After that, it wasn't necessary to have duplicate voc classes on every campus."

Van pointed to the blue doors. "So, the woodshop where the time capsule was made was in that wing."

"Yeah. They actually still have a wood shop and auto shop here. Run by ROP of course. We can go in there after we take a look at where the time capsule was buried."

Van and Jay descended several steps into the lower and much larger commons. Here the ceiling was at least twenty feet high, and although there was a roof, there was a feeling of openness as if there were no roof.

Jay stopped at the bottom of the steps and turned to the right where there was a large column about four foot square extending from the floor to the ceiling. "Before the infrastructure changed, there was a large planter here where we're standing between the upper and lower commons. If you look on the floor, you can see the outline of the old planter where newer concrete has been poured. This new column is right where the time capsule was located in that planter."

Pointing to the ceiling, Jay continued. "According to the architects of the changes, the roof seam between the lower and upper commons was a very weak point when the original school was built. The new column supports a new beam spanning the seventy-foot width of this area between the upper and lower quads."

Van stepped back. He was trying to envision what it must have looked like in 1972.

Jay said, "Unlike most of the other planters at that time, this planter had a safety fence around it on the upper side and along the descending steps on two sides. As a result, the planter didn't get abused much, and plants actually survived here."

"And the time capsule was placed here because it's between the two common areas?"

"Exactly. It's really the center of the campus. If you look out here across the lower campus, you can see several sets of colored doors leading into academic wings. Each set of doors is a different color with the academic focus of the wing noted in large letters. See, over there, where 'English' is written on the door. All the English classes are in that wing. There's a wing for social studies, math, science, art, and special programs."

"I see. So how does one get to the parking lots and athletic fields I noticed when I drove up?"

"There are exits from each wing to the outside. Also, if you look at the corners of the upper and lower commons, you'll see exits leading outside."

"So, you really have a totally enclosed school except for the athletic fields and parking lots."

"Right. Unlike most schools in Orange County, Nuevo is built more like an eastern school where snow conditions are common. Of course, this means there's a huge air-conditioning system to handle the open areas that would usually be outside for most schools. It was the weight of the roof-mounted air-conditioning system that forced the alterations in the late nineties."

Van turned his attention back to the pillar and eliminated planter. "The planter that was here had sides like those planters over there." Van pointed across the lower quad to a large planter that housed some scraggly plants.

"Yes, the lower quad side on this planter was about four feet high. All the planters had the same basic design; they were made with cream-colored brick housing walls about twelve inches thick. As a result, the top of each wall was ideal for sitting, which was the architect's intention."

"Were any other planters removed?"

"Oh yes, several have been removed, though not for the same reasons. As you walk around both quads, you'll notice places where there's an area of more recently laid concrete on the floor. That's probably because a planter was removed. Same thing in the academic wings where some planters have been removed."

The image of what it must have looked like before the planters were removed reminded him of something he had read in earlier reports. The planters were not stand-alone. "As I understand it from the investigator reports in 1999, the planters extended down into the soil below for drainage reasons."

"Yes, in a way. The soil below the six-inch slab you see throughout the school is very compacted, as you would expect. However, below each planter was a large layer of gravel with a drainage line that would allow water from the planter to be carried off and out under the slab. Otherwise water could seep out onto the concrete floor."

"The reports also indicate that when the planter was being prepared for the time capsule, the custodians originally anticipated the capsule would extend below the ground surface of this planter, so they dug down about six feet."

"Yes, I think that's correct. They actually dug down below the surface of the slab into the hard-packed soil and the gravel layer. Is that important?"

"I don't know. Is there anyone around who was on the custodial staff then?"

"No, the lead custodian then, James, passed away in the eighties, and I think most of the custodial staff at that time have retired. I suppose some are still alive. We can check."

Van nodded. "Don't know that they would remember, but I was just curious."

They walked the length of the lower commons and exited the rear of the school building. Along the way, they passed the locations of several previous planters that had been removed and replaced with a concrete slab.

They exited onto the rear athletic field area and walked along the back side of the school building for several yards before reentering the building into what was identified as the vocational arts wing. To the left, just outside and before entering, was a large compound that served as the auto shop. Just inside the entry doors and on the left was the auto shop classroom entrance, and on the right side was the woodshop entrance. Jay unlocked the door.

"Well, this is the woodshop. It looks very different than it did in the early years of the school. All the original equipment has been changed multiple times."

"Investigator Inskeep noted in his report that there was a large … he called it a *projects room*. Where is that?"

"Just over here." They walked to the back of the room where there was an eight-foot-wide double door. Jay unlocked the door and opened it. The two were met by a wall of what could be called, for lack of a better term, junk. "Wow, I haven't been in this room for years, but if memory serves me right, it's always been a mess. I think it was used to store anything the teacher, or in this case teachers over time, didn't want out in the classroom. As you can see, it's everything from student projects to old equipment."

Van too was surprised. "I can see what Inskeep meant when he said there could be a body in here and they would never find it." Jay just smiled. Every large institution had its junk room.

There was no way to navigate the room, which Jay said went back about twenty feet. It was literally a wall of junk.

"Was this where the prototype would have been stored?"

"Probably not initially. If they were using it as a model to build the actual time capsule, I think it would have been out on the floor. However, once the actual time capsule was built, I think the prototype would have been relegated to this room. But, of course, that's not what happened. Stuff doesn't end up in here for the short term."

"Who would have had a key to this room?"

"The teacher, of course … and also each member of the custodial crew, both those in the day and those who worked nights to clean the classrooms. Each administrator would have had a key as well. They have master keys to everything."

"Would any of the other shop teachers have had a key?"

"You mean like the auto shop or electronics or metal shop teachers? I doubt it. They each had their own storage room. Certainly the department chair would have."

"Would the storage room ever be left unlocked?"

"Never. It locks whenever it's closed. Takes a key to get in."

"And the classroom. Who had keys to this classroom?"

"Same people. The only other way to get a key would be to have one checked out to you by the principal's secretary, who was the custodian of keys."

"Where would she have kept the extra keys?"

"We have a safe in the front office. Only the principal, assistant principal for operations, and the secretary would be able to access it. I assume it was the same then as it is now. Pretty standard throughout the district."

"And keys are tightly controlled?"

"Especially in this school since it's all indoors, and once into the main building, one could access the many open classrooms back then."

"You mean the classrooms were left unlocked?"

"Actually, if you go into the academic wings, even the science wing, the original design of the school had no doors on the rooms. Only the vocational rooms, band and choir rooms, and PE facilities had doors."

"That's interesting. You say most rooms *had* no doors."

"Yeah, it began to change in the late seventies as teachers

complained. The original design was to be a very open campus. The wing halls are as wide as classrooms, and the theory was that every space was to be open and useful for instruction and learning. Also, within each wing are planters that were meant to give the feeling of openness."

"So all of this changed over time?"

"The issues of safety and security along with teacher preference eroded the openness. Eventually doors were added to all the rooms. Where originally one needed only to access the big building to gain access to most of the rooms, by the 1980s, one needed a key for each room."

"So, if I was a teacher here in 1973 and I taught English and came in on a weekend to do work, all I needed was a key to get into the main building, and then I would have access to almost every room except those in vocational arts and the other areas you mentioned."

"Yes, but you wouldn't have access to the gym, locker room, or offices in the wings."

"Offices in each wing?" Van showed surprise with his question.

"Because the classrooms were open, each wing had a room of cubicle office spaces assigned to each teacher. It was a communal office area. The idea was that a teacher had an office cubicle and could not call a particular classroom theirs. Multiple teachers could use the room during the day. During what would be a teacher's conference period, he or she could work in their office cubicle, and another teacher could use the room."

"What about the administration office area? You needed keys?"

"Every teacher has a key to the main office area that gives them access to the lounge and general office area. Administrators and counselors have their own private offices there."

"But except for the wing offices and certain private offices, a teacher could access much of the school. Even the main office area?" Van was thinking about the implications. "This was a very unique school architecturally—in the beginning, I mean."

Jay smiled and shrugged. "That it was, but now it's much more traditional."

"And getting keys was difficult."

"Giving out keys has always been a sacred practice. If you lose your keys, the consequence is expensive because in an enclosed school where everyone has a master key to enter from outside, all the locks would have to be rekeyed. If you lost keys, you had to answer to the assistant superintendent for personnel services. It's not something you want to do."

They were walking back across the upper commons and toward the main office when Van stopped. Something was turning over in his mind, and he did not want to lose it.

Jay stopped as well but said nothing.

Van looked around in all directions before turning to Jay. "When did the school start removing the plants from some of the planters and pouring a slab to cover the planter?"

"Well, let's see, I think the first one was done in about 1975. If you look over there in the lower quad where the so-called amphitheater is located, you'll see a planter on each side of the stage. Plants never did well there because students always stood in the planters for a better view during performances. So, early on, they removed the plants and put in a four-inch slab."

"So, over time, some planters were removed, and some were capped with a slab."

"That's pretty much what happened."

"Even in the academic wings?"

"Most of those were capped in the seventies because the plants just didn't do well. All are about ten feet long and five feet wide. They make great sitting areas for students, so they weren't removed, just capped."

"Do you think there's any record when each one was removed or capped?"

"I suppose district maintenance and operations may have that information. They do the work, and I assume they would have records. We could check."

"Yes, I'd like to know when each planter was either capped or removed. It would also help to have a map that showed where each capped or removed planter was located."

"Let me see what I can do. You think this is important to your investigation?"

Van was going on a hunch that had occurred to him quite suddenly. But it was best to keep his reasoning close. "Don't know, Jay. But I long ago learned to make few assumptions during an investigation. If you could obtain that information for me, it may be helpful."

They walked into the main office area. Jay bought a couple of bottles of iced tea from the vending machine in the teacher's lounge and gave one to Van.

Van noticed the panel of open boxes mounted along one wall of the lounge. By his quick calculation, there were about eight rows of boxes. Each box was about four inches high and twelve inches wide. A row had about ten boxes. "I calculate about eighty boxes against that wall. Are those staff mailboxes?"

"Yeah, each employee has a box with their name. Any mail, flyers, notices, need-to-know information, and just about anything else that will fit into a box can be passed to and from staff."

"Were they here when the school opened?"

"Yep."

"So anyone with access to this lounge, actually to the front office, had access to these boxes."

"Correct."

"Did that bother teachers? I mean, students, staff, even visitors and parents could come in."

"Well, I suppose it's been an issue but not enough to eliminate the practice. Most schools do the same thing. In fact, many teachers send their student aides to the front office to get things out of their mailbox or put something in another teacher's box."

Van had to smile. "So, teachers complained about privacy and security in their rooms and wanted doors but were willing to let this open mailbox practice exist. Interesting irony."

"I suppose it is. Never thought of it that way."

"So, if I wanted to leave a key to my room for another teacher or staff member, I could do so by just putting it in their box, and he or she could give it back when done by putting it in my box? There would be no need for in-person exchange."

"That's true. I'm sure that's been done, although it would be frowned upon."

"Why?"

"Because this isn't a secure room. Students are always in here stuffing things in the boxes. Any kind of advertisement for the student body, PTA, Booster's Club, and you name it ends up being stuffed into boxes here. Students distribute the mail. Like I said, teachers are always sending students up here to get things out of their box or to put something in another box."

Van was taken by the oddity of practice. "So, for employees, the school environment is a mixture of tight policies and loose practices."

Jay found the conclusion both humorous and serious. "A very perceptive observation, Investigator. You're always thinking, aren't you?"

"It comes with the job."

As they walked toward the principal's office, Van began to wonder about where Allison Connors taught. He needed to familiarize himself with her environment. He realized the tour had already taken considerable time, but one more stop was important.

—⟋⟍—

Back in his office by noon, Van immediately sat down to record observations. His visit to Nuevo proved valuable. Seeing the site of a crime is always preferable to reading what someone else says about it. Photos and detailed descriptions do not hold up to an actual visit.

Foremost was the fact that the campus was so open in 1973. Even today, in a security-conscious world, the campus seemed excessively open. But in 1973 it took only a couple of keys to access almost all of the campus. That Cindy's remains were deposited in the prototype capsule over the weekend seemed less than surprising. Before leaving, Van asked if there were any old records of which keys were checked out to which teachers and staff in 1973. Sylvia said there were lots of old files, and it would take time to see if those included any key checkout records. She was not confident of finding anything, but she would look.

It'll take time, thought Van. Of course, that was one of the standard lines from sources when one was investigating a very cold case. *The more distant the event, the more distant the evidence.* Nothing came easily when it came to relying on old witnesses, records, and evidence.

The removal and capping of planters was also intriguing. Something had caught Van's attention as he thought back to the moment it occurred to him that if someone could slip into the school to bury the prototype capsule, they could likewise use the capping of any planter as an opportunity to bury other things, maybe even another body. If records of the planter capping process suggested it started as early in the school's history as Jay suspected, Van wanted to know which planters were capped and when.

One other element of his visit was useful, not because it provided any revelations but because it was a personal experience for Van.

Just before taking leave from the school, Van asked where Allison Connors taught. Jay took Van to the English wing but did not instantly remember which room she had used. The teachers did move around during those early years. It was kind of like jockeying for position in a horse race, said Jay. It took a couple of years before teachers began to express passionate preferences for certain rooms. That passion grew even more as the doors were added to the rooms.

As they entered the English wing, Jay stopped and looked around. Jay was trying to take his mind back mentally and match a face with a room. "Thinking back, if I'm not mistaken, I believe Allison taught in this corner room." It turned out to be a room just inside the wing, next to a capped planter.

While Jay was trying to confirm in his mind which room Allison had taught in, Van sat on the planter and tried to imagine the wing in the early years with all the rooms having no doors and all the planters filled with plants. One could see that before doors were added, the entrance to each room was about six feet wide and open to the high ceiling. One could have easily walked down the very spacious hall and looked into each room, even seen what was happening at any given time. No doubt it would have been noisy since there were no doors to contain the classroom activities. Certainly the carpeted floors in the rooms and hall helped in that regard.

The planter walls were only about two feet high. Students could sit around the planters, but since they were not yet capped in the early seventies, students had to walk around them when passing along the hall. Van's recollection of his own high school days suggested movement in the wing would have been crowded and noisy between classes. Did the students really respect the planter, or did the plants get abused when students took a shortcut through a planter? *Probably the latter. Another reason the planters in these wings weren't practical.*

With capping, each planter became like one big brick-and-concrete table. Van could see where today the capped planter tops were a great sitting area.

Jay came back. "Yes, I'm sure that for several years Allison taught in this classroom."

"Do you have a key to the room?"

"Yes, this master key will open it." Jay opened the door, flipped on the lights, and stepped aside so Van could enter.

As he entered, Van let his senses take over. He relaxed and let his mind take it all in. It was a practice honed from experience in wide-ranging cases over years. He once described the practice as *sensory inventory.* He treated it as a skill. He had explained to his wife that it was like their honeymoon visit to Phantom Ranch at the bottom of the Grand Canyon. Standing along the edge of the Colorado River and gazing up at the endless line of stratified cliffs above had given Van some feel for how overwhelmed John Wesley Powell and his men must have been while floating through the unknown canyon. Van had read about the 1869 exploration, but nothing helped him connect with the expedition more than seeing what they saw. Despite all his reading, seeing what Powell saw was as close as he could get to those events, and it impacted his senses.

Standing in what was once the room of Allison Connors affected

Van's senses. It was as close as he could get to his prime suspect. At the time, Van knew it as a sensory connection with a person he knew by name but knew little about.

At the time, Van was conscious that she had walked every inch of the room. She had passed in and out of the doorway countless times, and she had taught an equally countless number of kids in the room. It was disturbing to think that she likely gave thought to heinous plans here as well.

He glanced around the room, imagining it as it could have been almost a half century earlier. She had stood where he was standing. Everything that she was as a teacher had been in this room. Van wondered, *Who are you? Where are you? Why did you kill those kids? Who else have you killed? Yours is a trail of murder, a trail of madness. We'll find that trail and find you.*

PART 3

—∭—

GOING IN A DIFFERENT DIRECTION

If passion drives you, let reason hold the reins.
—*Benjamin Franklin*

T HE WORLD OF literary self-help advice is full of clever sayings about overcoming obstacles through hard work. Who has not been told that *if at first you don't succeed, try and try again*? Every young school kid is told that success depends on a philosophy of *practice makes perfect*. Later, when one is a teenager, the advice is modified to give it a historical context by suggesting that the *Puritan ethic* is at the root of success.

Of course, at some point we all come to realize that the linear connection between trying and succeeding is not so straight. Experience often reminds us that pursuit of goals is sometimes accompanied by a healthy dose of failure and sometimes requires a little luck.

Failure is a great teacher. The question is whether the victim of failure is a good learner. If we are attuned to the lessons of failure, we soon learn that it is not a matter of just working harder toward our goal. It is a matter of working smarter.

Passion is also important in goal quests. But passion alone can be a double-edged sword. Although it is a valuable motivator, it can also cause one to be blind to reality and to lessons.

History is brimming with failures resulting from passionate minds that did not listen to what was happening around them as they marched forward toward goals and in the face of odds against them. The rubble of lost endeavors is filled with the bodies of those who were convinced they were right and need not listen to advice.

Just the same, history is also filled with examples of those humble and reasonable enough to constantly take stock of the lessons to be learned and the advice to be heeded. They may go slowly, but their tenacity is evident in the commitment and willingness to consider alternatives.

To Catch a Thief, as the 1955 Alfred Hitchcock movie suggests, sometimes requires divergence from the norms of investigative methods. It may require listening to a different line of thinking. It may take a thief to catch a thief but not always.

Success in solving a crime, especially one that has remained cold for decades, may require a willingness to consider alternative methods. It may require finding a different entrance into the world of the criminal in order to understand the motivation of an evil and misguided passion. It may require finding a new way forward, lest once again you settle for nothing. After all, as the Roman poet Lucretius suggested, ex nihilo nihil fit—nothing comes from nothing. The way forward may ask for something new.

CHAPTER 27

—∞—

SERGEANT PIERCE

Orange County Sheriff's Department
South County Substation

V AN PARKED AND entered the Employees Only door of the
department's South County facility. Sergeant Pierce was not in
his office but had put a Post-it on the door: *Van, have a seat. I went
to get us some iced tea.* Van had to smile; his reputation preceded
him. The sergeant had gone to the trouble of finding out about Van's
habits. It was a good sign. It's what cops do.

Upon the sergeant's return, initial greetings were followed by
the usual dance of questions and information swapping. There were
the customary inquires about history in the department. In such
encounters, it's all about your experience, your record. As expected,
they began with which academy class each had been in, their initial
assignment in the jail, and who they worked with. Then they moved
on to their years as deputies and again a discussion of their colleagues
at that time. All of this was the trail of credibility. The department
was a who-you-know environment. Establishing your credentials
with others was a matter of revealing your assignments and with
whom you had rubbed elbows.

This discussion of personal biography was followed by the usual,
"Did you know …?" Or, "Did you ever work with …?" Then, as
information came forth, there was the "Oh, I remember that case," or,

"Wasn't so-and-so involved in that?" It went on like that for several minutes.

These were formalities of importance. Any ability to work together amicably depended on these opening inquiries and sharing of foundational information. In the end, each would sense the limits of their potential to discuss the matters Van was bringing to the table. Without the dance beforehand, caution would prevail, and transparency in their discussion would be opaque.

Eventually Van moved the discussion toward his purpose. Van described the case and his current theory that the perp was a female teacher of substantial intellectual and physical prowess. He detailed what had been learned regarding the site of the VW burning and physical demands of leaving the area alone, especially at night. He shared the apparent hiking and backpacking expertise of the teacher and the earlier questionable death of her father in an alleged accident along the John Muir Trail. Van noted that at least one investigator at the time questioned the idea that it was an accident.

Finally, Van explained that his research suggested other people had disappeared under unknown and questionable circumstances in the Sierra, along the JMT. This was information gleaned from Google searches and inquiries with other agencies. Given that Allison apparently hiked the Sierra a good deal with her father, who died under dubious circumstances, it seemed reasonable to find out how common it was that people died in the backcountry.

Apparently it was not uncommon for people to be killed in an accident. However, most accidents were witnessed by others who were either unable to rescue the victim or unable to successfully render aid. In some cases, the body of a victim was discovered at a later date, usually by chance.

Van noted his take on it all. "It is interesting, however, that there have been, that I know of, at least four people who disappeared in the Sierra since the death of Archie Connors. All initially disappeared without a trace. In each case, there were no witnesses. One was found a year later in a river. But the cause of death has never been ascertained. A male disappeared, and no body has ever been found.

The bodies of a young couple who disappeared were later found by a packer. The couple was killed by blunt force trauma to the heads."

Van glanced at his notes. "Oh, yes. A female 'trail runner' disappeared on a one-day outing and has not been found. There was no backpacking involved. Not sure this fits into the picture."

Pierce was a good listener. He did not interrupt.

"I'm working on gathering more information about these, but quite frankly I have little to suggest it's a good chase since I cannot connect them to Allison Connors. Actually, I sometimes feel I'm grasping at straws.

"Fenton suggested I contact you because of your backpacking experience and my need for some help."

Pierce smiled. "Well, I would be glad to provide input, but I really think you need to talk with my dad and his friend Rob. They have lots of experience in the Sierra." There was a slight smile on the sergeant's face. "Actually, you wouldn't be the first law enforcement officer they've worked with."

"So I've heard. But give me your assessment. Would they be amenable to going to the site of Archie Connors's death, the location where the bodies of a couple were found, and maybe explore some OC trails of interest and give me their assessment of what they see and find?"

"It's certainly something they could do."

"My understanding is they've done some freelance work with the Inyo County sheriff."

"That they have. They're good friends with the retired sheriff Bob Pagliano. Mind you, Dad and his friend were never in law enforcement. My dad is a retired professor and high school administrator, and Rob owned a successful optical instrument company and is retired. For forty or fifty years, they've tramped the Sierra together. There are probably few trails they haven't hiked. People come to them all the time for input."

"What is it they did for Inyo County?"

"Two long stories. But let me summarize. The first involved their discovery of the body of a missing backcountry ranger. Although not

252 Trail of Madness

confirmed, they pretty much proved the death wasn't accidental as was initially determined. Second, a few years later, they were contacted by the wife of a man who died in the Los Angeles Aqueduct many years earlier. They were asked to look into it. Again, they revealed it was probably not an accident as the coroner had determined."

"Sounds like detective work to me."

"Not really. Dad and Rob just use a different style of searching for answers. The best way to describe it is to say they go into a slow wander. They ask the questions no one else is asking. They befriend people who give them information, and they poke their noses where others aren't likely to smell. They're kind of like hound dogs looking for a scent."

The unconventional style appealed to Van. "So you think they could help."

"I'm certain they could, but you have to talk with them. They both travel a bit, and my mom and Rob James's wife aren't real big on the two of them getting involved in any more Eastern Sierra investigations. I suggest you contact my dad first. He'll let you know if they're interested. If they are, you'll have to deal with them together."

"You're smiling. Is there a problem?"

"Yeah, those two could give you some real insight. Probably drive you nuts as well since they have this great ability to wander into fixes. Not the kind of trouble you and I are used to, but the kind that stirs the pot and raises new questions. Good stuff, actually."

"One thing I want to avoid is trouble. Can't have my case getting into the press."

"Don't worry." Pierce was smiling. "They want nothing to do with notoriety. It's not their style." Pierce raised his eyebrows and smiled again with a nod. "Some wine or beer, maybe, but not attention." Grabbing a piece of paper and a pen, he jotted a note. "Here's my dad's cell phone. Give me a couple of days to contact him, and then you can call. He and Mom are on a trip now. Plan on calling him after I give him a heads-up and then call you."

"I really appreciate your help, Ken, but I don't want to interrupt a trip."

Pierce waved off the comment. "Don't worry about it. Anything having to do with hiking, backpacking, or the Sierra will never be an inconvenience if it does not interfere with some other adventure. He'll gladly take your call. If they can do it, you'll have fun working with them. Oh, and here ..." Sergeant Pierce got up and retrieved a book from his shelf. "This is one of my dad's books. It's fiction and is situated in the Eastern Sierra and recounts the lives of two very different men—one a CPA and the other a large construction project supervisor—whose lives converge unexpectedly. Some information about the Eastern Sierra, building of the LA Aqueduct, and backpacking."

"Thanks. I'll get it back to you."

"Keep it. I have more copies. Dad gives them away."

Van glanced at the cover and looked up. "How do you pronounce your dad's first name?"

"It's Sti, as in eye."

"Interesting, don't think I have ever encountered the name before."

"It's my father's nickname."

The initial meeting with Sti and Rob took place in Van's office. Through the process of introductions and informal conversation, Van fell under the allure of the two friends. On the surface, they seemed to be just a couple of retirees. But listening to their comments, the use of history and literary clichés in their humor, and their use of uncommon, if not esoteric, terms, told him they were not to be undersold. There was shrewdness to their bearing. They were smart and did not miss much.

Van began by asking if they were familiar with the disappearance of two high school students following a prom in 1972. They were but had not heard much since the discovery of remains at a high school in the late nineties.

Van transitioned to some cautionary comments regarding the

delicate nature of his request and the need for any information he might share to be kept private. He alluded to the unorthodox nature of his request and his need to feel that Sti and Rob could be counted on to limit their comments, actions, and interactions to the parameters of his request.

Having received assurances, Van went on. "Let me share why it is that I could use your help." Van discussed what he had learned about a particular person of interest—a female teacher who was an especially accomplished hiker and backpacker. He did not call her a suspect, but he did not need to. Van knew the two friends would read between the lines. Van shared with them all that he knew about her and his suspicion that she might be living near the Sierra, though he knew that covered a lot of ground.

He recounted known disappearances along the JMT. Although he had no proof of a link between these and his suspect, he reasoned that his suspect could have been involved. What made this connection stronger was the way the suspect's father died. Van shared the story of Archie Connors's death and gave them the article from the *Inyo Register*. He also noted that blunt force trauma was common to all the deaths. Tenuous as it was, there could be a link.

"I'm sure you know that my theory is circumstantial and based on what many would call coincidental occurrences. However, I'm inclined to believe there's a very good chance that the person who killed our two students, Archie Connors, and perhaps others along the JMT was the same person—Archie's daughter."

Van reviewed what he knew about Allison and the preponderance of evidence that pointed to her. He concluded by noting, "We can't find her. She disappeared."

As his two guests were not in law enforcement, Van expected them to ask a lot of questions and seek clarification. They did not. He wondered if they were quiet because they were uncertain—or just quiet out of respect. Perhaps it was neither. The two were a bit perplexing.

"The one thing that troubles me is that it's hard to imagine that a woman acting alone could carry out these murders. Given your knowledge of backpacking, is it realistic to think that a female backpacker could do what I'm inclined to think would take two or more people?" He did not wait for an answer. "Let me amend that to include the idea that I think it not likely that a single woman, let alone a single man, could carry out what happened to these people deep in the backcountry. What do you think?"

Rob said, "There's a myth out there that women backpackers are few and that those who are, are studs. The reality is that Sti and I have encountered many women, lots of them in their fifties and sixties and even seventies who can hike the legs off of most men. They carry full packs and can hike with determination. Away from the trail, you would never guess that capability."

Sti chimed in, "They need not look like fireplugs. Many of the strong women hikers have little or no fat, they're rails, and they're rugged, and they can wear an evening gown to rival any celeb on the red carpet. Some even hike solo."

Rob added, "You have to understand, Van, the modern world of backpacking along the JMT is that of many people every day passing the same scenery. It's a very popular sport, and there are almost as many women doing it as men."

Van nodded. He was learning about a sport that he had never paid any attention to.

Sti continued. "Of course, that wasn't the case in the 1960s and '70s. The number of women was considerably fewer. During the last three or four decades, the number of female backpackers has skyrocketed."

Rob concluded, "To finish answering your question, yes, we think it possible that a woman could murder and dispose of people on the trail. Heaven knows how or why, but it is possible."

"Thank you for your candor."

Sti said, "But you didn't ask us here just to answer that question. The trainer in a local fitness gym could have told you that."

"No, I didn't. I want to draw on your collective knowledge and skill. I would like to ask you to go to a couple of the places where bodies have been found and search around. These places are no longer restricted sites, and I think it possible some evidence could have been left by those who conducted the investigations. In essence, I need you to be my eyes."

Rob wanted clarification. "Is there anything in particular you expect … let me restate that, would like to find?"

"Yes. I want to know if those investigating overlooked an earring."

The response caught the two off guard. Their facial expressions said as much. Van explained the earring on Cindy's remains. Van wanted Sti and Rob to sift through the soil at a particular site and answer his question.

Van acknowledged that his theory was a stretch. The suggestion of a link between a dead high school girl and her missing prom date with the disappearances and deaths of trail hikers was a risky bet at best. But he felt there was one thread of probability, and that involved the prime suspect who was a "strong backpacking fanatic." He had no idea about the motive, but his suspect had a strong proximity to the two teens and the Sierra backpackers. Some might call it coincidence, but until proven otherwise, it was a viable line of thinking. That was all he had.

"Investigator, going to the places is not a problem. Sti and I have probably been there before if it's anywhere near the JMT. But prowling around is another matter. We've done that sort of thing in the past. I'm sure you know that already."

"Yes, Sergeant Pierce explained your work with the Inyo Sheriff's Department. I took the liberty of contacting former sheriff Pagliano, and he assures me that the two of you were discreet and not likely to make a scene that would attract unnecessary attention."

Van added emphatically, "I want to make it clear I have no desire to put you in harm's way. It's just that I'm looking for a piece of evidence, albeit a very small piece of evidence, that could change the focus of my investigation. It could change everything. If it's possible to go to the precise site where two bodies were found, there is a chance, an outside chance I know, that evidence like the earring remains."

"Are we to assume you know what the earring looks like?"

"Yes, and before you went, I would give you a photo. I would also supply you with whatever records and information we can gather that would assist your search."

Sti said, "Investigator, you look to be fit. Why don't you accompany us to one or more of the sites." Van's eyebrows reacted, but Sti was determined to push the proposal forward. "Listen, we could go to wherever you want, search, take photos and notes, and write up reports for you. But you would be no wiser as a result. You want to understand a backcountry crime scene, you need to see it."

"Well, I don't know. I think I would just get in the way. Anyway, my theories about Allison Connors may be way off base, and the department might frown on such an adventure."

Sti did not let Van off the hook. "If you've come this far in your investigation, we can only assume your superiors are well aware of developments related to the Sierra. If they haven't called you off at this point, there's reason to believe they support where you're going with the investigation. Right?"

"I suppose ..."

"Well, we can make it easy for you. It would not be required that you hike. A good pack outfit can get you to most any place along the JMT in a day or two at the most. We would hike in and meet you. Your presence at one or two locations could benefit your thinking immeasurably."

Rob's comment was meant to get Van to step back and consider the issue from a different vantage. "You know, Investigator, you need to expand your experience with the outdoors. If it's true that your suspect is not only very experienced in the Sierra, it's likely also true that she's very experienced in the Santa Ana Mountains where the van was found. Having a perception of things from limited contact and photos and reports doesn't begin to cut it. Seeing is believing."

"I suppose you're both right, but I'll need to run this past my bosses."

Rob went on, "Look at it this way. If what you think proves to be the case, then any evidence or closure that results from your visit to a JMT crime scene is going to better position you to get a read on your suspect. If she's as good as I think you have suggested, then you're not going to get inside her mind without getting inside her world."

—m—

Later that evening, Van sipped his glass of wine and then set it aside and picked up the book by Dr. Pierce. Sitting in his favorite reading chair, the mellow and subdued sounds of Mozart in the background, he opened the book and began to read through the introductory pages. Sergeant Pierce had mentioned that although the book had a fictional story, it did provide some historical insights into the Owens Valley and the Eastern Sierra.

Several pages into the book, Van came across a map. It provided an aerial view of the Owens Valley and noted the small towns, the Owens River, the Los Angeles Aqueduct, and the major peaks that made up the eastern edge of the Sierra Nevada. The vertical territory of the map showed the town of Bishop at the northern end and the town of Lone Pine at the southern end. Having grown up in California, Van was aware of the general location of the Owens Valley, but his only prior experience with the Sierra had been visits to the resident national parks by way of the Central Valley. He had been to Death Valley, but he had never been in the Owens Valley.

The western side of the map focused on a portion of the Eastern Sierra backcountry and highlighted the John Muir Trail. At the northern end of the map, Van took note of Bishop Pass and the Middle Fork of the Kings River, which he remembered from his reading about the death of Archie Connors. Tracing the route of the JMT south, Van noted that it seemed to follow along the eastern edge of the Sierra and paralleled US 395 several miles to the east. The map seemed to indicate there were several trails that connected the JMT to the Owens Valley. It occurred to Van that at some point he should use Google Earth to get a closer look at the Eastern Sierra.

CHAPTER 28

SEARCHING AND REFLECTING

At Home, in the Office, and on the Road

S UNDAY AFTERNOONS PROVIDED a good time for contemplation. It was not that Van saved the day just for such thinking; it just happened. It was his nature to think reflectively, and many a late evening in the office or at home found him pondering his cases. But Sunday just seemed to be a good day to step back and consider the big picture and the sum of its parts.

His parents had been strongly religious, and Sunday afternoons were for relaxation, reading, a sumptuous family dinner, and discussion—a time for reflection. Van's experiences with Sunday school and church and family seemed to predispose him to using such time for deliberation. Since Anna Marie's death, there had been a tendency on his part to revert to his earlier Sunday-afternoon practices. He was aware more time was being spent reading and thinking.

Van enjoyed the pursuit associated with investigations, and spending time reflecting had proved valuable over time. Even so, there was a delicate balance in the practice. Too much thinking often inhibits the need for action. One needs to think to stimulate the optimum action but not so much as to lead to procrastination. He wanted to avoid the trap of paralysis by analysis. Timely follow-up to issues and questions is critical. So he was always aware of the need to stop and consider the implications of information and questions. He was also aware of the need to make progress. It was all about balance.

But Sundays had an advantage in that he was less likely to be interrupted by outside influences, or, as in the case of late evenings, by sleep. Sunday afternoons allowed him to sit back and consider the big picture in light of the details he had gathered. Van likened it to a complex thousand-piece jigsaw puzzle—when one is not rushed and has time to get up and wander around the puzzle and consider the relationships between pieces even though they are not yet connected, it is sometimes possible to see where things fit.

The combination of Sergeant Pierce's comments regarding the nature of backpacking in the Sierra and the subsequent interview with Sti and Rob left Van with some trepidation about his prime suspect, Allison Connors. His instincts said she lived in the mountains, or at least near them. She could live in one of the canyons of the Santa Ana range, but he doubted it. His hunch was that she lived close to the Sierra Nevada, where she was born and appeared to be most comfortable. He also suspected that if Allison was involved in the disappearance and deaths of others in addition to her father, the Sierra was her backyard. But she had to be in her seventies, and he was having difficulty imagining her living near and hiking the Sierra at will.

Perhaps, thought Van, *I've missed something. Allison's our best suspect. Maybe I've mistakenly assessed her. Could it be that Allison isn't who I think she is? There doesn't appear to have been a Sierra murder or missing backpacker in the last twenty years that could be associated with her or with the earlier missing backpackers. Could she have actually retreated from her earlier personality and now lives quietly and genteel-like beyond our reach? If that's so, I might be pursuing the wrong angle. Maybe she's dead. Am I chasing a figment?*

The balance between the known facts in an investigation and developing theories about possible suspects is a treacherous endeavor at best. The results have the potential to lead an investigation down the wrong, if not dangerous, path. It is a little like using football game films of next week's opponent as a basis for designing a game plan for that opponent. Such planning is only as good as the assumption that the opponent is predictable on the basis of the evidence. Most of what Van knew about Allison was old data suggested by the memory of others regarding events for which there was little more than conjecture for support.

Van was also aware that he was dangerously close to becoming too intimate with the case. Though he was not drawn to the case for the same reasons as Vargas in '72, he had to be careful to not let his gut overrule what his head knew. Vargas had been a victim of his own passion. Van was conscious of the results of being too deeply involved in the case and was constantly reminding himself to take a step back when connecting details with the big picture.

If, indeed, Allison Connors was responsible for the disappearances and deaths of Cindy and Carlos, and others in the Sierra, Van had to be careful not to allow assumptions to mislead his search for her. She had survived decades beyond the reach of law enforcement, and assumptions about her based on old data favored her current status.

All these years later, *she may not be what she seems* was a reoccurring theme in Van's thoughts.

Van's thoughts raced toward questions about Allison. *Who was Allison the child, the student? Who was she when her father died? Who was she in 1972? Who was she if she roamed the trails of the Sierra for three decades or more and was probably party to the disappearance of others? Who was she as she selected her victims?*

Who is Allison Connors today? Was she then as she seems now? Or has she changed? Why did she kill? Does she see logic in her actions?

As a student of his craft, Van had spent considerable time reading about the psychology of serial killers. But Allison Connors did not seem to fit the typology. There appeared to be no need for any recognition on her part. In fact, had not Nuevo High School been in need of architectural modifications, the remains of Cindy would probably not have been found until after Allison's own death.

Perhaps she was now dead. But he did not think so.

He was also aware that there were reasons Allison committed crimes. He did not yet know those reasons, but somewhere there was evidence to support a hypothesis. Any chance of apprehending and convicting her depended on developing credible evidence that not only linked her to Cindy and Carlos but provided an equally credible motive for her actions.

The death of Allison's father was at one extreme. She would not be the first to have killed a father under circumstances that appeared accidental. At the other extreme, it was likely the disappearances and deaths of others in the Sierra were not planned but just happened because the victims created circumstances of convenience for a deluded mind.

The key had to be Cindy and Carlos. Somewhere in their relationship was the reasoning for those killings that followed after that of Archie. Cindy and Carlos were close to the motive. Allison saw something in the two high school students that triggered her actions. Equally likely was the idea, and Karli Ryan agreed, that similar traits could have triggered Allison's actions in the murder of selected backpackers.

Van had no doubt the death of Archie Connors was no accident. In all likelihood, Archie's death was the first of Allison's murders. *How many murders followed? Who were they? When did the killing end? What was the common denominator?*

The answers to his questions were elusive, but he was confident that if he kept at it, each bit of insight would lead him to a greater understanding of Allison's motives and her current existence.

Somewhere in the Santa Ana Mountains were clues to the disappearance of Cindy and Carlos. The location of the VW van was not accidental or convenient. It was purposeful and therefore suggested a connection between the area and the murderer.

Similarly, the Sierra Nevada, especially the John Muir Trail, held some insight into Allison's motives. If the death of Archie was purposeful, there was reason to believe the motive held some meaning when one looked at her motives for the disappearances and deaths of the others.

Finally, scant as they may be all these years later, the merging of bits and pieces of information about Allison must, at some point, begin to provide a clearer picture of who she was in the past and who she was today. No doubt she no longer went by the name Allison Connors. However, Van was banking on the idea that Allison's intelligence was such that an alias would reflect some element of logic, if not irony, and not just a name pulled out of a hat.

Allison Connors was smart. She was brilliant. The only way he would find her was if he was at least equal to her talents. She would expect nothing less from anyone who pursued her.

As Van was wont to do, he returned to the issue of relationships. Finding Allison meant that he needed to understand her world, her intellectual world and her backpacking world. The first was an obscure, perhaps even hidden, world. Insight into the mental side of Allison's personality meant he needed to track down friends and associates. Of course, to do this he needed to locate where she lived and went to school. He needed high school and college records. He needed to continue talking with anyone who had known or encountered her. Roommates, teaching colleagues, and employers were all important.

He was well aware that tracking down any information on the young Allison Connors would not be easy. But he had no choice. If Allison was as bright as others suggested, then he would stand no chance of outsmarting her unless he could begin to understand her.

The second set of relationships was more tangible. He had to spend time coming to grips with the world of the backpacker, the world of the trail, the world of her interest in the outdoors.

Perhaps Sti and Rob were correct; he had to walk where Allison Connors had walked. Here he was not as confident as he was regarding the need to understand her intellect. It was more of a hunch than he was accustomed to acting on, but the location and circumstances of the VW along with the fact that she loved backpacking and was born in the Owens Valley suggested to Van that it was a credible hunch.

—⚍—

For several weeks, Van banged the phones in an effort to connect with some of Allison's former colleagues at NHS that he had not previously interviewed. He would have much rather met with them in person, but most no longer lived in the area. His approach was to phone and ask selected questions, the answers to which he could use as a screening device to determine those whom he did not need to continue interviewing and those he might want to talk with more.

He had a list of teachers, classified staff, and administrators who worked at Nuevo during Allison's tenure at the school. Only the younger teachers in 1972 were readily available, though they were now long retired. Most of the older teachers were very elderly now if they were alive. All three of the assistant principals, as well as the principal, were deceased. One custodial member was living, but he was not involved in burying the time capsule. Three of the clerical staff lived in Orange County, but they seemed to have little recollection of Allison other than she was "different and smart."

It had taken hours over many days to work his way through the list. In the end, his notes suggested scant new information. Van's bulleted notes summarized his findings.

- Always on time to school, never absent, and never left the school workday early.
- Followed all attendance, supervision, school, and classroom rules and regulations.
- Did not have problems with students and never referred any student to the front office.
- Was not the subject of any parent or student complaints.
- Consummate professional in her dress and behavior on campus and at campus events.
- Attended some faculty social events, but her behavior was always proper and did not betray her professional standing in the eyes of others. No one saw her consume alcohol.
- Never exercised her intelligence at the expense of others.
- None of those interviewed saw in her any potential to harm another—student or otherwise.
- An unknown quantity outside school.

It was the missing information that caught Van's attention. Everyone seemed to know that Allison was an exceptional athlete and backpacker, but no one seemed to know what she did in her off hours. They assumed she worked out and went hiking, but if she did, those who knew her never saw evidence of it.

What also struck Van as odd was the statement of one teacher that when Allison left school, she seemed to just disappear. "We all knew she lived in the area, but no one ever saw her outside school. No one seemed to know what she did with her free time, her vacation. She just disappeared. Never really talked about it."

Another comment caught his attention as well. Were it made by someone today, it would not seem out of place. In the early 1970s, he thought, it would have been a strange observation. "You know, Detective, Connors was different. Oh, yeah, she was smarter than the rest of us and a bit quirky, but I don't mean that. What I mean is that she watched what she ate, was physically fit, and struck a figure the rest of us could only envy. She was ahead of the health-craze curve."

To colleagues, Allison Connors was an enigma. The teacher, Miss Connors, was equally unknown. Students described her with platitudes of respect, and it appeared to Van that she was extremely competent and fair on the one hand and an unknown personality on the other.

Van could not help but think that those who encountered Allison Connors as a colleague or teacher saw only one dimension. Beyond what they observed, they knew nothing about her. They could only assume that her life away from school was much like her life at school. Van was already of the opinion that it was a deadly assumption.

Allison Connors was a person of contradictions. The Allison people saw was brilliant and a talented teacher. The Allison people did not see was a mystery that fostered speculation. She was the personification of paradox.

—⁓—

Fate plays a role in the life of police investigations. Sometimes it shines down and delivers unexpected rewards to those who are persistent. Other times, and perhaps most often, it frowns, and even the juiciest of leads hits a brick wall and investigative time yields only frustration.

In the case of Allison Connors, fate suddenly smiled, if only faintly at first. The result was a new source of information, a surprise source.

Van visited the Office of Student Records at Long Beach State and found, quite to his surprise, that many of the records from the school's early years had been digitized from old microfiche—saving him the potential of many hours of tedious searching. Of course, there was the usual dance of privacy issues that the officials threw up as a barrier. He had played this game before and always found the experience both reassuring and confounding. On the one hand, he could appreciate the need to protect privacy. He could only hope that his own privacy was protected with equal zeal. On the other hand, from an investigator's point of view, he was not asking for anything that was unreasonable. He was investigating a very old crime and was looking for information regarding a person of interest who had been a student in the 1960s.

He could get a warrant but hoped it would not be necessary. Van had long ago learned to play the *it could be worse* card if the authorities were resistant. He would explain that a warrant might give him free reign to cull through lots of records, but all he wanted was information about one student. His persistence resulted in being referred to one of the higher-ups in the university. After some explanation and some compliments, Van was given an opportunity to look at the records for Allison A. Connors.

The official transcripts were remarkable in a number of ways. First, the A for the middle name remained an initial with no hint of what it stood for. This was a bit perplexing until the university staff explained it was common even today.

A second frustration was the absence of information about where Allison had gone to high school. The records indicated only that she had been admitted as an honors student based on SAT and

ACT scores. Records that reflected any prior education at the high school level had long ago been destroyed since they were not deemed important.

He was completely surprised by the grades. He already knew Allison was regarded by Nuevo contemporaries as brilliant, but he soon learned why. Allison took a rigorous course of study with a major in English and a minor in history. There were no easy filler courses. She completed her course of study in four years and earned nothing less than a 4.0 GPA.

The transcript noted she was on the dean's list each semester and graduated with honors. When Van inquired about any awards or recognitions that may have been extended to Allison, he was told the records office had no information. It was recommended that he look through the yearbook for those years—the *Prospector*.

The *Prospector* included information about numerous awards given to students, but despite her GPA, there was no evidence Allison received any recognition. Van wondered if it was because she avoided such honors that she did not appear in the yearbooks. There were photos of graduates, but again, as with Nuevo High School, there were no photos of Allison. She was, even then, a mystery.

When he inquired about information regarding Allison as an athlete, Van was reminded that prior to 1972 NCAA, athletics for women was very limited. It was not until Congress enacted Title IX in that year that the scene for women's athletics began to change. The *Prospector* was testimony; there was little suggesting women had a role in athletics then. The women's athletic director helped Van locate some old records that indicated Allison was a distance runner on the intramural track and cross-country teams. She was a "Club" athlete. It was the designation for athletics that were not NCAA sanctioned and not a part of the official CCAA Conference competition schedule. Athletes on the club teams competed on an informal basis.

At the time, LBSU had a limited club program for women. Unfortunately, any records about athletes were limited to articles that may have appeared in the school newspaper, the *49er*.

Tucked away in a spring 1967 issue was an article titled "They Run without Notice." Written by a female student, the theme was equity support for female athletes. The article focused on several students committed to track success. There was a photo of several women running the university track; Allison was not named as one of those in the photo. However, the article referenced her.

A student who appeared in the photo was quoted, "Allison is the best out here. None of us can keep up with her. She's the reason we need formal status for women athletes. It's a shame she's not getting the recognition she deserves." The article went on to note that Allison could be found many early mornings running miles on the track, alone and without anyone coaching her. Those who had timed her unofficially said she could compete with many men at the longer distances.

But it was something else that caught Van's attention. Elizabeth Ambrose was identified as Allison's roommate. "I'm not an athlete, but if I was one, I would want to be like Allison. She's so determined. She's focused. She defines the scholar athlete. I'm glad to be her friend."

Was Elizabeth Ambrose alive? If she was, he had to find her.

CHAPTER 29

ELIZABETH AMBROSE

Belmont Shore, California

IT WAS A stroke of luck. Elizabeth Ambrose graduated from Long Beach State and married a fellow student with the same surname. Such was the rare fortune of an investigator. To make things even easier, she had been living in the same location in Belmont Shore, a quaint seaside community within the city of Long Beach, since 1975, the year she was married. Elizabeth and her husband were major donors to the school, and their whereabouts well known.

Close to the time of his meeting, he drove south on the main street through the oceanfront community of Belmont Shore, crossed the bridge at Bay Shore Drive, and dropped down into the area known as Naples. It was a maze of narrow streets and quaint custom-built houses that fronted on a system of canals. He followed Elizabeth's directions as he made his way through the network to the side street where she told him to park.

The walk across a small canal bridge and descent down the steps to the canal walkway leading to Elizabeth's house brought back a happy memory from years earlier when he and Anna Marie had been in the area to attend a party. The homes along the canals were decorated for Christmas, and they walked among the lights and festivities of the season. It was not something he was likely to ever forget. It was one of the happier times just before she got sick.

Elizabeth's house defined the good life. Like all the canal homes, it was on a narrow parcel, and it was expensive. Elizabeth's home looked to be newer, with two stories and a front that was mostly glass on both floors. A small raised porch led to an ornate door with a gold plaque that read simply "Ambrose."

He knocked and turned to take in the canal view while he waited.

"Investigator Vanarsdale, I see you did not have any difficulty finding the place."

"Not at all. In fact, I rather enjoyed the short walk along the canal from the bridge."

Van entered to find a room with an impeccable view and immaculate interior—a mixture of light colors that complemented the array of Impressionist paintings and elegant sculptures.

"Now, I know you will politely say no, so I insist you have tea or coffee. Which will it be?"

"Well, tea if you insist."

"Do you have a preference?"

"Earl Grey if you have it."

"Oh, yes, a good standard as teas go. Feel free to look around while I get our tea."

"Thanks. It is 'Elizabeth,' correct?"

"Oh yes, always Elizabeth." She was responding from the nearby kitchen. "Before I met Al, people called me Liz, but Al said my name had a regal touch. He preferred Elizabeth. So it is."

Van admired the view out the front window and took time to examine the paintings. The works were by unknown artists. The furniture and accoutrements were of fine quality, and Van thought the atmosphere comfortable, not lavish. The evident wealth was subtle and not garish.

"Here we go, Investigator." Elizabeth motioned for Van to sit in one of the chairs.

Elizabeth took a matching chair and set the tray on the small table between them. She poured him a cup of tea and then one for herself. "Sugar or cream?"

"No, thank you. I drink it black."

"Ah, so you have come by an appreciation of tea on your own and not because of a continental influence."

"Yes, just plain tea."

"Good, good." Elizabeth sipped her tea before setting it down. "Now, I know you are here to talk about Allison, but let me give you some background information. My husband always said, 'Context first and the details second.'"

"Said?"

"Yes, Al passed away several years ago. A good man." Elizabeth smiled. "Interesting thing about Al, he hated the more formal Alfred for himself but insisted on the formal Elizabeth for me. I guess I liked that about him. Anyway, he built a career out of his skill as a communicator. He used to tell the kids that when they were explaining something, they needed to always explain the setting and context before going into the details. Actually, I think he overdid it when they were young, but I know they practice that approach today. You know how it is. We don't realize the value of lessons when we're young, but we find ourselves practicing them when older."

"Yes, the power of early influence." The concept seemed appropriate given Van's purpose.

Noticing a family photo on a nearby table, Van asked the obligatory question. "You have three children?"

"Yes. We raised all here. It wasn't easy when they were very young. The water danger, you know. But we managed, and as they got older, they really enjoyed the water and sailing. They all graduated from Long Beach Wilson High School before going on to college. Then they moved into professions that have since taken them to distant places."

She paused and smiled at Van. *What a pleasant and accommodating woman*, thought Van. *Indeed, there is a regal quality to her.*

"Did Al know Allison as well?"

"Only a little, Investigator. Allison wasn't one to let people get close, especially a male."

Especially a male. Van found the comment full of meaning. Best to hold off on pursuing that issue until later. "Tell me about Allison."

"You know, I roomed with Allison Connors for two years. I thought I knew her as well as one could. But after we graduated, I never heard another word from her. She just disappeared. I have often wondered about Allison. She was the smartest person I have ever known, but her destiny seemed to be beyond my world. But I'm getting ahead of myself.

"Allison and I ended up as roommates by accident. I was sharing an apartment on Roswell with another girl. It was really a granny house behind the owner's home in a peaceful neighborhood. We were about two miles from the campus. I didn't have a car, but the bus ride was easy. When my roommate dropped out, I posted a Roommate Wanted notice on campus. Allison responded. She liked the idea that we each had our own room. Allison's room had a walk-in closet that she converted into what she called her study cave."

"Can you explain that?"

"Allison found a desk for the closet and fitted the closet with a bookshelf for all her books. She had lots of them, lots of privacy too."

"Lots of books of her own? Seems a bit strange for an undergraduate."

"Yes, it was. But Allison had read all of them."

"How many books do you think?"

"Investigator, I don't really know. But I would say there were probably six shelves, each about four feet long. Maybe a couple hundred."

"Do you remember what kinds of books?"

"Mostly great works of literature, philosophy, history, and some were actually in Latin or French."

"Do you think you could construct a list of some of the books you think were on the shelves?"

"I suppose so. I also remember there were some other books, not just books of literature but books of special interest."

"Such as?"

"Books about nature by people like John Muir. I remember his name because Allison had a small poster with a saying she credited to Muir. It was something about *hiking the mountains to get their tidings* or something like that. I'm sure you could Google it. Allison had made the poster herself, and there was a photo of a mountain glued to it. She said she found it in a magazine. She also said she had climbed the mountain, but it looked difficult to me. I was fascinated with that photo, though."

"What fascinated you?"

"At first I thought she was kidding about having climbed it. But with time I came to realize that Allison probably had climbed that and many more very difficult mountains in the Sierra Nevada. My image of her was that she was as strong and powerful as those mountains."

"Can you tell me why you came to that conclusion?"

"Yes, but let me back up a bit first. We first met at the student union. A family friend owned the apartment, and he expected me to vet any potential roommate. I was impressed with Allison, but following the owner's expectations and my mother's advice, I had some questions for her. You know, questions about boyfriends, partying, drinking, those kinds of things. Allison said she spent her time studying, working a part-time library job on campus, and running.

"She would actually run to and from the university. I know there was a group of other female students she would sometimes run with on campus. She worked returning books to the shelves in the library stacks in the late afternoon and then ran back to our apartment."

Van could picture the distance Allison would have had to travel. It was not flat.

"Later I discovered another interest, backpacking. Whenever we had extended breaks, she would disappear to the Sierra. On a few occasions, she would share a magazine article or photo about the Sierra Nevada and comment that she had climbed the featured peak. I was doubtful at first but soon discovered she could explain in detail how to climb the peak. On one occasion, *Life* magazine featured an article about several people killed in a fall on a treacherous Sierra peak. Allison explained what they did wrong and how they could have avoided the disaster.

"Anyway, when Allison moved in, she had few things other than the books and didn't have a car. She had lived in the dorms for two years but concluded it would cost her less by moving off campus. The first day she showed up at the Roswell apartment, she had everything in a backpack and was carrying two duffel bags. The pack looked very used. She called it a Kelty pack. At first I thought it was a Scottish name and spelled with a C. She corrected me and said that was the name of the company. The pack was olive-green. I remember the brand name because it was on a small triangular red label sewn to a flap at the top of the pack. If I saw it once, I saw it a million times—Kelty."

He knew nothing about backpacking and wasn't sure whether Elizabeth's information was valuable. He wrote down *Kelty pack*.

Van was intrigued by the backpack. "You said the pack was called a Kelty, and it looked very used."

"Believe me, Investigator, that pack had seen many miles. I'll never forget her arrival. It was packed with all kinds of things, and it looked so big, much bigger than one would expect. I thought it looked like one of those packs you see being worn by a Sherpa in those Himalayan expeditions. Allison wore it like it was light as a feather. She showed no sign that it weighed too much. When I found out she had hiked all the way from the university, I was dumbfounded. She acted like it was no big deal. When I think back on it, I have no doubt that she would have carried those boxes of books had the apartment owner not transported them for her."

"Was there a lot of backpacking gear?"

"That pack sat in the cave and was always packed and ready to go."

"Did you ever see the contents of the pack?"

"Yes. Let me think. A small stove that could fit in your hand. A sleeping pad, not an air mattress. I think she had a tent, but I never saw it set up. There was a plastic bowl and cup and other cooking items. She had what looked like a down jacket and a few hiking clothes items. She liked hiking in shorts, she said. There were some personal items in a nylon bag. There were other things, but I don't remember them all. But I can tell you she kept that gear in perfect condition. On several occasions, after she returned from one of her outings, I found her cleaning each item before placing it back in the pack.

"Oh yes, she had a sleeping bag she called a mummy bag, and she kept it hanging in the closet. She said the down fill would lose its loft if packed. All she had to do was stuff it in the pack before going. Her boots sat on the floor next to the pack."

"What about maps? Did she have maps?"

"Allison had a large file folder filled with topographic maps. On many occasions, I found her studying them. I found it interesting that she did not take them with her. It seemed she already knew where she was going and didn't need the maps."

"Given how she maintained her hiking gear and her maps, would you say Allison was a meticulous person?"

"I would say she was a minimalist and kept the things she had in good order. Allison's possessions were practical. She wasn't one to collect unneeded items. Everything she owned was taken care of."

"I see. How did the two of you get along?"

"Very well, though I think it was a one-sided understanding."

"Meaning?"

"Allison learned a lot about me. I learned little about her. What I mean is she was good at drawing things out of me. I'm not a real outward-going person, or at least I wasn't then. But I certainly was much more so than she. Allison would engage me in conversations that led me to reveal things about myself. I, in turn, couldn't really get much out of her. I learned more about her just by watching and listening for the messages between the lines."

"What kind of things did she draw out of you?"

"Well, she was always interested in who my friends were and who I was dating."

"Any specific things she was interested in?"

"I always felt like Allison had been appointed by my mother to watch over me. Now mind you, Investigator, my mother was a die-in-the-wool Catholic, a widow, a solid criminal defense attorney, and not one to suffer stupid mistakes. I went to an all-girls Catholic high school, and my mother kept close tabs on me. When I went to Long Beach State, she continued to do so, but she also encouraged me to live more independently. During my freshman and sophomore years, I probably slid back away from some of my mother's admonitions. When Allison came along, I got back on track."

"Can you give me an example?"

"Well, Allison was my alter ego. She had an uncanny ability to size up any of my dates. She didn't hesitate to advise me about who I should avoid."

The mention of alter ego seemed uncommonly insightful. It suggested to Van that Allison had a moral compass regarding human behavior, especially behavior involving others. But what really intrigued him was Allison's interest in Elizabeth's relationships. "How did you respond?"

"Actually, she was usually right. You see, my mother and father were very much in love, and the fundamental foundation of that love, according to my mother, was respect and confidence. My father was the consummate gentleman of honor. When a drunk driver killed him, my mother was devastated. I was twelve years old at the time and old enough to know what my mother lost. I vowed to honor my father by living up to his standards. Allison saw to it that I met this vow by not dating what she called *the dirts*, a derogatory term she used to describe guys who wanted only one thing, and you know what that is."

"*The dirts*. She used that phrase?"

"Yes, *the dirts* were the unsavory boys Allison told me to avoid."

"How did you respond to Allison's views?"

"I didn't disappoint, if that's what you're asking."

"I'm curious. How did Allison let her views be known?"

"She was very candid."

"Can you share an example?"

"Sure. She would say something like: 'Elizabeth, do you really know him? What do you know about him? Let me tell you what I know.' Things like that."

"Sounds like Allison had very set views about how young men should treat women."

"It was more than that. She had definite views on how women should act. A man taking advantage of a woman was as sinful as a woman who was loose. She didn't respect either."

"Did you ever know if Allison dated or had a boyfriend?"

"Never while she lived with me. I thought it odd at first, I guess. I eventually concluded she didn't have time to date or have relationships."

Elizabeth's insights were remarkable. He kept thinking about the implications for his investigation, for the relationship between Carlos and Cindy. It looked like Karli Ryan had hit the nail on the head. Allison's motive was somewhere in the milieu of emotions and drives that encompass the experiences of high school boyfriend and girlfriend relationships. The true picture of Allison A. Connors was beginning to emerge.

The conversation continued for some time along the lines of Elizabeth's perceptions of Allison's views on male and female relationships. Van realized that what he was hearing from Elizabeth was commentary on the thinking of someone whose code of reference provided deeply rooted determinants of the action to be taken if the code was not adhered to.

Van kept probing for examples of Allison's principles and judgments. As the discussion progressed, he became increasingly aware that Allison weighed the quality of male and female relationships. If they lived up to her expectations, all was well. If not, he was beginning to believe that Allison felt compelled to take some action. She would intervene.

It was all there; the motive was beginning to materialize.

He did not say anything to Elizabeth, but Van could not help but think that Elizabeth could thank her mother. Had Elizabeth violated Allison's code, she could easily have become a victim.

"I'm curious about the middle initial, A, in her name. I can't find it in any records."

"We only talked about it once. I asked her what the A stood for, and she said she shared her mother's middle name, Alexandra. I don't recall her elaborating on why she shortened it to a single letter. I guess it just saved space and time."

"Alexandra? I guess if it was her mother's name, that makes sense." As Van recalled, there was no Alexandra in Mary Jo Harden's name.

"Elizabeth, I want to take you back to that week in the summer of 1966 when Allison went backpacking with her father and he died in an accident. Do you remember that?"

"Yes, I do. I felt so sorry for her."

"Can you share with me your recollections?"

"Yes, Allison and I were finishing up summer school when her father called one evening. I took the phone call. We had a very long cord on the phone, so each of us could take the phone into our room. I remember an almost immediate change when I told her who was calling. I left the phone with Allison and closed the door."

"What can you tell me about how she responded?"

"Hard to explain. Her expression changed."

"Did she get angry?"

"I don't mean she was angry. No, it was more like she had expected the call and was obligated to talk with him but not happy."

"What made you think that?"

"She talked for some time. Probably ten minutes, and then she hung up. Ten minutes on the phone was a long time for Allison. When done, she brought the phone out and set it back down in the kitchen and returned to her studies. I couldn't read anything particular into her behavior at that time. I had my own tests to study for, so I didn't pursue the matter. However, about a half hour later, she came out and said she needed to call her father back and would I mind. She took the phone back into the cave."

Van wondered. Interaction of that nature suggested a conflict, followed by guilt, followed by an attempt to patch things up by calling back.

"A few minutes later, she brought the phone back to the kitchen. I'll never forget the look on her face. There was no anger. She was Allison Connors, in control. She told me that after her tests that week she would be leaving for several days to go backpacking with her father. Allison provided no more information. I knew she didn't want to talk more. I knew enough about Allison not to try and engage her in more talk."

"When did she leave?"

"When I came home from my last final three days later, she was gone. Allison wasn't big on saying goodbye. Everything was the same in her room and in the cave, except the pack was gone. She left a note saying she had bought some groceries and would be back in about a week. I remember thinking at the time that she wrote a note much as a mother would. It was as if she was saying, *I bought you some food to tide you over for a week until I get back.*"

"How did you find out about her father's death?"

"Allison called me about a week later. She said that her father had died in a freak accident and they had just brought his body out from the backcountry. She was staying in the Bishop area until he was buried and while she took care of some family things."

"Did she sound upset? Crying?"

"It was strange. I say that because it wasn't Allison's style to exhibit a lot of emotion. She seemed to be in control, something characteristic of Allison under stress. But she wasn't crying. At least it didn't sound like she had been or was crying."

"She said she was going to take care of some family things? Did she elaborate?"

"No, I knew her dad lived up there, and I just figured it natural that she, being an only child, would have things to do. She didn't provide any details."

"An only child?"

"Allison had no siblings. She told me that. She said she had a brother who died when she was young. I think around 1960 or several years before her mother died. I never learned more."

"She never mentioned a sister?"

"Oh, no. I'm quite sure she said she was an only child because her brother had died. I don't remember how old she was, just young."

"Did she talk about her mother?"

"No, not really. But I must confess, while Allison was gone hiking one weekend, I was doing a paper for a literature class and needed to look up something about Don Quixote. I didn't have the book and was certain I had seen one on her shelf, so I went looking. I found the book, and on opening it, I noticed it had a small message to Allison signed *Mom*. Out of curiosity, I looked and then found similar messages in other books. They were just signed with 'Mom.' In fact it occurred to me that Allison never called her mother by name. She was always just *Mom* or *my mom*."

"Do you recall what the notes said?"

"No, not exactly. That was a long time ago, Investigator. As I recall, they were short and along the lines of *This is for you, Allison*. It was pretty generic stuff. I didn't read them all."

Van was going to ask a question but sensed Elizabeth had something to add.

"Oh yes, now that I think about it, there were a couple of books where the note was addressed not to Allison but to Alexi, or Alexis, or something like that. I remember finding it unusual since it was the only reference, other than Allison's own explanation, to her middle name, Alexandra. I never encountered it again."

Alexi or *Alexis*. Again Van recorded the information. "Were there any signed by her father?"

"None. Allison never talked about her father. Would not talk about him. In fact, she mentioned him more when she called about his death than she had the whole time we roomed together. She backpacked with him once each year, but I think they were far from being close. I think she was only obliging her father by going backpacking."

Van thought to confirm a hunch. "Would you say they were estranged?"

"I think that would be a polite way of describing their relationship. Although, in all honesty, I really knew nothing about him."

"You say she never called her mother by name. Did she talk much about her mother?"

"I think she idolized her mother. When she referenced her mom, it was always to note that Mom was smart, Mom was well read, Mom knew people, Mom this and Mom that. Funny ..."

"How's that?"

"I sensed that Allison had been very close to her mother and wanted desperately to live up to her mother's expectations. However, other than the formal reference to 'Mom,' and her mother's middle name, I never really learned anything about her mother. I have often thought Allison probably would have liked to have a relationship with her mom as I had with mine."

"Were there any photos of her parents?"

"There were no photos of her parents or anyone else. I never saw any letters or memorabilia or family heirlooms. Allison's family was a mystery just as Allison was. Strange, isn't it?"

Van was not one to try to read meaning into comments when he could just as easily ask for clarification. "Strange in what way?"

"That you can live with someone, live close to them, for a couple years and never really know them. When you're young, those missing pieces in a relationship are of little importance because you both have your lives to live. It's only when you get older that the strangeness begins to surface. Eventually you begin to wonder how it is that something like that could have happened."

There was a curiosity in Elizabeth's tone. Van let her go on.

"I sometimes wondered if Allison was attending college not just for herself but to somehow vicariously obtain a degree for her mother. It's odd how one sees these things in others. I mean it's odd that we sense things about other people when we really don't understand them."

Van understood the perplexed reflection on Elizabeth's part. As an investigator seeking to identify and pursue a perpetrator, he knew that in the absence of good leads it was not uncommon to conjecture on the basis of very limited information. It was something done of necessity and not without risk. Elizabeth, all these years later, was remembering Allison on the basis of an experience controlled by Allison. Allison did not let people get close. She did not let people understand her.

"You said that Allison disappeared occasionally to go backpacking in the Sierra. Did she ever go backpacking in the local mountains?"

"I don't think so. Maybe, but I don't remember her backpacking locally. Though on occasion she went day hiking in Orange County."

"How do you know this?" He could hardly believe what he was hearing. Elizabeth was a gold mine of information. She was adding pieces to the puzzle.

"I think she once told me she knew the Santa Ana Mountains and liked to hike there when she didn't have time to go to her beloved Sierra."

"If she didn't have a car, how did she get to the local mountains or even the Sierra?"

"She got rides with students going home for holidays. Or she would hitchhike, ride the bus, or pay someone to give her a lift."

"Did Allison ever tell you where she grew up?"

"Not directly, but I gathered she grew up somewhere in Orange County because occasionally she would get mail that had been sent to a location in Orange County where the address was crossed out and our forwarding address on Roswell was written in."

"Do you remember the address in Orange County?"

"No, I can't recall that I even cared or looked closely at the time. I just seem to remember that but only vaguely. And it only happened a handful of times."

The mention of Orange County as a former residence would account for Allison's familiarity with the Santa Anas. Could she have lived in one of the canyons? If so, she would have gone to a nearby high school.

"High school?"

"That was peculiar. I could never get anything from her about her high school experience. I just assumed it was somewhere in Orange County as well."

"One other question, Elizabeth. Did Allison go to commencement?"

"I thought she was going. She had the cap and gown, and we had talked about hooking up after. She didn't show up. For a long time

I was angry because I never saw her after the ceremony. She just disappeared."

"Wouldn't she have had to do her student-teaching after graduation?"

"She was a teacher?" The surprise was written on Elizabeth's face. "I never knew. She must have gotten her credential somewhere else or lived somewhere else."

"No, she got it at Long Beach. So, you never saw her at Long Beach State again?"

"I got a job soon after graduation and relocated. It was several years before Al and I got married and moved back into the area. If Allison got her credential, I was not aware."

"And the books, what happened to them?"

"When my mother and I came back to the apartment after the commencement ceremony, everything that belonged to Allison was gone."

"No note or anything?"

"Yes, there was a note expressing sincere thanks for sharing the apartment and for my friendship. I don't know what I did with the note. I've looked for it. Actually the note was also interesting because it included a postscript, something like *tell your mom she did a good job.*"

"You never heard from her again?"

"Actually, several days after commencement, I received an envelope with no return address. It contained $200 in cash and another note of thanks that explained the money was a gift and asking me to forgive her for the abrupt departure. Very strange, don't you think, Investigator?"

"Yes, very."

The conversation moved forward with Van probing Elizabeth for any additional information. Already he had learned a great deal about Allison that was unknown prior to his visit.

The afternoon moved quickly, and at one point Van glanced at the mantel clock and was surprised to see they had been talking for over two hours. It was time to go. He could always come back. But Elizabeth had waited for this moment to ask a question.

"Investigator Van, I hope I have responded candidly to your questions."

"Yes, you have been very helpful, and I'm very grateful."

"Perhaps, then, you can share with me why you're so interested in Allison Connors."

Van knew Elizabeth Ambrose was not a threat that would go to the media, but he also knew there was a line he did not want to cross. The trick was to stay on the safe side of the line while at the same time respecting the entitlements of the interviewee who had some right to know why they were being questioned.

Van explained that he was working a cold murder case from many decades earlier. The case involved two missing high school students. The body of one was later discovered. No leads on the suspect had ever been found. Van went on to indicate that he was trying a different approach to the investigation by interviewing those who had been teachers, family, or friends of the two students. Because his predecessors had gathered considerable data, he was determined to find others who had not previously been interviewed. Allison was one of those.

"So, Allison went on to become a high school teacher." Elizabeth's tone betrayed her amazement.

"Yes, she was a high school English teacher. She left the school several years later and just disappeared. Allison Connors disappeared in 1978 and has not been heard from since."

"Is she a suspect?"

"Mrs. Ambrose, this case is so long ago that it's very difficult to say who's a possible suspect. Many witnesses and people of interest are long gone. At this point, I'm just trying to track down who I can."

"I can't help but think that given Allison's unique behavior and the nature of the questions you've asked me that she must be on the list of suspects. Correct?"

Van nodded but said nothing.

CHAPTER 30

LEARNING ABOUT HIKING

Santa Ana Mountains

V AN WENT OVER his checklist again before picking up the daypack and heading out the door.

The morning was cooler than expected. The sky was gray as the sun was below the horizon. The breeze that seemed to be coming off the ocean increased the chill in the air. Thankfully he had listened to Sergeant Pierce when he made his purchases at REI. The down vest and lightweight windbreaker would be needed today. Van realized that if it was chilly at home, it was probably more so in the mountains.

On the drive toward the Santa Ana Mountains, his thoughts returned to the topographic maps he had studied the evening before. Thankfully he had been able to get together with Barry McMurry and go over the route he was going to hike. Van was conscious that the last thing he needed would be to get lost and have to be rescued.

What concerned Van was the inadequacy of his skills. Barry taught him how to read the topographic maps and how to use a compass and his recently purchased GPS to orient himself with his surroundings and thereby identify just where he was on a map. He tried the GPS while walking in a nearby park and found it very useful. But in the mountains, he felt sure his orienteering skills would be put to the test.

Just don't get lost, he thought. He imagined the embarrassing image of newspaper headlines about a sheriff's department investigator being lost and rescued after a prolonged search.

Fenton had suggested he go with someone who knew more about hiking. Pierce suggested that his father would gladly go with him.

No, he had to go alone. The objective was twofold. First, Van wanted to become familiar with hiking alone in the Santa Anas. He was certain Cindy and Carlos had met their end there and that the responsible suspect, Allison Connors, was very adept at moving about in the range, even at night. Second, if he had any hope of understanding Allison, he must expose his senses to her world. To get close to her and have some understanding of her thinking, he had to approach her comfort level in the mountains.

It sounded so simple. See and connect with Allison's world and he could somehow connect with her. But he knew that was unreasonable thinking. He could never really get inside her head. Nor could he understand her way of thinking. The best he could hope for was enough experience along the trails of the mountains she hiked to open a small channel of insight into her.

Van wanted today's experience to enhance his thinking. He could not make headway with Allison as his prime suspect if he could not be open to new ways of thinking about the evidence. He must also be open to new questions that might guide his investigation. In the end, what he wanted from this outing was different perspectives on Allison's talents, her skills, and her world.

The concept of perspective was important to any comprehensive investigation. One needed to look at a case from multiple angles. The thought prompted Van's recollection of a comment by Stenzgard several weeks earlier. Van, along with Stenzgard, Fenton, and a couple of deputies were in a meeting regarding a missing person whose body had turned up in a small pond of a local golf course. Although there was some evidence to suggest a possible assault, the coroner and ME said they found very high alcohol elevations in the victim and could not rule out the kind of injuries often sustained by someone who is very drunk and has an accident. It looked to them like the victim had fallen down multiple times and then wandered onto the course during the night, fell into the pond, and drowned.

After some discussion that was tending toward accepting the findings, Stenzgard observed that there was a possible way to confirm or reject the report. He indicated he had taken the liberty of driving out to the golf course during a night when there was no moon. The course was pitch black. While walking toward the pond with a flashlight, he found the sprinkler system was on in various parts of the course. Then the sound of the sprinklers some distance away went silent, and just as quickly the sprinklers immediately around him came on.

In his hurry to avoid getting wet, Stenzgard had jogged away from the sprinklers and found himself faced with a fence along one edge of the course. On the opposite side of the fence was a narrow parking strip behind several buildings of a strip mall. The shipping bays behind each building had spotlights that seemed to extend their field of light across the asphalted area to the a six-foot chain-link fence and the edge of the golf course.

Stenzgard reasoned the shipping bays were monitored by security cameras, and he was wondering if the camera scans covered the distance across to the golf course fence. Perhaps the victim climbed the fence from the strip mall area to enter the course. The security cameras might provide some information.

Stenzgard's perspective proved right. The victim had been walking behind the strip mall about two in the morning when he encountered three men drinking and smoking. There was a violent confrontation. To escape, the victim ran toward the fence and climbed over it. The others chased him and also climbed the fence.

What happened on the opposite side of the fence, in the golf course, was not visible. However, if the sprinklers were on and the victim was being pursued, it was quite possible he unknowingly ran into the pond.

The security camera also showed the three pursuers returning back over the fence about ten minutes later. Two days later, a night shift deputy found one of the suspects drinking behind the strip mall. He was arrested, and the search continued for the other two suspects.

Perspective was critical to any analysis of evidence. Stenzgard understood that, and Van hoped his hiking outing would also provide some different perspectives. Perhaps this little excursion would not change things in the immediate investigation, but hopefully it would allow for a different view of evidence or circumstances further along.

—~~~—

At the eastern end of Silverado Canyon, Van parked his car and felt the full chill of the morning when he exited. He was not surprised as the elevation was 1,800 feet. Although he had his down vest on over his long-sleeved shirt, he reached into his pack and took out the windbreaker. He also put on a fleece head cap.

He quickly felt the comfort of the layers. He recalled the salesperson at the store telling him it was all about layering with the proper materials. Funny, he thought, everything he was wearing was synthetic except for the down in his vest. As a kid, it was all unheard of. For his mother, warmth was always about wearing wool, which Van never found to be comfortable material.

Looking around, there were no other vehicles. Van felt a bit self-conscious. Here he was decked out in gear that was all new. His pants were olive colored, and the bottoms of the legs could be zipped off to create shorts. His boots had about two miles of walking on them. The salesperson told him to wear them around the house and neighborhood to help break them in. Sti Pierce had told him that breaking in a pair of boots was a ritual. "How they fit in the store may be a far cry from how they fit when you're hiking. Find the problems before you go, not after." Van had meant to do more to break them in, but somehow it had not happened.

He locked the car and shouldered the pack. He remembered that the REI rep had told him how to adjust the straps so the pack rode comfortably. "You want to find the best fit for you."

It was a strange feeling. Van had hiked in parks and in places like the floor of Yosemite Valley with his wife and kids many years earlier. But those were casual affairs, and he never felt isolated or unprepared. Today was different. He was alone and headed up a trail where he might not encounter anyone. Should he get lost or injured, there would not be the throngs of people to take note and provide assistance.

He had water, food, first-aid supplies, maps, compass, GPS, and his cell phone. The latter may or may not be useful. He also had photocopies of the pages from a local hiking guidebook that described the route he would follow. He had studied the maps and the trail description. He knew where he was headed and could visualize the route.

There remained some angst in Van's mind. It was not the uneasiness of not knowing but the reality of something Barry had said. "When you're hiking, alone or with others in a remote area, there's always the potential of objective danger. It's the danger that you cannot control. You can plan, exercise caution, and seek to avoid danger. But Mother Nature has her own ways, and we're guests in her house. When a crisis strikes, we often don't see it coming. The skilled backcountry traveler will be just as surprised as the novice. The difference is that the former will have the knowledge and options to survive. The novice will panic and close off options. It doesn't mean the experienced hiker isn't afraid; it just means he or she has the experience needed to make good choices. What makes the potential of objective danger interesting is that it must be accommodated in order to gain experience. You only learn by doing."

Van walked across the parking area and toward the Forest Service sign. He glanced at the posted notices warning that water was not available along the trail. He also took stock of the large map that noted the routes of various trails in the area. Van would hike the Silverado Trail.

The Forest Service gate was closed, barring vehicle access to the Maple Springs Road. He walked around the gate and noticed the sign for his trail. It was 3.3 miles to Bedford Peak.

As if to relieve any uncertainties, Van glanced back at his car and then scanned the area at the end of the canyon road. All was quiet. No one was about except him.

He turned and started up the trail. It was a quarter after seven in the morning. The sky was blue. It was cold. But it was also beautiful. The rawness of the setting did not go unnoticed.

—⁓—

The hike to Bedford Peak had taken three hours. Van felt he could have done it in shorter time. The guidebook said it was a 6.6-mile round-trip that could take several hours. However, Van had not been in a hurry. He had purposefully taken his time to ensure he did not make any mistakes. Though he had to admit the trail was well marked, in good condition, and you would have had to ignore common sense to have gotten lost. The trail was really the remains of an old dirt road.

It had not been an easy hike. Van reasoned that he had gained about two thousand feet since leaving the trailhead. The climb up had been steep, and Van quickly noticed that the gain in altitude plus the steepness took a toll. The altitude did cause Van to breathe deeply. As he hiked, he experimented with his pace and eventually settled into one that allowed him to make progress with the least effect on his breathing. As a result, he went slowly.

Van learned early in the hike that the art of layering also facilitated shedding clothing as one's body heated up. A half mile along, he had removed the cap and turned the windbreaker sleeves up. Soon thereafter, he removed the windbreaker, and after another series of switchbacks, he removed the vest. But now on top, his body was quickly starting to cool down, and it was not an especially warm day. He reached into the pack and removed the windbreaker.

As he scanned the world around him, Van sensed pride at his accomplishment. It had not been easy, but he had done it alone and despite his early anxiety.

He had not encountered anyone along the trail, but Van could see that this was a popular hiking area. From Bedford Peak, trails diverged in two directions. To the north was a portion of the Main Divide Road that eventually connected with Black Star Canyon Road several miles to the northwest. The Main Divide Road also left Bedford Peak and continued in a southeast direction toward Santiago Peak, many miles away.

One of Van's reasons for the hike was to see the Main Divide Road. The guidebook noted that the road connected with all the other unimproved dirt roads and trails that crisscrossed the Santa Ana range. One could travel the Main Divide Road and drop down into many of the canyons off Santiago Canyon Road.

Van walked along the Main Divide Road in both directions for a couple hundred yards. Then he looked at his maps. It occurred to him that an excellent hiker, one in good shape and who knew the area, could navigate the region with little trouble, even at night.

For a long time, Van just stood and looked across the landscape. He studied the ground cover, the chaparral, the occasional stands of trees, the sporadic rock outcrops, and the intersecting and diverging canyons. It was a wild area, but it did not lack for personality. Van had little experience with mountains, but he suspected that each mountain area had its own personality of features—its geography, flora, fauna, and atmosphere. If you lived here, it was home. For someone raised in the canyons, these trails and roads and firebreaks could be as familiar as the streets and roads of any neighborhood. He considered the old saying, *we are where we live.*

After eating a snack and quenching his thirst, Van took another walk around the area. It was quiet. The sun was higher in the sky. The breeze was still up, but it produced no noise. Except for a small rodent that was quickly lost in the brush, the only other animal life were some birds soaring in a circle pattern some distance away. He thought they were vultures of some kind, but he knew little of such things.

Everything he could see was novel to him.

Like any hobby, passion brought with it a certain ease of engagement. He could see that while it was quite possible for the uninitiated to become disoriented and confused in this environment, it was equally possible that some, those for whom this area was home away from home, would wander as if it were their personal backyard. He sensed it was that way for Allison.

Checking his watch, Van noted it was just after eleven. He needed to start down. Before the day was out, he wanted to debrief and record his insights.

And yet he found that a certain part of him did not want to leave. The hike up alone had given him possession of the peak. It was his for the day. He felt no threats. Any anxiety that made him uncomfortable hours earlier had abated, and his aloneness was no longer the provocateur of uncertainty. Was it the act of accomplishment that fostered such feelings? Or was it a sense of security born of the pride and ego of the goal won? He did not know.

What he did know was that Allison Connors must have felt at home here. She would have been at home on these trails. This must have been her world. Somewhere within reach was her roots, her beliefs, and her motivations.

Moreover, Allison's deadly encounter with Cindy and Carlos was nearby. He was sure of it.

For the moment, his surroundings had become user friendly. Van shouldered the daypack. He glanced around to ensure he was leaving nothing and then took his first steps toward his car.

Back in his office, Van was aware his morning experience had stimulated thoughts regarding Allison. From Bedford Peak, he had looked in the direction of the old catering site, but it was hidden from view and miles away. However, the elevated view provided Van with some idea of the unique qualities required of anyone who could have managed to hike away from the vehicle. Allison could have hiked to Santiago Canyon Road and made her way to a hidden car or other destination. Somehow that did not seem likely. Allison was a hiker and would not trust the road as a legitimate escape route.

No, he doubted Allison even had a car in the area to return to.

Instincts told him that her comfort level and confidence off road would trump any need to travel the area in a vehicle. There were risks, and Allison did not appear to be one to risk exposure. In adopting such thinking, Van knew he was being drawn to the conclusion that Allison's familiarity with the area included the possibility that she had a residence or shelter in the mountains. What was the possibility?

Van knew that his suspicions about Allison's relationship with the Santa Ana range required some new inquiries. How many places were there to live in the area? Was it possible that Allison could have grown up living in one of the canyons such as Harding, Modjeska, Black Star, or even Silverado? Just his drive through Silverado Canyon suggested there could easily be a hundred places to reside in that canyon. These questions needed attention.

There was something else that kept creeping into Van's thoughts about Allison the hiker. Elizabeth Ambrose had said that Allison made many trips to the Sierra to hike while she was in college. It was also the location of her father's death. Was Allison just as skilled at moving about the Sierra as she was the Santa Ana range?

The hike to Bedford Peak opened lines of thinking. Perhaps a trip to the location of Archie Connor's death would do the same.

I have to go to the Sierra. No sooner had the thought occurred than he reached for his phone.

CHAPTER 31

THE ENIGMA

Home and Homicide Office

A S SOMETIMES HAPPENED, Van found himself unable to sleep because he had allowed his questions at work to make the drive home with him. His mind kept perseverating on thoughts about Allison Connors. Experience told him that whenever he found himself wrestling with conflicting thoughts on a case, it was wise to do nothing related to the case at home. The best medicine was distraction with a history book, mystery novel, a movie, or classical music.

Failure to take this approach had two possible outcomes. One, he would not be able to fall asleep. That did not happen tonight. Two, he would fall asleep and wake up to go to the restroom about one or two in the morning and not be able to get back to sleep. That is what happened.

Tonight he had opted to listen to classical music and try to relax before going to bed. What made it unfortunate was the choice of music—the piano concertos of Rachmaninoff. It was a long CD and featured the Russian pianist Valentina Lisitsa. Van had played it through twice, but his mind kept harping back to a series of questions about what made Allison Connors tick. Like Russian music and literature, Allison was both mysterious and dark.

Thinking back on it, Van knew he was his own worst enemy when he combined provocative classical music with reflective thoughts. He had made his visit to the restroom and now lay in bed trying to get back to sleep. He did this knowing full well the outcome.

After several minutes, Van glanced at the clock. It was 2:37 a.m. He got up, pulled on some sweatpants and a sweatshirt, and wandered to the kitchen.

He wasn't hungry, but habit found him opening and scanning the refrigerator. There was a half-empty bottle of Gatorade. He retrieved it, walked to the pantry, and grabbed a bag of restaurant-style tortilla chips. Both items in hand, he wandered down the hall, stopped at the furnace thermostat to turn up the heat, and then continued on to his study.

The previous morning, Van had spent time going over what he knew about Allison Connors. The list was long, but as a consequence of his recent outing in the Santa Ana Mountains, Van found himself troubled by the idea that Allison could walk away from her former life and not only leave no trace behind but also not revisit her former self. It had been thirty-some years with absolutely no reemergence as Allison Connors.

It seemed to Van that if the subconscious mind is so powerful it rules our behavior, then the first thirty-five years of Allison's life had left its mark subliminally. No doubt Allison's behavior since her disappearance must somehow reflect itself in perceptions molded during the first half of her life. If that were true, how could she just walk into a different life and do so without regard to the past? If the years before teaching molded her, how could the years since teaching be disconnected? Or was a name change the only real change?

It kept coming back to Van that Allison today could be just like the Allison of old except that her name had changed. Everything he had learned about Allison prior to 1978 suggested someone who was an enigma, a paradox.

Everyone Van had interviewed who knew Allison kept prompting the same thoughts. Allison was someone you could not really get to know. The only things you knew about her were those you saw.

Anything in her life before that moment of observation was not accessible.

It was like she came out of nowhere when she showed up at Long Beach State. She went back to nowhere when she left Nuevo. Actually, as Van saw it, Allison existed as people knew her between the time of her mother's death in 1963 and her departure in 1978. She existed in the norm of society all of fifteen years. The Allison anyone knew was visible for only fifteen of her seventy-plus years. That meant that 78 percent of her life was unknown.

The only word to describe it was *bizarre.*

Van had called Karli Ryan to inquire about his observations. In his conversation, he told Karli that as he saw it, Allison's life was divided into three periods. The first period was about nineteen years in length, from birth to 1963. He knew little about that period other than several general facts. She spent her early years in the Bishop area. Later her parents were separated; Allison and her mother lived somewhere in Orange County, and her father stayed in Bishop. She had a brother and sister, both had disappeared, and her mother committed suicide in 1963.

The second phase included her years in college and her employment at Nuevo High School. The Allison everyone knew in this phase was brilliant, exceptionally well read, an athlete, an expert backpacker, an extraordinary English teacher, and an enigma. She had no lasting friendships, and any relationships were superficial. The second phase was fifteen years.

The third phase started in 1978 and had lasted since. Other than the fact that Allison disappeared, he knew nothing about her. He could only speculate that she remained brilliant, continued to read, and was a good athlete and an avid backpacker.

Van wanted to know how powerful the first nineteen years could be in all of this.

Karli suggested it could have been very powerful. "Have you ever read the classic work by Philip Slater, *The Pursuit of Loneliness*? It first came out in the early seventies."

"You know, I think I remember it being popular when I was in college because the counterculture bunch were reading it. I never read it. Probably should have."

"Well, I suggest you read it. Slater poses some interesting implications for a child raised in an environment where the extremes of training are focused on independence. As he notes, 'Love and discipline can emanate from the same source.' It has a Spartan-like quality. Your lone suspect has long wanted very much to please the source."

Van was glad he recorded the conversation. Taking notes when Karli was on the stump was not easy, and anything he was likely to try to remember would probably be misrepresented later.

"Also, you may want to take a look at a more recent work, *Quiet*, by Susan Cain. Your suspect is a brilliant loner, but she didn't get that way by herself. Those early years were the critical piece. It appears she's a classic introvert who has mastered the ability to function in a very sociable world. You want to understand her, try these books."

Once off the phone, Van called a local bookstore. They had *Quiet* but did not have *The Pursuit of Loneliness*. After several more calls, he tracked it down in a bookstore in the county's largest shopping mall. He drove there and purchased both books.

Actually, that was his first mistake. The books in hand, he spent the afternoon reading Slater's book. When he finally headed home, Slater's frame of reference was working its magic on everything Van knew about Allison Connors. Van was not certain that he bought into everything Slater had to say, but some key points bore strongly on the personality of Allison.

Slater's thesis was critical of America's focus on raising kids to be independent. It fosters individualism at the expense of a democracy that needs more congruency. However, it was Slater's references to the extremes of training kids to be independent that struck Van as most profound. Was that the work of Allison's mother? Certainly it was not the father.

Allison was independent beyond normal benchmarks. Not only was she a loner, she worked hard to not develop any real friendships. And yet Van saw nothing in what he knew about Allison that suggested she was lonely. Had she been trained to so fend for herself that she saw no need for others? Obviously Allison was a bright kid whose mother helped her to become a brilliant student even though Allison had not formally attended school. Allison also became a gifted athlete and backpacker. How did she become so obsessive? All of this to what end?

If Slater was correct, extreme individualism promotes extreme isolation. If that were the case, Allison was a prime example. She lived in an atypical world that to her was completely normal, preferred, and worshiped.

Having said all of that, there was still the matter of motive. Allison may be a brilliant, independent, and hermit-like individual, but there had to be a motive for killing. Slater had a suggestion about that as well.

An excessive emphasis on individualism, says Slater, denies "the reality of human interdependence." Van extrapolated that the true loner, the individual who sees no need for social interdependence, finds fault with group or relational norms when they go wrong. Coupled with that is the need to place blame and rectify. Allison went well beyond Slater's individual.

The thought of needing to place blame and rectify kept playing over in Van's mind like a video loop in a news show. The implications were enormous and sinister. In Van's line of work, the only way to portray Allison was to describe her as a psychopath and a psychotic.

Under those circumstances, thought Van, the answer for the independent loner confronted with the unacceptable must be to either avoid the problem or terminate the problem. He did not like the inference of his thinking, but Van knew enough about history to know that as horrific as it might sound, there was a long narrative of people who saw nothing wrong with their heinous actions. Where most judged them evil, they saw themselves acting normal, perhaps even acting in the interest of all. Such is the nature of vengeance.

"Madness and vengeance." Van was talking out loud. He shook his head in disgust.

Could it be that Allison Connors was trained to act on certain motives? If that were the case, Allison had nineteen years of in-house training by her mother before going to college. It wasn't brainwashing. It was brain forming. By then she knew her calling. College was just the academic icing on the cake; it was a place to legitimize her talents and prepare for a future.

But why teach for nine years? Was there a purpose for those years? Or did the years at Nuevo represent something else? Was it an experiment with normalcy? Was the purpose to see what the real world was like or to get some experience in the real world before becoming enigmatic? Van doubted the latter view because the real world for Allison would have been the world she was trained to function within. He did not think Allison was ever equipped to live in his world.

And yet he could not escape the fact that Allison had lived in a social world for fifteen years. She knew how to live with other people, even though they would see her as different and odd. Or was it that Allison recognized she did not fit in and decided to change her person by moving on to a new world? Had she tried normalcy and failed? If so, Allison left Nuevo, adopted a new name, and moved elsewhere. She could reinvent herself at will.

Could she do that and still be a maven of the Sierra trails? Van was inclined to think she could. He was inclined to think that Allison Connors could move in and out of identities with the same ease as one who changes clothes to fit the occasion. Perhaps she had adopted a nom de guerre—a warrior name, a pseudonym to match her commitment to vengeance.

Sleep was not an option the rest of the night, and Van decided to go into the office, once again long before the day shift commenced.

They had grown accustomed to his early arrivals, so those on duty at five o'clock took little note. The sergeant nodded and smiled, as if to say "we were expecting you." Van acknowledged the salutation and made his way across the floor to his office.

As the computer booted, he made his hot Earl Grey.

The one accomplishment during his reflection in the early hours of the morning was the realization that he needed to make a couple of adjustments in his approach to finding Allison. He had to redouble his efforts to locate where Allison was raised in Orange County. The evidence strongly suggested she spent considerable time in the Santa Ana Mountains, and her childhood home had to provide reasonable access to the trails. He needed to have one of the civilian staff pursue this. He would give Deena the task.

He also had to take a closer look at Allison's forays into the Sierra. This would mean going to the Eastern Sierra and finding out where she was born and where she lived before moving to Orange County, as well as finding out more about the history of her parents. Based on his earlier inquiries with the Inyo County Sheriff's Department, Van did not anticipate the task would be easy.

Ultimately, Van would have to repeat his hiking experience; only this time it would take place in the Sierra. Preferably, it needed to take place on the JMT and include visiting the site where Archie Connors died.

Increasingly, Van felt his senses and his research were converging on the idea that Allison was now living under an alias somewhere near the Sierra. Of course, that suggested an infinite number of places where she could live. However, logic dictated she would opt to live in the Eastern Sierra, probably in the areas between Lone Pine to the south and Mammoth Lakes in the north. According to Sergeant Pierce, if she wanted easy access to the JMT, then the Eastern Sierra between these two cities was the ideal place to reside.

The Eastern Sierra was tied together along US Highway 395. It was a lot of area, but there was one caveat; Allison Connors was probably not living in too small of a community where her lack of a past drew attention. It was more likely that she lived in one of the few more sizeable towns like Lone Pine, Bishop, or Mammoth Lakes. Or, she lived in a most rural and isolated setting where she was virtually hidden from the rest of the world.

Regardless, she had to have access to the Sierra Nevada.

CHAPTER 32

INTO THE BACKCOUNTRY

*Bishop, California
and North Fork of the Kings River*

I T WAS LATE afternoon when Van finally neared the town of Bishop. Following directions provided by Sergeant Pierce, he had stopped at an Interagency Information Center just outside the town of Lone Pine, sixty miles south of Bishop. There he was able to familiarize himself with the geography and history of the Eastern Sierra and purchase some books he thought would provide some background about the region.

It had been hot in Lone Pine; Bishop was no different. Van was surprised that the Owens Valley, even though it was four thousand feet in elevation and next to a lot of twelve-thousand-foot peaks, was so hot. On the other hand, he had to admit that there was majesty to the area. From the valley, the sheer eastern front of the Sierra Nevada seemed to jut straight up from the valley floor.

In contrast, many of the peaks above had snow. Such juxtaposition was alien to Van. Something told him it wasn't alien to Allison. The contrast between the Santa Ana range and the Sierra was stark, but both were more than just familiar to her. It occurred to Van that his trip into the Santa Anas would pale in comparison to his trip into the Sierra backcountry.

Once again the reality of tomorrow's outing generated a sense of angst. And yet his earlier experience, combined with the fact that on this trip he would not be alone, suggested there was little reason for concern. Still, past practice encouraged him to temper expectations.

Growing up in Orange County, his only encounters with big cities were Los Angeles and San Francisco. Soon after he started working with the feds, he had occasion to go to New York City. The encounter awed him. He had never experienced anything like it. Walking the streets alone in the twilight was not frightening, but it did create a kind of anxiety. He remembered looking around at the throngs of people and realizing that they were very comfortable in the Big Apple. It also occurred to him that even though the big city was densely populated, one could live almost anonymously in it.

Van supposed the same was true with the wilderness. One could develop a comfort level that allowed for survival in the harshest of conditions where the uninitiated would easily succumb.

He wondered how he was going to feel if given time to be alone in the Sierra backcountry. Would he feel comfortable or would he be like the wealthy bond trader, Sherman McCoy, in Tom Wolfe's *Bonfire of the Vanities*, someone who got off at the wrong freeway exit in the wrong part of the city and found himself completely out of his comfort zone. He knew Allison felt comfortable in the wilds. Was the same true for Sti and Rob? He thought it was probably something one learned, since the wilderness was not a natural setting for most.

The hotel where he was to meet Sti and Rob was in the center of Bishop and across the street from the city park. The concentration of traffic and the numbers of people along the sidewalk were testimony that Bishop was the tourist center of the valley. The smaller towns to the south—Lone Pine, Independence, and Big Pine—could not equal the size and density of Bishop. And yet Bishop too seemed quaint and well suited to the cowboy-like environment of the valley.

—✳—

It was early evening, and Sti and Rob were hosting Van in the patio area of their ground-floor room at the Creekside Inn. Though the temperature was in the upper nineties, the heat was dry, and the early evening shade in the open courtyard of the hotel offered a pleasant place to sit and enjoy a glass of wine or beer. The gentle sound of Bishop Creek provided background.

The two retired friends were seemingly at home in the inn and the town. Although they came from very different backgrounds—Sti had been a high school teacher and later a professor, while Rob had owned an optical instrument company—the two had spent many years traipsing about the Owens Valley and the Eastern Sierra. A common interest in camping and backpacking had brought Sti and Rob into a friendship that spanned decades of exploring the region.

Both were physically fit and appeared younger than their seventy-plus years. For years Rob had been a cyclist, logging multiple days of long-distance rides every week. For Sti, exercise had included years of daily runs. Rob was the more outgoing of the two, though Sti, with his sense of humor, was never at a loss for words.

"How is it the two of you have this room with a view and shaded patio and I'm stuck with a view of the parking lot on the exposed side of the building where the sun's intensity makes opening the curtains and sitting on the porch impossible?"

Sti took a sip of his Mammoth Mountain Brewery, Double Nut Brown Porter and responded. "You see, Van, Rob and I are regulars here. Over the years, we've stayed here so often that the management thinks we're good for advertising. Wherever we go, we recommend the hotel. In return, they give us the best room options. Also, we're private sector—you're government sector. We pay full price; you pay government rates."

Van was sorry he asked.

Rob was quick to fill any void. "Van, don't get him started. You open the door with a question like that, and Sti will fill the room with a litany of cheap thinking. The last thing we need is him waxing philosophical."

As expected, Sti responded, "Give me a break."

"Oh, and that's one of his favorite sayings. Among others, which I'm sure you'll hear ad nauseam, it's a common and abused utterance."

A little taken aback by the general familiarity and levity of his hosts, whom he knew did not live anywhere near Bishop, Van could not help but be a little perplexed with the circumstances. "I was also wondering how it is that you were there to meet me when I entered the lobby."

Rob answered, "Oh, management was informed we were expecting you, and they called us when you pulled up in front. Your Crown Vic was a real giveaway."

"But how did you know that I liked Sauvignon Blanc and had it on ice here in your room?"

Sti and Rob just smiled and said nothing.

Getting no response, Van realized he must accept the warning given him by Sergeant Pierce. *"You'll find my dad and his friend Rob to be the ultimate mixture of intelligence, skill, wit, and absurdities. The last characteristic will drive you nuts."* He shook his head. "I guess I don't want to know. You guys are, as Sti's son suggested, different."

"Well, let's just say we have a real affinity for the Eastern Sierra and would never want you to have a bad experience at our expense. We've found that good planning is a prelude for good times." Rob ended his comments with a smile that bordered on slyness as he sipped his beer.

Rob glanced at his watch. "We best head up to the lobby. The sheriff should arrive any time."

In the lobby, Van knew the tall, lanky, clean-cut, older man wearing a golf hat was the retired sheriff. In the business, you developed a feel for knowing what a professional in law enforcement looked like. Command presence was evident even when they were retired.

"You must be Investigator Vanarsdale. It's good to finally meet you, although I don't have a clue why you would hang around these two reprobates." They all enjoyed a short laugh. Though subtle, the scene did not go unnoticed to others in the lobby.

"Well, it's good of you to join us, Sheriff."

"It's Bob. Just call me Bob." Aware that he was known in the town and attracting attention, Pagliano motioned the group over to a corner of the lobby where there were comfortable chairs and they would be out of the listening range of others.

"So, you have these two Owens Valley clones and wanderers doing some work for you."

"Yes. I've asked them to check out a couple of hunches. Our suspect has strong ties to the area from her childhood. I have reason to believe she remains closely connected with the Eastern Sierra and possibly backpacker disappearances along the John Muir Trail."

"The boys filled me in yesterday. I agree with your approach."

The comment was reassuring to Van. With Pagliano suggesting he was on the right track with his investigation, Van knew the job would be easier since he was an outsider operating here in another county's jurisdiction.

Pagliano picked up the slack. "I also talked with Brenda Robertson in Mammoth. I understand she worked for OCSD at one time and you knew her. She'll be helpful as well."

Van couldn't have asked for more. Investigations were often hindered when they crossed jurisdictions. It was the old territorial imperative theme. That would not be the case here.

"I have no doubt that these two will help you as well. Their methods are a bit strange sometimes, but they do get results." Pagliano went on to describe the help his office had received from Sti and Rob on two previous instances.

Van had already learned about both cases from Sergeant Pierce, but it was good to know from another professional that Sti and Rob were both skilled and discreet. They could be trusted.

The next morning, Sti and Rob rode with Van as they covered the twenty-six miles to the Rainbow Pack Station at Parchers, a small store and cabin compound a mile south of the Bishop Pass trailhead at South Lake. At nine thousand feet, the trailhead is a major entry point along the Eastern Sierra. A twelve-mile hike over twelve-thousand-foot Bishop Pass provides access to the approximate midpoint along the John Muir Trail.

Sti and Rob would hike in and meet Van, who would be packed into the location where Archie Connors had died. Along with the packer, the three would stay there for two nights before Van would exit the backcountry with the packer, return to Bishop, and drive home.

The plan was that after Van returned to the trailhead, Sti and Rob would backpack south along the JMT. Their goal was the location where the remains of two UC–Berkeley students had been recovered many years earlier. Though their task was to look for an earring, Sti and Rob had no illusions. It seemed a long shot at best.

Originally, when he realized the miles that would be covered and the altitude at which they would be hiking, Van was worried. Sti and Rob were seventy years of age. Thinking back on his minimal experience with altitude gain while hiking, he was not sure he could support their goals. Van called Sergeant Pierce and expressed his concern. Pierce laughed. "Are you kidding? Nothing to worry about." Van was not certain. He was a bit surprised at the cavalier response of the sergeant.

Van knew investigations, but he felt like a fish out of water. This was not like any other investigation. In the end, he reasoned that his decision to change the approach to investigating Allison Connors required that he be willing to accept some oddities, even risks.

The trip up to Bishop Pass found Van in awe of the scenery. He had seen photos and movies with such views, but nothing compared to seeing it in person. Van was overwhelmed by the grandeur.

The packer, Roary, rode at the front, followed by two mules packed with gear. Van followed behind. His horse needed no guiding or encouragement. It followed the others. Van thought the horse had been on the route so many times that it was all rote. As for Roary, he looked like a cowboy with his long mustache, worn and faded Levis, boots, and soiled Stetson whose original color was indefinable.

Van could tell they were nearing the pass as the train made its way around bends on a trail cut into the rock. But he was not prepared for the view that was suddenly thrust upon him. In front was a sign indicating Bishop Pass at 11,982 feet. Behind it the trail wound across the rocky pass landscape and seemed to drop out of view a hundred yards or so ahead. But it was the view beyond that startled. He knew from the maps that somewhere in front and thousands of feet below was the Middle Fork of the Kings River. It was a vast and deep canyon that he was not yet able to peer into. Beyond the canyon were towering peaks of rock and snow that touched the sky well above him. In simple terms, Van was blown away by the scene.

They took a short break at the pass. They had encountered some backpackers coming up, but there was no one else at the pass. After checking the rigging on each of the mules, the packer mounted, and they continued forward and down toward the Middle Fork.

The roar of the Kings was almost deafening. When Roary said, "Here we are," Van hardly heard him. "The directions from your friends indicate this is the spot where those people camped in 1966."

Van looked around. Rob and Sti were nowhere in sight. He could not imagine they passed the two. Perhaps Sergeant Pierce overestimated their capabilities.

The packer began to unpack the gear. Van dismounted and felt helpless and a bit alone. The packer did not talk much. Van was a bit anxious. What had happened to Sti and Rob?

Then it occurred to him that this was what Sti and Rob wanted. He needed to have the feeling of being isolated in the backcountry. He needed to let his senses take in the experience. Van began to scan the area. As he did so, it came to him that his ride into the canyon and his observations along the way suggested that the Sierra was consistently the same even as it changed with each setting. The trees, the rivers and creeks, the rocks, the shrubs and small plants, they were all here, but the scene was constantly changing. The same ingredients over and over even as each step along the way provided a different view.

The idea that he should look the area over prompted Van to pull out his maps. He had a topographic map with the location of the Archie Connors accident noted on it. This was where Allison's father died. *Her first murder?* he wondered. Much like his experience at Nuevo High School when he went into the room where Allison had taught, Van was aware that he was seeing what she had seen. He was walking where she had walked. The tenuous connection was there. It was a feeling. It was a remote and vague sensory experience, but it had value. Somewhere in all of this was a piece of Allison, a piece that spoke to her motives and actions. Van could only hope it would help his cause.

No sooner had Van taken a seat on a large rock well away from the sound of rushing water than Sti and Rob appeared out of nowhere.

"Sorry we weren't here when you arrived. We got tired of waiting and decided to hike up the canyon a ways to a hidden meadow we know. We would've been back on time, but Rob stopped to talk to some people. You'll find that Rob never passes up an opportunity to have a confab with anyone he meets along the trail. There have been many times when we were on a tight schedule and ended up late because of his conversation abilities."

"Look who's talking. Need I tell the investigator about how you befriended some homeless and drunk tramp at 9:00 a.m. in the middle of Bishop Park, only to scare off nearby tourists and beckon the response of the local deputy to inquire about what was going on?"

"I was just trying to be friendly. It is my sense of equity …"

"Are you guys always like this?"

"Like what?" asked Sti.

"Constantly bantering. How do you remain friends?"

Rob responded with a chuckle, "It's our wives. They've known each other since sixth grade. Sti and I met when the wives got together years later. We have to tolerate each other because our wives expect it."

"Yep, they had a choice and became friends. We came along long and never had a choice."

Van was sorry he asked. "Well, give me some idea what I'm looking at."

Using a topographic map, Sti and Rob explained where they were and the path of the JMT through the area. They went on to show how the area along the river had changed somewhat over the decades. This may have been the site of the death of Archie, but without photos of the area in 1966, it was impossible to recreate the scene. The only info they had to go on was the topo and accident description provided by Pagliano via input from Investigator Pollard and the *Inyo Register* article.

There was still a cut in the riverbank that dropped several feet down to the rushing water. If Archie had stumbled off that bank in the middle of the night, one could see how falling could have resulted in knocking him out if not severely injuring him. If he ended up in the water, it was no stretch to assume he could have drowned.

All three knew he could have just as easily been pushed.

"Is this typical scenery along the Muir Trail?"

Rob said, "Much of the time. Pretty characteristic of the big rivers flowing through narrow canyons like this. But this is one of the lower points along the trail. The forest is thick right here. Just north of here, the trail meanders through a couple of large meadows where the trail isn't right next to the river. It's much quieter there."

Van was following Rob's description on the map.

"And several miles downriver from here the trail cuts west, leaves the river, and climbs out of this canyon and follows Palisade Creek up into Palisade Basin where there are few trees and the terrain is very rugged and rocky.

"As you probably noticed today, as the trail climbs, it goes above the elevation where trees grow, like it was when you came over Bishop Pass. South of here, you're above timberline before going over Mather Pass at the upper end of the Palisade Basin. Likewise, if you were to follow the JMT upriver from here, you would go above tree line before going over Muir Pass."

Sti pointed out the two passes on the map. "Basically what we're saying is that what you see here and to the immediate north and south of here is a terrain that's repeated over and over along the John Muir Trail. It's terrain that's found everywhere in the Sierra Nevada."

"Are there many people in the area? You said you talked to some earlier. We saw some backpackers hiking in and out today."

Rob swiped his hand around the area. "Actually it is a bit surprising there's no one else camped near us. If you walk around this area along the river, you'll see where many people have camped over the years. National park and forest service people now discourage camping next to rivers and lakes, so you'll find more recent campsites upslope above us on some sandy benches." Rob pointed to an area several yards above. "There's an excellent campsite up there. Can't see it from here, but those who know will camp up there."

Van asked, "So, if you wanted to kill someone and dispose of their body, you would have to be careful others weren't camped nearby."

Sti said, "Remember, Archie's death occurred in 1966. Things were much different then. Today it would be hard to hike a whole day along the JMT without encountering several people going in either direction. In 1966, one could easily hike the whole length of this canyon from Muir Pass seven miles north of here and Mather Pass fourteen miles south of here and not see anyone."

Rob added, "And even if you did see someone, you could be pretty much assured that you could find a camp spot well away from them if that was your desire. It was much different then."

"Were there packers then?"

Rob responded in the affirmative. He noted it was probably a good bet that most of the trail use in places where one can access the backcountry on a day's ride from a trailhead amounted to just as many backpackers as stock packers in the forties, fifties, and sixties. That was not the case today because there were many more backpackers.

Van glanced over and watched the packer set up camp. He had unloaded the backpacks and set up two tents. The animals were picketed nearby. The packer was quiet and seemed to enjoy being alone and not being talked to. Van had the feeling while watching that there was a distance between the packer and Sti and Rob. There was no animosity there. They were just different people with different takes on life.

"The packer is quiet, almost aloof. Hardly said anything on our ride in."

Sti smiled and spoke admirably. "He's in his world. He loves this place as much as anyone, but he's used to spending considerable time alone. I guess it's a trait not unlike the range cowboy of old who often rode alone."

Rob reinforced Sti's comment. "They're good at what they do. Much maligned in recent years by those critical of the damage horses and mules do to the trails and meadows. The packer is often not popular with backpackers. However, have a problem back here, and it's usually the packer who's called on to bail people out. Tough to be critical of people who are part of a golden past that's rapidly disappearing."

As Sti walked over to his backpack, he turned and commented, "I think you'll find that our packer is a wealth of information about this area. You may want to get his take on things."

Rob and Sti moved off and set up their tents on the sandy bench about fifty yards away and above the trail.

The morning chill found Van wearing a down parka and drinking hot coffee provided by the packer. Looking up toward where Sti and Rob were camped, he noticed Rob sitting on a rock and reading a topographic map while he drank his coffee. The two friends were astute. Van sensed they, like him, cherished time alone to think.

Last evening, the packer, Roary, loosened up, and the four had a great conversation about the life of a packer. Roary had been born in Elko, Nevada, and moved to Wyoming when he was about ten. His dad was a manager on a ranch. "I just grew up with horses like my daddy did."

Roary's approach to life was simple. He had a truck and horse trailer. He had two horses and had, over the years, worked for many of the pack stations in the Eastern Sierra. He had gone to the University of California–Davis for two years before dropping out. "I just wanted to do what I'm doing. Never really wanted anything else. College is for lots of people. It just wasn't for me."

That morning, Roary indicated he had brought mail to take up the canyon a couple miles to a forest service trail crew camp and would be back shortly. Van had asked him if it would be a hard hike. The response was both humorous and a testimony to a packer's world. "No. My daddy always told me if something was further away than the length of a football field, well, best you saddle up and ride over there."

Once Roary had left, Sti and Rob spent some time helping Van become better acquainted with the JMT and what backpacking the trail entailed. They shared their equipment and explained how they prepared and packed trips. They also showed him how to find remote campsites well off the trail that were secluded and often went unnoticed by those only intent on covering miles.

He was curious about solo backpacking. Sti and Rob shared with him the realities of traveling the trails alone. Obviously the backcountry was always home to objective danger but no more so than the city streets. The key was knowledge, skill, and good decision making.

Van was surprised to learn that there were many backpackers who avoided the trails and hiked cross-country. The dangers were enhanced in cross-country hiking, but the rewards were great. Again, it came down to good choices and control of risks.

Rob said it best. "Van, a skilled backpacker, one with experience and confidence, can crisscross the backcountry for days with little regard for trails. If your suspect fits this mold, there's hardly any area of the Sierra Nevada that she couldn't access. She would go completely unnoticed. In fact, she could hike a route paralleling the JMT from Yosemite to Whitney and never be seen by those on the trail."

It all challenged Van's conventional senses.

After a morning of educating him on the backcountry, Sti and

Rob left him to spend some time alone. He did not have to ask them. They seemed to sense that he needed to get a feel for the environment by sitting and by wandering close to the trail. Van appreciated their confidence. They knew that one of his goals was to gain as much understanding as possible of the world wandered by Allison Connors. To do this, he needed time.

Tomorrow he would head out. Today he needed to absorb the Sierra backcountry.

—ഇ—

"How was the working vacation?"

"Well, Sarge, for reasons beyond the purpose of the trip, I found it one of the most refreshing, if not confusing, experiences of my life."

"Refreshing and confusing?"

"Never had such an experience and not likely to have one again. If I do, I'll probably have to carry my own gear."

Fenton shook his head. "What about the Ashae case? That's why you went."

"Pierce and James were right. I needed to go into the backcountry to appreciate what we're up against with our suspect. I now have a little understanding about what a physical and mental specimen she must have been in her prime. I can't really put myself into her head like Pierce and James could probably do, but I have a better sense about her comfort zone.

"Allison A. Connors, or whatever her name is now, is at her best when alone in the wilderness. She's a skilled hiker who can carry what most could not lift off the ground. She could do it for miles while gaining and losing thousands of feet in elevation. She's also smart—probably in that top 1 percent intellectually. No doubt she's in the top 1 percent physically."

"I wonder, Van, are we getting sidetracked with this emphasis on the Sierra backpacking element of Connors? I mean, it just seems to me that even if there is a connection, we would be hard-pressed to find any value in it. The chances of finding an earring after all these years is remote. Any remains discovered in the Sierra aren't likely to be preserved like Cindy's were in the time capsule. The whole area isn't our jurisdiction. Are we wasting our time?"

"Sarge, I've wrestled with those same questions. And I might agree with you were it not for a conversation I had two days ago with the packer.

"On the way out, we stopped at the top of this pass. It was almost twelve thousand feet, and there was no one else around. I knew the packer, Roary was his name, had been intimate with the Sierra for a long time, and I was curious about his take on missing persons in the backcountry.

"I was careful and asked how likely is it that a backpacker acting alone and with no formal weapon like a gun or a knife could kill two other backpackers and dispose of their bodies so that they're not found." Van picked up his notes. "You know, Sarge, in his own reflective way, his response was measured but convincing. He stopped what he was doing and said something like 'Mister, I've been in this business for going on twenty-seven years. I've seen all kinds of hikers. They come in all sizes. Some well prepared, others pathetic. Some are thrilled to be here, and others look to be running away from something. But all those people come from out there. I reckon all the malignancies of the towns and cities are carried in here by them. I guess if you want to kill, you'll find a way, and this here is as good a place as any.'"

Van looked at notes. "'But hiding a body?' I asked him. I'm paraphrasing again. He said, 'Look in back of you. Those mountains on the other side of the canyon where we camped. There's a lake up there, Ladder Lake. Getting to it isn't easy, and those who do are usually cross-country hiking. Over the years, a lot of people camped at that lake. But then a few years ago, a guy discovers the remains of a World War II plane. People had hiked by it many times and never seen it. They found the remains of the crew too. That plane and those remains were hidden in plain sight for over half a century. So, I reckon if someone killed a couple of backpackers, they could just as easily find a way to hide the bodies. Though I suspect time, like that plane, would make those bodies known."'

Van put his notes aside. "You know, Sarge, that packer got me thinking. The motive to kill those two teenagers in 1972 was probably related to the motive that drove Allison to kill her father. Years later, she left that world and went into her other world. Since then, her world has probably been exclusively the Sierra Nevada, more specifically the John Muir Trail. Whatever she saw in the relationship of those kids that prompted her to kill them she was likely to also see in some people she encountered in the backcountry. The same motive in a different setting. The same reaction on her part. Her world today is still the Eastern Sierra."

Fenton's response was a mix of humor and country wisdom. "Not so sure I would want to run into her on the street or in the library."

Van smiled and leaned back. "Sarge, she's in her seventies now. I doubt she's murdered anyone in the last ten or twenty-plus years. But in her prime, I don't think any of us would have wanted to encounter her on her turf."

"Think she's still out there?"

"Hell, Sarge, I don't know. But I kinda hope she is."

CHAPTER 33

A STRANGE ENCOUNTER

Along the Southern JMT

A FTER WAITING UNTIL Van departed with Roary, Sti and Rob started down the trail. Their plan was to work their way south to a small meadow near Baxter Creek about thirty-five miles distant.

In the afternoon of the next day, Sti and Rob arrived at the Bench Lake backcountry ranger station about a mile beyond where the JMT crossed the South Fork of the Kings River. An acquaintance, Randy McClintock, was the ranger in residence for the season. They found her entertaining a small group of Boy Scouts who had hiked in over Taboose Pass the previous day.

When the Scouts and their leaders moved on a short time later, the three friends sat down at the makeshift table to catch up.

Conversation moved to discussion of various rangers Sti and Rob knew. Backcountry rangers were moved around every couple of years, and over time they had fostered friendships with several. They were particularly interested in the previous Bench Lake area ranger, Martha Ray.

"She's big-time now. They moved her to a supervisor position. She works out of Giant Grove HQ and oversees all the backcountry rangers."

"Has she been here yet this year?" asked Sti.

"Not yet. They've had difficulties up north this season, and she's focused a lot on those."

"Oh, what kind of problems?"

"Vandalism for one. You know that lake above McClure Meadow about a mile?"

Sti noted the lake. "You mean 11,106?"

"Yeah, its now 11,092. That's the lake where they found human remains years ago. Well, the location has been kept isolated, but someone was up there earlier in the season and did some digging. Park Service has kept that location under wraps for years. They didn't want attention drawn to it because they never found all the remains. I guess it's been a mystery, but I don't know the whole score."

Sti and Rob were intrigued. Both were thinking the same thing. *A body was found at 11,106 many years ago, and this is the first we're hearing about it. Did Van know? Could this have been another victim of Van's suspect?*

Rob inquired. "We've never heard about this. What's the scoop?"

"Well, it's apparently out now. None of us in the backcountry had ever heard about it either. I guess it just got lost over time. Talked to the ranger over at Ray Lakes a couple of weeks ago, and he said that the remains were those of a well-known backpacker and mountaineer back in the seventies. His disappearance was shrouded in secrecy for years.

"Dan at McClure Meadow station made the discovery that the site was being tampered with. That was about a month ago. Since then, NPS has been trying to find out who's responsible."

Sti asked, "They find anyone?"

"Apparently no. Few hikers go up there. Actually, from what I hear, location of the remains is not really next to the lake. Guess that's why they've been able to keep it quiet."

Sti and Rob asked some follow-up questions, but neither wanted to come across as being too curious. They would discuss the matter later.

—m—

Later that evening, camped at Bench Lake, Sti and Rob sat down with their respective cups of tea and coffee to talk about Randy's revelations regarding the remains at Lake 11,106.

Rob said, "I don't think Van's aware of that body. As far as I remember, there are only the remains of three people, the two bodies discovered down by Baxter Creek, where we're headed, and the girl they found in the upper Kern. I remember he said there was a missing trail runner and a solo male hiker whose bodies had not been found. I guess this could be one of those. But I'm certain he indicated no additional bodies had been found."

"The strange part is that we never heard about the body." Sti's voice belied his level of suspicion. "They've kept that a secret, allegedly for reasons even unclear to Randy. I wonder if Van will be able to breach the secrecy. If he needs help, we have another card to play."

"You mean our friendship with Martha Ray?"

"Yep."

—m—

They arrived at Baxter Creek in late afternoon. They had covered about sixteen miles.

Years earlier, a packer, picketing his stock for the evening, discovered what initially looked like bones from an animal. The next morning, when he went to retrieve the stock, he took a closer look and noticed some pieces of clothing in the area. Realizing he may have found human remains, the packer reported his find upon returning to Kings Canyon a couple days later.

A team from the National Park Service was sent in to collect the remains. Ultimately about 90 percent of the remains of two people were found along with what was left of their gear. It had all been buried in a shallow pit formed when a large pine tree fell over and the root ball containing rocks and dirt was pulled from the earth.

Subsequently, it was determined that the two victims had been students from Berkeley who disappeared while backpacking in 1968—Enid Ackerman and Ingar Tolkenson.

Baxter Creek came down from several small lakes in a basin of the same name. The basin was two miles to the east and a thousand feet higher. An unmaintained trail went up past the lakes, over Baxter Pass, and down into the Owens Valley near the town of Independence. It was a long and hot trail and not one suited for stock. Sti and Rob had been over Baxter Pass a couple of times. Except for the Baxter Creek basin and the view, the trail did not have much going for it.

Rob pulled out a map, and they began searching for the location where the remains had been found. GPS coordinates indicated the site was west of the Muir Trail. The two moved well off the trail and removed their packs. Then they began to make their way toward the coordinates.

As it turned out, the location of the root ball pit where the remains were found was right on the GPS coordinates. It was a good ways from the trail but not especially hidden. It was also not in an area where people tended to camp. It was just a stroke of luck that the packer had found it.

Sti noticed the small steel stake in the ground on the edge of the pit. It was a permanent marker. However, the remains had been found many years earlier, and there was no evidence of the subsequent search. Authorities had obviously gone over the site thoroughly and removed all they could find. A hiker happening by would have no clue of what had transpired years earlier.

Sti and Rob were banking on the fact that since the remains and gear had been buried for years and disturbed on multiple occasions by rodents and other animals, it was likely that a few small things were not discovered by those sent in to make recoveries.

They went back and retrieved their backpacks and set up a small camp about fifty yards from the permanent marker. They were not visible from the trail. It was getting late in the day, and they spent what little time they had just giving the site a cursory look.

—ⵎⵎ—

Based on discussions the evening before, Sti and Rob reasoned that if there was an earring left behind, it was likely to be in the root ball pit, where it would have been left at the time the remains were originally buried. If those who later recovered the remains somehow displaced the earring to the area surrounding the pit, it would be an area too big to search. In that case, it was not likely to be found. They needed a focus. They would concentrate on the center of the pit, an area about six feet in diameter. Logic said the bodies had originally been placed in the center, and an earring was likely to end up immediately below. Their estimates depended on assumptions, but they knew they needed to limit the search area.

They spent the early morning taking photographs of the pit and surrounding area. Then Rob brought out the small twelve-by-twelve-inch rolled wire mesh they had brought with them. Using the small plastic hand shovel they carried for other purposes, they began to dump scoops of soil from the bottom of the pit and sift it through the mesh in a search they expected to be fruitless. Nevertheless, it was what they had been asked to do.

They were in no hurry and had no illusions about finding anything. All Van had told them was to look for an earring like the one in the photo he showed them.

Rob was methodical. He tested the softness of the soil with the shovel. He determined that at the bottom of the pit the soil was loose to a depth of about eight inches, give or take. Below that it was hard, and he surmised the hard soil was the original bottom of the pit after the tree fell. The eight inches of loose soil had to have accumulated since the pit was created and from the work of the early searchers.

It was tedious work, and a couple of times they came across some small pieces of cloth that were faded and disintegrating. After three hours, they did find a button. Anything they found that was not natural they put in a plastic bag. By the end of the day, they had two buttons, a grommet like those used in an old nylon poncho, and several small nondescript pieces of nylon and fabric. The search conducted years ago had been thorough.

They had found nothing to suggest an earring and decided that except for the area around a large boulder that sat on one side of the pit, about three feet upslope from the center, they had been pretty thorough. They were not surprised they had not found the earring.

Later, as Sti was cleaning up the cooking gear after dinner, Rob wandered back over to the pit. It was six in the evening, and he had no intention of sifting through any more soil, but he walked to the edge of the pit. As he stared up at the old pine tree root ball, it occurred to him that the boulder down in the pit had actually fallen from the root ball sometime well after the tree had been uprooted. In fact, the indentation in the root ball directly above the boulder suggested as much. It seemed reasonable to conclude that the boulder had dropped down into the pit in recent years because its original location in the root ball was well defined and not significantly eroded.

Rob walked into the pit and tested the boulder. It was firmly embedded in the soil but not so firm as to suggest it had been there a long time. He pushed, and it moved slightly. They had sifted the dirt around but not immediately adjacent to or under the boulder. They purposefully had not moved the boulder because they thought it had been there from the beginning. Rob used both hands to roll the boulder aside. The soil beneath was somewhat compact but not like the soil he found about eight inches below the surface of the middle of the pit.

With his fingers spread, Rob dragged his hand through the soil. It was compact but not as hard as he had expected. It confirmed that the boulder had fallen recently. He acquired a short stick and pushed deeper into the soil, loosening it. Then he dragged his hand like a rake through the soil. His index finger unearthed a small piece of nylon twine, which in turn forced a deep blue piece of rock to the surface.

Rob recognized the stone; it was turquoise. It had a teardrop shape and was not much larger than a pencil head eraser. He stopped. He did not want to disturb the soil unnecessarily. He turned his head toward the camp. "Sti, bring that wire mesh and the shovel here."

Five minutes later, the dirty turquoise stone was resting in Sti's hand. Rob poured some water over it, and Sti rubbed the rock clean.

The very small hole where the earring wire would have been threaded was evident but clogged with dirt.

Sti's comment summed the situation up. "This is a game changer. It's a good thing you wandered over here."

"Isn't that what we're good at?"

It would be dark in a couple hours, but they had much to talk about. When they finally turned in, it was late.

With the finding of the earring stone, it was not necessary to stay in the backcountry any longer. They would contact Van very late tomorrow night or the day after at the latest.

—⁓—

Sti was dead to the world and did not hear a sound.

Rob found himself waking to what he thought had been a sound, but he wasn't sure. At first confused, he just lay there and closed his eyes. He was comfortable on his back and did not move. But there was a soft rustling sound, and Rob quickly stared up at the tent wall and listened.

Rob heard no more sound and convinced himself that he was not really hearing anything important. Sti was a good twenty feet away in his own tent. Sti sometimes snored, but Rob did not hear anything. It was a very quiet night.

He thought perhaps he was imagining things and was about to turn over on his side when a vague shadow moved across the tent wall. He froze. All his senses went on high alert. His first thought was an animal, perhaps a bear. *Bears don't bother backpackers in the Sierra*, he thought. The shadow had been only momentary and had not returned. Rob lay still, watching the tent wall.

Then the shadow again moved across the tent wall. Rob started to think fast. *I put the bear spray in my boot. If I move fast, I can reach above my head where my boots are and grab the spray and be ready to use it in a matter of seconds.*

Rob was on edge. He listened. Several seconds went by, and then he heard the rustling sound he thought he heard earlier. *Something's in my pack. It has to be a bear; no other animal like a marmot would make that shadow on my tent.* And then there was the sound that confirmed Rob's suppressed fears—it was a slow unzipping sound. *Someone's in my pack.* It was a person.

Curiosity gave way to a creeping fear. Rob's heart was accelerating, and he was trying to not give in to panic. He tried to focus on his options.

It was a warm night, so Rob had not zipped his sleeping bag. He realized that he could easily retrieve the bear spray without making any sound. His hand crept up alongside his face and above his head several inches before it encountered his boots. Carefully he felt the first boot, but the spray was in the next boot. He moved his hand over and felt the spray canister. Rob picked it up. He knew that in order to use it, he would have to remove the safety pin.

Outside, the sound of a slow-moving zipper had stopped, and the rustling began again. The sound was close. His pack was about ten feet away and leaning against a tree. Whoever was searching his pack had opened one of the zipper pockets and was searching within. Rob saw no indication on the tent wall that a flashlight was being used. Someone was searching blindly.

Sensing he could use the rustling sound coming from his pack as a bit of a cover, Rob brought his hand and the bear canister down to his chest. He planned his next move. The big hang-up would be his tent entrance. It had a long zipper. He reasoned he could unzip it quickly and exit the tent's side entrance in perhaps three or four seconds. Then it would be another couple of seconds before he could stand and turn around toward where his pack was located. With the bear spray in hand, he could use it immediately if the pin was out.

Five seconds, he thought, *may be too long.* But he could not just pretend to sleep and ignore the intrusion.

Rob armed the canister.

Then the rustling stopped. Rob held his breath. Then a slow zipping sound again. Now was the time. Rob transferred the canister to his left hand and slowly reached for the door zipper with his right.

Before doing anything, he tried to imagine if there was anything he forgot. Once he started to move, he had to be unimpeded. His feet were not tangled in his bag. He did not need to unzip his bag; he could just throw it off. Everything had to be one fluid motion.

Door zipper in hand, Rob executed his plan. The unzipping of the tent sounded loud to Rob and seemed to take forever. The exit of the tent was not pretty as he turned and righted himself. He began yelling and spraying before he actually caught sight of a shadowy figure jumping up from a squat. The figure had been facing away from Rob and turned to glance quickly in Rob's direction before then turning away and starting to run. It all happened in a handful of seconds.

Sti, who had been sound asleep, came into reality amid yelling and the sound of heavy footsteps moving past his tent. Then the tent jerked violently, and he heard the sound of a slight grunt as something hit the ground. Then there was the sound of running steps again. And there was Rob yelling but not running.

And then it was silent.

Sti was on his knees, crawling out of his tent.

Rob was standing next to his backpack. His panting voice said it all. "Shit! Who was that?"

CHAPTER 34

———∽∿∿∽———

DEBRIEFING

Orange County Sheriff's Department

IT WAS AFTERNOON on the third day after their exit from the Sierra when Sti and Rob arrived at the Orange County Sheriff's Department in Santa Ana. Van met them and ushered them to his office.

Neither took a seat as they waited until Van had crossed around to his side of the desk. Then Sti dropped a white business envelope on the desk. The handwritten notation on the outside was simple: *Earring Stone*. The numbers immediately below were the exact GPS coordinates where the stone was found. The date and time of discovery were also noted.

Van smiled and sat down. They followed suit. Words were not needed. They had briefed him by phone, and he knew what to expect. He broke the seal with a knife. He had always been the patient type and did not hurry. He carefully slid the folded single sheet of paper from the envelope out onto his desk and unfolded it.

The smile got bigger. Van was looking at a small and slightly dirty turquoise rock about the size of a jelly bean with a teardrop shape. Van moved it around with his index finger and looked at it from several angles. He saw the hole was filled with dirt and reached into his desk drawer and removed a small safety pin. Poking it into the hole from both sides, he cleaned out the dirt. The hole was very small, and only the tip of the pin would fit. Talking to no one in particular, Van muttered, "The wire would have gone through here." As if to inspect the hole further, he held it up to the light. Then he set it back down on the piece of paper.

Van reached into a file on his desk and pulled out a large photo of the earring found in the time capsule. Though not a true match, the rock in the photo and the stone found by Sti and Rob were very similar. The wire hole confirmed the purpose.

More to himself, Van said, "Now we know," and then he looked up at Sti and Rob. "How in the world did you find this? It's a miracle. You actually found the proverbial needle."

Rob said, "Quite by accident, I assure you." He went on to recount in detail what had transpired. He stressed that he and Sti had no confidence they would find anything. Then he reached across the desk and handed Van a flash drive. "This has all our photos of the area where we found the earring rock and close-ups of the rock as we removed it."

Looking back at the teardrop, Van shook his head. "You were right, Sti, when you said this is a game changer." He picked up the turquoise rock again and held it in the palm of his hand as if he was weighing it. "So small but so important."

Van stood and reached across to shake their hands. "Thanks, guys. You cannot imagine what this means to the investigation." They responded with a mixture of expressions of appreciation. "Well, I know this didn't come easy, and your subsequent experience was far from pleasant. I think it best at this point we get Sergeant Fenton in here and fill him in if you have the time."

"We have all day."

Van placed the stone on the white paper, folded the paper, and placed it back in the envelope. "We also need the two of you to put together a full report for our purposes."

With that, Sti held up a large manila envelope and handed it to Van. "Our summary report and some printed photos and a map showing location details."

Van opened the envelope while at the same time calling Fenton's office. "Sarge, we're ready when you are. We can meet you in IR1." He hung up and then looked quickly at the contents before looking up at Sti and Rob.

"You two amaze me. Sure you don't want to give up your day job and work for us? This is very comprehensive. Well written."

In tandem, they responded, "Not a chance." Sti carried it a step farther. "Been there, done that."

"We're going down to an interview room where we have more space. With your permission, we'll tape your input. When that part of our discussion is complete, we can stop the taping and talk more informally."

As they walked toward the interview room, Van dropped the report off at the desk of one of the floor personnel. "Could you make two photocopies of this and bring it to IR1? Thanks."

—⚒—

Fenton greeted Sti and Rob, and the four sat down.

Van turned on the recorder and began with a series of questions regarding their identification and time line of events. Following that, he asked for them to discuss what transpired between their meeting in Bishop and their exit from the backcountry a week later.

When they discussed the discovery of the earring, they referenced the photos as well and brought out a large, shaded topographic map to give the two officers a clear picture where the events of that day and night took place. Alternating with input, Sti and Rob carefully and sequentially reviewed the details, not wanting to leave anything out.

With regard to the 2:19 a.m. intruder, they included photos taken immediately after the incident. These provided the two officers with a sense of the scene. Included were some photos taken the next morning that showed the boot prints of the intruder. The prints suggested lightweight hiking boots, but the shoe imprint was not clear and not enough to suggest the make.

The size of the footprint was small, suggesting the intruder could have been female. Having no ruler for scale, Rob had used the folded edge of a 7.5-minute series topographic map. The latitude markings were uniform along the side, and the traditional 1:24000 scale on the map would allow anyone to note the actual measurements of the print.

As best he could, Rob tried to provide some idea of what the intruder looked like. "As I noted in the report, I'm certain it was a female. I would say she was about six feet tall, maybe more but certainly not less. I say that because it occurred to me she was at least my height. She was thin, wearing short pants and a loose-fitting long-sleeved shirt with a down or fiber-filled vest. She wore boots.

"It was night, and any moonlight was filtered by the trees. Colors are a bit hard to specify, but my guess is that the shorts and shirt were probably in the khaki range. She wasn't wearing glasses, but she did have a skullcap of the kind lots of backpackers wear at night. It was a typical Sierra night in the middle of summer, not real cold. I don't recall seeing any logos that would suggest the name of any brand of attire. My sense was that the clothing wasn't new.

"I would say she was lean. Her legs were long. When I first glimpsed her, I was spraying the bear canister in her direction, and she was coming up from a squatting position next to my backpack. She had been facing the pack, and as she rose, she had to turn. I can still see the *deer in the headlights* look on her face. The eyes were big and had a look of surprise. Somehow I knew the face was that of a woman, a mature woman but not an elderly woman.

"I don't know how much, if any, of the spray got on her. Probably not much. She turned away from me quickly and started running. I had only that one look at her face. As she ran, it was evident she had what I would call a sleek figure. Certainly there was no fat. She was in good shape, and she moved quickly and deftly."

Van interrupted. "When you say deftly, what does that tell you?"

"Not clumsy. Whoever it was moved quickly and easily. Like a deer bolting into the trees."

"Thanks. Go on."

"Thinking back on her appearance, the cap made it difficult to judge, but the hair wasn't long. I don't recall seeing hair outside the cap. The surprise on her face makes it hard to pass judgment on her facial features.

"After about three strides, she tripped over one of the ropes on Sti's tent and went down momentarily. There was a cry of sorts but no discernible words. As fast as she went down, she was up and running. She was into the shadows of trees and out of sight within seconds."

Fenton was curious. "So this person comes into your camp and riffles through your packs. The report notes you found nothing missing."

"Yes, correct," said Rob.

Sti interjected, "I put almost everything into a stuff sack and take it into my tent. Not much left in my pack. Actually, nothing was removed."

"Unlike Sti, I don't take all my things into the tent. I think she probably spent more time searching my pack as a result. I saw no evidence she used a flashlight. There was only minimal moonlight. I examined the pack with my headlamp soon after she fled and found things moved but nothing removed."

Again Fenton pursued his interest. "So, given the nature of her search, could you say that she seemed to know what she was looking for and would not need a flashlight?"

Van stepped in. "You're suggesting she knew they had found the earring or something else in that hole, and she was searching for it."

"Yes, if she knew they had found the earring and she wanted it, then perhaps that's all she was searching for. Of course, that would be a huge task in the night with no flashlight and without removing things from the packs."

Forehead furrowed, Sti shared concern. "Sergeant, that's a bit scary, and we've talked about it. It suggests we were under observation the whole time."

"I know, but it sounds like this Allison, or whoever she is, has the skill set to do exactly that—see and not be seen. One other question. In the morning, did you look around and find anything she dropped or anything else she might have touched?"

Rob responded, "Yes, we looked and found absolutely no other trace of her. We even walked the entire perimeter of the area looking for something that would suggest the direction of her departure, but there was nothing. No additional footprints or anything."

Sti said, "One other issue, fingerprints. We knew at the time prints were a possibility if the intruder wasn't wearing gloves. However, it was next to impossible for us to preserve anything since we had nothing to do it with and we had to pack our gear for the trip out. You're welcome to have a go at our equipment, but she was probably smart enough to not leave any prints."

Van nodded. "I'll check with our people on the prints issue. In the meantime, if you could avoid handling your gear as much as possible. I'll get back to you sometime today on this."

Fenton looked at Van, and there was a grin on his face. "Van, you were right when you said you thought she could be on to us. She knows we're looking for her. That's good. When the hunted know they're being hunted, then they start reacting rather than living their life. She's playing our game now, not her own."

Van nodded. He understood Fenton's implication. Allison would now act in response to their investigation and not according to her own agenda. That is when those on the lam make mistakes. But he was not convinced. Allison was smart. "Well, at least we know she's alive."

"And taking chances," said Fenton.

"She wanted the earring. Are there other earrings? Does she want those as well?" The comments by Sti caused the others to turn and look at him.

The response from Van was telling. "We have three bodies and two earrings. I suspect that if we find other bodies, we may again find earrings. Is Allison Connors now collecting the calling cards she left behind years ago? That would be quite unusual for a serial killer."

Fenton asked, "Rob, do you think you remember enough about the intruder to help one of our artists try and develop a facial sketch? If you can, it would be a big help."

"I have thought about that option and tried to keep an image in my mind's eye. But in all honesty, all I see are the deer-in-the-headlight eyes and a stocking cap. I really don't think I can give much more. But if you wish, I can try."

"Well, if you're going to be around, we'll try and set something up."

They went on to discuss the hike out over Kearsarge Pass and the ride they hitched to the town of Independence where they reported the night intrusion incident to the Inyo County sheriff. Then they caught a northbound ride to Bishop where they spent the next two days before driving back to Orange County.

When they were done with the formal interview and statements, Van turned off the recording equipment, and both Van and the sergeant expressed thanks.

Fenton took the lead. "Well, I'm not a backpacker, but I would say you guys had one interesting experience. I do have a question. In the days before or after you found the earring, did you encounter any solo female hikers?"

Rob shared that they had met people on the trail prior to that night, but he felt sure that the person he saw at night was not any of the female backpackers they had seen along the trail. On the hike out, Rob looked closely at each female but saw nothing to suggest the intruder.

At this point, the conversation began to be questions and clarifications about their written report. Nothing new surfaced.

As the conversation tapered off, Rob and Sti let it be known there was one piece of information they did not include in the report because it was given to them in confidence by the Bench Lake backcountry ranger.

Sti noted Randy's revelation that the National Park Service had many years earlier found remains at what was then Lake 11,106 on the topographic maps. It was remote and near the JMT. For reasons not clear, the finding of the remains was a couple decades old and had never been made public. Recently, someone had revisited the site and had been digging.

Sti said, "Van, were you aware of a body being found near Lake 11,106? We don't remember any conversation with you about that."

Van was intrigued. "No, I wasn't aware. Can you show me where that lake is located?"

Rob opened Mount Henry and Mount Darwin topographic maps and pointed to the lake. "We don't know where near this lake the remains were found. You'll have to find that out. It's a remote lake and gets few visitors. Most hikers along the JMT don't have time for such deviation. Sti and I have been there a couple of times and never saw another backpacker at the lake. It's a good two- to three-day strenuous hike from the closest trailhead."

Sti added, "And we would appreciate it if you wouldn't reveal our source."

Van nodded. "We'll do our best to keep it close."

Rob chimed in. "Also, we do know an administrative ranger in the Kings Canyon–Sequoia National Park. I know she could prove very helpful, but we wouldn't want to contact her unless your inquiries meet a dead end."

Their meeting concluded with Van offering to take them to lunch. Sti and Rob begged off as they were going to meet with a friend who lived in Newport and would have a fine lunch and wine waiting for them.

Back in his office, Van asked if he could impose on Sti and Rob for one more favor.

Van took out some aerial photos of the Santa Ana Mountains taken in the 1970s. He pointed to where the burned-out van had been located. "If the two of you have some time, I would like your insight into how far someone could hike between about 1:00 a.m. and sunup. I have, as you can see, circled out distances of five and ten miles. However, distance and travel are two different measures. I'd like to know how far you think a fit female about thirty years of age, and an expert hiker, could have covered in five or six hours without hiking on the paved road."

They were not sure when they would have the time to pursue Van's request, but they would try.

CHAPTER 35

THE BREAK

Trabuco Canyon
Cleveland National Forest

Van was exhausted as he walked toward his office. One of the staff, Deena, was waving her arm to get his attention. She got up and intercepted him near his office door.

"I have some information for you, Investigator ..."

He did not want to rebuff Deena, but he desperately had to go to the restroom. "Deena, can you give me about ten minutes? I'm shot and need to unload these files and figure out where I am before I can do any work. Come by in about ten. Is that okay?"

"Sure, Investigator."

Van wasn't sure why Deena, unlike all the other civilian staff, insisted on calling him by his title rather than name. He had convinced most of the others to call him by name.

He went into his office and quickly dumped the files on his desk. Then, just as quickly, he went down the hall to the restroom.

On returning minutes later, Van was struck by the mess. The desk was in disarray. And the large tea he had ordered four hours earlier was right where he left it. *This is not a good day.*

The call from the night shift sergeant had come yesterday, Sunday evening, about ten o'clock. Neighbors had heard two gunshots come from the home of an elderly couple in Lake Forest. Deputies responded and found the couple dead. Van and Stenzgard got the summons. They arrived within minutes of each other, around eleven. They had been there all night.

Van came into the office about eight in the morning, having grabbed hot tea at the local Starbucks. He had an early meeting with Assistant DA Heidi Metzler. They had been working an attempted murder case for three months, and now the two witnesses were backing away from statements made during the early part of the investigation. Heidi was angry and using Van as a scapegoat.

Van thought by coming in early he could review some before the meeting, but the meeting turned out to be a very unpleasant two hours with Heidi. What made it even more trying was that he had left the large cup of tea in his office and did not have the caffeine lifeline at the meeting. He lifted the cup; it was room temperature. He drank it anyway. It was too expensive to waste.

Nothing he could do about Heidi's issues today. He needed to put together his share of last night's case. It looked to be a murder-suicide. The paperwork, of course, was no less complex. His day would be consumed by the case.

The old couple had been retired teachers for twenty-some years. She was ninety, and he was eighty-six. Son was killed in the early days of Desert Storm. Neighbor said the daughter had gotten into drugs and had fallen out of favor with the parents. Daughter had not been around much for years. The closest neighbor, the one who reported the shots, said the couple had suffered some financial setbacks. They had gone to church yesterday morning, came home, and were not seen or heard until the shots rang out.

Van and Stenzgard arrived to find the husband and wife sitting in adjacent reclining chairs. She was shot in the head, and he in the mouth. The gun was on his lap.

Forensics would do their thing, but Van knew, as did Stenzgard, it was a closed case already. He shot her and then turned the gun on himself. Van wondered, *What is it about some older couples that they run out of time in this life? They see things as hopeless and just want to move on.* It was sad. *Is that what happens when you lose your children? You lose the will to live?*

A soft knock on the door, and Van glanced up to see Deena. Had it been ten minutes?

"Investigator …"

"Deena, please, can you do me a big favor?" He picked up the cup. "I bought this several hours ago, and now it's room temperature. I need the caffeine and hate to waste it. Could you please see if you can find me some ice? Then we can do business."

"Sure, we have some in the workroom. I'll get some ice."

He turned on his computer and logged in. By then, Deena was back and put ice in the cup.

Van took a long drink and sighed.

"Thanks, Deena. I apologize if I came across short. It's been a long night and morning. Now, what was it you had for me?"

"You remember the request you made a month or so ago about those homes in Silverado and Modjeska Canyons?" Van nodded. "Well, I started by tracking down the names of all of the owners—you know, people who are listed on the tax rolls as owners. You had said to look for the name Connors, Archie, or Mary Jo. You also said to look for an Allison A. Connors."

Van's hopes jumped. "Did you make any connections?"

"No, there's no Connors and none of those first names. I mean, I was thorough, but nothing. For a lot of those places, the county has incomplete records. County recorder's office said the people we're looking for are, and I quote, 'canyon people' and are not like people in the flatlands." Deena raised her brows. "Whatever that means. So I decided to expand the search a bit. Sorry if I didn't say anything, but, you know, I decided to look in some of the other canyons, including Trabuco Canyon."

Van leaned forward.

"That's when things changed. You know, Silverado and Modjeska are private lands, Trabuco is Forest Service land. Homes there are on long-term leases. The ownership thing is a bit different, not always easy to follow. However, I discovered some very peculiar information.

It seems many, probably most, of the Trabuco homes have been there for many decades and have been owned by the same people or families. There are a couple of houses owned by the same people for over eighty years.

"When I thought about it, I wondered how someone who may have bought a home there as an adult eighty years ago could still be alive. I mean, they would have to have passed it on to someone in the family. That could mean a name change. A Connors surname could have owned a place, but an offspring could have a different name. You know, like marriage.

"Anyway, I called our contact in the county clerk's office. She got back to me and indicated that there has been little change in the title listed on most of those houses. Even though people have died, the family holds on to the place, and no change is made in the ownership. Because the houses are on government-leased land, the ownership and taxing process is complicated. Families can own a house for generations and not change the title. You know, as long as they pay taxes and lease fees to the feds, they're not questioned. No one seems to bother those people."

"And how is this all relevant?" asked Van.

"Because when they sent over some background history on ownership of the leases, an oddity popped up. I know it maybe doesn't make sense, but I noticed that in 1953 a Mary A. Hardin became the owner of one of the houses. At first that meant nothing because I was looking for a Mary Jo Connors. Then I noticed the name was changed in 1957 to Mary A. Hardin-Talonis. In 1960, it changed to Alexandria Talonis. Then in 1963, Alexis Talonis became the owner. She remains the owner today. Allison's name has a middle initial of A. Does that make sense?"

He had been listening, but the quick succession of names caught him off guard and was at first confusing. But one name stuck with him—Mary A. Hardin. The middle name was only an initial, A. Just as quickly the last name also resonated. Then the change in 1963 hit all of Van's senses. "Alexis Talonis? Do we know anything more?"

His mind immediately went back to the interview with Elizabeth Ambrose. "A for Alexis," he said to himself before Deena responded.

"No. Clerk says these places are so remote mail isn't delivered because the road often becomes impassable. Mail is sent to postal boxes most often. For some, the Trabuco home is a second home, so the mail goes to a primary residence or postal box somewhere else."

"Where's the postal box for this Alexis?"

"There's a collection of route field boxes located where TCR, I mean Trabuco Canyon Road, intersects Santiago Canyon Road."

"So people would have to drive some distance to get their mail. And the property tax payments for this Alexis Talonis?"

"Paid on time every year, without fail. There's a postal box listed for Hardin-Talonis. It hasn't been changed in over fifty years. But there's more. Can I sit?"

"Of course, rude of me. Please, sit." Van felt foolish. He knew that sometimes his attention to social graces was distracted when he began to think. "Deena, go on."

"I learned about some of this late last Friday, and you were out of the office, so I set it aside. But the area sounded interesting, and since Paul and I don't live far from the canyon, I suggested we take a ride out there on Saturday. Paul consented because I told him it would be a good test for his four-wheel-drive truck. And it was.

"The road is long and dusty. It's not an easy five-mile drive. When we got to the end of the road, where the so-called houses are, there's a makeshift parking area. You know, it looks like a lot of hikers park there who are headed up Saddleback and Holy-Jim Canyon. Apparently there's a waterfall somewhere up there. Owners of the houses also park there. But these aren't really houses, you know. Shacks would be a better term. Some are falling apart. Some have lots of graffiti. Not much appeal. Don't really know what attracts people to those places, you know what I mean?" Deena must have realized she had gotten off track because she turned back to her notes.

"Anyway, Paul and I walked around a little. Some places have numbers on them, but I didn't see anything to identify where the one owned by Alexis Talonis was. Then I saw an older woman doing some work in a flower garden, and I struck up a conversation with her. When I inquired about one owned by someone named Talonis, she looked confused. I told her it had originally been owned by a person named Hardin. Then she perked up and pointed way up the hill at a small, almost hidden shack that was isolated from all the others. It really looked rundown and hidden by overgrown shrubs."

Van marveled at the thoroughness of Deena's efforts. He fought the urge to question.

"She said that when she was young, a single mother and daughter lived there. The mother was named Hardin, Alexandria Hardin she thought. Every once in a while, an older boy came around. Word was he had run away from home years earlier."

Van was staring at her, and Deena hurried on with her comments. "I asked her when the mother and daughter lived there. She told me it was the 1950s and probably early 1960s."

Van was momentarily stunned. He could hardly believe what he was hearing and desperately wanted to interrupt. He didn't. He found himself biting his lip as he listened with rapt attention. His mind was moving fast, but he still wanted to hear the details from Deena.

"I asked if anyone had been around lately, and she said no. She hadn't seen anyone since about 2000. At that time she said a grown woman appeared one evening, but no one got a good look at her. The next day, this lady I was talking to said she decided to walk up and introduce herself. But as she was approaching the house, the woman came out with a big old backpack on, locked the door, and then hiked off. You know, she never saw the woman's face. She never saw her again, she said."

Van had been following the conversation, but his mind was racing ahead.

However, the sudden mention of the word "backpack" was like a bolt of lightning. Van suddenly found himself reacting physically and mentally. He did not want to miss anything Deena was saying, so he kept his reaction short. "Go on, Deena. This is great info."

"This lady, Mable, said that later her husband, Walter, went up to take a look. When he got back, he said that the water hadn't been turned on, the electricity was still turned off like it had been for years, and the propane tank still registered empty.

"Mable said that over the years since the 1980s people have said they saw a light in the cabin at night sometimes, but other than that day in 2000, no one has ever seen anyone around.

"Also, Mable said all the people who live on and off in their little community say the lady who owns the cabin is older and comes and goes only on foot. They've never seen a car, not since the early 1970s."

Van was on his feet. He knew what he had just heard was a breakthrough. With a smile and enthusiastic tone, Van set his thoughts in motion. "Deena, make me photo copies of the address and area map. Also, make photocopies of all of your notes on this matter. I need anything that identifies the house, tax collector plot map, whatever. I'll be back in a few. I'll need it all."

Van was thinking fast. "And, Deena, this is to take priority. Drop everything else you're doing and focus on this. Also, keep this to yourself. We don't want everyone to know."

As Deena turned to go, Van called after her. "Also, get me whatever you can find on Alexandria Talonis and Alexi Talonis." Deena did not turn. She just nodded and kept going.

He walked quickly over to Doug Fenton's office. "Ann, where's the sergeant?"

"At a meeting upstairs with the bigwigs. Don't expect him back for an hour or two. More if they all decide to go to lunch. The lieutenant is there also."

"Call him. I need him ASAP. I need the lieutenant as well."

"They're not going to like being interrupted, Investigator."

"They'll like it even less if I don't get them down here ASAP. Tell them it's a major break in the Ashae case. They'll come."

Van walked back to his office. He got out his map of the Trabuco Canyon area and noted the remoteness of the houses. Deena's comments kept playing over in his head. She had a "backpack." She is "older and comes and goes only on foot." It was her; it had to be Allison.

—⚬⚬⚬—

When Fenton walked in, Van was looking at a Google Earth view of the small enclave of Trabuco Canyon dwellings. The density of trees made it difficult to see any one clearly. He wasn't even sure what he was looking at.

"Gee, Van, you got some cojones. This best be damned good," said Fenton as he entered, followed by Vargas.

Van recounted the input from Deena. By that time, Deena had supplied some map information.

He was standing facing Fenton and Vargas as he spoke. "It's the name, Alexis, that seems to be the key. Elizabeth Ambrose, Allison's college roommate, told me that the initial A in Allison's name stood for Alexandria or Alexis. I know the last name Talonis isn't the same, but the uniqueness of Alexis just seems to be beyond coincidence. Also, Archie Connors's wife's name was Mary Jo Harden. This home was owned by a Mary Jo Harden before title was transferred to Mary A. Harden-Talonis and later to Alexandria Talonis."

The conviction was strong in Van's voice. "This is not coincidence. There's too much convergence here. This home was where Allison spent about ten years of her life before going to college. It was owned by her mom and transferred to Allison, albeit with another name, upon her mother's death. No one but Allison, carrying a backpack, has been there since."

Vargas seemed contemplative as he listened. Van knew that he was asking the lieutenant and Fenton to buy into conclusions most would regard as coincidence. He also knew that law enforcement saw coincidence differently than civilians.

"Okay," said Vargas, "what do you need from us?" The lieutenant was on board.

"Boss, I want deputies out there now to seal off the area. Keep everyone away from this house, no one on the property, deputies included. We need a warrant, but in the meantime I want it sealed off."

The lieutenant said, "I'll take care of the warrant. You guys take care of the rest and keep me advised." He started walking out the door and stopped. Turning back, Vargas looked at Van. "If this goes down, Van, it's good work on your part. But remember, I don't want the press on this yet. Keep it close. I'll keep the sheriff up to date."

Fenton took out his cell phone and made a couple of calls while standing just outside Van's office door. A few minutes later, he reentered the office. "They're on it. They suggested we also get the deputy on duty who works the county backcountry since he knows that area. I told them to get him there pronto. No lights, sirens, or excesses that could alert the press. Everything QT."

Van was thinking. "Doug, I know Stenzgard is lead on last night's case, but we all know that's going to end up being a murder suicide. I need him to be with me when we go there. No one on the force has his skill at assessing things at first sight. I need to know what he sees and thinks when we get our first look inside that house. Stenz has a cabin in Big Bear. He knows about cabins and mountain homes. He knows what to expect, what to look for. We need him."

Fenton stuck his head out the office door. "Deena, locate Stenzgard for me."

The lieutenant walked back in. "It occurred to me that you'll also need some dogs there. If the other body of those two missing kids was ever there, the dogs will find the evidence. Forensics will also be useful in that regard. I'll make the calls. I want this to get top priority." He walked out again but stopped again and turned when he saw Deena coming.

Deena said to Van, "Stenzgard went home for a shower and change of clothes. He'll be here in thirty minutes."

"Okay, you guys have this in hand. Keep me posted." With that, Vargas walked away again.

Van sat back in his chair and looked at Fenton. "Hope the boss can get a warrant quickly."

—ɱ—

An hour and a half later, they were on the rough dirt road into Trabuco Canyon. Van had briefed Stenzgard on their ride to the turnoff where they parked Stenzgard's Vic and loaded into the deputy's green-and-white four-wheel Jeep. Fenton sat up front, Van and Stenzgard in the rear. Van did not tell the deputy what it was all about, but deputies were used to being kept in the dark by investigators. Van did make some inquiries.

"You know a couple named Mable and Walter up there?"

"Oh yeah, everyone does. They're there most of the time. Everyone else is an absentee landlord. They call her Mel. They keep watch. Which place are you guys interested in?"

Van explained, and the deputy knew the place right away. "That place is isolated. Unlike most of the other places where the day hikers and recreationists walk indiscriminately through yards and peek into houses, that place gets no visitors. It's really isolated off and above all the others. I think the fact that it has poison oak growing all around it helps. Owner seems to know that and not trim it. I've never met 'em. Everyone says it's a woman. Place doesn't get vandalized like some of the others. People leave it alone."

The deputy's comments were fitting. A lone cabin owned by a lone woman. Both mysterious.

The deputy slowed as they approached the large steel pipe swing gate blocking any further travel down the road. A deputy waved them through. Off to the left and scattered along the hillside were dwellings, all small and couched among the many trees. There was a Forest Service sign designed to communicate information, warnings, trails, and cautions to hikers and those in the area just to picnic or have fun.

The parking area had fifteen to twenty vehicles, including several patrol cars and a Forest Service truck.

The deputy parked, and Fenton immediately got out and walked over toward another department officer, the sergeant in charge of patrol out of South County.

"Doug, must be damned important for you to come out here. What's this all about?"

"Walk with me, and I'll explain."

Van recognized the tactic. Fenton would explain the situation to the patrol sergeant out of hearing range of others. No need to broadcast anything.

Van looked around. He could see several deputies strategically placed, but he wondered just where the house was.

The deputy that drove them in turned to Van. "I know the Forest Service gal. I'll let her know that you're going to serve a warrant on a place and anticipate no problems. I can tell you from experience that when the time is appropriate, it would help if someone briefed her. USFS can help us sometimes. Best to keep on their good side."

Van nodded. "Sure, I agree. Let her know I'm the lead here and will talk with her a little later. In the meantime, I would appreciate it if the presence of any unnecessary personnel is kept to a minimum." It was not lost on Van that the off-road deputy had a future in the department. He understood the value of relations.

"Will do, Investigator." With that, the deputy wandered off.

Stenzgard approached. "Van, Doug is waving for us to come over." They walked across the small dirt parking lot to the base of a dirt road that served as a trail and climbed steeply up the hill and into a small canyon.

"Van, this is Sergeant Dohene." Short in stature, Dohene was a bit overweight, smartly groomed, and wore a smile that conveyed a friendly demeanor.

They shook hands and exchanged greetings as Stenz continued. "These deputies are his. He says there are several civilians in their cars awaiting him. Anyone who was already up here or came into the parking lot since has not been allowed to leave. He also says that he has asked any residents to stay in their houses until further notice."

Dohene was quiet and seemed content to let Stenz take the lead.

Finally he asked Van for some guidance. "Just need to know what you want done at this point. How long do you want to detain these people?"

Van expressed his appreciation for Dohene's help. "Have your deputies get names and addresses, other particulars, and some idea why they're here. Do not let any women who are older than sixty and single leave. Also, if they have a place here, ask them if they've ever seen anyone at house number 37. I don't know where it is yet, but I think it's one of the last houses up the canyon and on the right. Sits up high. If they have, get a statement and let them know someone will probably contact them."

Stenzgard turned to Dohene. "Wayne, we don't need anyone here who's not necessary. This could be a long day and evening. Thanks for your help."

Van wondered, *Is there anyone Stenzgard doesn't know within the department? Probably only very recent hires.* Anyway, Stenzgard was under control. He had a calming effect. Van reminded himself that today was what he had been waiting for. Best to take it slow. Surprisingly the mantra of his old Latin teacher popped into his head, *vincit qui patitur*—he prevails who is patient. A smile crossed Van's face.

He turned back to Dohene and Fenton. "Wayne, can you show us exactly which house we're looking for? I have all the details, but we haven't been here before."

"Sure, follow me."

Van was content to let Dohene and Fenton take the lead. He and Stenz followed along with two of Dohene's deputies and the backcountry deputy. It was a good climb up out of the parking area and into the assembly of dwellings.

Ten minutes later, they were standing below a very old and dilapidated picket fence when Dohene spoke. "This is it, Investigator, but watch out for the poison oak. It's everywhere. It's the best fence this place has. It's these shrubs with groups of three leaves." Talking to himself, the sergeant betrayed his Boy Scout education. "If it has three, let it be." The smile that followed was self-conscious. Then he stood aside.

The house was old and had not been improved upon in decades. The windows were covered with solid wood shutters that looked to not have been opened in years. The door at the front had two padlocks, one near the top and another about two feet from the bottom. The locks were on steel bars anchored in the framing of the house. One could not break into this house easily.

The wood house looked to be about thirty feet deep and twenty feet wide. The roof was metal, old corrugated aluminum now so black with corrosion it looked to be anything but metal. At some very distant past, the house was probably white, though that was just an assumption based on bits of paint here and there that looked to have no color. Everything on the outside of the house was in the worst of shape—worn, unkempt, and generally dilapidated. Plants and shrubs had taken over the yard and crowded around the sides of the house. The density of shrubs around the door gave the appearance of a setback porch at the entrance.

About twenty feet from the front entrance was what looked like an old fire pit with a ring of boulders around it. The yard included pieces of old wood, some kind of old chicken or bird cage, the wheel from an old car with the remains of a shredded tire, and an assortment of indescribable pieces of junk that were overgrown by weeds and shrubs, most of it poison oak.

"The warrant here yet?" asked Stenzgard. He was on his mobile set.

Someone in the parking lot responded, and it came through gravely. "On its way."

Stenzgard spoke again. "We're going to need a good set of bolt cutters to get in."

"Ask the Forest Service gal. She'll have one," Dohene said. "They're always having to cut off locks when people illegally put chains and fences across their access roads and firebreaks. I'll ask her. She'll feel needed then."

The backcountry deputy stepped forward with lopping shears. "Investigators, I carry these because I often have to trim poison oak and other shrubs in order to open gates, clear areas around signs, and other things. Want me to cut some of this stuff so you can get into the yard?"

Stenzgard told the deputy to go ahead and then patted him on the back. He added, "When you're done here, stop by my house. I've got some pruning that needs attention." The comment elicited some general laughter and eased the tense atmosphere.

Van's mind was rapidly absorbing the scene and the task before them. He turned to no one in particular. "When the dog gets here, I want to cover the grounds out front first. Then we'll cut the locks, and the dog and handler can case the inside before we go in. Once they're done, Stenz and I will go in. With those shutters in place, we're going to need some good lighting. Have forensic techs bring up some lights. Let's try to keep the number of personnel limited until we have a good handle on what's inside."

He thought a second and went on. "There's the potential for fifty years of evidence here, and I do not want to spoil any of it, so anything that looks like junk is to be given respect until the techs say otherwise. Stenz, you think of anything?"

Slowly, Stenzgard pointed to the fire pit. "I want that fire pit left alone." He turned to Van. "There's something phony about that pit. I'll let you know after I get a closer look."

Van knew bringing Stenzgard was a good decision. There is no substitute for the instincts of experience. The best thing that could happen in the department was keeping Stenzgard in investigations and not having him be promoted.

The wait for the warrant was not long. Dohene returned with a very large set of bolt cutters. The handler and dog were right behind. Dohene handed the warrant to Van. "It just arrived."

Van and Stenz walked alone up to the door. All their experience told them there was no one inside, but there was protocol. They knocked on the door and then waited. They banged on the door and announced their presence, noted they had a warrant, and asked that the door be opened and waited again. Everyone waited. They all knew the drill.

Van and Stenz then motioned the handler and dog forward to scan the grounds. They were searching for any scent that would suggest human remains were buried in the yard. The yard was small, and it took only about five minutes.

When the handler indicated there was nothing, Dohene went to the door and cut the two locks. The deadbolt steel bars did not move, so Dohene banged on them with the bolt cutter until they disengaged and slid away from the doorframe. Then he stepped back.

Patitur, thought Van. It would be dark inside and who knew what else. They did not need to rush in. Van reached out, and Dohene handed him the bolt cutters. Without standing in front of the door, he pushed on it with the extended bolt cutters. It did not move easily. As he pushed harder, the door swung in slowly, emitting the expected sounds all could hear.

Stenzgard held up a flashlight and shined it inside. It was so dark that the beam of light seemed to be swallowed in the cavity. Fenton came forward with a couple of larger flashlights.

Within a few seconds of looking, his eyes began to adapt, and he could begin to see things. The inside was a mess of nondescript chairs, a table, what looked to be some kind of sofa, a door into another room, and other things one would expect from an abandoned shack. He stepped back and motioned for the handler and dog to enter.

The dog seemed to know what was expected on entering. Van and Stenzgard followed.

Beams from the flashlights darted about, and Van caught only fleeting glimpses of the interior.

Van wondered, *Could this be where it all started?*

CHAPTER 36

TRABUCO HOUSE EVIDENCE

Trabuco Canyon and Homicide Office

V AN AND STENZGARD stepped inside and stood cautiously as they
moved their flashlights about. Everything suggested there had
been no occupant for years. It was a derelict space. Everything had
mounds of dust, and there were cobwebs everywhere.

It took the dog only a couple of minutes to cover the interior. The
dog soon found something, and the handler noted to Van and Stenz
that it was a small cloth bag in the closet in the bedroom. Visually it
was too small to be human remains, but the dog had singled it out.

Once the dog and handler left the building, Van and Stenzgard
looked around. Without good lighting, they could do little. Shortly,
forensic techs set up large portable lights at the entrance. It made all
the difference.

Careful not to contaminate evidence, they wore the obligatory
plastic gloves. Claudia had also insisted they wear masks because
the dust would be kicked up with their every move. Careful not to
displace anything, they scanned the scene.

Except for the creaking of the floor as they walked, all was silent.
Then Van heard the subtle and casual comment from Stenzgard who
was in the small back room. Van would never forget the comment. It
was a simple "Bingo!" followed by, "Van, you need to see this."

Stenzgard had found a small wooden jewelry box. Probably made from cedar, it had dust on top, but one could tell it had a varnish-like finish. It was old. Stenz, using the blade of a pocketknife lifted the lid to reveal the jewelry—earrings to be exact. They were protected from the dust, and Van immediately recognized their style. Though each was slightly different, they were all similar to the one found on Cindy, and each earring had a stone very much like the one uncovered by Sti and Rob. *Bingo* indeed.

It was strange. The box sat on a small dresser. The four dresser drawers were empty. There was nothing else in the room except a small bed stand and a bed with no mattress.

The box was a repository that served a purpose. It was as though the shack existed to protect a box of special earrings. The strangeness of it all expanded. The house was as furtive as its owner.

There were three sets of matching earrings along with a single earring. The basic design of all three sets was similar. They were for pierced ears, made of wire in an oval design, and each with a small, polished stone suspended from the oval piece of wire. There was the single earring with no matching partner that seemed to command Van's attention. Was the matching earring somewhere on a buried body, perhaps that of Carlos or another victim in the Sierra?

Van wondered how many earrings had been removed over the years and then left with bodies here in Orange County or along the JMT.

They continued to search. There was nothing else of consequence in the bedroom.

In the kitchen area, which was one side of the entrance room, there was scant cooking equipment consisting of a couple of pans, an old coffeepot, a handful of plates, some utensils, and a few other odds and ends. The items were distributed among a couple of kitchen drawers and a single cupboard with three shelves.

The only clothing consisted of two coats hanging from a nail. There was nothing in the very small bathroom. In the entrance room, there were no magazines, no toys, no old radio or TV, no decorations, no mirrors, no lamps, and no bulbs in the two overhead lights.

Except for the stuff bag found by the dog, the only closet was empty.

On one side of the entry room was a duffel bag with what looked to be old hiking and backpacking gear. Next to it were five cardboard boxes of books. The boxes were old and had no markings. They were neatly stacked against a wall.

Stenzgard said the backpacking items looked like old army/navy surplus stuff used in the fifties and sixties. Nothing that is used today.

Van had noticed immediately that the books were out of the ordinary. They included a collection of older kids' books that he did not immediately recognize. There were some classics by the likes of Shakespeare, Dumas, Homer, and Thomas Aquinas, among others. Also, there was Gilbert and Sullivan's *The Mikado*, and there was a Bible. There were also some books in French and Italian.

He could not escape the thought that the books were probably at one time among those on the shelves Allison had created in her study cave when she roomed with Elizabeth Ambrose. Van wanted to leaf through them, but he did not.

Van sensed that whoever had used the place intermittently over decades was careful not to displace things and to disturb as little dust as possible to give the impression the house was not used at all.

As they left the house, Stenzgard stopped and looked at the rake and shovel that leaned against the wall just inside the door.

"Van, this is peculiar. Follow me."

Stenz walked out to the fire pit he had noted earlier. He squatted down and turned over a couple of the fire-ring rocks. Looking up at Van, he said, "This fire pit was not built for fires. Get that Forest Service gal and backcountry deputy up here. Also, bring that dog back."

As the others walked over to hear the conversation, Stenzgard noted that the rocks lining the periphery of the fire ring did not have signs of charcoal or burn residue on them. "These rocks are clean." Stirring the surface of what was the fire pit area with a stick, he also noted, "If there had ever been a lot of ashes in the pit, they pretty much washed away long ago. In all likelihood, there's never been a fire in the pit. Any ashes here were probably placed to suggest it was a fire pit."

The others nodded acknowledgment, but Stenz was not finished. He then noted that the pit had sunk too far in the middle. The sinking extended about a foot outside the ring of boulders. Over many years, water had filled the pit, and it had probably settled a bit each year, suggesting the earth beneath had at one time been dug up and then replaced as when something is buried. Brushing loose soil in the middle of the pit away with a stick, he noted how the center of the pit, where the soil was more solid, was a good ten to twelve inches below grade.

Stenzgard ventured an interpretation. "It's my guess that any soil that may still be on that shovel in the house matches the soil below this pit. Also, something is or was buried here. I think forensics will find something here for us."

Van's heart had started to race. All he could think of was Carlos, a body.

The Forest Service representative showed up, and Van asked for her input.

"The fire danger here is acute. Open fires were banned many decades ago. But, of course, it's an ongoing battle since common sense is lost on many. However, the people living in the canyons tend to know the risks and have always cooperated."

Van asked, "Would you agree that this fire ring appears not to have been used for a fire?"

Borrowing the stick Stenz used, she stirred the soil and overturned several large rocks. "Yes. If it was ever used for a fire, I'm guessing it was fifty years ago or more."

Turning to Claudia, Van said, "The site's yours. Find out what the house and this fire ring have to tell us."

He had a meeting with those involved in the investigation later in the morning, so Van arrived at his office early to review his preliminary report on the search of the Trabuco house or the TC house, the unofficial names now in use. Van was of the opinion it should be *mystery house* because it seemed to suggest that mystery begat mystery.

He had spent two days writing the report. It was considerable even though it did not yet include all the input from forensics. He could not remember a report from any of his cases where he had spent so much time on details for which he had so little understanding. He also could not remember when what he thought was a breakthrough raised as many questions as it answered.

To begin with, the small sleeping bag stuff sack contained two large plastic bags. There were no remains in the bags. The bags were neatly folded, a detail oddity that did not escape his observation and that of Claudia.

Claudia suggested it was conceivable that the bags at one time contained human or animal remains or were used to transport remains many years earlier. She would let him know. However, what perplexed Van was why the plastic bags, if they had contained remains as some point, were not thrown away. Claudia reminded him that DNA was not part of criminal investigations until the 1980s, so even though she might find some trace evidence today, there was no chance of it happening in 1972. But that still did not explain why Allison had not eliminated the bags, unless it was another of her hang-ups with environmental issues. Maybe she could not dispose of something that was recyclable.

As for the two coats, forensics would look closely for DNA or other evidence.

Conversations with Claudia over the past two days revealed additional mysteries. Forensics was not able to pull prints from anything including the locks and bolts on the door, kitchen items, the shovel and rake, the duffel bag items, the boxes containing books, and several other places one would likely find prints.

Van recalled his conversation with Claudia near the end of the day at the Trabuco house. "Van, this house is full of contradictions.

It's clean of any prints but loaded with dust. Talk about irony. A clean and dusty shack. Go figure."

"So you didn't find much?"

"Van, come on, I didn't say that. We found plenty. We just didn't find what you want."

"Can you give me anything?"

"Sure, the dust. Believe it or not, we measured dust thickness to discover that the dust accumulation isn't uniform. The place has been visited from time to time over many years. For example, the boxes of books, the duffel bag, and some other items had less dust on them than other areas."

"So what does that tell you other than some items have been in the house longer?"

"Come on, Van, extrapolate. You're smarter than some of my techs, and they know why."

"The house gets used, but very little is disturbed."

"That's my boy."

"And is it safe to say that the box of earrings has signs of being the most recently used?"

"You hit the bull's-eye. That box has been accessed repeatedly."

"And the books. Do you have anything?"

"Well, those will take some time. I know you want to find prints there. I've told my people to be very careful and look for notes in the books and provide you with photocopies of anything."

"How long do you think it will take?"

"Van, come on, my people are not going to read the books. Quite frankly, those books aren't page-turners, so my neophytes won't be doing anything more than I've asked of them.

"Oh, and as for your partner Stenzgard's observation, the windows and shutters have probably not been opened in decades. They're so snug that only the slightest amount of sunlight penetrates to the interior. Someone could have been in the house at night, and any light would not easily be seen by others on the outside."

The issue of the fire ring was equally perplexing.

Forensics had found something, but it was not a body. It was more plastic trash bags, a bit different from those in the house but trash bags nonetheless. Also, Claudia was quick to state, "All things point to there being some human remains residue in these bags. We'll look closely, and I'll let you know."

Van mentioned he was looking for any residue to match a suspected victim. Claudia responded, "Get me some DNA from family members, and we'll see. No guarantees. It'll probably take weeks."

Thinking back on the events of that day, Van could not get away from the fact that Stenzgard was good, very good. Van's instincts about having Stenz along were on target. Even Fenton commented on the value. "The two of you make a good team. I'll have to remember that." Always one with a sense of humor, he added, "Give you guys the difficult ones."

They had not found a body, but they had found the earrings and quite possibly evidence suggesting that Cindy and/or Carlos may have been slain there, or at least their remains may have been there at one time.

Van was confident now that Allison A. Connors, a.k.a. Alexandria or Alexis Talonis, was their suspect. They need only track her down, but that was proving difficult.

Van finally turned his attention back to his purpose for coming in early. He picked up the report and began to review and edit his work.

—⟶ww—

Two hours later, Van met with Stenzgard, Fenton, Deena, and another support staff member. They convened in one of the interview rooms where there was space for all.

Fenton took the lead and asked what Deena had learned about the suspect, Allison Connors.

Deena said, "We can find no evidence of the whereabouts of Allison A. Connors. Same for the two aliases. Her last known address was the apartment in Orange, which we know is a dead end. In 1978, she owned a VW Vanagon, one of those pop-up tops. She had purchased it used from a long defunct dealership. The last time she renewed the license was in the summer of '79. There's no record of the van having been sold through conventional channels. The VIN hasn't surfaced since '79. No indications the van was in any accidents. It's just ceased to exist as far as the DMV is concerned."

"Driver's license?"

"Dead end. It was last renewed in 1977. No records of citations or renewal after that date."

Van felt the frustration. "When she left the district, was there any forwarding address other than the apartment in Orange?"

"None. Initially the apartment address was the only forwarding address. That never changed."

"What about retirement contributions? She was a teacher. They have to make contributions. If retired or drawing on the pension, wouldn't the state know where she was? Has she paid state and federal tax?"

"State Teachers Retirement says she pulled her untaxed deposits out after leaving the district in 1978. Paid her tax on that money, and they have no idea of her whereabouts since. Also, if you're wondering about her IRS and California taxes, she hasn't paid any since 1982."

Deena looked again at her notes. "The only addresses on anything were either the Orange apartment or a couple of temporary postal boxes at private locations in Orange. No records from any of those sources."

Van said, "Okay. Any death, county, or court records?"

Deena went on. "I've looked at every angle, and I can find nothing to indicate she lived past 1982. She just ceased to exist."

Deena's sense of futility was obvious. Van made it a point to thank her in front of the others. Certainly she was the one responsible for breaking the case open. He was especially appreciative of her initiative.

Van asked if the others had any suggestion where to look. Fenton suggested the teacher's credit union and banks. Deena indicated she had followed those lines and came up with nothing. Allison had a teacher's credit union account but closed it out after writing her last check to the California Franchise Tax Board in 1982.

When Van felt they had gone far enough with the Allison Connors discussion, he turned to the alternative names. "Okay, what about Alexandria or Alexis Talonis?"

Anita, the other support staff member, said, "Name of Alexi Talonis surfaced in 1963 as the new owner of the TC, I mean the Trabuco Canyon property. That name still exists in county records. Appears to not be a common name since there are two other people of that name in the county. The oldest of the two is only thirty-one. It's also the name the Forest Service has on record as the owner of the TC property. However, IRS and state franchise tax board don't have record of any Alexandria or Alexis Talonis in Orange County."

Anita took a drink of water. "I haven't heard whether the name appears elsewhere in the state. I'm using age as a screen. It'll probably be a day or two before I exhaust this search."

When Anita finished, they all looked at Van.

"I want to go back to the change from Allison to Alexandria and then Alexis. We know that Elizabeth Ambrose told me Allison's middle name was Alexandria. We can deduce that it's shortened to Alexis. Can we speculate Alexi is a further shortening?"

Stenzgard spoke up. "I talked with a friend who runs a funeral parlor about that idea many years ago when I was looking into an alias." Now they were all staring incredulously at Stenz. He addressed their interest with his usual slow and adroit approach. "Well, those people in the funeral business know names. My friend is always having to ask people what a middle initial in a name stands for. He says they often don't know even when the deceased are close friends or family members. Seems middle names get lost sometimes. He says that sometimes people just stop using a middle name, and it disappears over time. Sometimes people don't like their middle name and use only the initial. This is often the case when the middle name is after a father, mother, or other family member that has become the point of friction."

Fenton expressed his level of impatience. "So how does that help us?"

Not to be hurried, Stenz continued. "Well, now, it seems there are common uses for the initial A. If you're female and Anglo, as we know Allison was, it's usually Allison, Andria, or Alexandra. But my friend says these middle names are often truncated into alternatives so Allison becomes Ally, Andria becomes Andi, and Alexandra becomes Alexis. My friend thinks that often people who do not want to be known by their given name, say Alexandra for example, change it—in this case to Alex, which is a bit too male sounding, so it becomes Alexi or just Lexi. Thus, their given first name and middle name disappear."

They were used to Stenzgard's style. He was a storyteller. Everything had a context.

"So, our Allison A. Connors is Allison Alexandra Connors. If she wanted to disappear, she could drop the first name and become Alexis. Of course, the surname remains the same, so anonymity is really not possible by just changing the first name. So, especially if one is female, you take on your mother's maiden name. In Alexis's case, that would be Hardin, which her mother had gone back to after the divorce from Archie Connors. But Hardin appears elsewhere, tax and property ownership records, so the Hardin surname is not a good idea if she wants total anonymity."

Van could only smile. There was nothing like Stenz stepping through the logic of experience.

"So, what is Allison, a.k.a. Alexandra, a.k.a. Alexis, to do? She goes somewhere else in the family in search of a viable surname. Maybe it's her mother's maiden name, or even the maiden name of her grandmother. I bet if we search a bit, we'll find the origin of Talonis.

"Of course, we have to assume that along the way, over thirty-five years, whatever name Allison started with in 1978 has morphed. She could now be Alex or even Lexi. I guess we can assume it possible that Allison has become a different person many times over just by adopting old family surnames and morphing first names. She becomes new by keeping it in the family."

Van recognized Stenz's suggestion was a stretch. But he also realized Stenz seldom lost sight of context. If it had not been that Allison had disappeared, the stretch would be ignored. Perhaps she was now Alex or Alexi or Lexi.

"What makes this all plausible is that we," he nodded to the other staff members present, "didn't find any evidence of Lexi Talonis. Allison really wanted to disappear, so she picked an uncommon name and did not formalize even that." Stenzgard was done.

The group knew all too well that there were people who went unknown by changing their name and adopting a new persona. Usually they were escaping a troubled past, had run away from home, or were fugitives. To do so successfully, one had to shun all contact with former family and friends. Establishing a new life with a new name meant completely distancing one's self from the past. There could be no connection without risk. It almost always meant moving to a new location where one would not be noticed or recognized.

It was not a simple task. Moving and remaining a loner could attract attention. So the alternative was moving and blending in. After years of blending in, one could conceivably go completely unnoticed and be regarded as an insider in a community rather than an outsider.

With so much effort to gain obscurity, it seemed that if Allison A. Connors was now Alexi Talonis, she had failed to completely sever the tie to her childhood home in the canyon. For some reason, she was drawn back to the home, albeit on very rare occasions. And yet all knew they were no closer to locating Alexandra, Alexis, Alexi, Lexi, or whatever her name was now than they had been before they discovered the Trabuco home. There in was the mystery. Their suspect did not even act like most criminals who change their name and seek a new life.

Allison's sense of independence eschewed even the norms of a person reinventing herself.

Van realized they had strayed from the purpose of the meeting, and he sought to bring them back to its focus, the evidence at hand.

"Forensics hasn't gotten back to us on the plastic bags, books, earrings, or old army/navy stuff. However, Claudia says there are no prints." He turned to Stenz. "What about interviews with people who live in the canyon?"

Stenzgard reviewed the comments collected from deputy interviews with those in the area when the search was conducted. "The troops got nothing of value from the people they detained. I think the older couple, Mel and Walter, proved of most value. They've been there for decades, and on only a few occasions have they seen evidence that someone was in the house. In the last twenty-odd years, it's usually been at night, but only that one time in about 2000 did Mel actually see anyone—and even then, she didn't see a face."

Anita added, "Our sources indicate that the house has not had electrical service since 1979. The propane company has no record of when the tank was last filled. The gauge on the tank reads empty. The water service was shut off in 1979. The sewage is a septic tank. So, it's safe to say that if anyone has been there since 1979, they did so without the benefit of utilities."

"And yet the taxes have been paid as has the lease to the Forest Service, correct?" asked Fenton. The responses were nods. "Obviously, she didn't want to lose possession. The home is an important part of who she is. If it were not so, then I see no reason for her to visit it secretly on a periodic basis."

Deena responded, "Yes, and taxes are always paid on time, and the cashier's check always comes from a bank in New York City, the First City Trust Bank. The check is always from an A. A. Talonis. I have asked them for some assistance regarding who it is that requests the check and how it is that First City is involved. But you know how it is. A cashier's check requires only that there be cash collateral. No indisputable identification is required of those making a request."

"That's strange. New York, you say? It can't mean she lives in New York." Van jotted down *A.A. Talonis—First City Trust B.—NYC*. He needed to see if his fed friends could help. "Deena, see what you can get from First City Trust. Let me know if we need to call in the big guns to help. We can call in the feds for help on this one."

The Talonis name kept nagging at Van. "Allison allegedly had an older brother; he would have to be in his eighties now. She also had a sister. I wonder …"

Van was thinking, and the pause was long. The others waited. In this line of work, ideas came and went quickly during discussions of evidence and theories. They had all learned long ago to keep quiet when another was searching within.

"Mmm … maybe we need to do some work in Inyo County. I seem to recall that the sister lived there, and the brother was raised there before running away. I'll follow up on this. We can see if Talonis is a name out of the Owens Valley area."

"Van," said Fenton, "have you heard anything from your two friends who were going to look into travel to and from the catering site by trail? I ask because it seems to me if Allison was visiting the house from time to time, she apparently did so without driving. That would suggest a couple of things.

"First, she may have been moving about with limited use of a vehicle. She may be so strange as to actually walk, hitch a ride, or take public transportation. Is it possible she could travel between TC and the Sierra without needing a car?"

Van turned to Deena. "Deena, could you check that? Those two were going to spend some time in the field and let me know the feasibility of travel to and from the catering site. Do you have their number?" Deena nodded.

Fenton continued. "I was also thinking that even if she had a vehicle, like the old van, she could always park it somewhere and use trails and dirt roads and even firebreaks to move to and from the house. Even if she was using the old Vanagon we know she owned, which is possible though hard to believe, she could be using it as a home in a remote location and resorting to hiking as a means of transportation. I know it sounds crazy, but everything we've found so far involving Allison is strange."

Stenz was to the point. "So, partner, where do we go from here?"

The protocol, with Van in charge, dictated that whenever the discussion suggested the need for a decision, they all looked to Van.

"Through Sti and Rob, I've gotten to know the retired sheriff of Inyo County. It may be that he can provide some assistance in that regard. The more I think about it, the more it occurs to me that someone who wanted to spend the maximum of time in the Sierra would want to live nearby. On both the eastern and western side of the Sierra, there are areas of remoteness where one could easily live in a shack, abandoned facility, or even a vehicle without attracting attention."

Stenzgard spoke to Van's theory. "Kind of like old Charlie Manson and his gang did before being arrested by the Inyo County sheriff. A truly self-reliant individual could survive a long time like that so long as they're not known and there's no reason to keep track of them. I don't know how willing your retired sheriff is, but maybe Brenda or your two friends could help."

—⚋—

Walking back to his office, Deena caught up with Van.

"Investigator, you got a second?"

"Sure."

"Well, my mother had an older sister who was schizophrenic. Eventually she had to be hospitalized. We never talked about it because the stigma was too great, you know. But later when I was in college, my mother explained what had happened. Her sister grew into multiple personalities over time. Eventually the new person replaced the original person, and her sister was like a completely fictitious person." Deena paused before continuing. "Well, you know, I was wondering if we shouldn't talk to someone who knows abnormal psychology."

"You know, Deena, that's probably a good idea, and I know who I'm going to call. However, if you know someone who's skilled in this area, I would appreciate a referral."

"Okay, Investigator."

Van was going back to his office to call Karli Ryan.

—m—

Twenty-four hours later, Van was talking with Dr. Ryan.

"Yes, Van, it's quite possible that your suspect no longer thinks of herself as Allison Connors. It seems she has worked for thirty years or more to be someone else and has done so with a degree of effectiveness. However, I caution you not to buy into this idea blindly."

"What's the basis for caution?"

"It sounds to me like she lives 99 percent in her new personality, but there are some ties to the past that she hasn't let go. For one, there's the old house, which you say she's rarely returned to and then only for a day or two. There's a connection there, and it's probably related to when your suspect was young. I would guess it's the mother."

"Why the mother?"

"The earrings. The oddest item found in the house was the box of earrings. That's more than just odd. That's her tie with the mother. I suspect the earrings are symbols of her mother. I would also venture to guess that if you could find candid pictures of the mother, not those in a yearbook where they didn't allow such earrings to be worn in yearbook photos, you'll find those, if not similar, earrings."

"So far we haven't had much luck with this suspect or her family regarding photos. They all seem to have been camera shy." Van thought about the alternative. "Or she's destroyed them. If you want to reinvent yourself and want nothing of the past to suggest otherwise, would you destroy old photos?"

Karli responded that it was very possible, but she was already thinking about another angle. She shifted the conversation. "Didn't you tell me the mother took her own life?"

"Yes, but I don't know how since I've never been able to find a coroner's report. There's just a death certificate and sketchy newspaper obit."

"Well, I think your suspect, upon murdering, leaves a piece of her mother behind ..."

"That would suggest that she ..."

"Yes, she murders for revenge or for retribution. The earring is a way of paying tribute to the mother. It's as if your suspect is saying, 'This is for you, Mom.'"

"A tribute. A gruesome tribute."

"But you also told me you have nothing to suggest your suspect has killed for years."

"Actually, at this time, I have no information of missing hikers or known deaths after 1990."

"So maybe your suspect feels she has paid the debt. She has concluded her business and has no need to continue."

"All this sounds a bit too logical. Is there anything that makes the idea of a revenge killing a bit more certain?"

"Sure, and this is really the key—her name."

"Explain that."

"I'm surprised, Van. Given your reading and historical interest, you should have seen this. Have you read *Harry Potter*?"

"The books by that British author?"

"Yes. If you had, you would recognize the similarity between your suspect's adopted name and the use of Latin in the *Potter* books."

"Okay, I give. Explain please."

"Okay, the short course. Your suspect spells her last name as Talonis. Consider this, if she's willing to morph or alter a first name, it's possible she's playing the name game. What if Talonis was simply a play on the Latin word *talionis*? If that were the case, the root word would be *talio*, meaning retaliation. Of course, Lexi could be morphed to Lex. *Lex* is Latin translated to reference legality or, in this case, law."

It suddenly made sense, and Van blurted out his insight. "Yes, I should have seen this earlier, the *law of equivalent retribution*— lex talionis. By truncating her name from Alexandra to Lexi and adopting a new surname, our suspect was taking on the persona of judge, jury, and executioner."

"Van, she had to have a reason—a motive. It's somewhere in her relationship with her mom."

"That I don't have yet."

"But I would venture to guess that if you look at the mother and father, you'll find it. They were divorced. He was a known drunk and womanizer. She moved to Southern California, probably to distance herself from him. Your suspect lived with the mother and, according to your comments, was estranged from her father.

"Older brother runs away to get away from mom-and-dad conflict. Older sister turns to drugs. Baby of the family stays with mom. She sees the suffering mother, she sees the father at fault for mom's suicide, and she decides to revenge her mother's suicide. In fact, she seeks revenge for the whole relationship between mom and dad. If the mother had been abused by the father, well ... that could be causal. And she leaves a piece of mother with the victim."

Karli's ideas were swirling around in his head as Van tried to find the implications for what he already knew. "That explains how dad's death could be intentional and not an accident. But what about the others, the Muir Trail murders?"

"Look closely at the relationship between mom and dad. The hiking couple killed exhibited something in their actions that your suspect saw as wrong and warranted death as a punishment."

"So, when she saw people exhibit the kind of relationship her parents had, she reacted?"

"Yes. Maybe more. I think it's more than the mother being victimized by the father physically. She obviously hated her father for what he did. But it may also be that your suspect blames her mother for part of the relationship problem. It could be a vicarious thing. When your suspect sees other women allowing themselves to be taken advantage of by a man, her response is to conclude that person is being foolish like her mother was. Thus, to prevent the same outcome that affected her mother, she kills the person and thus prevents the outcome."

"Yes. She's a psychopath and a psychotic. Two sides to the vengeance coin."

"Yes, but there's a caveat. Van, your suspect is incredibly intelligent. She may be psychotic, but she's under control and appears to be rational and logical, as she sees those terms, in her thinking and actions, especially since she stopped killing. She thinks things through. How else could she launch and conclude a career of vengeful murder? Once she concluded her killing spree, she has probably not had an inkling of interest in killing. She has moved on. She's aware of being a pursued suspect. That's a game she'll play. But I doubt she poses a threat. She's older, perhaps not able to kill any longer."

"Doesn't quite fit the image of a serial killer. She may be elderly now, but she wasn't by 1990 or even after. Not sure I can buy into the idea that she no longer poses a threat."

"Remember, Van, she gave up teaching to pursue an alternative career. She wasn't hasty or impulsive. It was all planned. So is her approach to the final years of her life. It's all planned."

"Still, it seems strange to think that her perceptions of the world and her role in it should be so stilted, so removed from the norms of acceptable behavior."

"Go back to your books, Van. Shakespeare may have introduced us to madness, but Kant introduced us to the idea that our perceptions are the product of our experiences over time. Mad as Lexi may seem, she probably doesn't see herself as mad. Kant probably said it best when he suggested that there are things that serve as the status quo for most of us; then there are things as they are seen by others. She doesn't see as we do. For Lexi, perceptions are based on experiences that go back to her childhood. Those experiences are the most powerful motives for her. Those experiences drive her judgments and, as a result, her actions."

It was all falling into place. He knew the suspect—Lexi Talonis. He had the motive, revenge killing. He knew she was still alive. He had reason to believe she lived near the Sierra, probably the Eastern Sierra. He knew she had killed her father. He knew she killed Cindy and probably Carlos. He knew there was a young couple killed along the JMT by her. He strongly suspected there were other victims along the JMT. He suspected she had not killed in over two decades.

But, for all that, he was no closer to finding his suspect than he was before.

CHAPTER 37

THE BOOK COLLECTION

Homicide Office

I T HAD BEEN weeks since the TC search. Van was working other cases. It was the nature of working cold cases, the cycle of repeated starting and stopping.

The search of the house had been a success in many ways, and he felt frustrated he had not been able to devote more of his time to the Ashae case. However, he was relieved the search did not make the news. The case had been open for many years, and as long as it was not in the media, he and the department could take their time. He knew Claudia was also aware of the situation because it had taken longer than he anticipated to receive a completed forensics report. Forensics was overworked. Current cases got top priority.

The report on the house had come in this morning. He glanced at it but did not have the time to review it thoroughly. Perhaps this weekend.

He would take the files home and see what Claudia and her team had found, though she had already given him a verbal heads-up. He would also exercise. He reminded himself of his commitment to more exercise when at home. He had been trying to find a way to make sure there was balance between work at home and the importance of exercise. So far he had not been very diligent about keeping to the balance part of the equation.

Van turned back to his computer screen and some work he was doing on a recent case.

The not-so-subtle entrance of Stenzgard was noticed. Actually, it was a welcome diversion.

Stenz, in his casual style, walked in and took a seat. Stenz settled in and made himself comfortable. Always unhurried, his intent to share was evident before he opened his mouth.

"You know, Van, I am amazed how consistent certain behavior patterns are when everything says otherwise."

"What are you talking about?"

"You know that murder/suicide we handled a few weeks ago?"

"Yeah, the elderly couple, the Millers, a tragic ending for those poor people."

"That's what I mean. Never should've happened. Never would have, except for that daughter."

"The drug addict? She wasn't even in the state when it happened."

"But she was the cause."

"Okay, what am I missing?"

"It's like this. I'm trying to close that case out. I talked with the neighbors on multiple occasions. I couldn't understand why a couple like that would take the easy way out. Yeah, they had some financial problems like most people. But they owned the house. Didn't have a single loan outstanding. Sure, they like many others lost some retirement value in the '08 debacle, but it didn't render them poor. And they didn't have any impending health problems."

Stenz shifted in his seat as if to say his comfort level wasn't yet where it needed to be. Van knew enough to wait and listen.

"Not only that, they weren't really lonely. Their son was a hero in Desert Storm. Killed in combat and a hero in the eyes of his commanders, comrades, and the entire community. Every time the church, community, or military in Southern California had an event to honor military personnel, the parents were invited and their son, the hero, honored."

Stenzgard shook his head. Stenz was former military, and Van knew there was a soft place in Stenz's heart for the Millers.

"On the day they killed themselves, they had gone to church and their son was mentioned in the sermon, and gobs of people came up to them after and shook their hands and acknowledged how proud they must be for their son. You don't just kill yourself after that. Hell, Van, those people had every reason to be proud, not sad."

Van wondered where this was going.

"It doesn't make sense, Van. So, not being the real intellectual type, like you, I started asking questions. You know, the 'why' questions, the 'why not' questions, and the 'who would do this' questions. And then I began to hear things that helped me make sense."

"But we know no one else shot them. No one else was there at the time."

Stenz cocked his head to one side and raised his brow, as if to say "let me finish." Van did.

Stenz went on. "Only partially true. You see, neighbors had begun to note that the long-lost drug addict, the daughter, showed up several months before and then visited a couple of times between then and when they shot themselves. Not long visits, just your basic 'hi, how are you, I'm broke, can I have some money,' and leave visits.

"Asking questions, I eventually found out where the gun came from. The daughter had stolen it from an ex-boyfriend user. According to a neighbor, she gave it to the parents about four months before their deaths. Old Mrs. Miller told the neighbor that the daughter kept saying that the Millers needed a gun because the neighborhood wasn't safe.

"Now I'll probably never prove it, but I know what happened. That deceitful bitch kept pushing their button on the issue of their being old, useless, and hoarding all they owned. Son was dead. The daughter wanted it all. She pushed them to the edge of sanity and provided a way out."

Stenz shook his head while Van waited. "The son is a hero but dead. The daughter is an addict, an embarrassment, and she's still living. The Millers lost what was precious, and the daughter was the old albatross around their neck. They just gave up."

"Stenz, why are you telling me this?"

"Because your Ashae suspect is smart, and smart people think too much. It's like the Millers. They were both teachers. They may have been elderly, but they were intelligent and capable of logical thinking. But things take a turn in life, and over time they start obsessing about it. When they think too much, it gets in the way. They begin to wear themselves out and get depressed.

"You see, Van, people like me make a living asking questions because we know we're not smarter than the crazies who commit crimes. No, I don't solve murders because I'm smarter; I solve them because I'm dumb enough to know what I don't know and I have to ask questions."

He marveled. Stenz could use a story to note a point of view on a case far removed from the story.

"Your suspect was so smart she talked herself into insanity."

"That's an interesting perspective. And your point?"

"Ask the question. Why would she kill her father? The answer? Many reasons. He was a jerk and obviously treated the wife in such a way that it drove her first to a pregnancy that pushed them into marriage. Second, he pushed her into an abusive relationship; third, into a divorce; fourth, into her taking the kids and moving south; fifth, it drove the boy into running away and the middle kid into drugs; and finally it drove the mother to suicide. I'm guessing the youngest, your suspect, was also abused. But the youngest is also brilliant. And her brilliance gets her into trouble. She thinks she can correct all the wrongs that befell her mother. Think about all the great people who were very intelligent and became mad. It would not have happened if they would have dumbed down a bit. No, they thought they were smarter than the problems. They weren't."

Van responded. "Well, we all know she's super intelligent. But why kill all the other people, the kids and the people along the trail, probably others as well that we're not aware of?" Van knew Karli Ryan's view on this question, and he was inclined to agree with her, but he was intrigued that Stenz may have an alternative view.

"Because she's saving the world and potential offspring from the people she murders. She's a teacher. She sees this handsome nitwit who could date anyone taking this shy, innocent girl to prom. She knows why. He wants into her pants. This is what happened to her mom. Popular boy dates shy introvert, gets her pregnant, and the rest is a hellish history."

Leaning forward with his elbows on his knees, Stenz looked directly at Van. "Kill a couple who reflect her parents' mistakes, and she's preventing a repeat of history."

Van responded with the conclusion. "And once she kills the father, our suspect finds it easy to rationalize killing the next time. The Ashae and Fuentes kids are logical victims in her mind."

"Right, but the father is the key. As they say, once you've killed the first in war, all the others are easy."

"And for her, this was a war."

"You got it."

The conversation was short. Stenz came for a purpose, shared his point of view, and left. He did not belabor the point; just said his piece and moved on. It was classic Stenzgard. A man of few words, he thought through a conundrum and found an opportunity to share his unsophisticated and compelling thoughts with a colleague. Then he was back to his own tasks.

Stenz had a point. Van knew it would become part of his investigation frame of reference.

—⚶—

After Stenzgard left, Van could not refocus. He picked up the forensics report.

The key pieces were the plastic bags.

The two bags found in the house, one inside the other, had traces of lye. The bags could have been used to transport bones, but it did not appear they were used to house a body or body parts. There was no trace of human tissue. There was nothing sufficient to provide a source of DNA.

Of more significance were the bags found buried in the yard. They were newer bags than those in the house. The two yard bags were a ply used for construction projects–very thick and heavy. Forensics had found very small tissue traces inside, and they were testing them against DNA samples from Carlos's family. The process was slow, and it would be a while before results were in, but Claudia felt confident the remains were human.

It seemed to Van that even if a DNA match was found, it would only confirm what they were pretty sure of already, Carlos was also murdered. However, with no body and no idea of the whereabouts of Allison, the value of it all was limited.

The box of earrings was also unremarkable. The box could not be traced, nor could the earrings, other than to say they did have a sort of 1960s hippie look to their design. It seemed to Van that Mrs. Fuentes had noted the hippie look early on. The single earring did not match the one found on Cindy, nor the stone Sti and Rob had found, but it was of the same basic design.

Dust depths and coverage suggested, as Claudia suspected, the house had been used from time to time but at a very minimal level. Van wondered, *Did Alexi or Lexi, or whatever her name was, come home to get an earring when needed, or was her purpose otherwise?*

Claudia noted the house was about as strange an environment as she had ever investigated. Whoever had come and gone was conscious not to leave traces of anything behind. Even the clothing was nondescript, and there was nothing to sample for DNA.

The World War II surplus items revealed little. It looked like they had never been used. As for the cooking utensils, her team found no traces of food on any of them. The place was clean.

Van laid the report aside and thought about what he had read. He had some deadlines approaching, and his other cases beckoned. He needed to switch gears, but it was too late. His mind was focused on the Ashae case.

He turned the page to the section with the heading, "Books."

The books had revealed no prints, but the bindings suggested they were much used. Since the publication dates of some were in the 1940s and '50s, it was reasonable to conclude that they were purchased and read when Allison was young. The Bible was nothing special. It was not a family Bible, as it had no name or family tree references in it.

Several of the books had short messages addressed to Ally, Allison, or Alexis inside. All were signed "Mom." The report included a list of the messages and the book each was found in.

Van leafed through Claudia's report and found the addendum he wanted. It was a list of the books by title and author. There were seventy-three books in all, and they represented a diversified collection. There were both well-known works and some very obscure books. The collection was also a mixture of adult and teen and children's books.

As he scanned the books, Van noted common and less common works that caught his attention.

- *Shakespeare's Collected Works*
- *The Count of Monte Cristo*—Alexander Dumas
- *Divine Comedy: The Collected Books*—Dante Alighieri
- *Paradise Lost*—John Milton
- *The Cask of Amontillado: A Short Story*—Edgar Allan Poe
- *Medea*—Euripides
- *Don Giovanni: the Libretto*—Wolfgang Amadeus Mozart
- *The Bible*
- *Frankenstein*—Mary Shelley
- *The Writings of Thomas Aquinas*—Thomas Aquinas
- *The Mikado*—Gilbert and Sullivan
- *The Iliad* and *The Odyssey*—Homer
- *A Vindication of the Rights of Woman: with Strictures on Political and Moral Subjects*—Mary Wollstonecraft
- *The Collected Grimms' Fairy Tales*
- *The Story of Cinderella*
- *Snow White*
- *The Ugly Duckling*
- *The Little Engine That Could*
- *The Tale of Peter Rabbit*—Beatrix Potter
- *Three Little Pigs*

- *Little Red Riding Hood*
- *The Boy and the Bully*
- *Cassell's Latin Dictionary (1959)*

The list went on.

As he perused, his mind was considering the connections between all the books. What did they have in common? The works seemed so oddly collected, but Van was sure there was a connection, some logic. They had to be more than just a haphazard collection. His mind thought about the possible connections.

Shakespeare wrote comedy and tragedy. Well, the tragedy piece made sense. Homer's *Iliad* and *Odyssey* covered tragedy and everything else, if one liked to dwell on the foibles of human behavior. *The Count of Monte Cristo* by Dumas he did not know. Van vaguely remembered seeing a movie, but he had never read the book. He would have to Google it. Even more perplexing was the collection of writings by Thomas Aquinas. He knew Aquinas was a Catholic Church figure of importance and wrote in the medieval period. Maybe there was a connection with the Bible, which was also on the list. The Bible covered just about everything and probably had a connection to a lot of literature in the Western world.

Gilbert and Sullivan's *The Mikado* was not a mystery to Van. A fan of opera, he had over time become familiar with the works of Gilbert and Sullivan, though the two did not write classic opera. *The Mikado* was often used to advance the argument for letting the punishment fit the crime. That made some sense. Mozart's *Don Giovanni* was an opera, and though he had never seen it preformed, he recalled it focused on a young nobleman who was overly promiscuous.

Van knew Mary Shelley's work, *Frankenstein*, and he knew Edgar Allan Poe was strange and a bit mad, though the short story *The Cask of Amontillado* was unfamiliar to him. He had never read Milton's *Paradise Lost*, but he had read Dante's *Divine Comedy* in college and knew there were three books and recalled the journey through the various levels of hell as viewed through medieval eyes.

Recollections of these authors and works reminded Van of how often things he had taken for granted in school and college came back around to him as an adult. He had read a good deal of literature, but now when he needed insight based on his reading experience, he found himself needing Google, or better yet, Dr. Ryan. It did not escape him that he would also do well to consider reading some of the works.

A Vindication on the Rights of Women was unfamiliar to Van, as was the name of the author. It seemed a strange book mixed in with all the others.

The children's books were also a mixture that revealed little to Van. He recognized some of the books and remembered something about the stories. If memory served him right, most of them suggested a moral lesson. If Allison read these, he wondered how the moral of the story parts were ultimately lost on her.

Then it occurred to Van that perhaps, from Allison's point of view, the moral of the story for her may have been different. She did not see the moral intended by the author but the moral as defined by her mother. Stenz may have been right; Allison crafted a value system supported by a distorted reading of the literature.

Then again, Van thought that perhaps he had it all wrong. Maybe they were just the usual fare of children's books along with books the mother read and Allison read later. But he knew this was probably not the case. Together, the books made a statement, and he needed to uncover that.

He knew the pieces of the puzzle were coming together. His suspect had acted on a psychotic drive. Everything suggested a viable theory for the motive.

Van had a theory; he needed proof.

It had been several days since he had emailed Dr. Ryan with his plea for help in understanding the significance of the collection of literature. Van had intended to spend some time with Google and Wikipedia in an effort to see if there was insight value to the books collected at TC. As usual, more pressing cases demanded his time, and he had not followed through.

When Dr. Ryan's call came, Van was at his desk and on the verge of nodding off. It had been a long day of reading testimony and developing a report to the DA on a multiple murder case he was working with Stenzgard, who had a couple of days off. The computer screen was beginning to become a blur when the phone startled Van back to consciousness.

"You sound tired, Van."

"I am, but your call is a welcome break. I hope you have something that'll wake me up."

"I don't know about waking you up, but I believe we have more insight into your suspect."

"Well, I knew you would be better with the books than me. I just don't have the time to spend reading and thinking about all of them."

"I'm surprised, Van. The books, with a couple of exceptions, are classics and speak to a reader on many levels. One of those levels was clearly influential for your suspect. No doubt they were deemed important by her mother."

"What about the mother?"

"Van, do you remember being taught a lesson by your parents when they used some kind of story, or saying, aphorism, or proverb to teach the lesson?"

"You mean sayings like *look before you leap* or reading stories like 'The Little Engine That Could' to teach a kid about self-efficacy?"

"Of course, those would be good examples. I suspect that's what Allison's mother did as well. In many ways, I don't think her mother could have guessed just how effective she was."

"What does that mean, that she didn't realize Allison would be a killer?"

"No, that Allison would become a brilliant student of English literature as well as a murderer of exceptional talent."

"Interesting conclusion."

"Oh, Van, it's much more than just a conclusion. You see, Allison's mother very skillfully accomplished what people today suggest is the impact of violence in TV, movies, and video games. She planted a seed, watered it through stories and tales, and lived just long enough to know she had prepared her daughter well."

"To be a killer?"

"Not just a killer, an avenger, your Lexi—lex talionis."

Van recalled their previous discussion about the morphing of Allison's family of names to suggest a mission of vengeance. "Are you saying that all those books served that purpose?"

"The common element in those works of literature is revenge, retribution, or to put it simply, an eye for an eye. Let's start with the Bible, which features the eye for an eye concept in the book of Deuteronomy. Vengeance in Deuteronomy is legit under justifiable circumstances. Building on that, Allison's mother used the children's books to suggest it's okay to seek a form of vengeful justice. *Grimms' Fairy Tales*, the foundation for *Cinderella* and *Snow White*, are rife with such justice.

"All those little children's books provide a piece of this logic. Not in the violent way movies and TV do today but in subtle, subliminal ways that accumulate and set the stage for the more explicit stories such as *The Boy and the Bully* where the main character even contemplates the time when he will take revenge on the bully."

"So, Allison and her mother read this stuff ..."

"They didn't just read. They read over and over. They probably discussed what was read. It was the focus of their relationship. It became a sort of *groupthink* for the two."

"Same for the more adult books?"

"Even more so. Shakespeare's *Hamlet* and Dumas's *The Count of Monte Cristo* are nothing short of vengeance stories justified. But that's only the beginning. Mom was, in her own right, brilliant and not just the shy girl that Archie Connors impregnated. Her selection of an opera and an operetta are brilliant examples of multiple sources to justify vengeance. Who among us would think of that? Even I had to do some research on those sources.

"And then there's Euripides. The idea of Mary Jo preparing Allison to take vengeance on her behalf is not so far removed from

Medea, who uses her own children to bear the gifts containing poison that will kill her adulterous husband, Creon. How strange is that?"

Phone to his ear, Van listened as if Dr. Ryan was right in front of him. It never ceased to amaze him that human behavior had its roots in complexities so deep and often so distorted that even an experienced detective would have a hard time believing what he was hearing about motive. He could only listen and hope that later he would be able to remember what was said.

"Of course, Poe, Dante, and Milton were equally brilliant selections. The more I think about the conversations the mother and daughter must have had, the more I'm intrigued. I think their exchanges were so transforming at the highest cognitive level that the best of university literature professors could only hope to have such discussions with students a few times in their careers.

"I'll go so far as to say a youth leader in a totalitarian state couldn't be more effective in twisting and guiding a young mind. The case of Allison Connors is a classic, and I hope, once this case is concluded, we'll be able to study it in more depth because there's much to learn here."

"What about that one book on *The Vindication of the Rights of Women*? How does that fit in?"

"It's an old book, no longer in print. It was written in the late 1700s and is regarded as one of the earliest feminist works. At the time, there was nothing like it. How she got the book, what stock she placed in reading it, and whether Allison read it will remain a mystery."

"Why?"

"Because it speaks to the rational morality of equity, and there's nothing in it to suggest violence as a legitimate form of justice."

"So Stenzgard is right ..."

"Who's Stenzgard?"

"Another investigator who posits that Allison's mind was so brilliant that thinking was her undoing. He says she talked herself into madness. You think that's possible?"

"I'm not sure, Van. I have a couple of good research friends, Andi

Chris and Juju Vicks. Their research has focused on the correlation between brilliance, evil thinking, and criminal actions. Andi says the world of the perfect crime is predicated on brilliance, and she points to a history of literature founded on this thinking. Conan Doyle invented one such character—the infamous Professor Moriarty. I think all the great mystery writers have wrestled with the implications of such characters. You'll remember, of course, that Moriarty's rival is the equally brilliant and dark Sherlock Holmes, the very complex champion of good. The extremes of brilliance seem to pose the same threat of obsession and possible self-destruction. Perhaps your Lexi fits this mold.

"Juju's work is especially disturbing when you consider the actions of your suspect. The hypothesis is that while most of us see the perfect crime as a well-thought-out endeavor, in reality the brilliant mind is very opportunistic. A criminal with such brilliance is, following Juju's research, capable of committing very heinous crimes with little or no planning. There's something about your suspect that fits this theory."

He appreciated Dr. Ryan's digressions, but he wanted to come back to the connection between motive and the influence of Mary Jo. "So, it's possible she saw her mother and father in these other couples and knew it was her job to avenge what had happened to mother and thereby ensure the same thing wouldn't happen in the relationship of these couples. It's what she was trained to do. It's what her brilliance equipped her to accomplish."

"That's basically it," replied Dr. Ryan. "And she can do it on the fly."

"Kind of a lesson here, isn't there? It's not enough to teach someone to read. You need to also guide them to read in a balanced fashion so that they're not victimized by one genre."

"The old *reason in all things* approach."

"Anything else you learned from those books, Karli?"

"Well … yes, and I hesitate to go there because I'm not yet sure of the implications or how we should consider this …"

"Go ahead; this case can't get much more confusing."

"I'll let you be the judge. But my friend Andi surfaced this issue in a conversation we had about the books in your suspect's collection. If you look at all of the works of literature in that collection, I'm talking about the adult literature now, they're more than just vengeance tragedies. They're not open-ended conclusions. They conclude with tragedy. Vengeance is obtained, but that's not the end. Most of the lead characters in these stories go mad beyond what we think is expected. Sometimes they take their own lives and others with them.

"I caution you, Van. Allison, or Lexi as she sees herself now, is brilliantly damaged. You and I couldn't begin to understand where her mind is going. She lives in a world where anything her mind conjures is rationalized as acceptable to her.

"No doubt she knows you're on to her. She knows you. But she also knows that you don't know her. She's worked hard to remain an enigma, and in the end, that's her trump card."

Van acknowledged Karli's suspicions. "Well, we kind of already came to the conclusion that she's aware of our interest in her. But she hasn't killed for decades, and at her age, given her methods in the past, I'm not inclined to see her as much of a threat."

"Personally, Van, I think she has her future planned. She hasn't killed for about twenty-five years you say, and I'm inclined to think that's the result of her own plans. She no longer has a need to kill. At this point in her life, she goes into the future knowing she has accomplished what was intended."

"So what's your concern?"

"That you may upset these plans. In so doing, you may alter her anticipated future and force her into a corner like a wounded animal. If that happens, she may fight back."

"Then our retiring Lexi Talonis once again becomes lex talionis!"

"My concern precisely."

CHAPTER 38

—⚬—

GOING HOME?

Orange County Sheriff's Department

ROB UNFOLDED THE Cleveland National Forest maps. Rob had a cup of coffee. Sti shared Van's preference for the tea Van had brewed.

They were in a conference room on the third floor where a large table hosted the collection of maps. They pushed away the chairs so the three could stand and see the maps from above.

Rob started the discussion. "Van, we've been walking the trails, paths, dirt roads, and firebreaks of the area surrounding Silverado, Modjeska, and other adjacent canyons, including Trabuco Canyon. We paid close attention to possible links with the Trabuco Canyon house and the catering site. You can see in yellow highlight all the routes we've covered during the past couple months. You'll notice that for some we highlight only a portion of a trail or road because only a part of it was in our scope of interest. I should also note that some of these in yellow are trails and roads we traveled in the past and saw no reason to hike them again. Those in blue were not traveled because they didn't exist in 1972. You will also notice there are as yet lots of roads we haven't explored."

"You guys put in a lot of miles."

"That's fine by us. We helped you, and it was good exercise. We both win. Also, we drove most dirt roads as a way to cover more territory than we would have if we walked them all."

Sti pulled out a large spreadsheet. "We put together a matrix that shows the various routes from point A, which is always the VW burn site, to point B, the TC house. We have given each route a number that corresponds with the numbers on the map. We have noted the distance in each case, the probable time needed by an unburdened hiker to go from an A to B, and the difficulty of the hike, noted as easy, moderate, or strenuous."

"Unburdened meaning?"

"Not carrying a pack of any significance. Daypack would be okay."

Sti and Rob went on to share what they found regarding the various highlighted routes and the difficulty of travel. When they were finished, they waited for Van's comments.

"So, if our suspect walked from the VW burn site to Trabuco on the routes you think most probable"—he pointed to the map—"and if she left at say 2:00 a.m. and hiked at a pace of about twenty minutes per mile, she would have arrived at the house early morning, correct?"

"Yes," said Sti. "So long as she put in about three miles per hour and wasn't carrying any excessive weight and had water. She would be moving at a good pace, not an easy task at night, even with good moonlight. No time to rest either. It would have been a strenuous endeavor."

Rob added clarification. "According to newspapers, it was to be a clear night with a crescent moon. It probably provided enough light. Assuming the trails and dirt roads involved were in good condition, as they are today, she could have done it and arrived before anyone in the surrounding homes noticed. Of course, in 1972 the conditions could have been much different."

"Is it possible she could have driven on dirt roads only?"

Sti addressed the dilemma. "Possibly, but we're not convinced she did that. A vehicle, like her VW, would be difficult to drive on those roads, would have made considerable noise, and kicked up a lot of dust. Why would she risk that as opposed to risking little by hiking back?"

Van realized there were numerous possible scenarios in the hours after the prom. The evidence from Trabuco suggested Allison at some time probably had remains on the property. Where she encountered the two students and killed them was unknown. What he did know was that if the bodies were in the Fuentes VW at some time that night, they were off-loaded before it was driven to the catering site. After setting the VW afire, she had to either return to the TC house by walking, or by walking and retrieving her own van and driving to TC or back to her apartment in Orange. He was fairly confident she had walked away from the catering site. How far she walked was the unknown. It was all conjecture. But it was all he had. "So, you do think it possible that she hiked away from the catering site and could have covered considerable distance before dawn."

Rob said, "Investigatgor, there are a lot of places she could have parked a car and hiked back from the catering site to retrieve it. It's just that all the jockeying of vehicles—hers and the VW—would have taken a lot of time and exposed her to possible scrutiny."

Van wondered about other options. "What about these highlighted and even not highlighted routes that aren't a direct connection between the VW burning location and the house?"

Pointing to an example, Rob noted, "Well, you can see that they suggest one could navigate to the house from many different and remote places, including Corona, which is in Riverside County. If she had wanted, or wants to now, it's possible to make the trip over multiple routes.

"Also, keep in mind your suspect probably knows, or at least knew, this area better than almost anyone. If she lived in the area for some time, she probably hiked the hills around the house hundreds of times. There's the possibility that there are routes we're not familiar with. She would know them."

Sti picked up the thought. "Actually, this is also true in the Sierra. If she's as familiar with the Sierra as it appears she is, it's quite possible she can navigate around completely unnoticed. She doesn't need the JMT or any other formal route."

Van was confused. "But it seems to me, and I grant you it's based on my very limited experience over Bishop Pass, that there are no easy ways other than a trail."

"On the contrary," said Sti. "Many very good backpackers prefer to go cross-country and travel without a trail. Often they can cover distances faster than you and I on a trail because they're not bound by switchbacks and gradual contouring around or along slopes. In fact, it's very likely that she did so when we encountered her."

"So, if it's desired, a backpacker can avoid people."

Sti responded, "If they're skilled, yes. If all they do is stick to the trail, probably not. Of course there's one other element, and it's the environment. The chaparral of the Santa Ana Mountains is not always conducive to cross-country, off-trail hiking. It's different in the Sierra where the environment is much more open, especially at the higher elevations."

"So she could have followed the two of you to the Baxter site?"

"Maybe, but Sti and I have reasoned that it's likely we happened along when she was already in the area. Wondering what we were doing looking the area over closely and camping where we did piqued her concern. She watched, and when she saw we found something, she reacted."

The look on Sti's face reflected the concern in his remarks. "But if she followed us to the Baxter area, then the implications are ominous. She would have to know our purpose, or at least have reason to know we were in the area and she had cause to follow."

Van frowned. This was a line of thinking they had discussed before. If that were true, it meant Allison had inside information regarding the investigation. This was very troubling.

"Speaking of that, you earlier suggested she was not only a strong hiker but light on her feet. How did you describe her?"

Rob said, "Like a gazelle. I think she left by a route different than she entered our camp because she tripped over the tent line when leaving. But other than that, she was lithe on her feet and quick. Even if I had boots on, it's not likely I would have been able to follow."

"What do you mean by that?"

"When you hike and backpack as much as we do, you realize some people are just better than everyone else. They move with no excess waste of energy. They do so without appearing to work hard, despite the steepness of a slope or the altitude."

"I don't suppose there are many people like that." It was a statement Van assumed to be true.

Sti smiled as he responded. "Probably more than we think. Backpacking is a major sport now, and there are many great backpackers. They opt for backpacking and mountaineering rather than more traditional sports."

They discussed the Sierra maps and the route of the JMT. Van wanted to know how easy it was to go in and out of the Sierra. They noted that there were passes on the eastern side that made it possible, though some were very difficult. The trails to the passes were about a day to a day and a half of hiking apart along the JMT.

They also noted that someone like Allison probably knew many other routes that were not formal trails or even known cross-country routes, and she could enter and exit at will.

Van was concerned and voiced his opinion that she could present a danger for the two. Both Sti and Rob responded they had encountered danger many times in the Sierra but found that reason and cool heads prevail. She had snuck into their camp and had the chance for malice had it been her intent, and she left them alone.

"Well, if you two are available, I have another favor to ask."

Van explained that he was convinced Allison probably lived in the Eastern Sierra, but that was a big area and not an easy one to scan. "Former Sheriff Pagliano tells me the two of you are great at snooping about without getting into trouble."

Rob said, "I guess that's so, if you don't count the Harris caper and our last endeavor where a couple of country boys tried to harass us."

"Well, Allison obviously knows the two of you now. But she's a recluse and won't be looking for exposure. She knows you've seen at least a profile of her face and knows it's possible you've given a description to authorities. She can't very well chance an encounter.

"But you two know people in the valley, and perhaps some of them have seen something odd. Or perhaps they've noticed an old 1970 VW Vanagon she owns and may have parked somewhere in the valley. I'm convinced she lives in the Eastern Sierra because she was born there, her parents were from there, and she loves the Sierra. The west side doesn't make sense."

Again, Sti's humor was couched in his response. "Sure, we can snoop around, although it may require that you run interference with our wives. I think that over the years they've heard every excuse from us regarding why we need to go up to the OV or to the Sierra. I'm not sure we're as convincing as we used to be. The idea of us gallivanting off in pursuit of some seventy-year-old female super-hiker could raise some eyebrows."

Over the next half hour, the three worked out a tentative schedule for Sti and Rob to do some snooping around. Van also gave them more details about what he was looking for and what his people had developed regarding profile material on Allison, a.k.a. Alexi or Lexi.

Van cautioned the two against any bravado. When in doubt, back away. "If you see or suspect anything, immediately contact the Inyo sheriff and me. I want information, not intervention."

—⁙—

After Sti and Rob departed, Van sat alone in the conference room. They left the maps for him, and he was looking at them even as his mind was elsewhere. Something in today's discussion nagged him. Before today, Van had not given credence to the idea that Allison may have actually followed Sti and Rob to the Baxter site. Perhaps their observation that she happened to be there and they happened into her territory was not the case. Maybe she knew their purpose.

Van knew things often just happened. What appeared to be a coincidence was the product of the theory of large numbers. Given enough opportunities, the probability of things happening increases.

But Van was not given to coincidence. The thought that Allison could have known the intent of Sti and Rob had very worrying implications.

Was the JMT so much her territory that she just happened by because she was always around? *No*, he thought. *It's two hundred miles long. Why would she be there?* Was she doing what many had so long argued, that criminals are notorious for returning to the scene of the crime? If that was so, it would then be true that Allison went up and down the JMT, regularly visiting the places where she had murdered and buried victims. He did not think so. She was brilliant, not neurotic.

Was Allison the one who tampered with the Lake 11,106 victim, Reems? That reminded him; he had not heard back from the Park Service and needed to pursue that angle.

Returning to the scene of a crime soon after or even many years later was one thing. Doing it often was another matter.

Why would she search Sti's and Rob's packs unless she wanted what she knew they found—the earring? Did she know they were looking for it? She had to have known they found the earring. Had she also been looking for it? Was she checking to make sure the earring wasn't removed? He had a hard time thinking so.

She killed for revenge. She accomplished her task many times and left the tribute to her mother at each. So why would she want to retrieve an earring now?

Van stopped and held his hand up as if to tell someone else not to say anything. But the room was empty. He was frozen in thought and action. And then it was there, the thought that had been nagging him for the past hour.

Allison was getting old. She was fit and capable but getting older. Perhaps she even suffered some ailments. Age would be taking its toll. Her time was winding down. Even she had to know that her access to free movement about the backcountry would soon end. It all seemed consistent with the observations of Dr. Ryan. Perhaps that was why she had not, to Van's knowledge, killed anyone in the last couple decades. She was older and no longer had the hunting prowess of a younger Lexi. She knew she was no longer the hunter.

And if she was older, why the interest in retrieving the earrings? Was it because her job was done? Had she reached a point where she felt that the path she set off on in 1966 with the killing of Archie had reached its end? Was it time to reach some closure?

Like the convergence of ideas when a problem is being solved, Van found his mind racing through bits of information and ideas, all revolving around the idea of *closure*. For Allison, closure meant she had repaid her debt to her mother. She had been the good daughter, she had found her direction in the literature she and her mother had read, and now it was time to close the real book—time to end the story.

Perhaps Allison needed the earrings because she had to return them to her mother. Perhaps she had known all along this was her destiny, to return the earrings to the box in her mother's house. The thought was almost overwhelming to Van because the implications were huge.

It meant Allison would be going home one last time. *To die?* It was a question Van knew he had to share with Dr. Ryan. He remembered the cautious reasoning of Dr. Ryan's friends, Andi and Juju, about a tragic conclusion to Allison's life being parallel to much of the great literature.

He leaned back and considered his own questions. The great works of literature seem to raise an endless catalogue of questions about human behavior. For his purposes though, the questions about Allison's behavior could only be answered by Lexi. He had to find her.

Mentally musing about his take on the cyclical quality of events in the case, Van crafted his own take on the situation—it was his *full circle theory of madness*. Lexi was going home to Allison's roots.

PART 4

———∞———

CLOSING IN

A wounded animal is a dangerous animal.
—Anonymous

B RINGING CLOSURE TO arduous endeavors is never an easy task. Whether writing history or solving crimes, reaching a conclusion means fostering judgment. Then the pundits react. The historian must await the critics who will question methods, use of evidence, and findings. The detective must await as well but with some stipulations. In the legal system, it is always an issue of due process—the path from suspect to courtroom.

For historian and investigator, it begins with questions and the search for evidence. For both, there are protocols and theories that guide the search. It is also true, said historians Will and Ariel Durant, that "all formulas should be suspect. There is no one way."

The big difference, of course, between detective work and that of the historian is the potential menace of misinterpreted evidence. The historian need only worry about the post hoc critics. Police work, on the other hand, must accept the fact that the hunter is sometimes in jeopardy of becoming the hunted. Judgment need not wait until a conclusion.

The cornered criminal is more dangerous than the suspect unaware of those in the hunt. If it is true that those who have committed crimes are always looking over their shoulder, it is also true that in closing in on the criminal, law enforcement often must look over their own shoulder as well.

If it is also true that universal formulas of crime investigation are suspect, then the boundary between the hunter and the hunted remains vague, and the outcome equally uncertain. The only certainty is the unpredictable.

CHAPTER 39

RETURN TO NUEVO HIGH SCHOOL

I T WAS FRIDAY afternoon. Not much was happening on the floor. Fenton was not around. Van ambled down the hall.

Lieutenant Vargas was standing opposite his secretary's desk and dictating some instructions regarding the papers he was handing to her one at a time. Not wanting to intrude, Van walked on into the lieutenant's office and took a seat.

Vargas entered soon after and shut the door. He sensed the seriousness. "What's up, Van?"

"I need a favor, boss." Their relationship had moved to the casual stage, and Van referred to Vargas as *boss*, much as the others in the detail did.

"If I can, I will!"

Van went on to explain the logic behind his theory that the body of Carlos Fuentes was buried at Nuevo High School. Ever since the discovery of Cindy's remains in 1999, there was the sense among investigators that somewhere Carlos's body was buried. With the discovery of the former residence of Allison Connors in Trabuco Canyon and the revelation that both bodies had probably been initially buried or retained there, he began to focus on the high school.

Allison could not have buried him near her apartment in Orange, and it was not likely she took him as far as the Eastern Sierra. Given that Cindy was purposefully buried in the time capsule, it seemed only appropriate to consider that Carlos would also be buried with a purpose in mind and not just buried indiscriminately somewhere in the Santa Ana Mountains.

"When I visited the school several months ago, it occurred to me that his body could have been buried on the campus since there were several modifications to the campus in the years during which Allison was a teacher there. At the time, that was just a wild thought. A few days ago, I finally got a timeline from school district officials of some of the work done in the 1970s. Among the changes was the elimination and modification to several planters—planters just like the one the time capsule was buried in. There were lots of changes over time."

He could tell the lieutenant was listening, not just accommodating. "But it occurred to me that if she had buried his remains on campus, it was likely done in the most convenient of times. The most convenient time proved to also be the most convenient of locations as well."

Van knew the lieutenant was experienced and not given to accept the idea of easy extrapolation. Conclusions needed substance; they needed corroborating evidence. Knowing his argument was tenuous, Van stepped gingerly through his logic. He needed to convey reasonableness to his thinking, even if it was not foolproof.

"During spring break in 1978, a planter in the English classroom wing, and next to her classroom, was capped with a four-inch slab of cement. The cement would have to be poured and well set before students returned a week later. What makes this particular planter modification a reasonable focus was the fact that Allison left the district at the end of the school year, a month and a half later."

"Seems a bit of a stretch."

"Well, forensics indicates that the plastic bags retrieved from the pit at the Trabuco residence were vintage 1978. They were one of the early models of plastic trash bags being marketed for contractors. They were very heavy duty. They had only been on the market for a couple of months. Given the compaction of the soil at Trabuco, Claudia says the plastic trash bags were probably buried thirty-plus years. That would go back to the 1970s. I'm thinking they were used to transport the remains of Carlos. There's human tissue residue in the bags, and preliminary DNA results suggest the residue is that of Carlos. Claudia said she will have final results in a week, but she's confident the preliminary results are accurate. My thinking is that after the remains of Carlos were deposited in the capped planter, Allison returned to the house and buried the bags. Everything fits."

"Van, I share your reasoning, but this isn't just a case of let's go dig up a backyard looking for a body. We're talking about a high school. We're talking about a brick-and-concrete planter. That's high-profile stuff. I need more. Hell, I need a lot more."

"It would be easy to render my logic as a simple correlation, except for one thing. Cindy and Carlos were both students at Nuevo. Allison knew them as students, and that seemed important to her. She held Cindy's body for a year and then returned Cindy to the high school knowing it would be decades before the remains would be discovered. My thinking is that she wanted to return Carlos to the school as well, but it was all a matter of timing, and Allison was patient."

Van watched the lieutenant closely, trying to read his reactions.

"By 1978, Allison had already killed several people and had made a decision to leave teaching and pursue her next life as Alexi, and later Lexi. She needed to dispose of the remains of Carlos, and the decision of the school to cap the English wing planter provided opportunity and timing. Allison already knew the drill with work on planters. She had seen it happen to other planters on campus. The process took several days and was usually conducted over long weekends or holidays when students weren't around. As a teacher, she could be on campus during the capping, especially on weekends and at night when the project was not yet complete. There was time to bury the remains and replace the soil and pack it down before workers returned on a Monday." Van let his comments stand and looked for a response from Vargas.

Vargas was intrigued. "Like she did over the weekend when she buried Cindy's remains below the time capsule."

Van nodded.

The lieutenant sat back and stared at nothing in particular. "You share any of this with Fenton?"

"I shared the gist of it with him a few days ago. I think his concerns are much like yours. Would have gone into more detail with him today, but he won't be back in the office until next week. It's been nagging me for the past several days, so I took a chance that I could bounce it off of you. Oh, and Stenz knows, but of course he sees it much as I do."

"So, our suspect in 1978, knowing she is soon to leave the school, decides to dispose of the boy's body in a way that brings the whole thing full circle."

"That's correct, but I think the timing adds another compelling piece. I think it's full circle, as you say, because the timing was fortuitous. Carlos would be buried on the exact sixth anniversary weekend of the prom night when he and Cindy disappeared. Allison would have been very conscious of that reality. Both students would be back at school, and the timing, just before Allison departs, was right."

A second later, Van remembered another connection and said, "As Lexi, Allison has repeatedly been conscious of the 'bringing things full circle' approach. We know that with the earrings. Everything she does has a cycle to it, a certain logic that fits her frame of reference. She cannot leave Nuevo to pursue her next life in the Eastern Sierra without closing out the Ashae-Fuentes chapter. She has to return Carlos to Nuevo. As the Bard suggested, there was method to her madness."

The smile on the lieutenant's face said he was now convinced. "I take it you want to dig up that planter."

"You got it. But not initially."

Van could tell the lieutenant was looking for more. "Remember, with the imaging technology they have in forensics, we don't need to dig unless we see something. My research indicates Claudia's people could set up their equipment and give us a reading. That would take probably an hour, at most. If we see nothing, no need to dig. If we see something, we can dig."

Vargas picked up his phone and buzzed his secretary. "Charlene, get the sheriff on the line ASAP. Also, get the North County High School District superintendent; his name is …" He looked at Van for the name.

"Christopolus, Andre."

"Get Superintendent Christopolus on the line. I want him waiting on the line when I'm done with the sheriff. Thanks … oh, and get me Claudia in forensics as well."

Hanging up the phone, Vargas had a gleam in his eyes.

When they rolled into the parking lot at Nuevo High School at a quarter to eight in the morning, the forensics truck and three patrol cars were already there. There were a couple of other cars, a new BMW, no official plates yet, and an older model Toyota. Claudia, her assistant, and three deputies were off to the side talking as the lieutenant pulled up. Van knew that there were probably two or three forensic techs in the truck. They were nerds and not ones to waste time kibitzing when they could be working their computers.

Vargas was at his best. He immediately greeted the three deputies. He probably did not know them, but he knew the importance of recognizing the front lines even if they were young. Someday they could be working for the lieutenant or there could come the day when one of them might be of help to him. It was a great way to introduce himself and boost another's ego. Van knew he was watching a skilled leader at work.

Turning to the head of forensics, Vargas turned on his charm. "Claudia, we're going to have to quit meeting like this."

Claudia responded with her usual tone of sarcasm. "Well, Lieutenant, it's not like you have much of a choice. It's either me or my assistant here, and he's not nearly as good-looking as me." They all had a good laugh, even if it was at the expense of the assistant, Fernando, who had probably been in the department no more than a year but was no doubt used to such banter.

As the laughter subsided, a sedan pulled up and parked in the red zone directly in front of the school entrance. It was symbolic, thought Van. The superintendent was establishing his authority and privilege. Unfortunately, Superintendent Christopolus had not yet met *the* Lieutenant Vargas, who was superior at playing the power game.

Van had no doubt the passenger with the superintendent was a district maintenance official. That was confirmed when he exited holding a roll of construction blueprints.

Vargas went immediately to the superintendent for introductions.

"You must be Superintendent Christopolus." The pronunciation was perfect and commanding. "Vargas here. So good of you to allow us some time today." They shook hands. The superintendent introduced Martin Sanders as the director of facilities and operations.

Christopolus was tall and immaculately dressed in a vested suit. That it was Saturday seemed unimportant given the professional air in his manner and look. "I didn't know there would be so many of you. Is this level of presence really necessary?"

Vargas spoke with authority. "Oh yes, standard procedure. Actually we usually have a bit more presence, but I didn't want to draw too much attention to your school or alarm neighbors."

Subtle but commanding, thought Van. He knew there was humor in this, and those from the department were laughing internally. The smoothness of Vargas as he worked the situation was a lesson for the young deputies. Vargas had skillfully pulled rank on the superintendent. There was no doubt who was running the show.

"Well, yesterday you said that this was a necessary activity related to the remains that were found in 1999. I'm not sure what else there is to do on that since the time capsule no longer exists."

Vargas had been purposefully evasive the afternoon before when he talked with the superintendent. It was a standard rule when searching for evidence: don't tip your hat. "Well, I probably should have been more clear. You see, we suspect that there's some evidence buried in one of your other old planters, one that has since been covered with a slab in the English wing, and we would like to confirm or deny that theory."

"Oh my, that could mean a mess. Well, isn't there another way? We have school on Monday and wouldn't want disorder. I am sure there will be people on campus today. What will they think? I mean, we want to work with you, but couldn't this wait until a long holiday break?"

Vargas was in his element. "Well, justice has been put off long enough in this case, wouldn't you agree? I'm sure you want to help us out. If you insist, we can call the sheriff. However, I assure you she will side with me. After all, we could get a warrant to enter and dig up whatever we want, and you would be pushed aside if we did that. We want to work with you on this. I think this way is much better, don't you? Shall we go in?" Vargas didn't wait for an answer. He started toward the main entrance, and Superintendent Christopolus had no choice but to follow behind.

"Yes, yes, of course. I believe Cynthia, the principal, is already here." Christopolus was resigned to the situation.

Walking a short distance behind were Claudia and Fernando. Though Claudia carried a couple of evidence kits, Fernando had the task of carrying the larger gear, which Van knew included sophisticated imaging equipment, a computer, and portable printer.

As they walked, Van ran his hand against the hood of the BMW and the Toyota. It was a practice learned many years earlier as a deputy. The hood of the BMW was hot. Probably belonged to the principal whom Van had not met when he was here previously. As for the Toyota, he could only speculate it was someone on the custodial staff.

The hot BMW hood said a lot. Van could guess. The principal, wanting to make sure her desk and office were appropriately uncluttered and presentable, had driven hard to arrive early and get ready. Upon entering, his thinking was confirmed. Cynthia was dressed as though she were a CEO. It fit with the BMW. Not a hair out of place. Van knew her type. She was upwardly mobile, very self-assured, controlling, and would do the superintendent's bidding to a fault. *All of this on a Saturday morning*, thought Van.

Ever the charmer, Vargas was front and center with the principal. He shook her hand firmly as he commented, "It is good to meet you, Cynthia. I hope we won't be too disruptive, but I'm sure that working with your facilities people we'll get this over as quickly as possible."

As long as the superintendent was around, Cynthia was not going to say much. Van surmised they had not talked about the party line on this issue since neither could have anticipated what was happening. All the more reason to see the value in the decision on Vargas's part the evening before to not give specifics about what they were here to do.

Vargas asked Van to explain why they were here and the rationale behind the decision to inspect the English wing planter. Van knew what to say without saying too much. Also, he did not want to suggest that Jay Jensen was the one who really revealed the potential of the old planters and possible locations for additional remains.

As he was explaining to the three school district personnel, Van sensed that both the principal and the facilities director were not going to say anything. They nodded their understanding. Christopolus was clearly not happy, but he had been trumped and just listened. For Van, the art was to make everything sound logical without suggesting it was all based on a theory.

A few minutes later, as they walked to the English wing, the director of facilities noted that the planter slabs did not have rebar. Four-inch mesh wire had been used along with quickset cement. The planter in question had been poured in April 1978. He did not mention the specific date. Van knew the date would mean nothing to the director, principal, or superintendent.

Upon arrival in the English wing, it took a few minutes for Claudia and her assistant to set up. A portable table supported a laptop computer, a shoebox-sized imaging receiver, and a printer. A hardwired-imaging wand plugged into the receiver.

Vargas, Van, and two deputies stood by. The superintendent excused himself and the principal. They would be in the front office if need be. Both Vargas and Van recognized the tactic. The two had been caught off guard and needed time to figure out what to say when neighbors, students, staff, and parents began to kibitz about the presence of the sheriff's department on campus on a Saturday. No doubt the superintendent needed to contact his school board members and bring them up to speed before they heard it elsewhere.

Van was thinking. *If my hypothesis proves right, those two have little idea how much they're going to have to do to accommodate the press and inquisitive staff and parents in the days and weeks to come. Oh well, it's my job to solve crimes, not answer to the media for that.* Van was as much a user of the media information as anyone, but he very much disliked dealing directly with the media. The department had people to do that. Van could do his job and stay out from in front of cameras and microphones and lights.

Vargas, ever working the crowd, was cultivating a relationship with the director. He knew that people like the director could prove valuable, and when the boss was not around was a good time to extend thanks and acknowledge the expertise.

For his part, Van was again trying to visualize what the wing looked like when the planter had plants, the rooms had no entry doors, and the hall was carpeted and not tiled as it was now. Jay had said the original design was to encourage open space that would find the very wide carpeted halls used for instruction and learning. All that had changed.

After about fifteen minutes of scanning the planter, Claudia, listening through a headset and watching the computer screen, spoke without looking up. Her voice was raised, confident, and commanding. "Lieutenant, Investigator, we have something here."

Vargas, Van, and the director eagerly walked over to Claudia.

"Fernando, move a little to your right … stop. Now take one half step forward … stop. Okay, now sweep left and right and work your way backward for about three feet."

Claudia pointed to the screen. "As Fernando moves the imaging wand back and forth across the top of the slab, you'll see the crisscross of the wire mesh. You'll also see shadows, something like fathers see when they view a sonogram of the child their wife is carrying. As the images appear, the computer will record them. When Fernando is done, the computer will form a 3-D composite, and we'll get a look at what's below."

They waited. All were quiet. Claudia communicated with Fernando a couple of times; otherwise it was silent anticipation.

After several minutes, Fernando asked, "That sufficient?"

Claudia responded, "Yes," and Fernando stepped down off the two-foot-high planter, set the wand down, and walked over to Claudia. The computer was slowly compiling a picture.

A fuzzy gray-and-black-toned picture emerged on the screen. "There we go, gentlemen."

Vargas was anxious. "Don't keep us in suspense, Claudia. What are we looking at?"

"Bones, lots of them. They're stacked, unorganized, and at varying depths and angles."

"Do we know if they're human?" It was the director.

"They're human; either that or this school was the site for a bevy of apes at one time." Claudia's sarcastic humor was well known in the department, not so with the school district. Van tried to read the director. Was he informed or insulted?

Vargas asked. "How far down?"

"It looks like between about two and three feet below the surface of the slab." Showing the screen to Fernando, she said, "Wouldn't you say that's about right, Fernando?"

"Yes, two to two and a half feet deep and running lengthwise for about three feet and a width of about two feet. Looks to me like they were laid in a hole of those dimensions. You can tell because you'll notice the sides and ends where the bones line up abruptly against the edges of the hole." Fernando was smiling self-consciously when he finished.

"Lovely, Fernando. I always love the way Fernando makes sure the minute details are noted. He went to public schools in this county, Director, so you can take pride in his preciseness."

Vargas was convinced. "Okay, you know what to do. Dig them up."

The director spoke up. "You going to jackhammer the slab?"

Claudia was quick. "Yes, unless you have a better idea, which I doubt."

Fernando softened his boss's retort. "Actually, we'll use a concrete saw to cut out the exact area of concrete to be removed. Then we'll cut that area into one-foot-square sections. All together, we'll probably remove six twelve-inch-by-twelve-inch pieces. In the end, if you want, we will replace them or you can choose to just concrete the area."

With frankness to her voice, Claudia said, "See what I mean? Thanks, Fernando."

"Well, I need to let the superintendent know." The director was already exiting.

Vargas gave no ground. "Fine with me. While you're doing that, we're moving ahead. Claudia, get your people on this ASAP."

The forensics truck had everything in it they would need. Claudia told Fernando to pull the truck up to the nearest entrance and to have the forensic techs get things set up.

No doubt the sawing would produce noise and dust and raise the curiosity and concern of any teachers or coaches who may come to the school or were in the building. That was where the deputies outside came in.

Claudia requested a second van equipped to transport remains. Removing the bones would take time. They would be photographed and catalogued as they were removed and placed in a special container for transport to Claudia's lab. It was like an archeological dig.

With luck, they would be done sometime in the evening. For Van, Vargas, and the deputies, the waiting was the hard part.

After the director left in search of the superintendent, Van and Vargas had a discussion with Claudia. "Claudia, Van suspects we may find among the remains an earring." Van produced a photo to show Claudia. "Sift through this carefully. We found one with the girl's bones in 1999 and are likely to find one here. It's critical."

"Whatever you need, Lieutenant. We won't overlook anything. If that hippie earring is here, we'll find it. Just keep that superintendent and his loyal subjects off our backs as we do this. Nothing I hate worse than a bunch of lookie-loo bobbleheads on the sidelines."

"We'll do our best. Now that we know what we're dealing with, I'll get some more deputies here. Won't take long for news to get out that we've unearthed another body, and everyone will start talking about the prom caper again. It will be big news by tomorrow morning, if not tonight." Vargas was talking out loud to no one particular. They all knew the drill. "I best let the sheriff know. She's going to be besieged, and the public information officer will need to be ready to issue statements." With that, Vargas walked over to the other end of the wing and took out his cell phone.

Van knew not to follow. He also knew that he needed to be prepared to brief the PIO so that the company line on this matter suggested transparency without providing confidential or compromising information to the public.

The superintendent, director, and principal walked in about five minutes later. Christopolus was on his cell phone. He was explaining to his wife that he would probably not be home for a while. The principal looked a little bewildered. She was probably not even alive when the body was buried. The director seemed to be taking it in stride. Vargas was right. Letting the director be present when the computer screen showed the bones made the director feel a part of the project. Van wondered if it was an ego thing. Was the director somehow empowered because he had a better relationship with the sheriff's department? Well, he would at least have some good stories to tell colleagues.

Van nodded to Claudia, giving her the go-ahead to show the computer composite to the superintendent and principal. Once she explained it all, Van would then begin to use his authority at the crime scene and usher the three outside the wing. First, best to let them see the evidence so as to erase the mystery of the day and give the superintendent what he needed to talk with his board members and the press. The computer-generated photos were not to be made public, and Claudia had already confiscated them.

He could not help but wonder what all this would mean to the very proper-looking principal who would find Monday morning to be a turmoil of staff, student, and parent inquiries, rumors, and a thirst for information. She was young, probably under forty, and he wondered what kind of guidance the superintendent would give her regarding management of this situation.

Every organization had its defensive mode. Van wondered whether the school district would meet the reality of the discovery head on and acknowledge the importance of the sheriff's department in the matter, or would they flounder under the close scrutiny of the press.

After several minutes, Vargas had completed his phone call and returned to the milieu. To make the superintendent feel he and the district were not being shunned, Vargas tracked the superintendent down to explain what would happen. The department worked hard to walk a fine line between their work and keeping others informed so it could not be said the department had strong-armed them. It was all about minimizing the impact of dictatorial authority.

Working his magic, Vargas would let the superintendent know that the department would praise the district for its cooperation. The goal was to present a unified front. However, Vargas knew all too well that the news media would try to find something salacious in the whole thing. The department was used to the media hassle. He could only hope that the school district, for its part, would not buckle under the pressure.

Within an hour, the English wing was crawling with forensic techs and department support personnel. Claudia expected they would start removing the remains about two hours after the cutting ceased.

Outside, deputies had isolated the campus and kept both the public and employees out of the school. A sweep of the interior of the school had also ushered any staff, students, or others from within. With this, the world now knew something was going on at the school.

The PIO lieutenant and his staff were also present. They had to face the cameras and microphones and wanted a good feel for what was going on.

Entrance to the wing was cordoned off, and two deputies were at each end. A folding table with chairs was set up at the far end of the wing.

It was a waiting game.

Van wanted to know the process for placing the slab over the planter. The director stepped through the process, which had been completed during the spring break along with several other planters at the school. The planters would have been cleaned out, backfilled with dirt and sand that was packed down. That would have been done on the Friday before. Monday, the wire would have been put on top and the slab poured. That would give the rest of the holiday week to allow it to cure. As it turned out, the process left ample time over the weekend for the remains of Carlos to be buried.

Vargas was intrigued. "As easy as that, huh?"

"Lieutenant, this school is different. Because it's enclosed, people come here at all hours to work. It's not like our other schools. I've had custodial staff tell me about teachers who actually slept here overnight."

Turning to Van, Vargas mused out loud. "So, our suspect comes in late on one of the weekend days, Friday or Saturday or Sunday. She has the night to dig a hole, place the bones, backfill the hole, and leave it looking as she found it. With her prior experience in 1973, she would have known the risks and challenges going in."

Van nodded.

"Certainly speaks to her prowess." Vargas now began to think of the implications of the day's find. "Obviously, all this raises the ante. We have to find her. We now have two bodies. We know what happened. We know where it probably happened. We know who did it. What we don't know is where she is!"

Van knew the inference of the comment. The media would quickly raise the issue. *How is it that we know what happened and you haven't found the suspect?*

The name of the suspect might soon be out as well. Once people started putting the pieces of the puzzle together, it was likely that Allison's name would come to the forefront. Of course, other names could be there as well, but certainly Allison's name would be among them.

The media would begin to respond to rumors and speculation on the part of others. The news would say they vetted their sources, but those in law enforcement knew otherwise. The news only sold well if the story hinted at something salacious or sinister.

The sheriff would want to pull out all the stops and find the suspect. Van knew that was not going to be as easy as everyone thought. The pressure would flow like water from the media to the sheriff to the lieutenant to Fenton and then to Van. He had to keep this case in his hands if he was to pursue the course he wanted. The department would want him to take on additional assistance. Van liked working alone. He would have to be careful. He knew he could count on the help of Stenzgard but did not want any other help. He also knew Fenton, and probably Vargas, could be counted on for support of his approach.

There would be no relaxing music or exercising tonight. Though he desperately needed both, Van also knew his weekend was shot and the next several days would be long and demanding.

He also knew that since no one had a clue where Allison was living, after a few days the hot quality of the case would again cool down. The public had little interest in a very old case when the news was daily ripe with new cases of violence, graft, corruption, and other hot topics.

The trouble with success in his business was that it often equated to chaos. Investigating a homicide could be a methodical, thoughtful, and peaceful activity. But rewards of effective work could be dreaded. The madness of the crime, once solved, produced its own form of lunacy.

Allison would soon be aware that the body of Carlos and another earring had been found.

CHAPTER 40

SECOND ENCOUNTER

Sierra Nevada

THE EASTERN SIERRA is an expanse manifesting itself in both alpine and arid environments. Most of it is defined as an area including the eastern side of the Sierra Nevada range and the canyons and valleys that make up the lands between the town of Bridgeport in the north and Lone Pine in the south—a distance of 150 miles. For the most part, it extends east to the California border.

For someone intent on hiding, the Eastern Sierra affords ample opportunities, though he or she would need to be prepared to adapt to a region whose weather ranges from the bitter cold of snow in the winter to the sweltering heat of summer. However, the expanse is not so raw that he or she could easily evade detection forever. Few areas east of the Sierra range are so remote as to totally avoid scrutiny. US 395 runs the length, as does one of the world's iconic water projects—the Los Angeles Aqueduct. Along the way, roads, most of them unimproved, crisscross Eastern Sierra valleys and extend into the side canyons.

Towns are spaced well apart along the highway, and were it not for the LA Aqueduct and the strong recreational industry, the population of the region would be much smaller. Interest in skiing, hunting, fishing, camping, off-roading, cycling, climbing, and backpacking make the Eastern Sierra an outdoor enthusiast's mecca. The towns reflect a livelihood rooted in the recreational industry along with employment by the LA Department of Water and Power, municipal agencies, hotel services, and wilderness services such as the US Forest Service and Bureau of Land Management. While there are some alfalfa farms and ranches, these are generally isolated and limited in size.

In the Eastern Sierra, any remote areas well suited for isolated residence are well removed from the towns and well away from 395.

However, seeking solitude is not restricted to isolated locations. Solitude can be more about mind-set than location. In a town, it is possible to get lost among the crowds and live in solitude.

Sti and Rob were well acquainted with the Eastern Sierra. There was hardly a dirt road, canyon, or corner they had not visited during their decades of wandering. Van could not have picked a better source to aid in his search for Allison. The two friends had pursued very different careers, but they shared a love of the Eastern Sierra and everything it had to offer.

Finding Allison somewhere in the Eastern Sierra was a daunting task, and they were not trained investigators. But what they lacked in detective skills they more than made up for in other qualities, not the least of which was the use of instinct, curiosity, and experience. They were wanderers with a need to inquire when something caught their attention.

Knowing that finding Allison was a long shot, the two started with a set of assumptions.

First, Allison probably lived near the Sierra escarpment. Her love of the Sierra was such that she would want to be able to quickly access the backcountry on foot. Second, it was likely she lived somewhere between Mammoth Lakes to the north and Lone Pine to the south. The two towns were at the extreme ends of the JMT. Anywhere in between would offer quick access to the trail.

Also, the two reasoned that it was more likely that Allison lived between Bishop and Lone Pine, a distance of sixty miles and at opposite ends of the Owens Valley. She was born in Bishop and had at one time lived near Big Pine fifteen miles south of Bishop. The real high country of the JMT was along this region of the Eastern Sierra. Ideally, someone like Allison would want ready access to the central and most remote areas of the Sierra, the areas of the trail along which the deaths and disappearances had taken place.

With these parameters, Sti and Rob narrowed their field of inquiry. While on paper the area looked much more manageable than consideration of the entire region, the reality was that the task of searching was nonetheless demanding.

They were familiar enough with the valley to realize they could not just conduct a search unbeknownst to others. Despite its size, the valley was like a small town; people all seemed to know what was going on, especially if it involved behavior outside the norm.

It was true that each of the towns and crossroads communities had its own history and culture. However, they were all held together by a common history.

Change was slow in the Owens Valley, and it was noticed. Whether someone moved in or out, it was noticed, even by people well removed from the towns and communities. The same was true of births and deaths. Things large and small were noticed with equal curiosity. The independence of the valley was a source of pride, and little went on within that went unnoticed.

Sti and Rob reasoned that if one was seeking isolation, the towns were not the place to live. It was likely Allison lived in a shack on one of the old ranches. Perhaps she paid rent or was granted the privilege in exchange for guarding the place from vandalism. She could live in an abandoned trailer or in a small trailer parked on private property.

There was another interesting quality in the valley. Although residents would take notice of change and uncommon activity, that did not mean they would interfere. People tended to ignore things they deemed none of their business. If someone was in trouble with the law but was perceived to not be a problem, others might take notice, but they were just as likely to then adopt a sort of *live and let live* philosophy. If someone was the Robin Hood type, that was okay too.

It was also quite possible that a person could live within the valley on a seasonal basis. He or she may live other places during the rest of the year. Perhaps he or she followed a circuit that found him or her in the valley in the winter and in the backcountry in the summer and fall.

Given these factors, Sti and Rob decided to approach their search for Allison by using three guiding tactics.

1. Divide the valley into manageable search areas on a map and then check each off as they looked. They knew some areas would have nothing and others some possibilities. Already they were familiar with some regions, but they needed a systematic approach that allowed them to quickly ascertain what had and had not been scanned.
2. They also had acquaintances, people they knew in the valley. Many would share willingly, but Sti and Rob would be cautious and not too forward or pointed with their questions. They knew people in OV were very protective. They did not want attention and tended to be suspect of too many questions. They might tolerate a lot and protect the odd if they thought talking would disrupt the status quo.
3. Although they were searching, they knew that in reality it was little more than a scan. Respecting privacy, fences, and no trespassing posting required they go softly and focus on simple observations.

Using this approach, Sti and Rob felt that over time, weeks or months if needed, they could begin to narrow down a list of possible places Allison could reside full- or part-time.

With these guidelines in place, and with their usual casual and wandering approach, Sti and Rob began to look for Allison.

—ɯ—

After multiple visits to the valley, their large matrix map of the OV showed search areas crossed out, indicating they had determined that Allison was probably not living in that area. They tended to say "probably" because most often they did not want to trespass in order to take a thorough look. There were two places highlighted in yellow to note it was possible someone was or had recently lived in the area informally. Of course, despite the appearance of an organized search, they had no real idea what they were looking for. It very well could be their observations were bogus. They knew that, as did Van. They also knew that the task was almost impossible. They were not likely to cover all the areas.

At one point, well into their search, the two found themselves seated on folding chairs in the shade of a piñon pine in the late afternoon, high on the slopes of the Sierra escarpment on the west side of the valley. They were eating their favorite locally grown Chileno peppers and some trail mix while also enjoying a cold beer. The view was nothing they hadn't seen before, but it was everything they loved about the valley—vast, extremely quiet, beautiful, and relaxing.

Rob was staring off toward the east when he raised a question. As Rob was wont to do so often, it was really not a question as much as his introduction to a hypothesis. "What if Allison isn't the person we think we're looking for?"

Sti did not respond. He knew Rob was about to expound some idea.

"We have only one photo of her taken for the Nuevo yearbook in her first year as a teacher. It isn't even a good photo. And she avoided having her photo taken for ten years after, so that 1968 photo was used every year in the faculty section of the yearbook. The only other photo is a side shot, of poor quality, that was found in Carlos's stuff. It's been a half century plus since her photo was taken. We're looking for someone who hasn't existed since then.

"Look, she disappeared and adopted a new persona after 1978. Why would the old photo be of value? She must have also done everything to avoid being detected as the old Allison. Even when I saw her at Baxter Creek, it was only a partial face and only for a fleeting second in very bad lighting. I really haven't a clue as to what she looks like. Nobody has a clue."

"You don't think she lives here in the OV or at least in the Eastern Sierra?"

"I think she does. My point is she may be actually living in full view in one of the towns. Her transformation to a new name may be complete. She could be paying social security, taxes, bills, and the like. She could be completely integrated. It's been so long that people may not think of her as someone who moved into the valley. Many might think of her as a native."

"And how does this jibe with the wandering Alexi of the backcountry who makes occasional visits to the TC house? What about the trail murderer?"

"It's the Jekyll-Hyde thing. Most of the time she's seen as a regular member of the community. But when others aren't aware, she becomes Lexi. Her name, as most know her, may be something completely different here. Maybe she's Lexi only to us and has a sweet conventional name here. In all likelihood, she now looks nothing like we think she looks."

—⟶⟵—

It was late in an October afternoon when Van's cell phone rang.

"Van, Rob here. We have you on speaker phone."

"Where are you guys?"

"Sheriff's office substation in Lone Pine."

"Don't tell me you've gotten in trouble. Who's with you?"

"No one in here with us now. However, we just finished talking with a local deputy."

"Sounds serious to me."

"No, no, don't worry. We're just calling to update you on our search."

"You found her?"

"Well …" Sti said, "not in so many words. Strange circumstances in the wake of her activities would be a better way of saying we know about her."

Van was not certain how to respond. It seemed that Sti was always a little philosophical in responding to anomalous inquiries. "So, are you guys okay?"

Rob put Van at ease. "Oh yeah. We're fine and calling you because you instructed us to do so if anything developed."

A bit of frustration was evident in Van's response. "I'm all ears."

Sti and Rob related how they were camped the previous two days at the Lone Pine Creek Campground. On a whim, they decided to take a day hike up to Meysan Lake with the goal of possibly hiking up to Mount Irvine.

As it turned out, they were delayed the next morning and did not get to the trailhead until about nine in the morning. The trailhead is along Whitney Portal Road, about a half mile below the end of the road. From there, one has to hike through the lower end of the Portal Campground and then through an area that has several summer cabins on leased National Forest land. Eventually the trail starts after one passes the last of the cabins. From there, it is about three and a half miles to the lower lake. It is another mile to the upper lake. From the upper lake, it is a climb of about two thousand feet to the summit of Mount Irvine. It would be a long one-day round-trip.

There were no cars in the area when they parked and began walking toward the trailhead. The campground was empty, and the summer cabins were void of any vehicles or people. The forecast was for possible rain and a dusting of snow in a couple of days, though it was ideal weather for a day hike on a trail that was normally very hot and well used in the summer.

Rob took the lead in describing what happened. "As we were walking through the summer cabins, we saw no evidence of anyone. The cabins are very small, simple, rustic, and not much used during the winter. The cabins were already boarded up. Then, just as we passed the next to last cabin, Sti noticed a small red hydration pack, one of those backpacks cyclists and hikers use because it has a bladder for water and a sip hose for quick access. It was sitting on a flat log at the bottom of the steps up to the cabin. Sti pointed it out, and without leaving the path, we quickly glanced around, expecting to greet someone who lived there or was taking a break, but there was no one. So we went on.

"About fifty yards past the cabin, we reached the sign announcing the start of the trail and the usual regulations for use. Out of curiosity, Sti turned back and noticed the hydration pack was gone, yet we saw no one in the area. We knew someone had picked it up but thought they must have moved off in the other direction.

"Our hike to the lake was uneventful, and we made good time. However, the late start and impending weather change convinced us to turn around at Grass Lakes. We had a snack and relaxed. At about 1:00 p.m., we headed back down."

Van wondered where the story was going, but experience with Sti and Rob had taught him that they did not just communicate important information on a whim. No doubt they had discussed this phone call and the sequence of events to be relayed.

"Van, it was at this point that Sti and I began to see and later hear things that piqued our interest and reason for calling.

"The start of our return hike took us over to the edge of a ridge that allowed us to have a view down the canyon and the trail that would take us back to the trailhead. We stopped momentarily to take in the view when I spotted what looked to be a hiker headed up the trail toward us. The person was a good half mile or more away, so I took out my binoculars to get a better look. At that instant, the hiker turned around and headed down the trail, and all I saw was their back side. What caught my attention, Van, was the small red-and-white daypack.

"At first, we were amused and could only assume that the daypack was similar to the one we had seen three hours earlier. But we thought it odd the hiker had turned and was headed back down. At that point, we thought no more about the incident."

Sti took over the narrative. "When we got back to the trailhead and the cabin where we had seen the red hydration pack, there was an older man working on the storm door to the cabin's main entrance.

I greeted him and noted that I had seen his red pack earlier. His response caught us completely off guard.

"He told us he had only arrived two hours earlier after driving up from Los Angeles. He knew nothing about the red daypack. It wasn't his. Then he related a story that surprised us and is the reason we're calling you."

Sti went on to explain that the man was making changes to the locks on the door because someone had gotten inside. "I assumed he meant the cabin was broken into, but he insisted that someone had found the hidden key. There was no damage. He said that absolutely no one knew where the key was hidden. Whoever found and used it had lived in the cabin for about two weeks and left only the slightest evidence behind. He said something like, 'They didn't damage, break, take, or displace anything. They just used the cabin and left.'"

Van knew what Rob and Sti were saying. Allison was the one they had seen on the trail and had used the cabin.

Rob related how the owner told them he only knew about the problem because a neighbor who owned a nearby cabin and was up to close his own cabin for the winter noticed late one night a faint light coming from a small crack in one of the cabin winter shutters. There was no electricity for the cabin, so he went up to check for the source of the light the next morning. He found nothing, but the same thing happened the next night. That was when he called the owner from Lone Pine the next day.

"Van, we're calling you because the circumstances sound too much like what you shared with us regarding the house in Trabuco Canyon. The more we considered the strangeness of your comments as they compare with the descriptions of the cabin owner, our experience on the trail today, and our backcountry encounter, the more we began to conclude Allison had been there."

"Why are you at the substation in Lone Pine?"

The response from Sti was meant to put Van at ease. "The owner of the cabin called the sheriff's department, and they sent up a couple of deputies to take a report. They asked us to come in and file a report. However, we haven't mentioned anything about Allison, your case, or our work on your behalf.

"Van, the deputies who took the report noted they had, in recent years, received similar reports from cabin owners in Whitney Portal, Aspendell, and other locations. From our perspective, there can be little doubt. It has to be Allison. So, that's why we're calling."

The long pause on the phone before he spoke reflected Van's mixture of thinking about what he had just heard. "It's hard to believe she just happened to be there when you guys hiked by. Did you tell anyone you were going on the hike? Did you have to get a permit?"

"No on both questions." Rob's response explained their reasoning. "Interestingly, we think we just stumbled into a situation where Allison was already here. She couldn't have known we would be hiking that trail today. However, she knows us and knew who had seen her hydration pack. Allison doesn't expose herself, and perhaps this caught her off guard once again."

Van's thoughts were wrestling with competing issues, but one issue was of concern. "You said you saw her facing you on the trail, and then she turned around and headed down. That seems odd to me."

"Odd to us as well. We talked about it and have concluded that from where she was standing, she could see us just as easily as we could see her. No doubt she had seen us earlier when we passed the cabin. She was following us. When she saw us on the ridge, she knew her only option was to turn and hike down."

"Did you share all of this with the deputies?"

Sti explained that he and Rob had been completely honest with the deputies about the sequence of events. However, "We didn't share our suspicion that the individual was Allison. We just thought that at some point you're probably going to have conversations with your counterparts up here, and at that time you can provide a name."

Van was concerned. From his perspective, it was a close call. Though Allison had not displayed any malice, he was concerned that Sti and Rob could be in harm's way if things escalated. "Well, I want you guys out of there. I don't want you searching for her." The words and sense of angst in Van's tone made his wishes clear.

"I think we already found her," said Sti. "It's our bet that she's been secretly using these summer cabins without anyone knowing. Our guess is she can do this kind of thing at will and has probably a whole chain of places in the Eastern Sierra where she can go into hiding for an extended stay. This is corroborated by the deputy's comments that for several years owners have reported suspicions that someone has been staying in their cabins without any break-in, damage, or disruption."

"Well, I cannot risk your safety. From my point, you are no longer trying to locate Allison."

"Request noted. We are no longer working for you."

"I do not want you guys doing this." Van's voice belied his attempt at control.

"Noted."

The conclusion to the conversation left Van upset. He should have known the two would not take his advice and back off now.

—⁂—

It was late when Van arrived home. He was not hungry, but he was tired and irritated.

He was angry that he had gotten upset with Sti and Rob. They had done nothing wrong, certainly nothing to warrant his displeasure. They had simply taken a hike and were victims of a strange encounter. They did what he had asked them to do—contact the Inyo sheriff and call him.

He should have expected their response when he asked them to back off. Their form of experience with risk was the exception. They were not foolish and would not go looking for trouble. He realized that now; all the more reason for being upset for losing his cool.

He needed time to think.

Allison was in the Owens Valley. He knew this. Sti and Rob knew it. No doubt, Allison was well aware she was under suspicion.

Yet, it did not seem to bother her. Her actions were like the moves in a sophisticated game. She did not fire a salvo across their bow. She did not need to. She was confident in her decisions, movements, and anonymity. If she had wanted, she could have been much more vengeful.

In times like this, Van looked to seduce his body into relaxation and his thoughts into reflection by turning to music. He got up and wandered over to the electronics cabinet and turned on his tuner and turntable.

From the stack of records, he removed an old favorite. He had nothing against the CD. It was just the nostalgia of old LP records and the fact that he had a collection of favorites so familiar that he could never abandon the vinyl.

Van selected a 1950s Angel recording of highlights from Puccini's *Madame Butterfly* with Victoria De Los Angeles singing the part of Butterfly and Jussi Bjoerling as Pinkerton. It was an old monophonic and among those listened to when Van was young and just beginning to develop a taste for opera.

He kept the music soft as background.

Along with a glass of sauvignon blanc, he listened to music from act one. By the time the famous and long love duet between Butterfly and Pinkerton was playing, Van was already in another world.

Regardless of efforts to relax, Van found his thoughts drifting back to the Ashae case. It was the nature of perplexing issues that music-induced reflection should cause him to be consumed by those issues he found most troubling. When Anna Marie was sick, he had turned to music to relax, but music only took him to a world of sadness. Now, it took him to his cases.

Van stared into space. Alone with thoughts, he reviewed what he knew about Allison. Over and over, his thoughts cycled through the evidence and theories. Eventually, the burden of things he did not know about her seemed to take front stage in his thoughts. But with time, he drifted away from thoughts of Allison and back to the present.

As act two was beginning, the "One Fine Day" aria by Victoria De

Los Angeles reminded Van that tired as he was, he also understood that he was getting closer to Allison. Eventually they would catch her, and then it would be *un bel di*, a fine day. She would be held accountable for the deaths of Cindy, Carlos, and the others.

Van wondered, did it make sense to keep searching for Allison, or would it make more sense to try to draw her out? Whether by accident or design, she risked exposure when she encountered Sti and Rob. Could he somehow set a trap that would do what Sti and Rob had done by accident, cause her to surface?

CHAPTER 41

MONTHS LATER

Homicide Office

I T HAD BEEN months since the discovery of Carlos at Nuevo High School and weeks since the Whitney Portal incident of Sti and Rob. Claudia's team had completed their work on everything taken from the Trabuco House and Carlos's remains. Deena and Anita continued to search for leads regarding Allison and her various aliases. And as far as Van knew, Sti and Rob had not heeded his advice to avoid nosing around the valley in search of Allison. Although former sheriff Pagliano had let Van know that the two wanderers were not likely to create any problem.

Following the discovery of Carlos's remains, the local media were again tuned into the case. There was a flurry of speculation and commentary, but interest soon died, and the case went cold.

Of course it was not like Van had nothing to do. Caseloads go through cycles of intensity. When a new case comes along, it receives close attention on the theory that the hot trail cools fast in the hours and days immediately following a crime. Van knew that the entire homicide division was booked with work, and Fenton and Vargas were feeling the pressure from above to make headway on some key cases that were getting a lot of media attention. Current tragedy always sold more papers and airtime than the past.

Van was working with Stenzgard on one of the high-profile cases.

Stenzgard was good at staying focused and not being distracted by the press or, for that matter, the politics of the department. He worked his cases diligently, methodically, and by the book. Pursuing cases in this way allowed Stenz to handle multiple cases better than most. In many ways, Van found working with Stenz to be less stressful because there was predictability. He also found the traditional approaches of Stenz and others to be confining and not conducive to Van's tendency to want to work cases by seeking different perspectives by drawing on the input of others outside the proverbial *this is the way we do it* box.

Regardless, Stenz was one of the best people to bounce ideas off. Stenz was not patronizing and gave straight responses. Van was confident with the progress on all of his active cases, but he was increasingly concerned that the Ashae case was again at a dead end. Perhaps it was time to get input from Stenz and Fenton about their insights and suggestions.

Van finished filling Stenzgard in on progress in the Ashae case. "And that's what I meant when I said everything points to the suspect's identity, and everything points to the area where she's probably residing, but I haven't been able to find her."

They were in Van's office. At a quarter after nine, it was well into the workday for Van. For Stenzgard, it was just the start of the day. He tended to arrive midmorning and work into the evening. In his defense, Stenz often told people in the office, "I'm not awake in the morning. The crooks I need to talk with are night people, and they're not awake, so I need to find the common ground and that's usually the afternoon when they're awake or the evening when their shift is just starting." Whenever Stenz shared this point of view, people just shook their head or rolled their eyes. Hard to argue with Stenz.

Stenz had come in early to meet with Van. Sipping his hot coffee he had retrieved from the workroom, Stenz moved slowly into his commentary. "She seems to be predictably unpredictable, doesn't she?"

Such a tongue twister was prelude. Van knew enough about Stenz to not interrupt. He often opened with a conclusion before going on to share his thoughts. There was a story coming.

"I worked a case in San Clemente where this pair kept burglarizing small businesses. Went on a couple of years. Never had good surveillance photos, but we eventually determined they were a young male and female. On surveillance cameras, they were always casual or grubby like so many in that town. Beyond that, all we had was a feeling they lived in the area.

"Then one day we got a good surveillance video that allowed us to zoom in with clarity on what they were wearing. Both were in shorts and wearing those expensive name-brand leather flip-flops people down there wear. But we were inexperienced investigators and not patient enough to realize what the evidence was telling us. In fact, we didn't really see the value in what we thought was another useless video until an experienced colleague pointed something out. We had failed to notice what looked like a tan line above the ankles of one. The feet were not dark like the legs.

"With that little bit of information, we realized the two people we were looking for weren't the young slobs about town. The two we were looking for may have been in the sun, but they weren't the usual fare. They wore shoes and socks every day. Probably had regular jobs that required shoes. We began to realize that our two suspects probably knew the area and worked in a local business.

"Well, later we found out both of our suspects were delivery people for different businesses—one a pizza outfit and the other a small café that was doing a good order-out business. Together they got to see the inner workings of local businesses."

"How'd did you find them?"

"We didn't; they found us. All the burglaries took place between 10:00 p.m. and 1:00 a.m. We guessed they didn't work after 1:00 a.m. because they needed sleep before work the next day.

"One evening, a deputy helped a young couple with a flat tire on a side street in the area and noticed they were wearing flip-flops with visible tan lines just above the ankle."

"And you paid them a visit."

"Exactly. It all started when we realized our suspects weren't who we thought they were."

"Then you agree with my retired friends and Dr. Ryan. We're looking for the wrong image of our suspect. We've been looking for the classic recluse, the sort of isolated Unabomber type, the mental case who has withdrawn from society. It may actually be we're looking for the wrong person even though we're looking in the right area."

Stenz knew he had made his point. "I'm not saying she isn't strange or wacky; it may just be that the image we have of her is based only on the feats she exhibited when much younger and on the half-century-old images of what she looked like then."

This was why Van wanted to talk with Stenz. The dialogue got him thinking differently. "Do you think it possible that she lives more of a normal life now, even though she escapes to the wilds on occasion and roams the Sierra, even makes the very rare trip to the Trabuco house?"

"Van, anything is possible for a mind like your suspect. Damn, we know what she's capable of physically and mentally. We also know she's getting older. Most crazies don't live this long; they self-destruct. But it just seems to me that since she hasn't self-destructed, she has modified her ways to fit her age. You may want to talk to your psych friend about that."

"She knows she cannot take the risks and challenges that were routine years ago. Maybe Allison's earlier aggressive thinking has given way to reflection. She knows the risks and also knows she's no longer equal to those risks."

Stenz raised his eyebrows again and smiled. "It may also be true, and you have said this, Van, that she has entered a new phase. She's winding down her career of vengeful murder. She's moving toward retirement. She's collecting the earrings and preparing for closure."

"But she's still crazy."

"Certainly! Though maybe it's a more philosophical and mellow crazy. Shit, I don't know, Van. Ask your sources. This isn't my area."

"But you do think it possible, like your two young burglars in

San Clemente, that she's living what appears to be more like a normal life?"

"It's worth a try. What you've been doing isn't working. Believe me, I know what stubborn means. I keep reminding myself that I've been doing this too long and sometimes I need to step back from procedures and consider a new tactic. I think that's especially true with really old cases." Stenz started to get up but thought better of it.

He sat back down. "Oh, and one other thing. You may want to try getting one of those modern computer programs that can take a photo and then show you what happens to someone over a long time. I know the department has a gal that does that, but I saw this program on TV. You can do it with your own computer, with any photo. I know nothing about computers, but it was amazing. You could probably get several ideas of what she could look like today. Hell, she could be a raving elderly beauty or a haggard bitch. Who knows?"

Now Stenz did get up and started toward the door, talking as he went. "Now, I haven't had enough good coffee, so I'm going to head down the street and get a good cup, not the stuff they make here. I should be ready to start the day when I return."

At the door, Stenzgard stopped, tucked in his loose shirt, smiled at Van, and commented. "Want to look good for that spry young barista they have working there in the morning." With that, he was gone.

Van smiled. Stenz was one of the reasons he loved investigations. *You meet all types, and you can learn from each of them.* Stenz was the real thing.

Van looked at his watch and realized the fun of talking with Stenz had taken longer than he thought. He needed to spend the morning prepping for a day in court tomorrow.

—◆—

Deena had a smile on her face. "Investigator, you got a call from the retired sheriff in Bishop. I asked if it was an emergency, and he said no. Also, there was a call from the National Park Service. No message."

"Thanks, Deena." *Deena, always the professional. I've been here a year, and not once has it been my name. One would think 'Van' much easier to say than a polysyllabic title.*

Van called the Park Service first.

"Yes, Investigator Vanarsdale, thanks for returning my call. I apologize for the many months it has taken to get back to you."

Van's response was perfunctory. "Not at all. I fully understand. I'm sure your plate is full as well." *But not so full as to take six months,* thought Van.

"I know you originally didn't talk to anyone in this office, but Deputy Superintendent Wheeling has asked that I call you on this matter ..."

Van's ears burned. When reference was made to a request from the top brass in a major DC branch of government, it meant that the matter in question was as much about politics as it was about substance. What he was about to hear had been vetted by the sup's staff, probably attorneys, and was the party line on this issue.

"We would have gotten back to you earlier, but we have been so busy ..."

Van knew he was hearing official dogma. *Get to your point,* he thought.

"You know how it is. We're asked to do more with less, the sequester and all that ..."

Van could only shake his head in disgust and hold his tongue.

"Anyway, you asked about a body that was discovered in 1983 in Sequoia National Park near a lake with the name 11,106. Well, actually it's Lake 11,092 now, and that's probably why your request got slowed down ..."

Seriously? thought Van. But he kept quiet.

"You were right; a body was found then. At the time, we didn't know anyone was missing in the area since there had been no reports to that end. However, further investigation revealed it was the body of Charles Reems, an accomplished backpacker, who it was later discovered was AWOL from the military." There was a pause. "Are you getting all of this?"

"Yes, I am. Thank you. Continue."

"The Fresno Police Department and the US Army asked us to keep the lid on public information regarding discovery of Reems's body even though the death was determined to be an accident by our folks and by the Fresno County coroner. The reason for keeping it quiet was never made clear to us, but we obliged."

Interesting, thought Van. It was the old blame-someone-else ruse.

"Over the years, the case just faded from view. Frankly, it was so long ago that people just forgot about it. When early last summer it was discovered someone had been digging in the spot where the original remains were found, the initial thought was that it was an animal. So we sent some people up to take a look. Nothing of importance was found."

"So your folks who revisited the site found nothing?"

"Our people are good. They were thorough. They found *nada*."

"If someone went up there now, the site would not be protected and the NPS would not consider it trespassing or problematic to take a close look at the site?"

"What is it you're looking for, Investigator?"

"We're just following up on a possible suspect and possible homicides linked to that person. Thought maybe your victim could be someone connected to our suspect who has murdered people along the JMT."

"Along the JMT? Not sure I follow you."

"Well, we're looking for a piece of jewelry that's usually associated with our suspect's crimes. You wouldn't happen to know if an earring was found, would you?"

"No, it's not on the list of items found."

Van was thinking. *So they did go through the areas thoroughly and found things but nothing unusual from their point of view. That means Allison got there first.* The only thing she would have taken was an earring.

The appropriate closing comments concluded, Van ended the call.

Allison killed Charles Reems. There was just Reems, no hiking partner. That was different, but then there was the single female found in the Kern River. Allison was not above killing individuals as well as couples. Van could not avoid the conflicting motives.

The Reems and Fenwick cases were a bit perplexing when laid beside the other cases. If it was true that relationships were the key to understanding why Allison had killed Cindy and Carlos and probably the two Berkeley students, how did single killings fit into the picture?

Van thought back to a comment by Elisabeth Ambrose. Allison referenced men who sought to take advantage of a woman as "dirts." Archie took advantage of Allison's mother. Was he a dirt? Could it be that Reems encountered Allison along the trail and tried to make a move on her? Would she have seen him as a dirt and therefore killed him as she did her father? These were thoughts he had to run past Dr. Ryan.

—⟋⟍—

"Sheriff Pagliano, this is Investigator Vanarsdale."

"Van, thanks for returning my call. You were in court today. Boy, I don't miss that part of the job. Hated having to go to court; it was usually a waste of time. Well, you know that …"

Van knew the prevailing philosophy of law enforcement. It was a mixed bag. Being in court usually meant they caught the bad guy and now must suffer the slings and arrows of justice.

"Anyway, I have seen your two boys around recently. They say they're not working for you now, but of course I know them. To use their own description, they just love wandering and poking. Believe me, Van, they're good at it. If I were of a mind to open my own private investigative service, I'd hire them. Such nosing talent should be put to work."

"You're right; they are good, maybe too good."

"You mean that Whitney Portal encounter? That's nothing

compared to the things they've gotten into for me. I know, you feel a bit vulnerable with them out there nosing around, but they don't seek trouble. It may find them, but usually they do what's necessary to avoid it."

"I hope so. So what is it you called me about?"

"Yes. Well, I remembered a conversation we had when you were up here. If I recall, it was your finding that your suspect left an earring where she disposed of her victims."

"Yes, since then, we have found two earrings. Both accompanied remains."

"Well, the other day, I was in to visit Pollard, you know, the investigator who worked the Archie Connors case. He's not doing well, and his daughter told me that he was hoping I could drop by. He was a good deputy and detective, and I owe it to visit when I can.

"Anyway, I stopped in, and we visited. Before I left, he brought up the old Archie Connors case. Said that he had been thinking about it ever since your friend Brenda Robertson discussed it with him. Ryan said that a day after they brought Archie's body out, he went to where Archie lived in an old shack on the Triple Peak Ranch and found it a mess. They did a cursory search but found nothing really useful. Several days later, he went back to search for some personal information so he could complete the investigation report. He said that it was odd on the second visit because the place had been cleaned up, very neat, bed was made, and everything was pretty much in order. The strange part was that sitting on the bed were two earrings."

For the second time today, Van's interest was piqued. "You say two earrings?"

"Yes. Ryan said they didn't think anything of it since Archie was a womanizer. They thought it was from one of his girlfriends paying tribute after learning of his death. He asked the guys on the ranch if they had seen anything. Whoever cleaned the place was not seen."

"Do you know what ever happened to the earrings?"

"No. Ryan said they were collected along with a few other personal items and boxed. Ryan said there was never any reason to reference the box because the coroner concluded the death was an accident.

It was his recollection that no family member ever asked about the items."

"Is there anyone who could search around now?"

"Well, I've looked. There's nothing. When they built the new headquarters, much of that old stuff disappeared."

Later Van thought back on the two phone conversations. *What a day*, he thought. *Progress when you least expect. Go to court and waste time. Come back to the office, and a couple of phone calls become gold mines.* It was the way of investigations.

CHAPTER 42

A Plan

Orange County Sheriff's Department

"OKAY, VAN. FENTON tells me you have a plan. He also says, and these are his words, 'It's a bit out there.' I'm not big on risky ideas. So I need to be convinced." Vargas leaned back. "But I want to begin by having you recap exactly what we have on your suspect. If I'm to get the sheriff on board with any plan, I need to convince her we have no choice."

Van had decided any commentary regarding the conduct of prior department investigations was not in order. He began with the death of Archie Connors in 1966 and then traced the sequence of known disappearances and deaths that followed. He had to link the disappearances and deaths in the Sierra with their prime suspect. Vargas needed to see that any hope of finding Allison meant they had to go to the Eastern Sierra. She was not going to come to them.

He summarized the seven known deaths linked to Allison—Enid, Ingmar, Carlos, Cindy, Monique, Charles, and Connors. Blunt force head trauma was common to all. With the exception of Monique Fenwick, they knew the earrings were also a common element. As for the motive in each, there were also some common elements. Allison saw in the relationships of Enid and Ingmar the same thing she saw with Carlos and Cindy—a replay of her parents. Monique and her hiking partner appeared to have the kind of relationship Allison could not tolerate. Charles Reems probably tried to make advances on Allison and paid the price. As for Archie, he was her first victim, and he stood for everything Allison found abhorrent.

At present, they were in possession of three earrings and were aware of two more but did not have possession of them and were not likely to ever have possession. They had been lost. Van explained that the current thinking suggested Allison was now in the process of collecting the earrings and possibly returning them to the box in the Trabuco house.

He noted that an understanding of Allison had begun to emerge. Increasingly the evidence suggested that her mental state morphed as she went through various stages to the point where the original Allison A. Connors disappeared and was eventually replaced with the current a.k.a. of Lexi Talonis, although that was probably not her current name. Most likely, she had blended into the Eastern Sierra environment and was a typical citizen living under another alias.

Van stressed that everything pointed to her being psychotic. She was mad. He noted that Allison's extreme intelligence rendered her unique in that regard and not easily compared to the traditional qualities associated with psychotic behavior. Van cited some examples of Allison's behavior that set her apart. He also noted that all of this added up to someone who was both predictable and unpredictable.

Van then quickly reviewed the findings of evidence uncovered at the Trabuco house.

Vargas said, "So you think your suspect is living a sort of Jekyll-Hyde life and has melded into Owens Valley society and probably remains unnoticed. If so, that begs the question of how you're going to find her. I would like to think that what you have told me suggests she's like Whitey Bolger; she's hiding in plain sight."

Stenzgard spoke. "Lieutenant, she's there. It's not so much a matter of finding her as a matter of encouraging her eccentricities. She'll continue to act normal unless she perceives that the Mr. Hyde part of her needs to take action."

Eccentricities? Fenton and Van were staring at Stenzgard. They knew Stenz could be edifying, but his wording was unusual. He was waxing philosophical. The broad smile on the face of Vargas made it clear the lieutenant loved it. All of them knew enough not to interrupt.

"Van and his resources, including those two investigator wannabes who are older than me, have done a great job of isolating her persona. As Van can tell you, our suspect is in sort of a *return to the fold* mode." Stenz was giving Van an opening to pursue a key theory as yet undiscussed with the lieutenant. All eyes turned to Van.

Van took his cue. "Stenz is referencing the idea that has begun to emerge. We think a combination of factors have led her to begin moving toward some kind of closure to her career as a vengeance murderer. This first came to our attention gradually as we realized a substantial gap in Allison's homicide pattern. It seems possible there have been no disappearances or murders since the discovery in 1999. Quite possibly none since about 1990.

"Second, our suspect has a deep attachment to her mother and things associated with her mother, such as the earrings, books, and the home. The Owens Valley is another attachment. I have studied the comments written by Allison's mother that are found in several of the books recovered from the house. Though the actual wording seems harmless on the surface, it is clear that the books and stories have a common theme. They suggest the mother purposefully guided Allison's education and positioned her for the vengeful role evident in her psychopathic behavior after the mother's suicide. Many of the books are the classics you would want a brilliant student to read, though some do maintain a focus on the concept of vengeance.

"For the big picture, there's a kind of predictability in that we're fairly sure she's collecting the earrings and preparing to somehow return them to the house, to the jewelry box we found, even though she undoubtedly knows we have searched the house, took the box, and are watching the house. On the other hand, the devil is in the details. Her actions are also unpredictable. She may be psychotic, but she's not stupid. Allison is calculating. She knows we're on to her and probably has a good idea how close we are in finding her. It's not likely she'll drop her guard.

"Although she's capable of very aggressive, violent, and antisocial actions, she seems fascinatingly capable of controlling her behavior. Her motives and the madness of her actions are specific to her relationship with her mother and her perceptions about the relationship of her mother to the ex-husband and father, Archie Connors."

As he began to bring his comments to a close, Van relaxed and took a drink before he continued. "We think Allison lives somewhat of a normal life in the valley and the Sierra backcountry. For reasons only she understands, her killing days appear to be over. This may also be tied to her age; but from what we know, Allison remains strong, lithe, and quick on her feet. She is really capable of continuing as she has in the past but chooses not to do so."

Van turned to his final point. "I think Allison's mind-set has changed. She has become reflective, if that is possible for her kind of mind, and she's beginning to focus on a sort of full-circle closure if you will. Whether or not she's once again reinventing herself is uncertain. What is certain is that she knows she's not the woman of twenty or so years ago and knows she has to make some changes. Most importantly, Allison knows the motives of her earlier actions of vengeance are no longer operable. My discussions with others suggest that she may feel some sense of fulfillment and contentment with having achieved an intended goal. She has fulfilled her purpose and must now reach some form of closure."

With that, Van relaxed and leaned back in his chair.

The lieutenant said, "But what about the incidents where your two friends were followed by her? That doesn't sound like a retreat from her past ways."

"Actually, Pierce and James are convinced she wasn't trying to kill them. She had encountered them in the backcountry. Whether by accident or design, we don't know. They found what she wanted, an earring. She apparently tried to retrieve the earring but failed. When she encountered them again near Whitney Portal, she did nothing threatening. Both believe that had she wanted to harm them, she probably had ample opportunity on multiple occasions."

He thought about not making his next comment but then decided it was an interesting insight suggested by Dr. Ryan. "You know, guys, it sounds bizarre, but my sources may be right in suggesting that there's a certain level of respect for Pierce and James by Allison. They're her age, and they share her wanderlust approach to life and love of the Owens Valley and Sierra. She knows they abhor her behavior. She knows that they would not hesitate a second to see her apprehended and prosecuted. But she also knows that they have a certain respect for her independent nature and love of wandering. There's a certain kindred spirit. Strange, isn't it."

There was some quiet affirmation from the others.

Vargas showed disgust. "Damn, I know she's strange, and I sympathize with the idea of trying to find her in her own domain, but I just wonder if she isn't too smart for us."

Stenzgard offered a bit of advice in the way only he could do so. "Lieutenant, her type is crazy to begin with. When they take up the killing profession, they're even crazier. But she has been at this business for almost fifty years, and she's a master. She switched gears before, and she's doing it again. She's also smart. We'll get her, but not because we're smarter and not because she'll make a mistake. We'll find her when she wants us to find her and not before."

There was always some time for a bit of levity, and the lieutenant was not going to miss this opportunity. "Damn, Fenton, is this the same Stenzgard you keep touting as the department's own Colombo? He's too damned smart for the rest of us. He should be working upstairs with the thinkers and not down here where the work is done." Even Stenzgard laughed. It was another of his traits. He could laugh at himself and did not mind being the focus of humor.

The levity was essential to the team approach.

Fenton wanted to make sure the lieutenant understood that even though the team had an idea where things were headed, they were far from prepared for it. "Having talked about this a good deal, we're confident she knows we have discovered her house. But those are assumptions on our part given the time span since the search and our observations of her behavior patterns. If she can collect the earrings and return them to their place of origin, then she can say vengeance has been served. How she will do it is a big question."

There was a lull in the conversation. Vargas was jotting a note, and the others remained quiet until Van felt that since this was his case, he needed to speak.

"In a way, she'll retire. At least, given her age, she may not see a need to continue and perhaps has already planned to take her own life and join her mother whose ashes, it turns out, are probably scattered at the TC property." Van's comment caused everyone to look his way.

Vargas asked, "Her mother's ashes at the TC house? How do we know that?"

"It's a probability. Deena learned that the mother was cremated and Allison took possession of the ashes. By 1963, the home in Big Pine had fallen down and was replaced by a large barn on the property. Scattering ashes there was not probable. However, among the books we found in the TC house was a book of poems. One section included works by John Keats. In the space between two of Keats poems, "Ode on a Grecian Urn" and "Ode to Psyche," is a note underlined and circled." Van picked up his iPad. "The note says *Alexi, I want to stay at home. Keep me close where you can come to visit.* It isn't signed, but we assume it's the mother. On the inside cover of the book is a note to Alexi signed by her mother. It was a common practice with many of the books we found in the TC house. Since there was no body, just the ashes, the logical conclusion is the ashes are scattered at the TC site, thus providing reason to return home."

Vargas was clearly astounded. "Jeez. And you think you can find her before this so-called ending takes place? How?"

"Earrings ..."

"The ones in the jewelry box?"

Fenton answered. "No, we would like to lure her curiosity and interest in the style of earrings."

Van went on to explain the plan. "By marketing similar earrings. If we can find a good way to sell some earrings in Bishop that look very much like the ones her mother wore and which she has used, it's possible we can draw her out. She may not be able to pass up the chance to purchase them, or at least look closely at them. Or she may not want what she regards as imposters about. Hopefully the task of marketing will do the job."

"But how likely is she to visit a jewelry store?"

"Not likely. We wouldn't sell them there. Our idea is to have a very subtle display and sale of them at the monthly Crafts in the Park Fair that's held in Bishop during the spring, summer, and fall. It's a big deal in the town. Kind of place such earrings are sold. Allison is the kind of person who would visit that event, because it's community and something now in her comfort zone."

"And you think this will work?" asked Vargas.

"At this time, we don't have a better idea. We're hoping you will get the sheriff to contact her Inyo counterpart and help us put all of this in place for the upcoming season."

"Sounds like a stretch, but if that's all we have to go with now, I guess it's worth the try. I'll see what I can do. But first I need a full plan developed that I can share as a hard copy with the boss. She'll want to see it's well developed with a high probability of success. She'll also want to feel that it's a plan that won't embarrass the department should it not succeed. I need it in writing, ASAP."

Walking back toward their respective offices, Fenton spoke to Van and Stenzgard. "Van, I need you to plan on not being present at those craft fairs, at least in the beginning. This will be a cooperative effort with Inyo. We don't want to get in their way. When I talked with Bob Pagliano, he said the sheriff would be supportive but would also be reticent about outsiders getting too involved. With Pagliano helping put it all together, the Inyo department is not taken away from its own issues just to help us. Pagliano will work with you to make this go; however, I want you to make sure you keep me informed on every aspect of putting this thing in place."

"Not a problem, boss."

"Stenz, you're not involved in putting this together. If they get lucky in Inyo and turn up something, Van will be out of here for several days. If that happens, I'm going to request that you help Van with his cases if there is a problem. That okay with you?"

"Not a problem here."

—〰—

Working a case on another jurisdiction's turf is always challenging.

Once the two sheriffs agreed to a cooperative effort, the task of putting the operation in place was given to contact people, one in each department. The leverage was with Inyo because the operation would be on their turf and would be run by their people.

Van was the contact person for OC. His counterpart was a young investigator who had worked drug details and stings but had no experience of the type Van was proposing. Fortunately, the Inyo sheriff consented to permitting former sheriff, Bob Pagliano, to serve as liaison to the operation. The young Inyo County investigator knew a gift horse when he saw it and increasingly acquiesced to Pagliano's suggestions.

The big hurdle was determining whether to create a false vendor or to try to tag on to an existing one. Van was not a purist, but he was not keen on a nonprofessional on point with the sale of earrings meant to attract the attention of a suspect of Allison's talent. However, his counterpart in Inyo was a bit more informal and felt that if Allison was as skilled as Van contended, she would spot a fake a mile away. It would be better to let someone who sold on a regular basis hold down the fort.

Pagliano was a realist. He noted that if the plan was to be effective, they needed to be ready to wait several months for a response. The fair was on the second weekend of each month and ran from April through September. There was an additional weekend for Memorial Day in May and Labor Day in September.

Though Inyo had surveillance capabilities, they were already taxed on the craft fair weekends. Van agreed to provide additional equipment. This would be especially useful on the Memorial Day and Labor Day weekends when Inyo's equipment would be needed elsewhere in town. Memorial Day weekend was Bishop's local annual Mule Days celebration, and on Labor Day weekend, the city played host to the Tri-County Fair. Both weekends packed the town.

—⁓—

Setting up the craft fair plan was stressful for Van, and it was evident to others in the department. Just before the first weekend fair, Stenz paid Van a visit. Van had grown accustomed to the Stenzgard drop-in chats. He knew that Stenz was very experienced at what he did, and he welcomed the story approach to handing out advice.

"Van, you're good at what you do. You're a better-than-good investigator, even if your methods are a bit unconventional. However, putting this operation into place isn't about investigating. It's about *schmoozing*." As expected, Stenz flopped down in the vacant chair of Van's office. Van settled in to listen.

"Years ago, I was working a drug sales ring case in one of the exclusive areas of South County. You think there's good money in drug trafficking, you should see what happens to prices in the very upper-class neighborhoods. We're talking big money. Anyway, after working the case for a while, we realized that the drugs and money were flowing through a house on Coronado Island in San Diego. Now, if you know that area, you know that we're talking people who live in very expensive homes. They're not your typical drug traffickers, and they're not living in your typical drug-trafficking homes.

"We needed to work with San Diego PD. Of course, what we wanted was to conduct surveillance on some Coronado residences and try to pin down the house and its occupants. Well, yours truly was young and a bit impetuous and impatient. I think those are good words. My partner and our sergeant were experienced and much wiser and patient. They put together a plan that allowed SDPD to take the lead, even though SDPD wasn't really interested in our case. They had other issues on the burner, so our plan got second shift.

"My partner and my boss knew this. They knew that if it had

been their choice, they would have done things differently. Well, to make the story shorter, on the night we launched the operation, I got impatient and exceeded my authority. Not a lot, mind you, but enough that it could have compromised the whole thing.

"I'll never forget the sergeant. He located me on the island, told me to get into his car, drove down to a vacant beach on the extreme south end of the island, parked, and told me to get out. Then, where the world couldn't hear, he verbally reamed me so bad it almost actually hurt my ass. I will never forget the words, 'This case is not about you, Stenzgard. It's about those shits committing the crime. Our job is to catch them. When you put your ass ahead of SDPD in this operation, you're working for the badass, not us.' His final comment was, 'Damn it, grow up, Investigator.' He left me there alone, and I had to walk miles back to my car. Believe me, it was a long walk. When I got back, the operation was over.

"Van, we need Inyo. They don't need us. The best you can do is let them be in control and take all the glory. In the end, if we get Allison, you can take personal satisfaction. We all know what we're doing now wouldn't have happened if you hadn't taken over the case. If Inyo gets all the glory, so be it. You're close to this case. Don't get too close."

The input from Stenz was not unfamiliar to Van. Coming up through the system, deputies and investigators were reminded to be dispassionate about cases. *Work the case, don't let the case work you* was a common mantra. Stenz was well aware that he was not telling Van something new. Stenz was just doing what he needed to do, serve as an alter ego. It was something Stenz was very good at. He had that uncanny ability to find the appropriate moment to tell a story and convey a message.

—ɷ—

Everything was ready to go when the first Crafts in the Park Fair weekend of the year came round in April.

The first two weekends of the monthly fair in April and May sparked little interest in the earrings among attendees. A few people looked and handled the earrings, but they were usually much younger than seventy. Everyone who did stop by the booth was on camera, several cameras in fact, so there was a record. But as yet, there was no one who even came close to purchasing. Van was concerned and not sure the plan would accomplish what was intended. Pagliano kept reminding him that it could take several months to get results.

As Memorial Day weekend approached, Van was antsy and glad he had agreed to take some time off and drive to Bishop. Maybe being near the fair, if not actually involved in the operation, would make him feel more a part of things. He hated waiting in the wings.

CHAPTER 43

—ᴍᴍ—

MEMORIAL DAY WEEKEND

Bishop, California

MEMORIAL DAY WEEKEND was an annual celebration in Bishop. It was Mule Days, and thousands flocked to the city for a wide range of events that included the arts and crafts fair, a parade, activities at the tri-county fairgrounds, and a myriad of other events, including numerous pancake breakfasts and horseshoe contests. The mule was important in Owens Valley history because it was used extensively in building the Los Angeles Aqueduct and was the backbone of the backcountry packing industry. Mule Days was billed as the largest gathering of mules in the country, and past governors, television celebrities, war heroes, and others of note had led the annual parade as grand marshal.

For the tourist industry, Mule Days kicked off the summer season, and a good crowd was a financial shot in the arm for local business.

Sti and Rob were invited to stay with the retired sheriff. It was a real treat since the sheriff lived in one of the classic ranch houses in West Bishop. It was within walking distance of the town activities, and the two would not have to battle the crowds for parking rights.

Sti and Rob convinced Van to stay with Ellen and Harry Harker who owned a cabin in Aspendell. At eight thousand feet elevation, it was a small mountain community along Bishop Creek and about seventeen miles from Bishop, a twenty-minute drive. The Harkers were elderly and long-time friends of Sti and Rob. They loved having a guest to shuttle around to weekend events and to share their well-situated cabin. Should anything develop, Van would be readily available.

The weekend went well for Van, and he found the company of the Harkers to be informative but not demanding of attention. They let him enjoy both the uniqueness of Mule Days and the time to wander the gentle trails around their cabin.

But Van could not escape the reason he was there. Allison was somewhere near. He could only hope the earring trap would work.

As the weekend progressed, Van was dogged with the feeling that he was so close to Allison and yet so far away. No doubt she knew who he was, and in a haunting way, he sensed she would recognize him on sight. He, on the other hand, would not know if he was looking directly at Allison. A nagging thought was that she was watching him from among the crowd.

If she passed the booth where the earrings were on display, would she stop? Would she be drawn to the similarities, or would she see through the ruse? For Van, it was a necessary risk. Did Allison see the risk on her part, or was it a game for her?

From time to time as the weekend progressed, Van found himself thinking repeatedly, *Where are you? I know you're here. Do you know that I'm here?*

When Memorial Day wound down Monday afternoon, the vendors in the city park dismantled their booths, and in short order the park was vacant except for the trash and wear on the grounds.

There were volumes of surveillance data to review. There was also a general feeling among those assigned to monitor the designated booth that no one looking like any of the hypothetical drawings of an aged Allison had visited the booth. Women had come by and picked up and examined many of the items in the booth, including the earrings. But no one merited closer examination. Allison had not taken the bait. It looked like they had come up empty.

Tuesday morning found Sti and Rob joining Van and the Harkers for breakfast. The day was clear, beautiful, and warm. They all sat on the deck overlooking Bishop Creek and enjoyed postbreakfast coffee and tea. They were expecting Pagliano to join them at any time.

Van was quiet and seemed lost in thought. The holiday weekend had not gone as he wished. Though he had to admit that his hopes were probably too high. He had expected a breakthrough in finding Allison, but it did not happen. On the other hand, Van admitted to himself that he had a much better understanding of the Owens Valley culture and population. He also had a better understanding of the redeeming qualities of downtime in the Sierra. Working to avoid obsessing on the outcomes of the search for Allison, Van looked hard at the scene that stretched out below the cabin. Just on the other side of the small meadow, he could see glimpses of Bishop Creek as it made its way swiftly through the trees and shrubs along its bank. He thought he saw someone fishing, but the trees interrupted his view. *It's peaceful here*, he thought.

Van had indicated he would head home later in the day. If Pagliano brought any positive information regarding the search for Allison, Van would stick around as they considered the next step. Regardless, they all could tell Van was not the type to enjoy extended vacations. A couple of days away from the office, and he got antsy. He had not yet come under the full allure of the Eastern Sierra.

The sound of a diesel engine interrupted the interlude, and Ellen went to see who might have arrived. Pagliano drove a late-model SUV, and it would certainly not be him.

Ellen returned to the back deck a few minutes later carrying a FedEx box. "It was a delivery truck, Harry. Who in the world would send us a package from Bishop as overnight delivery?"

"Don't know, hon. Open it and find out."

Ellen went back into the cabin. A minute later she returned with the open box. "Strange!" She was holding a package and envelope. "There's a letter inside addressed to Investigator Vanarsdale."

Van was quick to his feet. His instincts took over. The years with the fed counterterrorism culture had nursed instincts and skills for just such occasions. The others were almost startled by his quick movement.

"Ellen, I want you to hand me the letter. Then I want you to set the package down here." He pointed to the small table next to his chair. "All of you, I want you to go back into the house immediately and stay well away from the windows. We don't know who this is from or what it is. Give me a couple of minutes to look all of this over before we go any further."

Once the others retreated to the cabin, Van took a deep breath and let his anxiety abate before taking action. His initial thought was focused on the package, but on second thought, the box was already open, so Van was confident it was not an explosive device. The fact that the letter was inside the box reinforced his thinking. Yet it was best to be safe.

Letter in hand, Van looked at the typed address. His training had taught him how to inspect a sealed envelope. He looked closely at the edges. He held it up to the light; it looked to be a multiple-page letter, nothing more. He rubbed his thumb across the entire surface. There was nothing inside but a letter. Turning the letter over to check the seal, he read the typed note on the back side. "*Not to worry, Investigator. That would not be my style. Also, you will not find any fingerprints on the letter, envelope, or items enclosed, so there is no need to exercise the normal protocols. It is important you read the letter before you go through the items in the box.*"

He could feel his heart pounding with anticipation. "It's her," he said to himself.

Van breathed deeply and let his body relax. It was a practice he had developed many years earlier when he learned that in his line of work there were moments of high drama when tension consumed him and could impair his thinking and actions should he not take control. A few seconds of self-calming effort, and Van knew he could move ahead.

Pulling out his small pocketknife, Van slit the letter at the bottom and looked carefully inside. There was only a folded multiple-page letter. He removed the letter and opened it. It was typed.

Raising his voice, Van said, "You can all come out now."

As they arrived back on the deck, Van was reading the letter. They remained quiet.

Aside, Van commented as he nodded toward Sti and Rob: "Letter is addressed to the two of you as well." Then he went back to reading. A couple of minutes later, Van handed the first page to Sti as he went on to the second page. And so it went as all three read the letter.

Investigator Vanarsdale, Dr. Pierce, and Mr. James:

I apologize for this informal introduction. Under other circumstances, I would have preferred to meet in person. But that is not possible. This personal letter and package will have to serve as a humble alternative.

Thank you, Investigator, for opening this letter. I know you were probably reluctant to do so, as it was addressed to you. However, since the package was opened without incident, I was pretty sure you would be willing to open the letter. As you can see, my intentions are purely personal, and there is nothing nefarious.

No doubt you all harbor a host of questions that surface upon receiving this letter and package. I shall do my best to answer some of them. However, on the chance that I do not, please accept my apology. It just means I was not as thorough in anticipating your inquiries.

Let me begin by acknowledging respect for each of you. Investigator, you are a worthy opponent and an honest one. I know you have a reputation for pursuing cases in an unorthodox way. Others could learn a lot from your approach. Sti and Rob, as friends commonly reference you, we have met on multiple occasions. On one occasion, it was in Bishop and only very informally and without your knowledge. On three other occasions, it was in the backcountry and just in passing. All four encounters were many years ago. The recent two encounters do not count. Both were rude on my part. Please accept my regrets.

As you no doubt have deduced, I have been living in the Eastern Sierra for many years. After leaving the OC, it was only natural that I should return to my roots. However, it was necessary to do so under another name, and I think you would agree that there has been some success with that effort. However, what you do not know is that there were three names.

I am telling you this because you will find out anyway. The first name was Mary Jo, and she has lived in a small one-bedroom and bath shack in Mammoth for about twenty-seven years where she has worked for the Mountain. No, not as a ski instructor or ski patrol member, which would have been nice but not practical. Rather, Mary Jo has been working on the night cleaning crew four days per week. You will find my identification enclosed, and I would appreciate it if you could convey to Mammoth Mountain personnel that I will not be returning next ski season. My keys are also enclosed.

The next name was that of a very elderly widow living in a rear-yard guest cottage not far from the center of Bishop. Ester has a fictitious son in nearby Nevada whom she visits quite often for days at a time, which accounts for her periods of absence. Ester is looked on fondly by the local church guilds.

The person you would have found most interesting to meet was Meredith, or Mar as colleagues call her. Mar works in records at the county court house in Independence. At one time, it was a three-days-per-week job, but with the struggling economy, it was cut to two days per week. For some that would have presented a problem, but Meredith has two other lives, and it actually helped her. She lives in a nice rental off Line Street in Bishop. I have included her county employee ID card as well as her keys.

When you find each of these sites, you will find them neat and void of anything valuable regarding my case. What you need is enclosed. I have cleaned the three dwellings well, and I left money for the owners of each. They will want to clean before renting, and the funds will help with that.

You can see that it was not necessary to hide. One can actually hide best among people. Multiple identities keeps one busy, and boredom is not an option if one is intent on maintaining anonymity. There were a few times when the lives of two crossed and there was a risk of exposure, but as time went on, I became better and better at balancing three lives.

Of course, there was always the Sierra. Mary Jo did not work outside of ski season, so that left more time for trips into the backcountry. I am not telling you anything new by noting that I have been able to travel the Sierra Nevada at will. To this day I can disappear into the backcountry with ease and have access to numerous caches of food and equipment. You could drop me off naked anywhere in the Sierra, and I would be fully clothed, equipped, and fed within hours.

Obviously you now know how it is that I seemed to have some idea of Sti's and Rob's movements, not to mention my knowledge that the three of you would be at the Harker mountain cabin this Memorial Day weekend. You see, even though Mar works only two days per week, she has access to the county computer network, which means access to calendars and emails, without permission, of course.

I know you also have some questions about the JMT disappearances and deaths. Enclosed you will find a small journal. Beginning with the years following my mother's death, I have documented every act of reckoning. With the exception of the beast, my father, you will find details regarding why I am responsible for the deaths of nine other people. I will not take the time to discuss those here. Let's just say each is justified, but the more complete rationale is contained in the journal.

Discussion of the murders brings us to the earrings. The answer is yes; I left earrings with each death as contrition to my mom. The beast, a most despicable and evil man, victimized her. He made a slave of her and drove her to an early death. But you all know she was also very smart. I am testimony to her brilliance. On the day I spread her ashes on the soil of her house in Trabuco Canyon, I vowed that should I ever see anyone else whose relationship stood to end up like that of my mother and the beast, I would put them out of their misery. Their mistakes would not be passed to offspring.

I had thought that Cindy's remains would not be found for fifty years. But it is just as well they were found after twenty-seven years. I realized then that it was time to end my endeavors on behalf of my mother. So, as you know, I began to retrieve each earring so that I could bring closure by returning them to the wooden box you now have in evidence.

I knew that I could not get the earrings left with Carlos and Cindy, but I felt sure that I could retrieve the others. I was not counting on Sti and Rob, so I have come up short. However, you will find enclosed the two from my father's bed, one from a couple buried near Charlotte Lake, one from the girl found in the Kern, and the earring left with Charles Reems. You have the one from the Baxter Creek couple. There is one that I have not been able to retrieve, and it will probably be some years before that earring comes to light, if ever. I also have one that I have not enclosed. You will get it soon enough.

I know the enclosed earrings are evidence, but I think it best they be added to the ones you now have in the wooden box. That is where they belong.

As a side note, I did see the earrings at the craft fair in Bishop in April and May. I am sure the surveillance cameras reflect that I did not pick them up. It was a good idea on your part, but I noticed quickly they were lookalikes. Sorry, boys.

Oh, before I forget. As I noted on the envelope, there are no fingerprints on the package items or letter. Of course, you already knew that or you would not have read the letter.

In closing, I have included three other items in this package.

To you, Investigator, I leave my personal copy of *Hamlet*. You will note it is very old. It was printed in London in 1770 and is valuable. Take care of it. Most people would find it fitting that I say *Hamlet* is one of the great works of literature. But I assure you my preference is not based on Hamlet's madness. It is based on my belief that Hamlet speaks for all of us when we find ourselves trying to understand things in life that "puzzle the will."

Dr. Pierce, I know your love of books and writing. I have read your articles and books. You will find enclosed a first-edition signed copy of Robert Pirsig's

Zen and the Art of Motorcycle Maintenance. It is one of the best works of the twentieth century and one of which I know you are fond.

Mr. James, I am well aware of your love of cycling and skiing. I once observed you telemarking at Mammoth and I was much impressed. Enclosed you will find an original opening-day ticket for Mammoth Mountain. You will note Dave McCoy has signed it. I assure you, it was not stolen. I have owned it for many years.

In closing, let me assure you that Allison A. Connors died long ago, and Lexi Talonis will cease to exist with the ending of this letter. It is not likely any of you shall ever see me again. You already know that if I wish to remain beyond reach, I can do so. That will be the case for the future.

For now, to quote one of the American greats, it is time to go. "I have other lives to live and have spent quite enough time at this one."

The best of life and love to each of you,
The former Lexi Talonis.

Having finished reading, Van let Sti and Rob do so while he picked up his cup of coffee and walked to the edge of the deck and stared off toward the creek. He could no longer see the person he saw fishing earlier. Soon he turned to face the others. "That final quote about other lives to live, who is that from?"

Sti responded, "Thoreau. Near the end of *Walden,* Thoreau, having extolled the virtues of living in the woods, answers the question he knows all will ask. They will want to know why he left the woods if it was paradise. She has modified the quote a bit, but the meaning is the same."

More to himself, Van mused, "She's telling us she's leaving to pursue yet another life, another lie, if you will. She has lived here for decades as three different people. No one noticed. Now she's going

somewhere else. Given her skill, she'll make it work again. Hmm."
Van sipped his coffee. "We came so close. And now she's gone."

Van walked back to the table and looked again at the letter. Then
he picked up the box and unfolded the bubble wrap. Inside he found
a small plastic container with earrings. Each had a small tag attached,
identifying the victim or victims with which it was associated. Inside
a separate envelope, there were two personal ID tags. One was a
court house issue. The other was for Mammoth Mountain. Both had
photos, and both photos were different. Picking them up, Van looked
at the faces, and there was no sign of the Allison he knew from a 1968
photo or the computer renderings of an aged Allison.

Van also noted the names on the IDs. They were consistent with
her information in the letter.

There was a key ring with three keys. They were probably the keys
to the three places she had lived. There were two other sets of keys
with each labeled to note whether they were for county offices or for
Mammoth Mountain purposes.

At the bottom of the box were three books and a plastic container
like the ones baseball card collectors use. The signed Mammoth
Mountain ticket was inside the plastic container. Van picked up the
four items.

He handed the ticket to James. "I wonder how she got that. It's in
good condition."

He then looked at the first edition of Pirsig's book. "Never read
this book. If it is what she claims it to be, I guess I should at some
point." He handed it over to Sti.

Looking at the old leather-bound copy of *Hamlet*, Van seemed
reluctant to open it. He held it and stared at it as he looked it over.
Then, to no one in particular, he said, "Years ago, as a kid, I went
to the home of my uncle after his graveside service. Most of the
people were adults, so I just wandered around the house looking for
something to do. My uncle loved photography and had a collection
of cameras in his study. I was looking at them and picked up one that
looked old. I thought it looked funny. My aunt came in, and she told
me that my uncle had used all the cameras. Then she said the one I

was holding was the first camera he had owned. She pointed to an old black-and-white photo of my aunt on the desk. She said he had taken the photo with the camera I was holding. You know, it was strange. I remember feeling like I was holding a piece of my uncle in my hand. It was like he was there, in my hand. I still have the camera. It's my lasting connection with him.

"I kind of feel like that now. This book is the mind of Allison. If I want to really understand her, I need to read this book. Not another book of *Hamlet* but this book. Strange, isn't it?"

There were nods from the others.

Then Van picked up the journal. It was black and very worn. "In a way, I don't want to read this. Strange, holding *Hamlet* in one hand and this journal in the other. I doubt even Shakespeare could imagine the horrors between the covers of this journal. Ironic." Van replaced the journal in the box. "I shall wait until a better time to open it and read."

To Sti and Rob, Van commented. "Gentlemen, I'm afraid you're both holding evidence. I must ask you to put the items back in the box. I will turn this all over to my people when I get back to OC. The letter too is evidence, but I would like to make a couple of photocopies. Harry, is there somewhere that I can make photocopies?"

"Certainly. My study has an all-in-one printer/copier. We can use it."

"Thanks. Pagliano should be here soon. If you would just put the original back in the envelope when you're done, Harry, I would appreciate it."

Van took a sip of coffee. "I think I'll take a walk. I won't go far so tell Pagliano I should be back shortly. Just need some time to think."

Minutes later, Van was walking along the path that crossed the meadow and intercepted the creek downslope from the cabin. There seemed to be no purpose; he was just wandering.

CHAPTER 44

—⦿—

AFTERMATH

Aspendell, Owens Valley, and Orange County

V AN'S WALK TOOK him downstream along the North Fork of
Bishop Creek as it wound its way through the trees and the
scattered cabins of Aspendell. There were some upscale homes,
but most of the dwellings were fifty years old or more and better
described as cabins. There were a few full-time residents. The rest
of the places were used primarily in the nonwinter months. Access
during the winter was a function of weather. Though even in the
winter the small community, with its isolation and beauty, had an
appeal to those interested in avoiding the complexities of a mountain
dwelling near a ski resort.

Van nodded to a young boy fishing, and then he noticed the
boy's father several yards downstream. As a youngster, Van had liked
fishing, but his father died when Van was in seventh grade, and he
never had the opportunity to fish again. It occurred to him that
there was a certain therapy to fishing, and time both stood still and
flew by. It was a strange paradox that Van had only experienced for
a short time.

From a distance, he watched the boy and his father fish for a
while and noticed how the two seemed to be on the same page in
what they were doing and without needing to talk above the noise
of the stream. The swift water seemed menacing, but the father was

obviously confident his son knew what to do. Father and son fishing defined the saying about a chip off the old block.

There was a certain regret in the observation. Van's son was now in his thirties. They had done things together, Little League mostly. They had tried Scouts, but it did not work. They should have fished more. You can have fun even when you do not catch anything.

It occurred to Van that investigating crimes was like fishing. You tried to read the evidence and catch the bad guy. In fishing, you read the water. In both cases, the bait or lure became important. If you played it right, you could hook one; if not, you went home empty. The difference seemed to be that in fishing, one could go home empty and call it a good day.

If you were fishing for big fish, Van thought the game probably took on different meaning. The quality of equipment and the skill of the fisherman were probably critical. He wondered if stealth became important. He knew some fishermen might even have to wade into the very water where the fish were located. Did that mean only the crafty were successful in bringing home the hard-to-catch fish? He smiled at his own insight; sometimes fishing required undercover work in the water.

The irony of the weekend was evident, and Van had to smile. *Went fishing for Allison and was skunked.* He shook his head and wandered on.

Van began to move further down the stream when he heard the loud "Dad!" and he glanced back to see the boy's pole bent and the father holding the net as his son reeled in a fish. When the fish had been landed, the smiles of the boy and the father were soundless communication that carried volumes of information. Then the father knelt down and released the fish, and father and son stood and prepared for the next fish. There had been a moment of elation; they would try for more moments.

Van was aware of the implications for his line of work. That was the difference between fishing and catching criminals. For the fisherman, the thrill is in the hunt and the catch; then he can let the fish go if he wishes, before going on to do it all again. A day of successful fishing could be a day of repeated hunt, catch, and release cycles. For Van, a day of work seldom resulted in success. And when he did manage a catch, there was no release. No, when there was a catch, regardless of how much work went into it and regardless of how much time it took, the real work began. It was catch and convict.

Walking back to the Harker cabin, Van was aware just how refreshing it was in Aspendell, and he thought that this would be a good place to come and get away from it all. He could even take up fishing again. He would like that.

—⁓—

Pagliano had arrived in Van's absence. He had read the letter and was on the deck with the others. It was a gorgeous day, and sitting outside was preferable. They watched as Van made his way up the path to the cabin.

Coming up the steps, Van sensed his friends were awaiting his thoughts. He looked up as he mounted the final step. "I guess it's like fishing," he said. "Some days you catch 'em, and some days you get skunked. I would have liked to catch that big one in the pond, but it was not to be."

"Van, I've seen some strange cases in my day, but this beats them all." Pagliano was shaking his head.

Sti, Rob, and the Harkers just listened. The two professionals carried on a conversation for a several minutes before Van turned to the Harkers.

"You have a great place here. I watched a boy and father fishing down there. There was a peace that seemed to prevail in their world along the stream. It made me remember how much I loved fishing and spending time with my father as a boy. I haven't thought about that part of my life for years. Tragedy nudged me to push it aside because it hurt too much after my father died.

"But now I see that I should have really embraced it." There was a pause as Van considered a question. "I was wondering, would it be possible for me to stay here a couple days? I have lots of vacation time that has to be used or I lose it. But more importantly, I need some time to unwind. As my partner in the office keeps reminding me, I tend to take my cases very seriously, too seriously sometimes. This case has been one of those. I need to get some time away before going back to the office to wrap things up. I might even try fishing again."

Harry responded enthusiastically. "Absolutely! You can purchase a license up the road at Cardinal Lodge, and we have all the equipment you would need to fish. The place is yours. We could not be happier to be your host."

"Well, I will need this afternoon to make some calls to my sergeant and to my partner." Pointing to the package, he said, "Some of this stuff is evidence that I'll have to take back with me along with perhaps some surveillance tape duplicates if our suspect shows up in any of it, though from the sounds of the letter, I doubt we'll find anything."

Pagliano said, "What about those house keys? The department will want to start searching for the three locations, and it looks like those keys may make it possible to avoid forced entry."

Van reached into the box and pulled out the keys. "These won't do us any good." He handed them to Pagliano. "I would just like to have a look inside the three places if you find them over the next several days while I'm here. Also, you have a photocopy of the letter. It may be of use as you search. No doubt Brenda Robertson up at Mammoth will want in on the act as well since it sounds like one of the places Allison lived is up there."

"I'll talk with Brenda, and I'm sure the sheriff will welcome your preview of any facilities we find. He'll be more focused on Meredith's role as a county employee." Pagliano knew the county employee revelation would shake things up in the department. He had a vague memory of her but could not remember ever really interacting with her.

Van picked up the books and looked through them quickly. "The journal is going to be a gold mine, and since it was sent to us, I need to take it back with me, Bob. However, I know my people will make copies of it, and I will send you and Inyo SD copies."

"Thanks. I'll let the sheriff know."

Turning to Rob and Sti, he said, "I'm not sure what will happen with the Mammoth Mountain ticket or the motorcycle maintenance book, but rest assured I'll take the position that they're your property as gifts. But I must take them back with me for the time being."

Rob said, "No problem. It is what it is."

"I'll let you know." Van picked up the work of *Hamlet*. "I know that I will be spending a great deal of time with the contents of the journal, but it's this work of Shakespeare that intrigues me the most. Haven't read *Hamlet* since college and really don't remember it. But as I said before, in these pages is the thinking of Allison Connors as a young woman and Lexi Talonis as a grown and older lady. It may be evidence, but it's evidence that I'm going to spend considerable time studying."

A lover of books, Sti found Van's interest in *Hamlet* interesting. "Perhaps none of Shakespeare's works has been more analyzed or oft quoted as *Hamlet*. If I'm not mistaken, Allison has quoted *Hamlet* in her letter when she suggests Hamlet speaks for all in saying our search for understanding 'puzzles the will.' I think it's from Hamlet's famous *to be or not to be* soliloquy. It makes me wonder whether Allison sees herself in Hamlet's thinking or finds Hamlet providing a rationale for her thinking."

Harry was wondering along similar lines. "Or, it could be that young Allison started out as a student of Hamlet's logic and ended up as Lexi thinking like Hamlet. Either way, it's clear that Shakespeare provides a road into the backwoods of her mind. I can only imagine the complexity of such a person."

To Van, the discussion was refreshing. He had long held to the belief that the classics contained the great lessons of life. Perhaps it was not an accident that he had been handed the Ashae case. The task of finding Allison somehow required a certain understanding of, if not devotion to, the liberal arts. Patel, Ryan, Sti and Rob, the Harkers, and even Stenzgard seemed to lend support to that idea. As for his own perspective, Van could not help but think of his adversary as a conundrum. She was brilliant and could have been a great researcher and teacher. But she was also mad. She was testimony to the idea that interpretation and perception ruled the potential of literature and the arts. Such sources could guide the moral and immoral alike.

—m—

Van and Pagliano took leave of the others to discuss shutting down the joint operation.

Later, Pagliano called the sheriff. He knew the information he would be sharing would result in immediate activity in the department. He also knew that if it had not been for the joint operation with OCSD, the reality of an inside source working for the county would probably not have come to anyone's attention soon, if ever. Nevertheless, the proverbial shit was about to hit the fan. Pagliano knew his role on the sidelines was about to change.

Van got ahold of Sergeant Fenton, and they worked through the process of terminating the surveillance and subsequent review of the tapes from the long weekend. Fenton, in turn, would talk with Vargas.

As a courtesy, Van shared the nature of evidence received in the FedEx package with Pagliano. However, it was agreed that keys, ID tags, and a copy of the letter were the important items for ICSD. The original letter and remaining items in the package would go to OC as evidence. Copies of the contents would be made available to ICSD later.

ICSD would move forward immediately to locate the two residences in the Bishop area, and they would contact Mammoth Lakes Police regarding the alleged residence there. They would also turn over the keys from Mammoth Mountain to the police. Brenda could take care of contacting Mammoth Mountain personnel. She would also look into whether the signed ticket was real and whether it may have been stolen.

When the joint discussion was completed, Bob Pagliano bid goodbye to the others and headed down toward Bishop before going on to the sheriff's department in Independence.

Later Van took a call from Fenton, and the two reviewed the

briefing he and Fenton would give to the lieutenant on a conference call later in the day. Van also asked for a couple of days off before he returned to the office. The sergeant told him there was no problem, especially since Van may have access to one or more of Allison's nearby residences. Then they talked generally about Van's take on the letter and how best to proceed with the evidence.

"Sarge, I think it would be a good idea for the next several days to have a detail keep a close eye on the TC house. Maybe even ask that older couple, the ones who are semipermanent residents, to keep their eyes open and let the department know if they see anyone at the house or in the area. I don't think anything will happen, but best to be safe."

"Okay. You think she could be headed down here?"

"No, she would assume we would be on the alert. If the letter is taken literally, it would seem that she's relocating out of the Eastern Sierra. My guess is that she wants to remain in close contact with the Sierra and will relocate to the west side, the Central Valley perhaps."

"Listen, Van, I know this hasn't worked as you had hoped, but you got too close for her comfort, and that put her on the run. She's crazy and unpredictable, but I would wager that she will slip up somewhere along the line. She blended into the Eastern Sierra culture because she was familiar with it. We don't know yet whether she'll be successful elsewhere. If nothing else, you have helped ICSD learn about someone who was a liability for them."

"I know, boss, and at least her journal will give us considerable work to do."

"You have taken this case farther than anyone here dreamed possible and in doing so answered a lot of questions. For some of the victims' families, there is now some closure, something that they have not had for decades."

"Thanks, Sarge. I'm going to go now and take another walk. I have found walking here is good for the soul. I will call tomorrow and be back in the office by late Thursday."

"Take your time, Van. You've earned it."

—⁓—

The remainder of Van's day was filled with walking and thinking. He had gotten directions from Harry and walked the mile up to Cardinal Lodge where he purchased a fishing license and had a casual conversation with a couple of teenagers who had caught their limit on the creek that day. They gave Van some tips about fishing the creek and told him to not worry about getting an early-morning start.

"These fish are stock, man," said one boy. "They don't act like native trout. Best to wait 'til about 10:00 a.m. and then fish a few hours. Go back in the evening. That's what we're doing."

"What are you guys using for bait?"

"Everything—worms, eggs, cheese. They all work."

"What about lures?"

"Naw, those have the treble hooks, and it's too easy to get snagged. Water's moving fast, and you can't control where the thing goes. Naw, don't use a lure, man. Go with a sure thing."

"Yeah, and look for the little eddies. You know, those are little pools, and the trout sit in there, you know."

"Yeah, like behind rocks. If you see a big rock in the stream, the fish will stay on the downstream side. Let your bait float down and around the rock. You'll hook 'em every time, you know what I mean?"

The kids were enthusiastic. They talked like pros, although their vernacular left something to be desired. Van had no idea who they were or whether they were really providing valuable information, but he did know they were having fun. *Kids, they're so transparent.* It reminded him of the old Flip Wilson line, "What you see is what you get."

Leaving the boys and heading back to the Harker cabin, it occurred to Van that Cindy and Carlos were about the same age as the two boys when they disappeared. Were they like those two boys—enthusiastic, talkative, matter-of-fact, self-appointed experts on fun? If they were, Allison had ended it all. Surely the two boys he had just talked with were not without their faults, as was also the case with Cindy and Carlos. But the two boys would have a chance to grow through those difficulties and learn and become adults for good or bad. Cindy and Carlos never had that chance.

Looking at jars of bait and the box of worms he had purchased, Van knew the boys were right. One had to read the river, try various kinds of bait, and keep at it. Accept the fact that the prey behaves differently than you think. Best to go after them on their own terms.

Yet again, Van found his thoughts of fishing finding an inroad to his reflections about Allison. He had tried to go after her on her own turf. She managed to read his intent and avoid. But she was no ordinary fish; she was older and experienced at avoiding capture.

He thought too about the earrings. There were too many earrings in the box, and those in the box did not account for all of the earrings there were. Each earring represented a life fished out of the water before its time. Van could not let Allison, or Lexi, or whatever she would choose to use as a name, feed at will and not pay the consequences. He would find her. Progress might be slow, but he would find her.

He had to keep fishing.

—⟋⟍—

Two days later, Van drove south to the town of Lone Pine. He had left Aspendell at seven in the morning and made several stops along the way to see sights suggested by Sti and Rob. *They aren't even residents of the Eastern Sierra, and yet they could sell the area at a travel show better than any native.* He had stopped at the Paiute Indian Visitor Center, Keough Hot Springs, Manzanar National Monument, the cemetery for victims of the 1872 earthquake, the Alabama hills, and a couple of spots along the aqueduct. His next stop was the Movie Museum and then the Interagency Visitor Center at the south end of town. Then it would be a long drive to OC.

It was just after midday, and Van was eating a snack at the

McDonald's next to the Movie Museum. As he did so, his thoughts drifted back to Aspendell.

Yesterday he had spent several hours fishing along the river. He did not "kill 'em" as the boys had, but then he really did not care. He was just enjoying fishing. He caught three. One he released. The other two swallowed the hook, and he had to keep them. He would have to learn how to set the hook when fishing so that he could just catch and release with consistency.

Ellen Harker fixed a big meal in the evening and invited Sti and Rob to join them. She cooked the two trout as well, and Van ate his first stream trout since he was a young boy.

After dinner, in the twilight, Sti and Rob accompanied him on a walk around the Aspendell loop road.

Passing two boys, Van greeted them, and they responded with a greeting as well. "Hey, man, like how'd you do today? We killed 'em."

"I caught a couple. Thanks for the tips." The boys walked on.

"Friends of yours?" asked Rob.

"A couple of kids I talked to yesterday. Gave me some great fishing tips. As you can see, real professionals."

They laughed.

"I owe the two of you a big thanks."

"You don't owe us anything. It was our pleasure. As Rob likes to say, *it keeps us out of trouble.*"

"I know, but the two of you are different, not odd but different in that you seem to enjoy the challenge of finding out by doing rather than talking. I've noticed that you tell people you're just wandering, but in reality it's not a willy-nilly approach. You sort of wander with a method."

It was a philosophy Sti and Rob had shared with many others over the years. Not surprisingly, Sti picked up the initial response. "We like to call it purposeful wandering. For us, that means wandering is an art form and not an unconscious endeavor. I have often likened it to chaos theory. On the surface, much of what happens in nature looks to be random and chaotic. But below the surface, a close examination reveals an intricate infrastructure, a purpose."

Rob chuckled. "See what happens, Van, when you give Sti the pulpit? He reverts to his professorial roots and begins to lecture."

"Give me a break."

Van laughed. "You always say that."

"And he says much more. Too much! Sti has a laundry list of phrases he invokes in conversations, as if they provide some closure, when in fact they exacerbate circumstances. But seriously, our approach to wandering is to poke around with an open mind on the one hand and purpose on the other. It's a delicate balance, and it often leads to some interesting discoveries."

Van was not in the mood for extended repartee, and he sought an end. "Anyway, I do appreciate all you've done to assist me. I have your email addresses and your phone numbers as well as home addresses and will keep you advised of any progress. Needless to say, this case is not like any other I have worked. I don't know if it will ever be completed, but I do intend to stay on it. It may be that I will need your services again, and if I do, I hope you're available."

The walk ended, and Sti and Rob said their goodbyes to Van and to the Harkers. Van walked with the two out to Rob's big Bronco. They shook hands and parted.

As they drove away Van thought, *I inherit the Ashae case, and it takes me into a new world and new friendships. Before then, the Eastern Sierra and Owens Valley weren't even on my radar. People like the Harkers and Pagliano were the kind of friends others had. And Sti and Rob, well they redefined retirement and friendship. And I never would have fished again.*

—⁂—

Van finished his iced tea and began walking to the Movie Museum. It was hot, but that was the Owens Valley in summer. Like all the buildings here, it would be cool inside the museum.

His cell phone rang, and he glanced at the number. It was Sergeant Fenton.

"Sarge, what's up?" He sounded like one of those teenage boys.

"Van, where are you? Still in Bishop?"

"No, no, I'm in Lone Pine and headed home."

"Well, your case is on again."

"Are we talking the Ashae case?"

"Yep. Listen, I know you've a three-hour drive ahead, but stop by the office. I'll be here."

The *why* hung in the air like a heavy storm cloud. "Are you going to tell me what's happening?"

"I just got off the phone with the Cleveland National Forest fire chief. Last night they were called to a fire where the VW was burned back in '72. When they got there, it was a VW van fully engulfed in flames. It had been burning very hot for some time. They got it under control. And later this morning, they took a closer look at it. They noted the VIN and traced it. They saw it had a red flag on it, and you're the contact person."

"It couldn't be Allison's old VW can could it? That thing is old."

"It is. It has one of those fiberglass pop-tops and the tire mounted on the front. It's all burned to a crisp. And so is the body inside."

"Body?" The term was like a shock to his system. "Do we know whose?"

"No, forensics is out there now. Claudia said it will take some time. There's not much left. She has nothing to go on yet. I asked her to put it at the top of the list, and she said she would."

"Who could it be?" The frantic wonder was evident in Van's voice. "Allison?"

"But her letter. Her intentions. I can't imagine. Doesn't make sense. She would have gone home to do it."

"There's one other thing, Van. Claudia found one of those burn-proof file boxes beneath the van. It's locked, but a key was sitting on top."

"Jeez ..."

"There's more. Deeply etched into the top of the box is your name. It's intended for you. I have Claudia's people bringing the box here.

I'm going to have it put in your office along with the key. When you get here, we'll take a look."

"And your money is on Allison as the victim?"

"Afraid so."

CHAPTER 45

———✺———

COMING FULL CIRCLE

BEFORE REACHING THE outskirts of Orange County, Van called Sergeant Fenton to tell him he was going to stop at the old catering site first. He wanted to see the burned Vanagon before it was removed. Fenton said he would meet Van there.

As he rolled up to the entrance to the site off Santiago Canyon Road, he lowered the window to provide identification, but the deputy recognized Van and waved him through. Anxious as he was to get to the catering site, Van took the recognition as a signal that he was becoming known among deputies outside downtown. *That's good,* he thought.

Fenton was already on site and talking with a forensic tech. Two other deputies posted at the site stood by. There was a Forest Service truck, and its occupant was doing paperwork.

Van just stared at the burned-out vehicle. First impressions were important, and the first impression was that the Vanagon was parked exactly where the '72 VW had been parked, exactly! It was not an accident. He was looking at the work of Allison. Any other conclusion was not possible.

Van shook hands with Fenton. A second tech was conducting some work on the van, and a third tech was taking photos. The body had been removed and transported.

A flatbed tow truck stood off to the side. The truck was owned by the department. When the techs completed their work, the van would be transported to an impound yard for further study.

"Claudia said these folks will be done shortly. We want the van out of here before dark." Fenton was pointing to debris scattered about. "Forestry says that it was an especially hot fire when they got here, and it took some time to get it out. The things scattered about aren't from any explosion, just the result of trying to put the fire out, they said."

"When was it called in?"

"Called in by a driver on Santiago Canyon at 2:37 a.m. Driver said it was like a ball of fire when he saw it. Forestry says it had probably already been burning for several minutes when the driver noticed it. By the time the Forest Service and a nearby unit from Orange got here, the van was pretty much destroyed."

"Claudia say anything about her observations?"

"She said that tests would probably reveal that an accelerant and chemical boosters were used to ensure the fire was thorough and intense. She said there was no explosion."

"Just like 1972. Tank was drained to reduce explosion effect, and nothing was left to chance."

"Yep, looks like Allison's work."

"Claudia give you anything on the body identification?"

"I asked her if she thought it was male or female, and she said that there was just no way of knowing at this time. I think her words were 'it's beyond burnt toast.'"

"Sounds like her. Anything besides the box recovered?"

"Just the set of keys. They were laying on top of the box."

Van walked around what had been a 1968 VW. He could not recall a vehicle involved in a fire that was as destroyed as this one.

"If Allison is here it seems likely she stored it nearby. Can't imagine she drove it from Bishop or Mammoth." *It's perplexing,* thought Van. "Then again, maybe she did. She's different."

The inside was a mess, and Van recalled that this kind of VW camper did not have a middle seat. It was a camper package with a rear seat that folded down into a bed. The interior pieces were made of wood and plastic. It was all obliterated. There was nothing left to define the prior state of things inside. The pop-up top was gone, melted, and the top was open to the sky.

"Where was the body?"

"Laying on what had been the bed. It burned to the floor, and everything around it melted as it burned. Claudia said it was ghastly."

"The box is at HQ?"

"Yeah, it's in your office along with the keys. I told Deena to keep your office locked and allow no one to enter without my authorization."

"Thanks, I've seen enough here."

Walking back to their cars, Van paused a second and looked back at the van. Then he looked off toward the northeast and then back at the van. "Sarge, I'll meet you back at HQ. I want to check something out first."

"Need any help?"

"No, but you're welcome to follow. I want to get the binoculars first."

Binoculars in hand, Van started walking east and then a bit to the north and up a steep slope. After a couple hundred yards, he stopped. Fenton followed.

"Man, I'm out of shape, Van. Doesn't this bother you? You're not much younger than me."

"I've been walking at eight thousand feet for the past week. Acclimatized a bit I guess." Van made a mental note. *Another reason to get a place in the Eastern Sierra. Good exercise.* He began scanning the area to the east and south of the burned van.

"What are you looking for?"

"Don't know. Just a hunch I guess …"

Fenton let him look.

"Sarge, take a look." He handed the binoculars over and then pointed down the slope. "See that old fence down there by what looks to be an old water trough for stock? Follow the fence to the east about to where the open space surrounding the catering area ends. At that point, you're about a hundred yards from the van. You can see a steel post sticking up just where the dense sage and other shrubs start. See it?"

"Give me a second. Yes, I'm following the fence. Okay, there's the steel post. It's rusted and has what looks like a small sign on it."

"Yes."

"Mmm. What about it?"

"You can't read the sign, but it says No Trespassing—Private Property. Lots of bullet holes in the sign. Pretty much the norm for signs out here."

Then, as if pointing and describing a post immediately in front of him, Van went on. "Now look below the sign on the steel post. Do you see a blue cloth or something tied around it near the bottom?"

"Yeah, I got it."

"Remember the cloth. Now, you can just make out a small path leading east from that post. Can you see it?"

"I think so. Hard to tell it's a path from here. Too many shadows."

"It's there. Now follow that path if you can for about two hundred yards, and it eventually runs into what looks like an old dirt road that goes off to the east and then begins to turn southeast about a quarter mile away."

"Yea, I think I can see all of that. What about it?"

"Follow me."

They walked back down toward the site of the VW. Once there, Van walked over toward the steel post. He stopped about five feet from the post and held out his arm to stop Fenton. "How recent does that blue cloth look to you?"

"Like it was torn from something and tied here today. It's not faded at all."

"Good observation, Sarge. No wonder they put you in charge of us." Van was smiling. It was more than a smile at Fenton's expense. It was a smile sparked by what had been discovered. That kind of humor was not his forte, but Stenz, Rob, and Sti had been rubbing off on him. He turned to Fenton.

"Sarge, yesterday I accompanied Pagliano to a small guesthouse on the outskirts of Bishop. It was found by investigators in the early morning. It was one of Allison's two residences in Bishop. They had not yet located the other. Anyway, they let me look around before they started their search. The tablecloth on a small table in the one room house was blue. Clearly visible to anyone entering that house was the fact that a piece of cloth, one full side of the tablecloth, had been torn off recently. If the tablecloth was about four feet square, then a piece a foot wide by four feet long was ripped from it. It was one of the first things I noticed."

"And you think this is a piece?"

"I know it is. I also know there's more somewhere. There are probably several pieces about the same size as this one. They're all torn from that one-by-four piece."

"Okay, you're going somewhere with this. Where?"

"I'm guessing that if we follow this path and link up with that old dirt road and follow it southeast, we will eventually find another piece of cloth marking where a trail or another dirt road departs. Following a string of these pieces of cloth, we would eventually find ourselves at the Trabuco house."

"That far? Holy crap."

"Allison is telling us how she got from here to the house in 1972."

"Unbelievable! What made you think to look for this?"

"Just a hunch. Ever since we discovered the TC house, Allison has been answering questions. The letter was a big question-and-answer session. I think the box will be another."

"And she knew this has been one of your questions."

"I think so."

"You're not going to follow it, are you?"

"Nope, I'm not, but I know a couple of people who will and who will document it well."

"Your two wanderers?"

"Yep. Let's head downtown."

"You know, Van, if that body is Allison, you have solved a very cold case."

"I don't know just how much I have solved yet."

"Let's put it this way. It has been four decades as a cold case. Along the way, other missing person cold cases have been added to it. Were it not for you and your persistent, albeit unorthodox methods, they would all still be cold and likely to remain so for a long time, perhaps forever. People in the department will know that. They'll talk about it. I hope you're prepared for the attention."

"Sarge, think you could protect me a bit from all of that? You know me. It's not my style."

"Van, I know you won't bask in it all. I know you don't want the attention. But you also know that we take our victories when we can. This is a victory. The sheriff and the lieutenant and others will want to celebrate, and they cannot do it without you."

"And the media?"

"Them too."

"Well, we can deal with that later. Let's see what's in that box for now."

As they walked back, Fenton said, "I've been in this business a long time, Van. One thing I know is that good investigators are all alike; they like solving the crime. They could care less about the accolades. You're one of the good ones. Take what comes your way and then move on."

—◊◊◊—

Driving to OCSD offices in downtown Santa Ana was not easy in late afternoon. Van decided to stop at a food mart at Santiago Canyon Road and Jamboree Road and buy an iced tea.

Taking his time, he could think. He had the feeling Allison was about to reveal much more when he opened the box in his office. He had the journal, and that would provide much-needed information and timelines about all the murders, perhaps some they did not yet know about. But the box had to contain something unexpected.

In the back of his mind, Van knew that things were about to change for him. Fenton had been right. The Ashae-Fuentes case would attract a lot of attention. It could also be that some of the backcountry murders would attract attention from other towns where the victims had lived. Perhaps Stenz could give him some pointers about being in the spotlight.

Van parked in the basement garage and took the stairs up to the homicide floor. There was the usual movement of personnel along the corridor and the usual greetings in passing. *Nothing different,* he thought as he approached the entrance to homicide.

Inside, people were at work, and at first there was no change, and then as he crossed the room toward his office, there were the smiles, there was silence. People knew; they all knew. He smiled back and nodded to each. Deena had the biggest smile, and she quietly addressed him. "Congratulations, Investigator." He unlocked his office and stepped in. The box was sitting on his desk; there was a white towel below to protect the desk. The ring of blackened keys was there.

Deena had followed him in. "Sergeant wants you to let him know when you're ready to open the box. He wants to make sure someone from forensics does the opening and is here to make a record."

"Okay, Deena. Give me a few minutes. Oh, can you see if Stenzgard is around? If he is, ask him if he has a minute to see me."

"Yes, Investigator."

"Deena, it's Van."

"No, sir. Today it's *The Investigator Vanarsdale!*" She smiled and left.

Van closed his door and stood looking at the box. Then he glanced around his office. *This is my world,* he thought. *I hope that doesn't change.*

Fenton came in. They were waiting for Claudia and decided to discuss Van's experiences in Bishop in recent days. They talked about Allison, but they also digressed, and Van shared his experience fishing in Aspendell. Fenton was a fisherman, and Van enjoyed the conversation about fishing, equipment, types of fish, and places to fish. It was the first time he and the sergeant had really talked anything but shop.

Then the conversation turned to Sti and Rob.

"Well, the two of them certainly helped with this case."

"Actually, Sarge, it was much more than that. They opened my eyes to what I have been missing since Anna Marie died. I have been so focused on work as an outlet that I forgot to have fun. In their own very subtle, perhaps sneaky way, they introduced me to the Eastern Sierra. They took me back to my boyhood. I owe them."

"They don't seem the type to collect."

"They're not."

Claudia, along with a camera-toting tech, entered with her usual flare. "Okay, boys, the vacation is over. Let's see what's in the box. Alfredo …" She picked up the keys and tossed them to Alfredo. "Here—open the box. Then you can look inside, Van."

Forensics set up a camera to record the activity.

The box was unlocked, and Alfredo opened it and stepped aside to let Van view its contents. The contents were unscathed. The box had provided sufficient insulation from the fire.

There was a letter that Van removed. While the others stood by, he opened it and read in silence.

Investigator,

We meet again, and so soon. Well, as I am sure you know, this has all been part of a larger plan. If you are reading this, the plan has been successfully executed. More importantly, for you and for me there is closure.

I do not know whether you have had time to read the journal. If you have, you know that answers are there regarding the who, when, and where of the victims. You have already concluded investigations into some of them, but the journal provides the needed details for the remaining.

But the purpose of this letter is to bring a different closure. You have found the VW, the one I have owned since 1974. I have had it in the Eastern Sierra all these years. It was seldom driven. As you know, I pretty much relied on public transportation, lifts, and an occasional hitchhike to move to and from Orange County. I drove it down on Memorial Day and parked it at a nearby ranch off Santiago Road. I spent Monday, Tuesday, and much of Wednesday night at the Trabuco house, as you call it. I know you have the place being watched, but you also know me. I like a good game.

You probably have also noted that the VW was in the exact same position as was the VW in 1972. One of the plus sides of eidetic imagery is that you never forget things.

To answer the big question, yes, the body inside is mine. Hopefully the fire went as planned and there is really nothing left of the VW or of me.

I should have very much liked to end things at the house. But that was quite impossible. To do so would have risked igniting a much larger fire in the canyon when the house burned down. You know from 1972 that I am very conscious of environmental impact issues. Also, I would not want to put all the other homes in the canyon at risk.

However, I do have a request. My mother's ashes are scattered at the house. If there is any possible way, I would like you to do two things for me. When my body remains are released from forensics, I would like it to be totally cremated. If it is not too much trouble, I would like you to scatter half of the ashes at the house. My big favor is to ask Sti and Rob to scatter the remaining ashes along the JMT. I know all of this sounds a bit morose, but I figure it is a reasonable request since I have provided details of the victims and I have removed myself from existence. In essence, I have closed your very cold case.

As for the earrings, I left an earring at the site of each burial, except in the case of my father; he got two, but they were left on his bed. If there was a couple, they got one earring. If it was a single victim, again I used only one earring.

In some instances, I did not have an earring with me when a victim was buried. In those cases, I went home and retrieved an earring from the box. Thus, there could be substantial time between burial and deposit of the earring.

The enclosed earring goes with one of the remaining unpaired earrings. It is one of the two my mother was wearing at the time of her death. I removed them from her body before it was taken away. In the box you found at the house, you found three pairs and two single unmatched earrings. This is the other half of one of the singles. That leaves you with one unmatched earring.

If it would not be too much trouble, now that it does not matter, adding the enclosed earring, which represents my death, to the box, along with the ones in the package you received and the ones you already possess, I can say that the ordeal is over. There is one exception. In the future, when the foundation for the backcountry ranger station at Bench Lake is removed someday, you will find an earring for the last victim noted in the journal. I would like to have provided you with a body to go with that earring, but that was not possible. I do not now know the whereabouts of the body. Perhaps you can track it down; if not, the earring will have to do. It matches your one remaining single.

I hope all of this brings closure to your efforts as well.

I am sorry you had to find a mess at the house several months ago. It is my fault that the house was such a mess. I had long meant to clean it up. Mom would have wanted that. But I failed to do so. Hopefully, when you visit it next, you will find that I have cleaned it thoroughly and it is once again a respectful home that will serve another family well.

One other thing. I am sure you found the blue cloth marking the start of the route from the VW to the house. I thought you and your two wandering friends would enjoy seeing how it was done in 1972. If not, at least you know what I did.

In closing this letter, I restate my previous comments. You have been a worthy adversary, one that I respect. Had it not been for you, the agony of many years of memories would continue with uncertainty for me. With your help, all is now a closed book.

Enjoy your time in the Eastern Sierra; I know you will go back.

Allison

Van mumbled, "I'll see what I can do." Van had no desire to check the small smile that crept across his face. She was Allison again. She had come full circle.

Van passed the letter over to Fenton and then picked up the remaining earring.

—⚊—

Claudia took the box and its contents. When her crew was done, they would log everything in as evidence. Van could access it as needed.

"Sarge, I know this is a bit out there, but I have a request. You know from the earlier letter and photos I faxed you that the Mammoth ticket was intended for Rob and the book for Sti. I'm hoping I can follow through on that. I know there are protocols but would appreciate anything you can do to expedite putting those items in their hands."

"I'll see what I can do. Won't happen soon, but in time, it may be possible."

"And the *Hamlet* book, I would just like to read it. I know I could find a contemporary copy, but there are markings in that book, and it was personal to Allison. I need to read it. I think it's a rare copy, and I have no intentions of profiting from it. I just want to read it. Think you can help there as well."

"I would think, as lead on this case, you have every right to spend as much time with evidence as possible so as to ensure your final reports are accurate. Will that work for you?"

"I believe so."

Fenton left, and Van sat down at his desk. It was now evening, and he was tired.

Stenz had waited until Fenton had departed before crossing the room to Van's office. "Hey, there's a star out here with your name on it." It was classic Stenzgard. He walked in and took his usual position.

"That's what I wanted to talk to you about. I'm not looking forward to the star treatment, Stenz."

Stenzgard smiled and waved Van off. "Van, the good ones never do."

"But if Fenton is right, there will be media, the higher-ups wanting photos and statements, and even press from the towns where some victims were from. I don't need that."

"Van, let me tell you a story." Stenz shifted and got more comfortable.

Van smiled. He expected nothing less.

"Fresh out of the academy, they put me with a patrol mentor, Martin Davidson. He was a department legend. A week later, we're on an early-morning patrol when a call came through for a 211 in progress. Martin hit the gas, and we headed to the scene while monitoring the communication coming from other deputies closer to the scene. Then, a couple blocks away, he turns suddenly down a side street and tells me to be ready to jump out. A few seconds later, he enters an alley and stops the car and yells at me to exit and stay behind the door with my weapon out.

"No sooner was I out than here come the bad guys running around a corner and toward us. The short of it, we had them. You see, Martin anticipated what they would do, and he was right.

"Well, after several other deputies show up and the arrests take place and the perps are transported, Martin tells me to get in the squad car. Then he says, 'Stenzgard, the press are going to show up. They're going to want to tout the two of us as heroes. But you're going to keep your mouth shut. You and I are going to be like great NFL quarterbacks. We're going to say nothing about what we've done. We're going to give all the credit to the linemen. We're going to say we just happened to be here and it was the deputies chasing the bad guys that deserve the credit.'

"I wanted to argue, but Martin shut me down. He said that we were hired to do a job, not to be heroes or in the limelight. If we couldn't just smile and give others the credit, we weren't doing our job.

"Van, just smile, give credit to all those people in the outer office and those deputies out there and the folks in Inyo County. When you do that, you take the air out of the media sails. They want sensationalism. Not taking on the role of hero gives them no story. Be polite, but point to everyone else. You'll enjoy the results much more."

Stenzgard lifted himself out of the chair in preparation to leave and then thought of one more element. "Remember, Van, you did all of this for the sake of those two kids in '72 and all the other victims of madness and murder along that trail. This isn't about you."

"Yeah, Cindy and Carlos ... and the JMT bunch. You're right. Thanks, Stenz."

Stenzgard was halfway out the door when Van said, "Say, Stenz, how would you like to take a ride with me tomorrow?"

Stenz turned back. "Where to?"

"Trabuco Canyon."

"To see a house?"

"To see *the house*. I have it on good authority that it's been cleaned up and is ready to be put on the market. Thought we should render our judgment before that happens. After all, no one now alive knows that house like we do."

"I think I can manage it if we don't go too early and have time to grab some coffee along the way. Just let me know." With that, Stenzgard was ambling away.

Uncapping his tea and taking a sip, Van leaned back in his chair. He had to smile. Indeed, today had been *un bel di*, one fine day.

Epilogue

I F, AS THE Samuel Johnson quote in the introduction suggests, morality is subject to the motives upon which one acts, then morality is an existential reality. As such, it results from deliberation and decision, and perhaps it is sometimes misguided by personal bias.

Aristotle provided an alternative view, contending that morality is rooted in what is right rather than in the vestiges of established norms or codes.

Of course, morality today is probably more rightly defined by a combination of elements, including traditions, laws, and intangibles often referenced to circumstances. Unfortunately, all of this suggests morality is relative; it is subject to the vagaries of context. Modern court cases in democratic societies suggest as much. The circumstances of morality in today's world imply a morality that is sometimes illusive and not easily defined.

But these arguments aside, society has laws, and those who choose to violate are subject to judgment and penalty. Be the perpetrator of moral violations sane or mad, the reality is that the system of laws makes no exceptions for the guilty; it only makes concessions on the matter of consequences.

The mad, of course, do not see it this way—especially those whose brilliance transcends logic. To the brilliant, well-read, and poetic psychotic, such thinking suggests the ends easily justify the means.

When vengeance is a motive rooted in perceptions of what is right, logic is the arm of retribution.

Of course, there are those charged with bringing the perpetrator of heinous crimes to justice. For those so assigned, the task is especially difficult when the culprit is an enigma and not drawn to a need for attention or benefits. The task is made even more difficult when a pattern of vengeance is concluded and the responsible party moves on and dissolves into the normal world. In such circumstances, a cold case soon becomes lost to time.

Investigator Vanarsdale was handed such a case. But unlike his predecessors, his approach to finding the responsible party was uncharacteristic. He recognized early on that he was not equal to the brilliance of Allison Connors. Though he did have one thing in common with his quarry; he too was an introvert. However, unlike his adversary, he had grown beyond his own shortcomings to accept that reaching out to others for assistance was valued. Unlike Allison, Van respected the insights and judgments of others to solve problems. While he was not without opinions, he was willing to work within the system to resolve disputed points.

Van also differed from his adversary in one other major way; he knew he could not control the future. At best he could only pursue accountability for actions of the past and thereby influence the future. Allison, of course, was the past acting on the future as judge and jury.

Allison's path in life was haunted by a brilliant intelligence under the influence of flawed logic and deeply rooted and misguided understandings. For some time, she walked in two worlds and managed multiple identities. She was most comfortable alone and in the company of her own logic along the trails. Her world was the raw components of wilderness. The terrain of the Sierra backcountry became her home of choice and the hallowed ground of her actions— the trail of madness, the trail of murder.

Those in pursuit realized that the methods for finding Allison would not be found in conventional wisdom. Nor could she be found by adopting Allison's madness and methods. No, Allison could only be found by working to close the gap of understanding between

Allison and her victims and between Allison the suspect and Lexi the mad. The more that was understood, the more the gap closed until the trail of madness reached a terminus of Allison's choosing.

As Van and his colleagues, friends, and sources came to realize, there was no victory. There was only a final earring. The sane cannot walk the trail of madness; they can only study and try to understand.

Afterword

T*RAIL OF MADNESS* is a work of fiction. As such, liberty was taken in writing a story set in both Orange County and the Eastern Sierra of California. All the characters are fictitious.

The root of the story comes from an experience in the early 1970s. I was a teacher at a high school that buried a time capsule soon after the school was built. Twenty-five years later, I was the principal when the capsule was opened. During the weeks leading to the opening, I had a running banter with several students regarding the possible contents. There was much speculation. The idea of a body was never discussed, but it occurred to me that such a finding would make for an interesting mystery.

Years later, when I began to write my story, the intention was a mystery focused on the work of a unique investigator named Van Vanarsdale. I wanted an investigator whose methods were not the public persona of the profession. He would be a reflective intellectual with a literary frame of reference. He would be an introvert who had learned to interact effectively with others.

The suspect had to be the counterpart to Van's skills, an antagonist who would take Van out of his comfort zone and into a world of new experience. For this story, the madness of the suspect needed some self-imposed parameters. Hence, she was a person of brilliance whose introverted nature thrives in the wilderness but is adaptable to some level of normalcy as needed.

To those who have asked how I write my stories, I often say I begin with an idea and then let the story take over. The book takes on a life of its own. I just try to hold the reins and exercise some control. It is not always easy. It is this quality of independence that allowed Sti and Rob to elbow into the story. They had been with me before. I know hiking in Orange County, Eastern Sierra backpacking, and the John Muir Trail. As such, Van was bound to run into the two retired wanderers at some point in the pursuit.

The place names in Orange County are real, although Trabuco Canyon is represented much as it was in 1972 rather than as it is today. There are homes at the end of the road, but no particular one matches the story line. Although the catering site location exists, it has not been used for catering purposes in decades.

Nuevo High School and corresponding school district do not exist, though I have drawn on experience as a teacher, principal, district administrator, and university professor in North Orange County.

The Orange County Sheriff's Department does not investigate many murders in a year, but I made the homicide department more robust, suggested a larger caseload, and altered the work environment.

The Owens Valley and John Muir Trail regions of the Eastern Sierra are accurately represented. For purposes of the story, the Inyo County sheriff serves the town of Bishop, which in reality has its own police department. Mule Days takes place annually in Bishop and has been represented much as it is.

Aspendell is a small collection of cabins and homes along Bishop Creek. Cardinal Lodge is about a half mile upstream.

As for the JMT, it is continually improved to accommodate the growing number of users. Increased backcountry use has been accompanied by an increase in accidents, although the deaths and disappearances in this book are fictitious.

Finally, the idea for the earring has an interesting history. My brother Ron and I were teenagers when we hiked the JMT alone. We camped one night at a place called Tully Hole. We arrived late and hurriedly set up camp, using a large flat slab of granite as a sort of stand-up table for cooking. The following morning while packing my gear, I discovered a small earring atop the slab. Like earrings in the story, it was a loop of wire with a small turquoise stone hanging below. I kept the earring for no particular reason. When I got home, I cleaned it and put it away with other items. Sometime over the years, I lost track of the earring. But I have hiked through Tully Hole several times since, and I always recall the earring when I locate the campsite and see the slab of granite.

I have long been intrigued about who might have owned the earring before I found it. There were not many female backpackers along the JMT in 1960 when I found the earring, but I developed an image of someone who was very feminine and a strong backpacker.

And so a story developed, and I write what I know.